Books by B.

UNDYING MERCENARIES
Steel World
Dust World
Tech World
Machine World
Death World

STAR FORCE SERIES
Swarm
Extinction
Rebellion
Conquest
Battle Station
Empire
Annihilation
Storm Assault
The Dead Sun
Outcast
Exile
Gauntlet

OTHER SF BOOKS
Starfire
Element-X

Visit BVLarson.com for more information.

Dreadnought

(Lost Colonies Book #2)
by
B. V. Larson

LOST COLONIES TRILOGY
Battle Cruiser
Dreadnought

Copyright © 2015 by the author.

This book is a work of fiction. Names, characters, places and incidents are either products of the author's imagination or used fictitiously. Any resemblance to actual events, locales or persons, living or dead, is entirely coincidental. All rights reserved. No part of this publication can be reproduced or transmitted in any form or by any means, without permission in writing from the author.

ISBN-13: 978-1519504272
ISBN-10: 1519504276
BISAC: Fiction / Science Fiction / Military

-1-

Defiant was a captured battle cruiser. She was the only ship of any real size in Star Guard. Shaped like the head of an axe and thickly armored, she dwarfed the rest of the vessels in the fleet. While dry-docked at Araminta Station she took up several berths, and special accommodations had been built just to house her.

I'd spent the last eleven months refitting the monstrous warship while she floated some two hundred and fifty kilometers above the Earth's surface. A year after her capture, we were close to completing the task. We'd installed our own control systems, new weapons and improved quarters for our personnel.

It was early in the morning, just before breakfast, when disaster struck.

"We have a problem, sir," Rumbold told me in an uncharacteristically quiet voice.

I wheeled away from the mirror in my quarters to stare at him. There were streaks of shaving cream on my face, but I ignored them.

"How did you get in here, Rumbold?" I asked.

"Perhaps you left the door unlocked…?" he suggested. His florid face attempted a flickering smile.

"No, I didn't. But let's forget about that. What are you talking about? What's the problem?"

His puffy cheeks twitched. "I'm talking about the ship, sir. *Defiant*."

I took a deep breath and let it out. I turned back to my mirror. All four corners of the reflective glass displayed shifting images and data. A ghosting effect allowed the surface to play back my own face at the same time it showed information streams from all over the ship.

I touched the upper left corner of the mirror, expanding the data feed coming from engineering. They were installing stabilizers down there. The ship's rough ride was legendary, and we'd worked hard to make it more comfortable. While the Betas who'd designed and built this ship didn't seem to be adversely affected, normal humans born on Earth were often driven to unconsciousness under heavy acceleration.

Positive data ran in ribbons along the edges of the display I'd activated, and the central graphic was depicted entirely in green. After a quick perusal, I determined there was no hint of a delay in the project.

Next, I tapped the upper right corner of the mirror. I was immediately provided with a live feed and watched as supplies were loaded into *Defiant*'s hold. Every conceivable foodstuff, tool and spare part had already been procured, emplaced and secured. Personal effects of crewmen and emergency equipment were up next. Again, there was no problem that I could detect.

Rumbold cleared his throat. "You know, sir, I think you're the only man aboard who shaves with a razor and foam. Even I use a consumptive nanite gel. Much faster and cleaner, you know."

"You know I'm a traditionalist, Rumbold. The feel of tiny robots crawling over my face is disturbing. The refreshing nature of water and soap—you should try it sometime."

I touched the third corner. The mirror instantly displayed the ship's command deck, which had been gutted and retooled. Dozens of new instruments hung from every surface. All seemed operational. While I perused the data, I tidied up my shave one-handed.

The fourth sub-screen displayed armament. Missiles choked the magazines. Heavy particle cannons were mounted all along the hull, connected like Christmas ornaments by strings of heavy cable.

I stopped and cocked my head askew. "I'm not seeing the problem, Rumbold," I said.

"Right sir… uh, I mean… no sir."

I turned to face him fully. He was an oldster, a veteran of Earth's navy. His life had been extended to a hundred and sixty years. Despite this, he usually managed to be quick-witted and even cagey at times. I was tired of his hinting around.

"Well spit it out Chief, you've got us both looking foolish!"

He wrung his cap, which was in his sweating hands.

"It's the bridge-drive," he blurted. "The engineers say it's inoperable."

I could tell he hadn't wanted to tell me, but I respected that he'd spoken a painful truth. Rumbold was a poor diplomat, at least when he was bringing bad news to me. The bearing of ill-tidings to a superior officer was clearly not on this man's lengthy list of skills.

His statement, however, surprised me. If I'd been forced to guess, I would have thought he'd tell me the stabilizers wouldn't interface with the navigational computer, or that the Earth-made missiles weren't going to fire properly from the Beta-built tubes. We'd had several mishaps during testing of all these systems.

"Well," I said, "we haven't really tested the bridge-drive yet. Perhaps when we get out there—"

Rumbold was shaking his head. "No sir. That's not going to happen. The engineers are certain. They say it has to do with the nav computer. The ship's star map memory was wiped, remember? They say we can't jump without a clear, valid destination loaded in. Without that data…"

"Ah-ha!" I boomed. "I see it all now, Rumbold. You don't have to worry any further."

"I don't, sir?" he asked in confusion.

"Not at all. You see, the engineers have finally figured out that we're going to have to make a blind jump into an unknown hyperspace when we engage the bridge-drive. That's entirely as expected. There's nothing to worry about."

"Really? They were quite insistent—"

I'd already placed a hand on his shoulder and begun steering him out the door he'd snuck into moments earlier.

"Fear not, Rumbold. They've got the shivers, nothing more. Engineers don't like the unknown. Who does? Their worries are unfounded. We'll fly this ship wherever we want to with Zye's help. Go back and tell them that for me, will you?"

"Yes, Captain…"

I propelled him out the door and into the passage. He cranked his head around to look at me dubiously.

"And Rumbold," I said sternly, "tell them not to talk you into bringing me their bad news the next time they think they have some. That sort of tactic is undignified and unprofessional."

"I'll tell them that, Captain."

Rumbold hurried away down the long, curving passage, and I closed the door thoughtfully.

As I polished every detail of my kit until it shined, there came a timid tapping on the door.

I strode to it and caused it to dissolve.

A trio of engineering people stood there before me. The tallest was a young woman with tight, twisted lips. She was clearly their leader. The other two were squatty fellows who hung back in the passageway despite the fact there was nowhere to hide.

"Commander O'Donnell," I said, nodding to the leader. "I trust you're here with good news?"

"I'm afraid I'm not, Captain. We *can't* fly this ship. At least, we can't fly her out of this star system."

"And can you tell me why not?" I boomed, raising my voice suddenly. Despite my volume, my tone was still controlled rather than angry.

She winced a little. "Because we don't know where we're going. You can't engage the—"

"Wrong," I interrupted. "I fully intend to engage the drive without setting all the variables. That's how ships like this one explore the cosmos."

"In *theory*, Captain," she admitted, "but as a practical matter, the ship only has the ability to detect the existence of an ER bridge—not where that bridge goes. When we get to the end of the hyperspace tube, we might be sucked into a black hole, or irradiated to death by a massive blue star. The possibilities are limitless!"

I stared at her for a moment, then smiled.

"Look," I said, "the admiralty has given me a mandate. I'm to take this ship to a new system and explore the place. I intend to carry out their orders. If you—"

"I'd like to transfer out, sir," she said suddenly, stiffly. "I didn't sign on for suicide."

"You are, of course, free to do so."

I shut the door in their faces by turning it into a solid. The air seemed to transform into a wall in less than a second.

The trio outside in the passage wasn't happy, but I didn't care. This ship had to fly.

Irritated, I allowed them an appropriate length of time to slink away. Using those moments, I considered the difference between the careful and the spineless, as well as their near equal association to number-jockeys.

Once I thought they must be gone, I burst into the passageway myself and headed up the empty passage toward the command deck.

Before I got there, my com implant began buzzing. Stopping in mid-step, I activated it, and a vid began to play on my retina.

An admiral was superimposed upon the passageway as if he stood in front of me.

"Admiral Halsey," I said, forcing a smile. "I'm very busy, sir, if you don't mind—"

"Sparhawk, your entire engineering staff has just requested transfer! Did you know about this?"

"Commander O'Donnell did hint that she—"

"This is unacceptable," Halsey complained. "I can't reassign new people to *Defiant*. Not at this late date. You're about to fly, man. You know that, don't you?"

"That is my intention."

"Without your top engineers?"

"You seem to be under the mistaken impression that I approve of their transfer requests," I said. "I don't."

"Ah," Halsey said. "I get it. You sent your whiny babies on up the line to me, is that it? Well done. I'll handle them."

"Thank you, sir," I said.

His image faded from my vision. Less than a minute later I took my seat in the central chair, which was located on a raised portion of the command deck. The three central seats used spinning gyroscopic systems to orient the occupants in whatever direction was required during maneuvers. I hoped we wouldn't have to engage that feature anytime again soon as the results could be nauseating.

I spent the next half-hour going through checklists and testing every piece of equipment on the command deck. Much of it was new or had been upgraded. Many of the computer systems had been replaced with human-standard systems that were easier for my crew to operate.

This made everyone aboard happy except for a single individual.

"Captain," Lieutenant Zye said, coming to loom over my chair.

I'd had the engineers reconstruct my seat so that it no longer dwarfed me. Unfortunately, Zye still did.

She was a woman—of a sort. Her people were known as Betas. They were a clone race, and they were all physically identical to one another. Designed to survive on a hostile high-gravity world, they were universally made up of large, powerful females. They were attractive with Asian features, but daunting to look upon due to the fact they stood nearly two meters tall. There were reportedly a few males living on their homeworld, but I'd never met one.

Beta minds, unlike their bodies, weren't all the same. As I understood it, there were three primary types of Beta. Most were simple clones. They were unimaginative and made excellent soldiers. One in a thousand were known as Alphas, more intelligent and varied of talent.

But then... there were the Rogues.

Zye was a Rogue. In attempting to create a superior Alpha, the cloning vats had tried a mutation in the genes controlling her neurological structure. As was often the case, Zye's mutation had been judged to be unproductive. She'd been scheduled for termination when we'd rescued her, and she'd since joined my crew.

"What is it, Zye?" I asked her.

"I don't like the new control boards. My fingers are too large for them. My touch—I'm constantly tapping on the wrong thing."

"Fortunately," I said, "your original station has been preserved. From there, you can access all the operational systems you've been assigned to."

She looked annoyed. "I would like full access to *every* system. Perhaps you could allow me to remotely log in to other stations from mine?"

She'd touched upon the problem. Zye was a hacker of some skill. She'd been instrumental in getting *Defiant* to obey us initially, but now those special talents weren't necessary. She'd been corralled by the techs and given restrictions. Naturally, she found this upsetting.

"I'll see what I can do about raising your priority level a notch," I promised.

"You'll see what you can do? Why not just order this thing done?"

"I'll talk to Commander O'Donnell about it."

Zye's face tightened. She wasn't a naturally expressive person, but when you got to know her, you could read her emotions. I knew immediately she didn't like Commander O'Donnell.

"I hate that engineer, and she hates me," she stated flatly. "I know that you're too smart for this to be an accident. Therefore, I understand. You wish me to be diminished and castigated. I must accept your disapproval."

"Zye—"

"No need to apologize, Captain!" she said quickly. "It would only further embarrass both of us."

She wheeled and stalked off to her station. I looked after her, frowning.

The truth was Zye was right. Commander O'Donnell *had* been the one to initially propose implementing the new permission levels. O'Donnell had objected to Zye's unprecedented access as a junior officer—especially since she was a colonist. The idea that a Beta had the power to get into all of the ship's central systems seemed preposterous to the techs.

I'd gone along with the new restrictions as they'd seemed logical enough. We were no longer in emergency-mode, dragging *Defiant* back to Earth any way we could. There had to be order, and a reasonable division of responsibility.

Still, Zye's reaction troubled me. I hadn't intended the change to be an insult, or a statement suggesting I mistrusted her.

Settling back into my routine again, I reviewed the reports. As far as I was concerned, everything was going along as planned. The ship would be ready to leave dry-dock within a matter of days.

My com implant buzzed again in my head—and I almost ignored it. The implant's tone, which directly stimulated my auditory nerves, indicated the call was a personal one.

Who would call me while I was on duty? My parents had little enough respect for my commission, but they knew better than to call me while I was on my own command deck.

Of course, it could be my girlfriend, the Lady Chloe of House Astra. There was no identification on the call, but that didn't rule her out. We'd had clandestine interactions in the past.

That thought perked me up. I glanced around to see if anyone was watching. No one was. They were all too busy debugging the new interface feeds.

My implant sounded a tone again. Surreptitiously, I answered the call.

A disturbing image popped up before me. I don't know what I'd expected to see, but I was sure this wasn't even on the list.

The caller was indeed Lady Astra. Her face and person were as lovely as ever. Her large eyes, high cheek bones and finely shaped body were fully displayed.

These positive elements of the image faded in importance when I saw the thick arm that was snaked around her soft, pale throat. A weapon had been placed against her head as well. The black muzzle was flared at the end—a PAG.

"William," she said in a hitching voice. She wasn't crying, but she was clearly stressed. "They've entered House Astra. My agents couldn't stop them. I'm calling you to inform you of my love and best wishes. My only regret is that we won't meet again. If—"

Suddenly, her words were cut off. The bicep around her neck had flexed. The motion squeezed her throat, and she gave a choking cry.

The fiend that held her lifted his cowled head then. He'd been hiding his face behind her shoulder.

"That wasn't what you were supposed to say, you bitch!" he rasped. "I should kill you right now."

My heart was pumping. All around me my crewmen bustled and worked with quiet competence. The horrific scene I was witnessing was mine and mine alone to deal with. None of them could share my private vision, much less help her. They were all as helpless as I was.

Fighting to keep my wits about me, I spoke.

"Intruder," I demanded, "who are you, and what do you want?"

"You, Sparhawk. I want you. Come down here right now. Come and bargain for your Lady's life. Don't bring troops with you. If you do, I'll kill her."

I narrowed my eyes, thinking fast. "I'll do as you ask, if you identify yourself."

The cowl shifted then. I thought to see—but no, it couldn't be.

Then the cowl fell back fully, and I recognized the man's face. It was none other than Edvar Janik, a smuggler I'd dealt with in the past.

It was Edvar who'd been storing Beta clone embryos in the snows of Antarctica. When we'd first met, he'd been working for the Stroj.

But Zye had killed him on that occasion. How had he survived?

"The last time we met," I said aloud, "I seem to recall that Zye broke your neck in a fury."

He rasped again, and it was an odd sound. A chuckle? Perhaps.

Pulling his cowl away from his neck, he showed me the scars and stitching that encircled his throat. The region was a livid red.

"I see," I said. "Very well. True to my word, I will come."

"Remember, Sparhawk—come alone!"

I closed the channel and stood up. I almost ran into Zye as I did so. She was suddenly standing near my chair.

"What's wrong?" she demanded.

"Nothing," I said. "I've been called down to Earth that's all. Look after things up here for me, will you Zye?"

Full of suspicion, her eyes followed me as I got up from my command chair.

-2-

It's good to be in charge at times—and this was one of those times. I didn't have to get permission from a higher ranking officer to leave the deck, I simply stood up and cleared my throat.

"First Officer Durris," I said loudly.

Durris turned from his boards, looking at me with an upraised eyebrow. "Captain?"

"I'm heading down to Earth. You have command of *Defiant* in my absence. Keep all our refitting operations in motion. Plan on leaving orbit on schedule in thirty-nine hours. I shall return before that time."

"Yes sir…" he said, frowning.

People had begun to look up from their work and take notice. It was to my credit, I supposed, that they were surprised to hear I was leaving the ship when we were so close to departure. There were many confused looks, and I counted several frowns. A few crewmen even awarded me an open-mouthed stare.

But only one of them dared to give me an argument.

"Sir?" Durris asked, stepping after me. "What about our engineering people?"

"Commander O'Donnell and her team will be returning to serve aboard *Defiant*," I said. "Her transfer request has been denied. They've all had their transfers denied."

"But I haven't seen anything from CENTCOM on that," he objected. "My duty rosters still indicate—"

"First Officer," I interrupted firmly. "They've been denied."

He stared at me for a half-second, then nodded. "I understand, sir."

I turned to leave the deck, but I found him following me.

"Captain?" he asked quietly. "I gathered from your orders that you'll be gone for some time... May I ask what this is all about?"

"Yes, you may ask—but I won't answer. I have business to attend to down on Earth. I'll be back as soon as I'm able. Keep the schedule, manage it tightly, and don't take any nonsense from O'Donnell."

"A family matter, Captain?" Durris asked.

I shrugged noncommittally. My family was one of the Great Houses of Earth. My father, Sparhawk the Elder, was a Public Servant. He'd lost his bid to win the World Presidency, but he was still a major political player on Earth.

The chief consequence of my family background was that everyone assumed all my problems were political in nature. The truth was I did my best to avoid the tangled in-fighting between the ruling families.

"Right sir," Durris said, tossing me a salute. "I won't disappoint you. Good luck with... whatever it is."

He turned around and bumped into Zye, who'd come up behind him to stand alarmingly close. For such a large person, she could move with remarkable grace and stealth.

"Excuse me," he said and hurried back to his navigational table.

"Zye," I said when we were alone, "I'm going down to Earth. I'd like you to stay here and help Durris aboard ship."

Her expression was flat and unimpressed. "I'm going with you."

"Even if I give you a direct order?" I asked.

"Please, don't do that."

I sighed, then turned to head for the sky-lift. The ship was still docked with Araminta Station. We took the tube to the central wheel and headed for the sky-lift in the center of the orbital structure. It was a long way down from there to Earth, but we'd done it many times before.

Together, we stood in the sky-lift's large lobby, waiting for a car to arrive. During this time, I was very aware of Zye's scrutiny. She was trying to figure out this odd situation. She wasn't a sophisticated woman, but she was a dogged one.

"You're in some kind of trouble, I gather?" she asked. "Or perhaps it's your parents?"

"It's not my family," I said, glancing at her. "It's Chloe."

She stiffened at the name. Zye tolerated Chloe Astra, but she didn't like her much. Some might have said she was jealous. If she was, she'd never made her feelings completely clear to me.

"I see," she said. "What do you need me to do?"

I laughed. "I've already told you. I'd prefer that you stayed aboard *Defiant* to help Durris."

"No, I meant—"

"I know what you meant, Zye."

I considered taking her into my full confidence. In modern times, law and order were tricky things on Earth. Normal people depended on the Guard or their local constabulary to dispense protection and justice. But among the Great Houses, which included both Sparhawk and Astra, things went differently. We had what amounted to private security forces, and we lived by a different set of rules.

If I contacted the official authorities, for example, that fact would immediately become a public matter. Every detail—real or imagined—would be leaked to the press by someone seeking a payment. Media would then descend upon House Astra. Camera drones would peep into each of the mansion's thousand windows before the first officer showed up on the grounds.

At that point, it would be obvious to Janik I hadn't followed his instructions. If I called for help there was no way I could keep control of the situation. He would be alerted and the conflict would escalate. Chloe might well die before I could reach House Astra.

No, this had to be done carefully. I would see what he wanted and then attempt to extricate Chloe from his grasp. Hopefully, this could be done without bloodshed.

Zye watched me closely as I thought things over.

"Zyc," I said apologetically, "I don't think I can take you with me this time. The situation is delicate."

She eyed me with a mixture of disapproval and growing concern. I knew I could use her help, and that made turning her down all the more difficult. She was always a good person to have at my back in a fight.

I wasn't sure I wanted her along this time, however. She'd been the one who had throttled Janik in the first place when we'd caught up with him in Europe. She hated the man due to his mistreatment of Beta "children"—meaning frozen embryos from her home planet. If she learned he was involved, things were bound to turn violent.

"You're going to House Astra," she said, "and you wish to do so alone?

"Yes."

"Now I understand. You're seeking a final farewell sexual encounter with Lady Astra. I've read of such things."

I wanted to protest as her suggestion was both rude and inaccurate. My mouth opened, but I managed to shut it again.

"You cleverly fooled the crew, sir," she continued. "I must compliment you on that point. None of them suspect the truth."

I managed to stop myself before arguing. If she believed the situation was purely personal, that served my purposes well.

"I'm glad you understand," I said at last. "Now, I believe the sky-lift has just arrived. If you would kindly head back to the ship—"

"I still want to accompany you to the surface. If I may, Captain?"

Looking her over, I considered. If I refused her now, she might become suspicious all over again. That might lead to further inquiries, the precise thing I was trying to avoid. The truth was there was little for her to do aboard *Defiant* anyway, now that her permissions had been reduced. Durris would probably find he could work with more focused zeal without her brooding presence on the command deck.

"Very well," I said at last. "Let's go."

We boarded the next car and began the long descent. At first, the falling sensation was sickening, but I soon adjusted.

The ride down through the mesosphere into the stratosphere went smoothly. It wasn't until we hit the upper troposphere that the sky-lift began to jiggle and bump.

Zye had stopped questioning me, and for that I was grateful. I didn't like misleading her. I wasn't good a discussing anything other than the truth, and I suspected I might be caught at any moment.

Fortunately, Zye could stand in one spot for hours doing nothing other than breathing and blinking now and then. This appeared to be one of those occasions when she felt no need to participate in small talk.

We made it another few kilometers down into the night sky, watching a stirring brew of dark clouds gather below. They seemed to be clustered around the umbilical itself.

"Looks wet down there," Zye commented, following my gaze.

"Yes, a storm is brewing."

"Perhaps you should delay your trip to House Astra."

I glanced at her. "Why?"

"Don't you two enjoy mating outdoors?"

I made a choking sound. "We've only done so once—have you been spying on me, Zye?"

She shrugged. "Spying seems like an inappropriate term. It's my job to guard your person."

The lights in the sky-lift flickered then, and the umbilical shivered. I heard a distant rumble of thunder from below us.

"Odd…" I said. "I don't recall seeing a thunderstorm on the schedule for tonight. Weather control is going to get defunded if they can't manage to keep a proper storm-schedule."

Zye frowned. Her eyes were unfocused, and I knew she was getting a call on her implant. She'd only just gotten fitted for it. She hadn't relished the process or the result.

She stared ahead, and she spoke woodenly. "Yes, he's here. No, his implant seems to be functioning."

"Who is it, Zye?" I asked quietly. "Durris?"

She shook her head. "No. It's Lady Astra."

That dumbfounded me. "She can't get through to my implant directly?"

"No."

"Relay the signal over to me. Share it."

"How do I do that?"

Trying to control my impatience, I helped her through the steps with the interface. Most humans became adept with implants when they were children. Zye was an exception as such devices were unknown on her planet of birth.

Finally, Lady Astra could be seen standing in front of the two of us. I was at a loss. There was no sign of her attacker, no gun to her head—I didn't know what to think.

"William?" she asked. "Why are you on the sky-lift? Are you coming down to see me?"

"Yes," I said, "but what happened to Janik?"

"Who?"

"Edvar Janik. Listen Chloe, you might be in danger. Either that, or you're someone else who's trying to fool me. I talked to you not an hour ago. I saw a man hold a gun to your head. Are you all right?"

"I'm fine," she said worriedly. "There aren't any strangers here. My agents have secured the grounds for the night. I'll order them to double the guard and seal the entrances."

My eyes narrowed in suspicion. Could this be part of someone's trick? I was on my guard now.

"What were you wearing the first night I met you?" I asked her.

She looked embarrassed. She looked at Zye, who stood stoically at my side. "My nightgown, as I recall."

"Correct. I believe you are the real Chloe... but how could someone have hacked my implant? Guard technology is the best."

"Captain," Zye interrupted, "can I assume you have deceived me? That you're not heading to Earth for a sexual encounter with this woman?"

Both Chloe and I looked embarrassed. "I'm sorry if I misled you, Zye. But I received a message—supposedly from Chloe—that said she was in danger. Now she appears to be fine, and I'm at a loss to explain this."

"The key question now," Zye said, "is who did this and why? Apparently they didn't actually kidnap Lady Astra, but they want you to believe they did."

I nodded, thinking hard. "They sent me a fake message attempting to make me come back down to Earth alone. That can only mean they're after me—not you, Chloe."

Lightning flashed outside. The strike was quite close.

"The weather system," I said suddenly. "Something's gone wrong. Chloe, check the reports. Is there any information concerning this freak storm?"

I repeated the question, but Chloe's holographic image had frozen in place. Soon, she vanished entirely. Chloe was gone. Her image no longer flickered on my retina. Only Zye stood at my side.

The umbilical shook again, and the lift shook with it. Looking down, I was surprised to see the tube. A large bulge rippled upward along its length, like a soap bubble that was about to burst.

I knew I shouldn't be able to see the umbilical at all from this height. When you were up higher, due to a slight curvature and various atmospheric conditions, you could occasionally catch a glimpse of it—but now that we were down so low it should have been out of sight under our feet.

"Away from the walls!" I shouted, backing away from the shimmering force-fields and glass-like polymers.

Other passengers around us on the car were pressing their foreheads against the inner membrane, straining to get a better view. They looked at me in surprise.

"Back away!" I repeated. "Move to the center of the car!"

A few of them did as I ordered. Most ignored me or glanced around in confusion.

Zye's heavy hand was on my shoulder. Following my own advice, we moved to the center of the car.

"What's wrong, Guardsman?" a kid with big eyes asked me.

"I don't know, but this situation is unsafe."

Something struck the outer membrane then, making it flash and shift colors. The car lost power and people cried out, staggering backward. The floor tipped, and then the emergency lights came on. The car stopped descending, and the sudden braking drove many to their knees.

Tones I'd never heard before on the sky-lift began to wail—emergency klaxons.

So far as I knew, the transportation system had never had a major accident since its construction. Then again, I was pretty sure this wasn't an accident.

"That was a power-bolt," Zye said. "It struck the tube. This can't be an accident."

"No," I said with certainty in my voice. "They have to be tracking me, and they're firing at the tube. There's no other explanation."

Zye looked at me. "How could they be tracking you?"

"My implant... Zye, you'll have to rip it out."

Implants were located at the top of the spinal column, at the base of the skull. There was an external nodule, a soft nub that could be used to access the wetware. Occasionally the units failed or required updates that couldn't be done through software downloads.

"I hate these things," Zye said, reaching back and touching her own implant. "I should never have let them ram a spike into my brain."

The tube wall flashed orange and magenta. A stronger hit had been scored. People screamed and fell to the floor. High-altitude air shot into the cab in a single freezing gust. The protective membranes must have failed for just a fraction of a second.

Could that have been their plan? Something so simple? Puncture the membrane long enough to allow the atmosphere to escape, to inject the thin, freezing air from twenty kilometers up into the cab to do the killing for them? If they managed it, I realized it would look like an accident. The deaths would be blamed on the freak storm. A lightning strike—perhaps that would be their cover story.

Reaching back to the base of my neck, I pinched the fleshy bulb that I found there. It slipped from my fingers as I tugged.

"Rip it out, Zye!" I shouted. "I can't get a grip."

She grabbed me, turned me around and put a massive thumb and forefinger on the bulb. "This is going to hurt," she said.

"Do it."

She did it. Her hands were at least as strong as mine, and she had a better angle. She tugged at the implant, and it ripped loose like a fleshy root. The threaded plug gave way as did the skin covering the region. Blood crawled down my back in a warm gush.

It felt as if part of my scalp had been torn free, which was fairly accurate. I was stunned by the shocking agony that followed. I almost pitched forward on my face when she let go of me, but I managed to keep on my feet.

"Are you all right?" she asked, looming close and looking concerned.

"I've been better," I admitted.

"Here it is," she said.

A warm slimy bulb was slapped into my palm. It felt like a hot tadpole, and it wriggled slightly in my grasp.

"Thanks," I said, "with any luck, they won't be able to—"

Another bolt struck. This one was closer and more focused than the earlier shots. Maybe they were getting impatient, or desperate.

A hole was punched through the force-field walls of the umbilical this time. The rupture was about as big around as a man's head.

The hole glowed and sparked. The smart polymers and force-fields tried to stretch, to cover the wound in the skin of the shielding, but they were slow to do so.

Could the entire umbilical be losing power? The cars had stopped moving, but that was standard procedure during one of these rare breakdowns.

Hearing a whistling sound, I realized the warm atmosphere of the cab was gushing out. We were too high up. No one could survive long without an oxygen tank at this altitude.

Staggering forward, I stepped toward the wound in the skin of the umbilical. Zye grasped for my shoulder, but I shrugged her off.

She was shouting something, but I didn't catch it. There were too many screaming passengers. The whistling roar of our life-giving air fleeing the car soon grew even louder than the cries of dying innocents.

I reached the hot opening. It looked like a melted hole in a sheet of glass. It was as if a giant blowtorch had been placed against a window until it turned molten and glowed orange.

Cocking back my hand, I threw my implant through the opening. It sailed out into space and dropped into storm clouds far below.

-3-

After I threw the wet piece of biotechnological hardware out into the open air, I collapsed on the sky-car's deck.

I was hazily aware of being dragged from the ruptured membrane to a safer spot in the center of the car by Zye. My body was cold and numb.

Later, I could recall seeing Zye's determined face above mine as she dragged me away. The screaming passengers had quieted. They were dying, with most of the air sucked from their lungs. They lay slumped on the deck, moving feebly, mouths gaping like beached fish. Their lips were blue and their eyes were wide with shock.

We were all dying, even Zye. But she'd been engineered to survive where others might perish. Hers were a people designed to live through great hardship. She fitted an oxygen mask over my face, and a tiny puff of life-giving gas hissed into my mouth. The masks had been released from the ceiling when the cab depressurized. She then moved around the deck, taking breaths from each mask before fitting it over the face of another fallen passenger.

Blood loss, the lack of oxygen and the sheer numbing cold overwhelmed me. I lost consciousness.

* * *

"It was the lack of blood, not oxygen, that almost got him," a voice said.

I swam awake. At least, that's what it felt like. It was as if I was at the bottom of the ocean, and the voices around me were on the distant surface.

My lips moved, and I made a croaking sound. I was surrounded by three people: a doctor, Zye and Chloe.

"He's coming around," Zye said. "If his brain isn't damaged, he may yet prove useful."

Such cold words... I knew Zye wasn't cold toward me. Others didn't understand that her practical outlook didn't mean she was utterly devoid of passion. She was just a realist, rather than a person driven by emotion.

"That's a terrible thing to say," Chloe scolded. "He's going to be fine."

Zye didn't answer.

I looked at Chloe. "Chloe?" I asked.

"I'm here, William."

"What happened?"

"You suffered an episode. They hacked your implant. You saw images that weren't real, that's all."

Oddly enough, this made sense to me. The images projected on my retina by my implant were never actually *real* after all. They looked real—as real as rain, as real as my own face in the mirror. But they weren't actually there. They were illusions generated by software.

I'd never considered the possibility before, but I saw no technical reason why someone couldn't manufacture sensory data and transmit it. Any implant user would be easily fooled. We were used to trusting our implants as wholeheartedly as we trusted our own eyes.

"But why?" the doctor's voice asked. "I'm still puzzled by that question. Why would anyone go to such trouble to deceive and kill Captain Sparhawk?"

"Because he's the best," Chloe said.

That response made me smile. She was a loyal friend, as well as a lover.

"Can we take him home now, doctor?" Chloe asked sweetly.

"No," he said firmly, "I don't think so. He's suffered serious trauma. We'll have to keep him overnight at least—for the autodoc to evaluate and monitor him."

I closed my eyes to rest. In the meantime, Chloe made no verbal response to the doctor... But there was a sound—an odd sound. It was like that of scuffling feet. I was left with the impression that someone had left the room in a hurry.

Opening my eyes again, I found they were focusing fully at last. I finally had control of them. The room still seemed overly bright, however.

"I can barely see you," I said.

Chloe came near, filling my vision. "I'm here," she said.

I smiled more fully... but then my smile faded.

Something was wrong. Her face—she was lovely, as always, but her hair was wrong. She hadn't worn that hairstyle for a month at least. In fact, if I had to guess, her hair was quite a bit longer than it had been the last time I'd seen her. Could she have altered it?

My heart began to pound. Was I dreaming? Was I being afflicted by a new projected illusion? I didn't think that was possible, as my implant was gone.

Numb fingers twitched and moved upward, slithering over white hospital sheets. I dragged my hand up toward the back of my neck.

A huge hand descended and clasped my errant fingers. It was Zye's hand. She leaned over me as well, and she frowned.

"Are you feeling well, Captain Sparhawk?" she asked.

That's when I knew. That huge face didn't belong to Zye. Chloe wasn't Chloe, either. They were both wrong.

Zye's expression, her tone, her lack of concern, her attempt to restrict my movement—it was all wrong.

Under normal circumstances, Zye implicitly accepted my authority as her Captain. That was the way of any Beta. They were nothing if not disciplined. Even as a Rogue among her people, she was more of a rule-follower than most of my crewmen.

I swallowed in a dry throat and asked for water. It was provided by the Zye-person. Chloe continued to beam at me as if nothing was wrong.

Making a decision, I chose to play along. I didn't know why anyone would go to such lengths to fool me, but I figured they must be prepared to do just about anything to continue their plans.

Forcing a smile, I blinked and sighed. "It's good to see you two," I said. "When can I get out of here?"

"That's exactly why we've come," Chloe said. "To discharge you. You have to thumbprint the release at the desk, and we'll be on our way."

I nodded. "Excellent. Help me up, will you Zye?"

She did so with hands that were possibly even stronger than those I remembered. As a large male and a member of Star Guard, I'd always stayed in shape. Zye was naturally strong, being a woman structured for heavy gravity, but she'd been in space for a long time. She'd weakened somewhat compared to a Beta from her homeland.

I could tell immediately when those big fingers grasped me and squeezed that this version of Zye was in her prime. She'd be a difficult opponent.

My mind raced as the two women helped me out of my bed and into my clothes. I surreptitiously looked for the doctor I'd heard speak when I'd awakened—but there was no sign of him.

The first clue as to the doctor's whereabouts came when I examined the Zye-impersonator's hand. There was a neat red crescent there—could it be a bite mark on the webbing between the thumb and forefinger? It stood to reason.

While pulling on my pants, I naturally looked down. I dropped my key-fob while doing so and bent low to pick it up. This gave me the opportunity to glance under the hospital bed.

When I spotted the twisted body of an oldster crammed under there I almost blew it and shouted in surprise. The man's eyes stared, his swollen tongue was purple, and it protruded from the mouth.

Regaining my composure, I straightened and shoved the fob back into my pocket.

"Feeling better now," I lied with a smile. I never liked to lie, but these were undeniably special circumstances.

The Zye-clone—clearly another Beta pretending to be Zye—gave me a hard look, but then she took hold of my arm as if to offer support. She propelled me physically toward the exit.

My mind churned. If they had the gall to kill the doctor, why not kill me as well?

It must have something to do with my family's fame, I decided. They didn't want media exposure. The death of a Sparhawk would bring plenty of media attention, but an outright murder—a public assassination—that would bring an investigation from the highest levels. Whoever was behind this didn't want that.

So, what would their plan most likely be? To get me out of the hospital and make me disappear? To drop my corpse into the darkest corner of the ocean? Or maybe they had another plausible accident prepared—it had to be something like that.

Naturally, I feared for Chloe and Zye as well as myself. There was a good chance they were already dead. I wanted to grab these villains and force them to tell me what they'd done to the two women they were imitating.

But I couldn't do that. They had the upper hand, and the Beta was a killer. I was still weak, even if I was feeling better every minute. To help my friends I had to stay in the game and play it smart.

"What happened, Zye?" I asked. "After the accident on the sky-car I mean? I don't remember how it ended once I passed out."

"You don't recall?" she asked. "There was an accident, yes. Bad things happened. People died, but you lived. They brought you here afterward."

I stared at her for a fraction of a second too long, but then smiled. I'd forgotten that most Betas weren't imaginative. They weren't very smart, if the truth were to be told. Zye was a Rogue, or more specifically, a maladjusted Alpha. That meant she was smarter than the average member of her race.

This Beta's slow wits gave me an idea. Her people were easily fooled. Zye had managed it countless times, by her own admissions.

"I see," I said. "Fine. Let's get out of here."

That suited my escorts well. They led me toward the tubes, which whisked us all away on a mobile disk to the ground floor. We approached a guard on the way to the front doors. The Beta holding my arm with her thick strong fingers frowned at the guard.

Under no circumstances did I want to let these two get me out of the building. The hospital was a Star Guard facility, which meant there were armed people in authority here. I decided now was as good a time as any to take drastic action.

As we passed the bored guard, who was tapping at a computer scroll, I slipped out of the Beta's grasp. I lunged at the guard and grabbed his sidearm.

It was a gamble, and it failed to work. The guard's weapon was a smart weapon. A beeping sound went off as it attempted to alert its owner to the theft.

The guard was already more than aware of the problem. He wrestled with me immediately.

To my good fortune, the man was older and out of shape. He had a paunch, a red face that spoke of an overuse of caffeine and other stimulants, and I'd taken him by surprise.

Instead of incapacitating me or calling for help, he grabbed for his gun to take it back.

"Hey! Security, I've got one from the crazy ward!"

By wrapping his hands around the gun with mine, he activated the weapon. When the day's events were reviewed, I had no doubt the man's trainers would discipline him.

As it was, his reaction turned out to be timely.

The Beta killer wheeled on me. Her big hands came up and clasped around my neck. I could feel the fantastic power in those fingers. They were like claws of iron. My throat could not possibly withstand the pressure for more than a few seconds.

The gun, pressed tightly between the Beta and I, went off in my hand. It was fully automatic, and it was loaded with lethal ammo.

A string of popping sounds rang from the walls of the lobby. People screamed and ran, some hobbling due to injuries or illness.

The Beta's eyes bulged in shock. The weapon had placed seven shots, kicking up higher with each blast and raking her body at point-blank range. Her chest and throat were a red ruin.

The iron fingers around my throat relaxed reluctantly, and she slid to the floor without a word.

"Sweet Jesus," sobbed the guard. "Give me my gun, you murdering fuck!"

I didn't obey him. I couldn't. Chloe's twin had now reversed her course. She'd almost reached the exit, but had turned around as if changing her mind. She stepped toward me slowly, hands outstretched in supplication.

"No, William," she said, her face running with tears, "you killed your friend! Please put the gun down. *Please*, William."

I looked at her, and I hesitated. I shouldn't have, but it's harder than you think to kill your lady-love.

Her eyes did it, in the end. They had that plastic look. The same look the Stroj assassins eyes sometimes had when they were close enough to stare into.

"On your knees, Stroj," I ordered. "You're under arrest."

The guard looked at me as if I was insane. He also looked as if he was having a heart attack. His face was redder than ever.

He stopped trying to tear the gun out of my grasp. He looked at the Beta on the floor and at Chloe.

"You're Sparhawk, aren't you?" he asked in confusion. "Why did you kill your Beta friend?"

"She's a fake," I said. "They both are. Take over and arrest this creature."

Chloe took another step toward me.

"Stop!" I ordered her, stepping back. "Guard, shoot her if she takes another step."

Chloe shook her head. "You wouldn't do that," she said. "Not to me."

I indicated the dead Beta on the floor. "Are you sure, Stroj?"

She did glance down, and the undeniable truth must have convinced her.

The creature that had been Chloe underwent a transformation. Not of physical form, but of aspect, demeanor and expression. She snarled at me in frustration.

"You're not getting out of this star system alive, Sparhawk!" she said.

Then, without further warning, Chloe exploded.

-4-

After being arrested, debriefed and reluctantly released, I was placed back into a hospital bed. I had new rips in my flesh to prove how hard a day I was having.

The real Zye showed up three hours later, after the sun had fallen below the horizon outside my window.

I eyed her warily. She looked me over in return with equal concern.

"Are you all right?" she asked. "I heard there was trouble."

"Where have you been, Zye?" I asked, unable to hide my new, distrustful attitude toward visitors.

Behind Zye in the hallway two of my father's agents stood with their hands in their jackets. The leader was Jillian, a mean woman who would kill anyone who threatened me. Her male partner was large, expressionless and all business.

"I'm sorry, Captain," Zye said. "Please believe me. We were rescued by emergency air cars. Medical people helped you into a car. I let them take us, and I traveled with you to this hospital. It was here in this building they lied to me. They convinced me I must undergo an examination in order to continue working in Star Guard."

For a moment, she hung her head in shame. "I can't believe such a simple trick fooled me... as a Rogue, I find this humiliating."

I repressed a smile. Zye fancied herself a master of deception. In truth, her tricks were always heavy-handed in nature.

"It's not your fault," I said. "You're new to this planet and to Star Guard. They won't fool you again."

Zye stepped closer and moved her face close to mine. She spoke in a hushed voice.

Out in the hallway, my father's agents frowned, and they too leaned into the doorway to watch her closely. They weren't about to let another assassin make an attempt on my life.

"What of the two outside?" Zye asked me. "Are you sure they're legitimate?"

"I know them from my father's estate. Besides, I don't think the enemy has had the time to come up with a third plan to put into action yet."

Zye's face registered confusion. "A third plan?"

"Yes," I said. "I think the attack on the sky-lift was an elaborate attempt to kill me while making it look like an accident. The second plan failed as well, a direct kidnapping and slaying."

"How could that have worked?" Zye asked thoughtfully. "No, wait, don't answer that. I know how I would have done it."

"How?" I asked, honestly curious.

Zye shrugged. "A simple thing, really. They had only to get the three of you into an air car and drive it into the ground."

I blinked at her in surprise, but then I nodded slowly.

"The Stroj," I said. "She would have done it. The Beta might not be so keen on self-destruction."

"No, probably not," Zye admitted. "She must have known she was kidnapping you, but not how it was going to end."

Thinking that over, I realized the enemy Stroj had a strategic advantage. They didn't mind dying for their cause if they could do significant damage through self-sacrifice.

"Zye," I said, "I was under the impression that there were no other Betas or Stroj on Earth."

"So was I," she said. "But the Stroj are tricky. Even trickier than I am."

"That might be the case—" I began but then there was a commotion out in the hallway.

Zye immediately moved to cover the door. Painfully, I climbed out of the hospital bed. Fortunately, the Stroj assassin's explosion had been too far from my person to do serious damage. I'd suffered only burns and contusions. I was, however, heavily sprayed with nu-skin. The fast-growing flesh substitute tore in places when I moved quickly.

Jillian pushed her face into the room. Zye and she eyed one another coldly for a moment.

"It's a Star Guard officer," Jillian said. "Should I let him in?"

"Yes, if he's passed the metal detectors."

"That may not be good enough," Zye interjected quickly. "They vary in composition. Some have polymer-based internal components."

Jillian glanced at Zye, then at me. "It's your call, sir."

"Let him in."

There was some rough complaining in the hallway as the man was inspected and ushered into the hospital room.

I almost hoped the visitor did turn out to be a Stroj imposter when I saw who they'd been patting down and irritating. A red-faced Admiral Halsey confronted me. He was my superior, one of the top commanders of Star Guard.

"Private goons, Sparhawk?" he demanded. "You've got the balls to doubt your own commanders?"

"I'm sorry, sir," I began.

"Well, don't be," he said, cutting me off. "With all the shit you've been through, I can hardly blame you. May I come in?"

As he was already standing in my hospital room, I made a gracious gesture. He began to speak then, and while he did so Zye and Jillian both gave him suspicious glances now and then.

"Fortunately for you, I'm not a Stroj," Halsey assured me. "They don't seem to love you much do they?"

"They don't seem to, Admiral," I said. "They've gone to a lot of trouble to take me out. It seems excessive."

"This time I think the enemy is playing the game right. They know you're one of our best and brightest. Sure, the Guard has always leaned on you. You're a man from a Great House invading the ranks of Star Guard. It's bound to make jealousy and envy spring up in the hearts of every mean-spirited man."

I thought of reminding him he'd been quite high on that list of distinguished doubters, but I passed on the idea.

"Again, my apologies," he said. "It's clear there are forces here on Earth, forces allied with colonists, who don't want us to leave this star system."

Turning that thought over in my mind, I quickly decided he was right.

"You've got a point, sir," I said. "I've been wondering about that for some time now. Why haven't we attempted to leave the Solar System again?"

"Political reasons, mostly," Halsey admitted. "People were burned by the loss of all contact with other star systems. The Cataclysm triggered an economic and social collapse. We turned inward, and we began to think that was a good thing. Powers arose who benefited from the status quo."

He eyed me significantly.

"You're talking about the Great Houses," I said.

He nodded slowly. "Think about it. We've got longevity combined with legal cloning and the ability to pass on that power to progeny—we've become a planet controlled by dynasties. Long term familial power has become institutionalized with the help of our technology."

I shifted uncomfortably and began to dress as he spoke. He caught my mood.

"Heretical talk, I know," he said. "But now that we've made contact with other worlds, people are wondering again, questioning. That's precisely what the Great Houses didn't want."

"Do you think it was a conspiracy?" I asked. "Or maybe just an evolutionary shift in thinking over time?"

He shrugged. "It could have been either. I'm a student of history... did you know that, Sparhawk?"

"No sir," I said, pulling my sleeves on painfully. They rasped over my flaking skin. My teeth bared themselves in discomfort.

"Well, I am. History teaches us that every society has its blind spots, evils they perform without question. They come to believe their barbaric practices are hallowed traditions. Think of the Romans with their blood-sports in the coliseum. Or the

Mayans, who sacrificed thousands of innocents to please their heartless gods. Even the Americans, more recently, came to believe in—"

"Sir?" I interrupted, now fully dressed. "May I ask what this has to do with the matter at hand? We have Stroj agents on Earth again, sir. That much is clear, and they appear to have Betas helping them."

"Eh? Yes, well... you're obviously correct. The general belief at Central Command is that this was an isolated sleeper cell. A group of undiscovered enemy agents that took action to exact revenge upon the man who defeated them in battle last time."

I looked at him. "Is that what you believe?" I asked.

"Hell no. Two renegades can't hack implants, blast holes in the umbilical and break into a hospital bent on assassination. It takes an organization to do all that."

I nodded. "I agree, Admiral. I agree."

"Good!" he shouted, clapping me on the back.

The blow was painful, but I kept a wincing smile on my face.

"Now," he boomed, "get back up to that ship. Get her underway and get the hell out of this system. Find your way to Beta. The emissaries are waiting aboard your vessel now."

My expression shifted into a frown. "Emissaries, sir?"

He laughed. "What? Did you think the government would let *you* represent Earth? What if you started a fight with the first colonist you met? You're good at that—at least, that's your rep."

"I see," I said unhappily. "I'll transport these emissaries to a colony world and make contact. Now, if you'll excuse me, sir—"

"There will be no excuses this time. There's a color guard waiting out in the hallway, and a pinnace on the roof."

That startled me. "A pinnace, sir?"

"Yes. To hell with the umbilical. Take my personal transport up to your ship and get going."

Nodding, I walked down the hallway. With great effort, I managed not to limp.

Behind me followed a grim-faced group. Jillian, her partner, Zye and a team of four marines all walked with visible tension. They were looking everywhere at once, and eyeing everyone but me.

How had I become the center of controversy again? Why had the enemy singled me out? After all, even if they did manage to kill me, Star Guard was certain to appoint a new captain to my post aboard *Defiant* and send him out into the unknown to explore.

There was more to this situation on Earth than I understood, that much was clear. I decided to put it behind me as best I could. At this point, I relished a nice calm journey into the wilds of interstellar space.

-5-

When the pinnace reached *Defiant* and docked with her, I was shocked to realize how much time had passed. Of the thirty-nine hours I'd promised Durris I'd return within, only two remained. I'd spent a full day in the hospital without knowing it. We would have to fly to the departure point in all haste to exit the system on schedule.

As I rushed to the command deck, teeth gritting with each painful step, another thought occurred to me: Chloe hadn't come to visit me.

I'd been stretched out on a hospital bed for nearly two days, but she'd never come to see me.

I'm no expert at relationships, but I knew this simple fact couldn't be positive. I ducked into my office and contacted her on my implant.

A tiny, irritating vibration ran up through the base of my skull. My implant had been restored and upgraded while I was unconscious. The new version seemed to be more intrusive— but that might just have been a side-effect of the swelling at the insertion-point.

The call kept buzzing, but she wasn't picking up. I glanced at my chronometer, there was so little time left. Perhaps I could call later when I was just about to leave Earth orbit.

But then, just before I gave up and disconnected, the call was answered.

"William?" Chloe asked. "Are you all right?"

"Yes—at least, I am now. I've been in bed for days, but I pulled through."

"I'm very happy to hear that. I was so worried."

"Chloe…" I said, summoning up the courage to say what must be said next, "I'm going to be gone. Gone for a long time, I suspect."

"I know," she said. "I'll miss you."

"Will you wait for me?" I asked, blurting out the words. I hadn't meant to say it that way. It sounded weak and pleading. I'd meant to indicate that I barely cared—but I did.

"William…" she said slowly. "I don't know what to say."

Suddenly, I understood. She'd already moved on. She'd made up her mind during the months I was away in space. Not knowing if I was alive or dead had been too much for her.

Possibly, she'd taken on another lover to speed things along.

"I see," I said stiffly. "I'm sorry to have troubled you with this call."

"Don't be like that, William. We can still be friends."

"Of course."

"Be well, be safe. Come home to Earth again."

"I fully intend to. Goodbye, Chloe of Astra."

"Goodbye, William of Sparhawk," she responded automatically, with equal formality.

The connection closed. I took a deep breath. I felt irritated and saddened all at the same time. But part of me felt liberated as well. Since Chloe had taken over her mother's position as a Public Servant, she'd grown steadily more preoccupied and distant.

After a brief internal struggle, I managed not to curse aloud. I told myself sternly that it might all be for the best.

Forcing myself to get moving again, I refused to sit in my office and brood. I found Durris in my chair, and relieved him with a tap on the shoulder and a friendly nod. He was red-eyed, and his head hung from his neck like a drooping plant.

"Are you sure you're all right, sir?" he asked me, looking me over with a tired, but critical, eye.

"Better than you, by the looks of it," I told him. "You're to report to your bunk for at least twelve hours."

"Yes, Captain—and thank you, sir."

He left, and I watched him walk away. I had no doubt he'd spent virtually every hour I'd been absent at his post. It gave me a guilty pang to think of it.

"Oh, by the way," he said in passing, "the ambassador is on C-deck. She'd like to meet with you and have a formal dinner gathering."

"Right…" I said, having almost forgotten about carrying an emissary to the stars, "I must welcome her aboard. But she'll have to wait for now, I must get this ship underway."

He left, and I turned back to my duties. I was full of questions about the ambassador, naturally. I knew she was a she, but that was about it.

I didn't ask Durris any more questions about this ambassador as I had too much to do. Pleasantries would have to wait.

Once I was sure *Defiant* was ready to fly, I had the helmsman back her away from Araminta Station. A few minutes later we zoomed away under heavy acceleration.

The sensation of a moving ship under my feet caused me to smile. It was good to be back in business.

Our real acceleration rate was around thirty Gs, but due to our dampeners, we felt only a fraction of it. Still, the weight of our own bodies was uncomfortable.

"Let's head for the departure point," I ordered, and the navigators laid in an appropriate course.

Defiant was Earth's only ship capable of interstellar travel. We'd long been out of contact with our colonies—it had been nearly a century and a half, in fact. It was something of a thrill for all aboard to know that history was about to be changed dramatically.

Using *Defiant's* sensors, we'd previously identified several possible ER bridges out past Jupiter. In the past, before solar flares had ruptured the existing network of bridges to other systems, these bridges could be found closer to the Sun. The Cataclysm had washed away those easy-to-reach links like sand bars in a flood.

"ETA to the departure point?" I asked the helmsman.

I frowned in surprise when I saw who was in the pilot's chair. Rumbold had spun around to face me.

"Sixteen hours, sir," he said. "We'll barely make it. I suggest we give the inertial dampeners a workout."

"Rumbold? Didn't I assign you to the damage control deck?"

"You did indeed, sir," he admitted. "But we only have two other trained pilots aboard, and they're off-duty."

"Ah, I see. You edged yourself back onto the roster for take-off. Is that it?"

"Just trying to help out, Captain."

"Right. Well, lay in the course and apply thrust as evenly as you can. We have a guest aboard."

Once the ship was underway, the droning of the engines built to a continuous roar. The stresses on the hull and our bodies increased simultaneously.

I'd sounded the all-hands warning, but I hadn't carefully checked upon the status of our formal companion. Complaints were, therefore, not long in coming.

"Sir," Lieutenant Commander Yamada said, spinning her chair around to face me. Like many of my crew she'd been recently promoted, but she hadn't let that go to her head. "Our diplomatic guest is unhappy. She's sending me complaints approximately every minute."

My face tightened. I supposed this was an unavoidable reality. Any ambassador wanted to be fawned over and groomed until she felt well-treated. I wasn't looking forward to the task, but fortunately, my upbringing had prepared me for it.

"Bring her up to the command deck," I told Yamada. "She can take a look at what we're doing up here in person."

Yamada looked dubious, but she relayed my summons to C-Deck.

We continued our flight, slipping past the Moon in less than an hour. As the ambassador didn't show up immediately, I dared to hope she wouldn't bother to come to the command deck at all—but my hopes didn't last long.

"Captain Sparhawk?" asked a woman's voice from behind me. The voice was a familiar one—shockingly familiar.

The ambassador was an older woman dressed in a black gown. The color and the garment were almost a uniform for any member of her Great House. I knew her quite well as my mother had been born a Grantholm.

"Lady Grantholm?" I said, standing up and bowing to her. I almost lost my footing—the acceleration had us all at a disadvantage. Despite the dampeners we were at one-point-seven Gs of thrust and rising.

"This acceleration is wholly unacceptable," she said in a severe tone. "I want you to slow this ship down—or turn on the dampeners. Whatever it takes."

I straightened from my bow and saw she was struggling not to grab onto the rail that ran around the inner region of the command deck. Finally, she swayed and reached for it. Supporting herself with two pale claws, she bared her teeth at me.

"If I don't miss my guess, we're *still* increasing our rate of acceleration," she said.

"We are, madam," I admitted.

"Whatever for?"

"Two excellent reasons: First, we're on a time schedule. In order to reach the departure point at the moment CENTCOM has instructed me to do so, we have to move at speed."

"Surely they'll understand a delay," she said. "You've been through quite an ordeal, I gather."

"That's my job, Lady. Any Guardsman would be required to do the same."

"False pride," she muttered. "What's your second reason, Sparhawk?"

"My understanding of ER physics," I said. "The recommended velocity wasn't chosen at random. When we reach the departure point, it isn't good enough that we float there motionless, waiting for an opening. We have to breach a membrane—a barrier between space and hyperspace. Only at that perfect moment can we engage the bridge-drive. The prerequisite speed is being built up right now."

"I had no idea this would be such a trial," she complained.

"I had no idea a Grantholm person could be so adverse to discomfort."

Her eyes flashed at me. Every Grantholm alive prided themselves on the rugged nature of people from their House. Compared to most upper class types, they were a capable lot, but they weren't accustomed to the rigors of the Guard.

"All right," Grantholm said, wheezing. "I'll return to my cabin. Have an oxygen bottle sent down, would you?"

"Immediately, madam."

She left with poor grace. I returned to my seat and Rumbold rolled his bulging eyes around to land on me.

"That wasn't diplomacy!" he exclaimed. "You spat at each other like two alley cats."

"Two cats from rival houses, you mean," I said.

"Why would they assign such a person to the task of playing ambassador? You might as well give Zye the job."

I chuckled at the thought. Zye's concept of diplomacy was limited in the extreme.

"Appointments of this sort are rarely based on merit," I admitted. "She's well-connected, and she wanted the job. I doubt anyone had the guts to refuse her request."

"She wants to go into space," Rumbold said thoughtfully, "but she can't handle an extra half-G of acceleration…? This doesn't bode well."

"No," I agreed, "it doesn't."

The hours went by quickly, as did the inner planets. We passed the orbit of Mars, tilted above the plane of the ecliptic to miss the asteroid belt, and soon thereafter Jupiter was looming.

We'd traveled an amazing distance in a short time. The full power of *Defiant*'s engines was startling. When I'd flown her home to Earth nearly a year ago, she'd been a limping wreck. Now, she was in prime condition.

As we approached Jupiter's orbital lane and passed it, we came into the region of space where the ER bridges lurked. The existence of these channels into hyperspace had first been proposed by Einstein and Rosen in the early twentieth century. They'd later become popularized with the term "wormhole."

As in so many cases in theoretical physics, the practical realities didn't match the theory exactly, but the bridges were close enough in nature to warrant the naming credit. Rather than being a warped connection between two points in space and relating to a black hole, the entry points were more numerous and less deadly. They appeared as fractures in space, rather than holes. They did, however, operate to connect two spots in normal space.

Once entered into, a given ER bridge led the explorers on an exciting journey, during which they had to locate and pierce the exit point. The bridges were called bridges because they operated in two directions, with fixed entry and exit points in normal space.

The only difficulty came when one explored a new bridge for the first time. There was no known way to detect ahead of time where the exit might lead—or even where it was, exactly. In most cases, the other end was located near a large gravitational force. After all, there had to be something big enough to cause the fracture in the first place—but even this detail wasn't always dependable.

"Guardsmen," I said, engaging the ship's public address system. "This is your captain speaking. We're about to embark on a dangerous mission. No one from Earth has activated an ER bridge in a hundred and fifty long years. It's time that changed."

All over the ship, people stopped what they were doing and listened. I couldn't blame them. It might be one of the last things they ever heard.

Defiant thrummed under our feet and hands. We could feel her power. Thus far, she'd flown with eagerness, never seeming to reach a speed she could not surpass. She was a fine ship, and I was glad to be her captain.

"We're about to enter an ER bridge into the unknown," I continued. "Throughout time, humans have sought to push their limits, to explore new places no one has ever seen before. This opportunity awaits us today. With luck, we'll find a friendly colony on the far side of this bridge and establish a positive relationship with them. It's time to cross your fingers as we have only minutes left."

"Sir," Zye said suddenly. "I have a security alert on my boards."

I spun my chair around and faced her. "Explain."

"There's someone in the aft hold. The entrance is unauthorized."

My mind raced. The aft hold? That was hardly a critical portion of the ship. Why would anyone…?

"Lieutenant Morris," I said, contacting him on a private channel. "We have a situation in the aft hold. Investigate and report."

"I'm on it, sir," he said. "We got the alert, too. We're already scrambling and on our way. I have to admit though, I didn't expect this."

"Didn't expect what?" I asked. "What do you think this breach is about?"

"The lifeboats, sir. Has to be. There's nothing else down there but foodstuffs and extra gear."

Life boats? I wasn't sure what to make of it.

"What do you think they want to do with our lifeboats?" I asked.

"Disable them, probably," he said, grunting and blowing his labored breath over the microphone. I could tell he was running through the ship ahead of his squad.

"Sabotage? Now?"

"When else? If you want to destroy a ship that's attempting to cross a bridge, what better time is there than to do it when she's screaming toward departure point and can't stop?"

"When else indeed…" I said.

After a few seconds thought, I made a decision. "Morris, if you sense the ship is in danger don't hesitate to use deadly force."

He chuckled. "You read my mind, Captain. For the record, don't feel bad if things get messy. I'd already decided to play it that way. Morris out."

"Captain," Zye called to me. "Permission to join the security team?"

"No," I said. "I need you on the command deck, Lieutenant."

Disappointed, she went back to her duties.

"Give me a visual on Morris and his team, please," I told Yamada. "Split the screen with the aft hold."

"Can't show the hold, sir. Whoever is down there has disabled the cameras."

With a growing sense of concern, I watched as the main forward screen lit up. Instead of displaying Jupiter sliding by, it now showed Morris and his team from the point of view of their helmet cameras. A trio of troops appeared. They were wearing black body-shell armor with heavy weapons mounted on their chest plates.

This impressed me. It took time to get into a body-shell unit, and this emergency had only been detected a minute or two ago. That meant Morris was really on the ball—or that he was paranoid.

Knowing him well, I suspected the latter. He'd prepared ahead of time, assuming something would go wrong and require heavy armor just as *Defiant* plunged into the breach. As was often the case, his instincts had proven correct.

Morris waved his lead marine ahead. I wondered briefly why there were only three of them in action. The ship had a complement of sixteen marines. Perhaps he'd only suited up a few of them and placed the rest in other strategic gear and positions. Whatever the case, the first marine applied explosives to the hatch after it failed to open. She kicked it in after the hinges were blown, and…

I don't know what I'd expected, but it wasn't what happened next. The three were sucked into the chamber with a sudden gush of air.

"Is the hold depressurized?" I demanded.

"It must be, sir," Yamada said.

"Why didn't the computer show that? There's nothing on the boards. It's all green."

"I don't know, sir," she said helplessly.

"The saboteurs must have fooled with the system," Zye said. "They've hacked the ship's monitoring system."

I took direct control of the screen input. I double-tapped on Morris' camera. He was spinning, falling in a black pit that an hour ago had been my aft hold. It was hard to tell what was going on, but from the flailing limbs and cursing, I gathered the troops were at least still alive.

Rumbold spun around at that point. He looked at me with red-rimmed eyes. "Sir, I recommend we abort entry into hyperspace."

I looked at Yamada. "If we divert, can we turn around and make a second run at this departure point?"

She shook her head. "We're going too fast. We'll overshoot. It will take about ten hours to get back into position—the departure point we were ordered to utilize may have shifted by then."

Baring my teeth, I slammed a fist on the console.

"Dammit! Who's working so hard to stop this mission?"

No one answered my question.

"Morris!" I shouted. "Can you hear me? What's your status?"

Nothing came back for several seconds.

"We've only got six minutes left before we're committed, sir," Yamada said.

I waved her off, trying to get a scratchy message from Morris.

"There's some kind of interference in here," he said. "We're alive, but they sure scared the—"

The system spat static for several seconds.

"Morris?" I called. "Lieutenant?"

"—no way they should have been able to do this without someone noticing. It's amazing how far—."

The signal faded away.

"Morris," I said, "I'm not getting everything you're saying. Are you in danger?"

"Danger? No sir, the danger has left the ship, I'd say."

Yamada waved for my attention. "Captain, if we're going to abort, we have to do it now. The departure point is directly ahead. We have to—"

I wheeled to Rumbold. "Helm, steer us fractionally off-center. I want to be in a position to either hit the edge of the departure point—or veer more and miss it entirely. Buy me some time to decide."

Rumbold looked scared. Maybe he was regretting whatever manipulations he'd performed to get himself back into the pilot's chair for this historic occasion. His eyes boggled and he lifted his hands toward the controls hesitantly.

"That's a tall order, Captain… but I'll try."

"Just do it. Morris, get out of that hold. Report when you're in the clear. You have seconds—"

I saw something then, something coming from the screens. Muzzle flashes began. Silent firing of heavy, chest-mounted guns. My marines were in action.

"Get out of there, Morris. Pull back to the hatch. And tell me what you're shooting at!"

"—can't get—"

More buzzing. I got up from my chair. Zye stood with me. I swung my eyes toward the timer. Five minutes? There was no time to armor-up myself.

"Deploy the reserves to support Morris," I commanded the rest of the security team.

"Are we going down there, sir?" Zye asked.

I could tell from her demeanor that she was spoiling for a fight. On screen, more flashes flared brilliantly in the dark hold. Silent yellow fire spit across the screen—but what the hell could they be shooting at?

Sitting back down with a force of will, I gestured for Zye to join me. She did so reluctantly.

"I've sent in reserve troops. We have to let them do their jobs. Morris, can you hear me?"

"Yes sir," he answered at last. I could hear him panting. I also heard heavy equipment moving.

Activating his helmet camera again, I frowned at the scene. He was dragging a corpse. The body-shell armor was still intact, but the head was missing. It was the woman he'd sent in first.

"They ambushed us," Morris said in between gulps of air. "Both sides. Someone must have set them up for—I don't get it, sir."

"*Who* ambushed you?" I demanded as calmly as I could.

"Not who, what. They were repair robots. Three of them. They came in with welding torches and pinchers. We shot them—but they're pretty tough bastards. They'd been reprogrammed to kill anyone who came into the hold."

I spun toward Zye. "Who's authorized to do that? To reprogram those robots?"

"We can't alter their base programming," she said. "Only the Stroj can do that."

Suddenly, I understood the situation. It was as if an explosion had gone off in my brain.

"Yamada locate the three engineering personnel that requested transfers off this vessel. Where are they right now?"

"You mean O'Donnell's team? Checking... They're all three in the aft hold, sir."

I moved to her station and stared at the data. "Morris? Is it possible anyone else is alive down there?"

"I doubt it, sir. The chamber was depressurized. It was hard vacuum. Oh, one other thing, one of the lifeboats was missing."

Yamada checked her boards closely. She shook her head. "The hold doesn't show that. But then again, it shows it's warm and pressurized, too. Someone has hacked everything down there."

"Who could do it? Besides O'Donnell?"

"Maybe me, Zye, or some of Rumbold's people. But I doubt it."

"It was the engineering team," I said with growing certainty. "That's why they wanted off the ship. Looks like they finally got their way."

"Sir," Rumbold said. He was sweating and stressing over the controls. "I've done what I can, but if we're going to miss this departure point, we have to veer off right now. What's your decision?"

I looked up at the forward screen. A faint luminescence lit up a large circular area in the center of it. Could that be the entry?

Taking a full second, I considered my options. Abort and retry, or sail into the unknown? The engineers had almost certainly sabotaged more than the aft hold. To fly now could be suicide.

But then again, for some reason an enemy very much wanted me not to take this particular path at this particular time.

Call it Sparhawk stubbornness, but I couldn't bring myself to turn away now.

"Steady as she goes, Rumbold," I said, climbing back into my harness. "Alert the crew. We're hitting the barrier in less than one minute."

Rumbold veered gently back on course, targeting the very center of the anomaly ahead.

When we hit it at last, I felt it. Everyone aboard sensed our passage from one form of existence to another. It made my skin crawl, and it seemed to tug at every hair on my head individually for a moment. It was like walking into a resistance, a field, an invisible barrier that pressed against the flesh and the mind, but which had no effect on the hardware around us.

And then we broke through it, entering into another state of the universe.

-6-

When mankind found the first ER bridge between the stars, we'd sent in robotic probes. The probes had never returned.

Finally, a human-run expedition dared annihilation and breached the entry point. What they'd found were a half-dozen wandering machines, unable to navigate as they had no point of reference.

Hyperspace was unlike normal space in that it was really a state of being—arguably a state of nonexistence. The robotic systems had been built on the premise that they would enter the bridge and exit the far side after a short interval simply by following their original course.

This turned out not to be the case. The twisted nature of hyperspace required course alterations to find the exit. Unfortunately, navigational systems found themselves without reference points as there were no stars or other objects to detect. Basic Newtonian physics still applied, allowing vessels to travel along the bridge under power, but which way was the correct direction? How fast was your ship going? Where, exactly, was the exit to be found?

Without points of reference, these things were unclear. The robotic ships hadn't been programmed with AI that was intellectual enough to solve the problem.

Fortunately, the brave science team who'd dared to face what seemed like certain death were capable of independent, creative thought. They started off by creating what they referred to later as a "bread crumb" path. A large number of small transponders were dropped in sequence. By placing them at regular intervals, a ship's crew could determine both their relative speed of motion and their direction of flight.

It was soon discovered that hyperspace was inconsistent by nature. Going in a supposedly straight line left a curving set of transponders in the ship's wake. After much careful work and nonlinear mathematics the engineers aboard were able to come up with an equation that described the curve created by the sequence of dropped points. Using this complex polynomial, it was then possible to predict the location of the exit.

"Unload the first tracking device," I ordered.

Yamada tapped at her screen and we watched tensely. All of us had viewed historical accounts, and we'd been trained in this process. But actually *doing it* was another thing entirely in my opinion.

The first transponder was dropped in our wake, and it seemed to curve off to starboard.

"We've got a gentle curve so far," she said, "about thirteen degrees over the next hour, judging from very limited data."

"Is there any reason not to follow our mission parameters?" I asked.

"No sir. I'll drop them at regular intervals. With luck, we'll pick up the pattern. If it's simple enough, we'll find the way out."

I dared to smile. "Good. Proceed."

Hearing the hatch dissolve open behind me, I spun my chair and saw Lady Grantholm approaching the center of the command deck again. She frowned at the blank screens and quiet instruments.

"We've stopped?" she asked. "Sparhawk, have you gone mad? Why have you stopped this ship? Why are we drifting?"

"We're actually moving at great speed, madam," I said. "At least in relative terms. We're in hyperspace. It's quite calm here in most cases."

Her face underwent a transformation. She moved across the command deck to stand directly between me and the forward screen. It was a breach of etiquette and regulations to block the captain's view, but I let it slide.

She stood tall and stared at the blank nothingness. Now and then, a spot seemed to shimmer, going from pure black to a deep umber, then back again.

"This is it?" she asked, her voice hushed.

I stood up and moved to join her. "A perfect nothingness. By comparison, normal space is crowded with gasses, dust and debris."

"It's oppressive," she said, "I don't like it. How long must we stay in this limbo?"

"Until we find the way out."

She turned to look at me in alarm. "You don't know where we're going?"

"No madam, not in any traditional sense. We don't yet know where the exit to this maze is located. Nor do I know what we'll encounter when we leave this quiet eye of the storm and reenter normal space once again."

"Insanity," she muttered. "Why would anyone place themselves in such jeopardy?"

I chuckled. "I might ask you that question. I'm a member of Star Guard. I go where I must. I've been ordered to explore this bridge, and I'm determined to do it. Why did you volunteer to come along as our emissary?"

She cast me a dark glance. "We'll talk about that later. Will you treat me to dinner?"

"Consider yourself invited to the Captain's table, Lady," I said.

"Thank you, William. At least you're not a typical ruffian Guardsman. I only hope your navigational skills are as good as your manners."

She shook her head and began to walk away. Now that the G-forces were normal, she was no longer hunched by the weight of her own slight body. She stood tall and proud as she swept by me.

Staring after her for a moment, I turned to Yamada. "Commander, how long do you expect this to take?"

She shook her head and fooled with calculations. "I've got very little to go on, sir. We've only dropped two points of reference. They're deviating, but only by a fairly typical amount according to our historical records. I'll go out on a limb and call this bridge 'average' just for the sake of argument."

"Which gives us about eighty hours to figure out the equation."

"Right—if this bridge works the way they did in the past. We really don't know."

"All right then, you have the watch. I'm going to check on the rest of the ship."

I'd barely taken two steps when Zye stood and began to follow me.

I glanced over my shoulder, frowning. "I didn't relieve you yet from your duties on the command deck, Zye."

"No sir."

"Do you have a special reason for following me?" I prompted. I naturally knew the answer before I asked the question. Zye had been rattled by the attempts on my life. She was determined not to let me get ambushed when I was out of her sight—not even aboard my own ship in hyperspace.

"I think it would be for the best, sir," she said. "I've got nothing to do on the deck as far as tactical ops go, in any case."

She had me there. No targets or potential targets were on any screen.

"Very well," I said, "please accompany me. We'll see for ourselves what happened in the aft hold."

Before we'd made it halfway down the main passageway, Zye stepped ahead of me and opened the door to the armory. "Don't you think we should stop here first, sir?"

I hesitated, then nodded. A few minutes later found me in a tactical body shell. Zye herself was too large for human body-shells, so she took a chest cannon off its mount and cradled it like a rifle.

Smiling, I led the way down to meet up with Marine Lieutenant Morris. He wasn't surprised to see us.

"Everything's secure down here now, Captain," he said.

"Are the robots neutralized?"

"They've been switched off remotely, but—"

"Then the situation isn't secure. We must assume the worst. The engineering team abandoned ship on us. No wonder they wanted to transfer out so badly. They weren't planning to be aboard when their trap went off."

"The engineering people, huh?" Morris asked, shaking his head. "O'Donnell was always a bitch, but... well, you just can't tell. Is she working for a rival House? Or was she a Stroj?"

I shrugged. "It could be either. But I don't know why any of the Great Houses of Earth would try so hard to damage this ship."

Morris chuckled "Don't be naïve, Captain. You're an anomaly among the upper classes."

I gave him a sharp look.

"Don't get me wrong," he said quickly. "This crew loves you, and we've come to realize you're a capable commander. But the Houses of Earth have nothing to gain and everything to lose if we establish contact with our lost colonies again."

"Political upheaval isn't an automatic result in cases of cross-cultural contact," I argued.

"Maybe not, but when you're already winning the game, there's little advantage in changing the rules."

Conceding his point, I tapped on the bulkhead that led into the aft hold. "What are the conditions in there right now?"

"As best we can tell the hold depressurized several hours ago. There were two dead crewmen inside when we stormed the place."

"Dead crewmen? I didn't see any reports of that nature."

"Yeah, well, we didn't see it was depressurized, either. Someone must have screwed up the sensors and possibly our central computer as well."

Slamming down my visor, I tapped on the bulkhead again. "Seal off this corridor and open the hold."

He sighed. When everyone was breathing canned oxygen, the door dissolved open silently.

The hold was coated in frost. Now that *Defiant* was no longer accelerating, debris floated everywhere in a profusion. It looked like an ice storm had hit and frozen everything in place. A broken power saw drifted by my faceplate, its cord severed and showing exposed copper wires.

Zye's hand shot out and grabbed the power tool, shoving it away from me. I marveled at this. She was even more jumpy than usual.

Morris went in first. He'd brought down more marines, and three of them spread out around the hold, shining their suit lights in every direction with their weapons at the ready. Nothing ambushed them.

I moved forward to step into the frosty chamber next.

Zye's hand shot out again, barring my way. "There's no need for a personal inspection, sir."

Brushing her aside, I stepped into the hold. My chest cannon swiveled this way and that. The software was tracking my eyes as I looked around and aimed at everything I examined.

Once we'd determined that the repair robots were deactivated and the hold was otherwise deserted, I examined the bodies of my fallen crewmen. In addition to the lost marine, there were two dead spacers from the loading crews. They wore black suits and shocked looks on their frosted-over features.

"They were caught by surprise, that's clear," Morris said. "They didn't even have a chance to put on their helmets."

I knelt and examined the bodies more closely. Zye stepped up behind me, and I felt her watchful presence. I knew she was probably frowning in concern, not wanting me to suffer the same fate as these hapless spacers, but I pretended not to notice.

"Ah," I said, noting a dark patch on the nearest man's uniform. "An entry wound. They were shot or—"

"Maybe not," Zye said, lowering her bulk to kneel beside me. "I've seen wounds like this before."

Without asking, she rolled the corpse over. It moved stiffly and unnaturally, being both frozen and weightless.

"There," I said, "the exit wound. Very similar in diameter."

"Yes…" she said doubtfully, "I guess you're right."

"If they hadn't been shot, then what else might have caused damage like this?" I asked her.

"I'm sure the medical people can tell us once we've sounded the all-clear, sir," Morris interjected.

I ignored him, frowning at Zye.

"If we can find more wounds I'd be more certain," she said.

We examined the second body, scooting away the first so it drifted toward a stack of strapped-down crates.

"That's different," I said, looking at the second corpse. It was the body of a woman. She had her helmet on, but it hadn't seemed to help her. "There are three entry wounds here, all around the left breast."

We rolled her over and found no exits this time.

"We must remove her suit," Zye said.

She produced a knife and slashed away the shirt. What I saw under there was alarming. The woman's chest had a large gap in it. I could see into the chest cavity itself. It looked as if one of her ribs had ripped itself loose from her body and punctured her skin.

"I get it," I said with sudden insight. "They took a trophy. A rib."

Zye nodded somberly. "Yes. This is almost definitely the work of a Stroj team of saboteurs."

"They were probably ordered not to take body parts, but I guess old habits die hard."

The Stroj were an odd people. They'd become part cybernetic in order to survive on their newly adopted colony world, and over time they'd come to believe beings made entirely of flesh were inferior.

They still, however, seemed to be fascinated with their past as full-fledged human beings. They often took trophies such as scalps, skin-patches and teeth to adorn themselves. The female marine was no exception. She'd been slain by surprise and had a rib plucked from her torso as she lay dying.

"I hate the Stroj," Morris said, breathing hard over his mouthpiece. "I hope we kill them all when we find their home planet."

Zye glanced at him in surprise.

"An ambitious goal," she said, "but a logical one considering the facts. There are only two possible conclusions to this conflict in the long term. Either we will destroy the Stroj, or they destroy us."

We left the bodies to the medical staffers then, after making sure the repair robots were thoroughly inoperable.

"These repair machines are untrustworthy," I said. "They were built by the Stroj after all, right Zye?"

"That is what I said."

"Right. They were a trade good you purchased from the Stroj long ago. Now, these robots have turned on my crew."

Zye tapped at her faceplate thoughtfully. "I too, find this fact disturbing. When we Betas originally forged a deal with the Stroj, our engineers determined the robots couldn't possibly attack any Beta. Perhaps our Alphas miscalculated."

"Maybe," I said. "Or maybe the Stroj followed the letter of the agreement you had with them. They can't attack Betas—but they can attack Earth men."

She conceded that this might be the case. When the hold was declared clear of enemies we retired to our conference room. There were many things to discuss and plans to be made.

The intrusion of the Stroj onto my ship changed everything from the point of view of Earth, but did little to alter our mission. *Defiant* must find a way out of hyperspace and determine where she was after she came out.

Would there be Stroj ships waiting for us when we exited hyperspace at last? Or something far more deadly? We had no way of knowing.

-7-

The intrusion of the Stroj onto my ship changed everything from the point of view of Earth, but did little to alter our mission. As *Defiant's* captain, my first priority was to find a way out of hyperspace and determine where we were once we came out—that had not changed.

Would there be Stroj ships waiting for us when we exited hyperspace at last? Or perhaps something even more deadly? We had no way of knowing.

Defiant's crew had grown to nearly three hundred individuals by the time we'd left Earth, but it was a tribute to the ship's size that the decks still felt empty at times. Marching down the passages to a spacious conference room, I joined a meeting that was already in progress.

XO Durris was guiding the group, but he sat down when I entered the room. He'd reported back to duty sooner than I would have liked, but he'd at least gotten a little sleep. Given the treacherous attack on our hold, he had a good reason to join us, so I didn't order him back to his bunk.

The topic of discussion was the attack itself, and its ramifications.

"It's my opinion, sir," Durris said as he sat ramrod straight in his chair, "that the enemy probably planted some kind of explosive device on the ship before exiting. Their hasty departure makes no sense otherwise."

"If you're right," I said, "they probably did it long ago."

Durris blinked at me. "Why do you think that, sir?"

"Recall their behavior before we left Earth. They picked fights with me, with you—with every officer on the ship. Let me ask this: did any of you like O'Donnell or her team?"

They all shook their heads.

"Just so," I continued. "They purposefully worked to irritate us, then they requested a transfer off *Defiant* before we left orbit. It must have seemed like a sure thing—but we didn't let them go."

Rumbold leaned forward and cleared his throat. "I was meaning to ask you about that part, Captain… why didn't you let O'Donnell and her people bug out when they wanted to?"

"Because Halsey wouldn't allow it. We didn't have time to train anyone else for the job."

The group nodded.

Durris spoke up next. "If these suppositions are true," he said, "we're still in danger. After all, they must have jumped ship for a reason."

"I agree," I said. "We'll have to search the ship from the top to the bottom. Yamada, go over everything these three engineers did. Pull files on security camera data, the works. We have to know what they might have compromised. It might not be a bomb, but rather a simple weakening of a vital component. We just don't know."

Everyone looked alarmed as they pondered the magnitude of searching this vast ship to find an unknown fault. We'd considered the matter to be at an end. We'd assumed that once the Stroj were off the ship they were no longer a danger—but we couldn't count on it.

The Stroj had operated right under our noses. Even though we'd all failed to detect them, I could tell Zye was feeling responsible. She was our chief of security, after all. She probably felt she should have caught the attack before it happened.

"You're right, sir," Zye said with a grim expression. "Anything could have been compromised. They wouldn't have left the ship if their work hadn't been done. I'll review every log I can dig up on their activities. There must be some kind of a record…"

"Good," I said, then I turned to Durris. "First Officer, I want you to spearhead the effort."

"I don't know if I'm right for the job, sir," he said. "I've already been fooled once. Perhaps another would be—"

"No," I said firmly.

Durris was being Durris again. He was an excellent officer, but he was a little too quick to blame himself for every error. This made him meticulous and thorough—but also somewhat lacking in self-confidence. That was probably the primary reason he'd yet to earn a command of his own.

"I have every confidence in you," I continued, speaking in a firm voice. "I have confidence in *all* of you. Remember, I missed the enemy spies too. This is our chance to rectify that error."

The meeting broke up, and I moved on to even less savory duties. Gathering most of the ship's complement of spacers, I committed our three lost comrades to float eternally in hyperspace. I wondered, as I shot them out into a formless gray void between vague reference points, whether their souls would ever find true peace out here.

That evening, a tone sounded at my cabin door. I'd removed my overcoat, but I quickly put it back on again and let the coat cinch-up its ties. It wouldn't do for a crewman to see me lounging after having conducted a painful funeral.

The door chimed a second time before I reached it. Could that be irritation shining through in the attitude of my visitor? That was my impression.

I dissolved the door and looked at Lady Grantholm in surprise.

"Dinner…" I said after we'd stared at one another for a few seconds.

"That's why I'm here, yes," she said. She knit her brows together giving me an up-down look of disapproval. "Don't tell me you forgot, William? I'm your Great Aunt. Captain or not, one would think—"

"I'm sorry, Lady. Won't you enter and dine with me?"

She swept by me with a sniff. Seeing there was no food laid out, much less a sumptuous repast fitting her station, she muttered under her breath.

"What was that, Lady?"

"I said one would think you'd forgotten your upbringing. Are you a Sparhawk, or a simple guardsman?"

"Both, madam," I said evenly, but the truth was, she was getting on my nerves. "You must excuse my distraction. I lost three crewmen and learned three others were traitors today."

Grantholm stepped away and made a fluttering gesture over her shoulder with painted fingers. "Commoners, William. Don't tie up your mind or your emotions with them. They live short, brutal lives. They're important of course—but not worthy of grief for a person of your station."

My jaw muscles clenched. "I disagree," I said. "Vehemently."

She glanced at me and pursed her lips. "Let's discuss more important matters. We have things to iron out between us."

"Such as?"

"Your role and mine as we exit this bridge. You're in command of this ship. You rule your crew and this vessel in every respect."

"I'm glad you understand the situation thoroughly."

"But," she said loudly. She flicked up one of her painted fingers toward my cabin's ceiling. The tip was a glossy lavender. "*I* command this mission beyond the limits of this ship's hull."

I frowned at her. "Meaning?"

"Don't be dense, Sparhawk. I mean if we meet other colonists, I'll do the talking. You're to stand by silently, flying your ship with dignity. Do you understand?"

"I take it from your overly dramatic statements that you think I might try to upstage you somehow?"

She tilted her head to the left. "You have a certain reputation. You bulled your way back to Earth in this ship, and you earned command of her. But that doesn't mean you're a king. You're a captain in Star Guard—that's all. The position is comparable to that of a ferry pilot."

"A ferry pilot?" I demanded incredulously.

"I'm sorry if I may seem rude. I find it's best to speak bluntly when important details of command are being worked out."

"There's nothing to work out," I said. "I'm in command of *Defiant*. I plan to leave the diplomacy up to you, Ambassador. Nothing else has ever entered my mind."

"Excellent. Now, what are we eating?"

I ordered up a platter of pine-spiced meats, dried fruit and a bottle of sparkling wine. This last item raised Grantholm's eyebrows, but she accepted a glass from the cabin steward without complaint.

Once we were in a more social atmosphere, the Lady's attitude softened. She turned the conversation to House Astra—and more specifically, my intentions toward the Lady of that House.

"Chloe is a fine-looking girl," she said. "She's young, but she seems to be level-headed. The loss of her mother was tragic."

I knew as a matter of fact that my Aunt hadn't been able to stand the Elder Lady of House Astra, but I gave no hint of this. Powerful people from rival Houses always believed it was the best course to praise the dead.

"That said," she continued, "I think you should drop your dalliances with her. What's wrong with a nice Grantholm girl? House Astra individuals are our traditional enemies."

I nearly spit a cream-stuffed croissant back onto the platter with the rest. Chloe had ended our relationship officially, but that didn't mean I wanted my Aunt telling me who to consort with.

"What?" I demanded. "Listen here, Aunt—"

"—Ambassador," she corrected quickly.

"Ambassador Grantholm," I amended, "I'm in charge of more than this ship. I'm in charge of my private life as well."

She made a small sniffing noise and drank her wine. "Never mind then, boy. I was just testing your resolve."

"What?"

"I wanted to get a reaction out of you. I can see you're serious about guiding your own destiny."

"I am," I said, "let me assure you."

She nodded slowly. "Good enough then."

"Lady, on another point, I do wish you'd start treating me in a manner appropriate to my station."

For the first time, she looked surprised. "Whatever do you mean?"

"I'm a Star Guard captain. Despite my young age, I am in command of the only Earth starship capable of interstellar travel. That makes me a critical member of our military. I'm *not* a ferry pilot."

She shrugged. "I'm well aware of your career accomplishments, but I don't see how I've mistreated you."

"You haven't mistreated me—not exactly. But you're behaving as if I'm still a teen at a family gathering. A favored son, perhaps, or an entertaining youth with a spark of talent. I'm far more than that now."

She stared at me for a second. "Perhaps you're right, William. You should remember that I'm an oldster, after all. Once one goes past the first century of life, it becomes more difficult to accept the rapid growth of the young into adulthood. Now, if you'd be so kind as to allow me to retire. I'm afraid I've been fatigued by this journey, and I must leave you now."

"A pity," I said, but despite the anger I was feeling, I realized I'd at least managed to finally engage her in a real conversation.

I saw her out. When she'd gone, I up-ended the half-empty bottle of sparkling wine. The nerve of the woman! She'd pushed and pushed until I'd been forced to push back.

I was left wondering what she might have demanded next if I'd agreed to stop seeing Chloe. She'd said something about Grantholm girls—maybe she'd have asked that I start courting one of her own daughters.

They were not ugly women, but they had questionable track records in terms of romance. All of them had been married more than once—unions which hadn't lasted. They were pushy like their mother, twice my age, and my cousins by blood. The entire idea was preposterous.

I soon fell into a deep sleep and dreamt of women in black gowns demanding things from me. In the morning, I awoke groggy but determined.

A shower and a careful morning routine improved my mood dramatically—but I was still determined. Lady

Grantholm wasn't going to treat me like an errand boy on my own ship any longer.

-8-

It took a full week to find the exit out of hyperspace. In the end, we'd managed to map out the polynomial curve and plotted our way to our destination. Only a nine-degree variation in our course was required to hit the exit squarely—but after travelling a billion kilometers, such a small variance made a great deal of difference.

"Steady on," I ordered. "Helmsman, you're speeding up. I ordered no acceleration on the final approach."

"Sorry sir," Rumbold replied. "I must have missed that point in the briefing."

Frowning, I looked at him in surprise. "Rumbold? How did you get back into that chair? Where's my pilot? Did you do away with her?"

"I was simply next on the roster, sir," he said without looking over his shoulder at me. "She must have stepped out and called for a replacement. Perhaps she's not feeling well. Hyperspace can do that to people—or so I've heard."

"Hmm," I said thoughtfully. Once had been a coincidence. Twice… Rumbold must have pulled something to get his rump back into the pilot's seat on both the entry and the exit from hyperspace.

Slightly annoyed, I considered ordering him below decks and summoning my regular pilot. After a moment's further consideration however, I dropped the idea. After all, he'd done well when we'd entered the bridge initially. Technically, that made him the most experienced living pilot in Star Guard when it came to steering a vessel through the dangerous transition into hyperspace.

What concerned me now, however, was our successful exit from the ER bridge. We had no idea where we'd end up. If rapid course adjustments were to become suddenly necessary…

"All right," I said. "You can stay in the pilot's chair today. But if any more roster changes are made on future occasions, I'll bust you down to swabbing decks with a power-mop."

"Understood, Captain," he said with visible relief.

"Time, Yamada?"

"Displaying it now. Our calculations should be correct to within a two-second span."

One of the alarming things about hyperspace was the tendency of the entry and exit points to shift during flight. They were hard to find in the first place—and they were moving targets.

We watched as the timer ticked down. Now and then it froze for two or three seconds, recalculating. At other times it jumped forward a few heartbeats. It was disconcerting.

"Requesting permission to increase speed by five percent, Captain," Rumbold said. "We're going fast enough to puncture the barrier, but we've got very little margin. If it shifts away just as we reach the point of no return—"

"Permission denied," I said smoothly. "I want to be able to maneuver when we come out if we have to evade something."

"Understood, sir."

After watching Rumbold for a few moments thoughtfully, I looked over at Zye. "Lieutenant, I want you to keep an eye on our pilot. If he fails to perform in some way, you have my permission to intercede and take over his station."

"A wise precaution," she said.

Rumbold muttered something I didn't catch. He kept his hands on the controls and his eyes on the screens.

Then suddenly, the clock surged forward. It went from forty seconds to seven. Everyone on the command deck gasped.

"There!" Rumbold shouted. "A huge shift!"

"Yes—but the exit moved closer to us," Zye said. "So far every shift has brought it closer."

"You can't count on that…" he muttered.

There was no more time for talk. We hit the barrier a few moments later and broke through into normal space.

The process of exiting hyperspace was somewhat more jarring than what one experiences when entering. I think it was mostly a psychological thing. Going from a universe full of stars to a dark vacant place was less alarming than switching from blankness and quiet into the swirling maelstrom of our home universe.

What riveted the attention of everyone on the deck was the looming presence of a vast, orange-colored star. It was close—too close.

"Prepare for evasive action," I said.

"Which way, sir?" Rumbold asked.

My crew was already trying to come up with answers in this regard.

"Durris, give him a course," I said, trying to sound calm. The gamma radiation readings were already on the rise. The star would cook us if we got too close.

My XO had the in-flight duty of operating tactical navigation. That meant he was in charge of deciding our short-term flight path. He worked with his screen making rapid calculations.

"The star's corona is venting from the northern pole," Yamada said from the sensor boards, "I'd recommend we dive south."

"Sir, there's a planet-sized body in that direction," Durris said. "It appears to be artificial in nature."

They all looked at me. Already, I could feel a gravitational tug. We were within the star's reach. Soon, that would make maneuvering more difficult.

"Dive south," I ordered Rumbold. "Head for the artificial construct. It's probably located there for a good reason."

The ship swooped sickeningly. Rumbold wasn't sparing any power. Fortunately, *Defiant* had plenty of it.

The next half-hour was harrowing, but we managed to get ourselves onto a stable flight path. We skirted the star, decelerating continuously. Our target was the strange structure that sat locked in a synchronous orbit below the star's southern pole.

By the time we felt our situation was no longer immediately dangerous, we'd made a series of discoveries about the alien system.

"There are no records of this star system in our Earth documents," Yamada said with certainty. "To our knowledge no one from Earth has ever been here before."

"How far are we from the Solar System?" I asked.

"About thirty-five light-years," Durris answered for the navigational team. "As far as we can tell, this is Gliese-32, a star system marked for exploration, but which was never definitively scouted before the Cataclysm."

"Well, start recording people," I said. "Sensors, what do we have?"

"It's an odd system by any measure," Yamada said. "There are apparently no large planets. There are only asteroids and planetoids. The star itself is mildly unstable. It's ejecting gas in regular intervals—serious flares."

That concerned me. It was a storm of flares that had jumbled our network of ER bridges more than a century back in our star system. If this star was unstable, wouldn't it possibly disrupt the local bridges in this region of space? The most alarming thing about that possibility was the thought that we might be trapped here, unable to backtrack through the same route to Earth.

I mentioned none of this to the crew. They were smart people, and they could interpret the data as well as I could.

"I assume the artificial planet is built in that location for a reason?" I asked.

"Yes," Yamada answered. "It's in the Goldilocks zone, well-placed for liquid water to form on the surface. Even more significantly, it seems like the flares never travel in that direction."

Nodding thoughtfully, I got out of my seat and began to pace. "Makes sense. They came here and found a dangerous star. With nowhere to land, they built their own home in the one spot that's calm within this stormy system. The question is:

why didn't they keep traveling? Surely, there must be better systems than this one to colonize."

"Sir?" Yamada asked me, "I've got the standard greeting file queued-up. Should I begin broadcasting to the artificial satellite?"

My lips compressed tightly. This was a big decision. "I'm going to have to ask you to hold that option for now. I think we should know more before—"

"You'll do no such thing, Sparhawk!" shouted a voice from the rear of the command deck.

Everyone looked. It was Lady Grantholm, and she was almost trembling with rage.

"I thought we had an agreement," she said loudly. "You fly the ship, and you let me handle the diplomacy. I think no one can argue that thus far, I've upheld my end of the bargain."

"This isn't about a bargain, Ambassador," I said. "We're talking about the safety of this ship and crew. We don't know anything about these locals. They could be aliens. They could be hostile—"

"They most certainly will be if you don't broadcast our peaceful intentions!" she said. "Imagine this situation from their point of view. An unknown ship has just appeared in their system. Without a moment's hesitation, this ship targets their meager satellite and heads directly toward it. Worse, we haven't said a word in greeting."

She'd made good points, but my instincts told me to proceed with caution.

"Madam," I said, "let me investigate further. If we see no sign of hostility—then…"

"Captain, I would like to see you privately," she demanded.

With a sigh, I followed her into the adjacent ready-room. We sat across from one another.

"Here's what I'm willing to do," she said when we were alone. "I'm going to allow you to save face—this time. But don't test me again."

Blinking, I offered her a drink. "Allow me? Do I have to remind you who's in command of this ship, Lady?"

She smiled wickedly. "The ship, yes—but not the mission. Here are my orders… *Our* orders."

She handed me a computer scroll which I took dubiously. I read for a few moments, and I felt a chill settle in my guts.

"I see," I said.

"You read it all?"

"Just the pertinent parts."

"I'm authorized to take direct command of this mission, in every detail, if there is a diplomatic crisis brewing."

"There's no diplomatic anything yet," I said. "We haven't even determined if there's anyone alive on that station. They've made no transmissions, no attempts to talk to us."

"As the interloper, that's our obligation, not theirs," she said. "As to the definition of a diplomatic crisis, the person who's tasked with making that determination is me."

"Yes... as I said, I read it."

"You accept my authority in this situation?"

"It seems I have no choice. But let me ask you: how did you get such an order authorized and approved without my knowing about it?"

"That was part of the conditions by which I agreed to go on this suicidal mission," she explained. "You didn't seriously think I was going to play the elderly aunt in the back room while my nephew ran the show, did you?"

"Now that you mention it, that sort of role did seem out of place for you."

She nodded. "I see we understand one another at last. Now, let me explain to you how we're going to proceed. You'll go back onto the command deck alone and order Yamada to start transmitting the diplomatic greeting. I'll exit through the other door and move back to my quarters. If the natives in this system respond, I'll return."

"How does this sequence of events improve the situation?" I asked.

She shrugged. "Your crew will see you giving orders. I'll have vanished. Don't you think that's better than having me standing there like a harpy, looking over your shoulder to make sure you're doing it right?"

I had to admit, she had a point there. I accepted her conditions as I had no other easy options.

Returning to the command deck alone, I gave the orders. The transmission began. It left me with a hollow, worried feeling in the pit of my stomach.

If I'd had a leg to stand on, I'd have defied her no matter what the orders from Earth said. As *Defiant*'s Captain, I had the right to safeguard her crew and her hull.

The trouble was, the local population had shown no sign of hostility as of yet. I was therefore honor-bound to follow Grantholm's orders.

As soon as the situation changed, however, I vowed to realign the rules more to my liking.

-9-

No one questioned my orders to begin transmitting the diplomatic address. Using a dozen languages and a hundred binary protocols, the canned message spoke of universal peace and harmony. It requested a response from any and all listeners every minute or two, providing long pauses in between. During these intervals Yamada waited tensely for any hint of a reply.

Nothing came back to us. Not even a blip.

A full hour passed, after which Lady Grantholm returned to the deck in irritation.

"What's wrong?" she demanded. "That message was crafted to elicit a sure-fire response. It's been tested on dozens of cultures and political factions. It never fails."

Yamada spoke first. "Perhaps they're not human."

"Preposterous," the ambassador scoffed, advancing to lean on the railing and leer in frustration at the forward screens. "We've never met an alien species capable of building something like that artificial structure. We've found nothing but a few bugs and plants."

"Maybe everyone aboard is dead," Zye suggested.

Grantholm turned toward her. She nodded thoughtfully, "That stands to reason!"

She wheeled on me next. "Sparhawk, your Beta is a thinker. I see now why you've so wisely added her to your team."

"I'm glad you approve," I said dryly.

She walked to the forward screen and examined the data carefully. "I'm no expert," she admitted, "but this system looks like a deathtrap to me. One unexpected flare-up from that star could have licked this station—just once mind you—and turned it into a giant microwave oven."

Such an explanation had already occurred to me. The thought was cringe-worthy, but I couldn't deny the possibility.

"Well then," I said, "what should we do next? Diplomatically speaking, I mean?"

"We'll keep broadcasting the message," she said, looking at me thoughtfully. "What do you think we should do tactically?"

"We'll approach the station in a non-threatening fashion. We'll keep our gun ports closed and our engines at half-power. Hopefully, they'll respond before we reach them. If not... I suggest we investigate the station."

"Board a derelict structure?" she asked, impressed. "Perhaps the Grantholm blood *is* strong in your veins. We were explorers once, you know."

In my memory of family lore, the Sparhawks had discovered just as many worlds as had the Grantholms back in the days of family-financed expeditions. I decided not to bring that up, however.

"We're in agreement, then," I said. "Steady as she goes, helm."

Lady Grantholm retreated from the deck after exacting a promise from me that I'd contact her the moment the situation changed.

"Looks like you've hammered out a working relationship with the old battle-axe," Rumbold said when she'd left. "If you don't mind my saying so, sir."

"We understand one another," I agreed. "Is there still nothing in the way of a response, Yamada?"

"Nothing sir. Not even a—hold on."

I spun my chair to face her. She placed her hands on her headset and tilted her to one side. Her expression was one of intense concentration. I could tell she was trying to pick up an auditory signal and trying to ignore competing sounds.

"Are they saying something?" I asked after several long seconds.

Yamada shook her head. "I'm not sure."

"Zye, tap into Yamada's feed. In fact, pipe it to everyone, please."

A moment later I joined them, listening to the raw data stream. All I heard was a tinny knocking sound. As if a hammer was tapping on sheet metal.

"What's that? What kind of a feed are we picking up?"

"It's not a transmission," Yamada said. "I'm pinging the surface of the structure with low-powered lasers. The surface appears to be vibrating rhythmically. Every few seconds, the entire structure shakes a little. I don't understand it."

"So, these noises are an interpolation of what it sounds like on the orbiting station?"

"Right. If you were standing inside the structure, you'd hear something like this, only much louder."

Turning back to the forward screen, I magnified the image to its maximum. The shape was that of a spinning polyhedron. There were two hundred and forty facets to the structure, each of them a triangular plane. Viewed as a single entity, the station looked almost spherical.

As we watched, it slowly twirled around. We watched for a full minute before something significant changed.

"Captain!" Rumbold shouted. "One of the facets—it's an opening. Something small is coming out of it—a whole bunch of somethings."

From this distance it was hard to be sure about what we were looking at, but it was undeniably true that there were small objects coming out of the station. A black, triangular mouth had yawned open, and it was spitting out items with regularity.

I listened to the rhythmic knocking sound again. The beat of the knocking sounds matched the appearance of small objects.

"They're launching something," I said, "that much is clear."

"Missiles?" Rumbold asked.

"No," Zye said with certainty. "They're fighters. They're taking up positions off to one side of the station, massing up into a large formation."

"Fighters," I said, putting down my headset. "Apparently, our diplomatic message has failed to impress these people, whoever they are."

I began to order a logical series of counter steps. Two minutes later Lady Grantholm made another appearance.

"What's this?" she demanded. "Announcing war on our newly discovered neighbors, Sparhawk?"

"We're taking defensive precautions. All *Defiant's* shields are up, and we're pumping defensive drones out of the aft tanks."

"Well, suck them back up into your hold!" she ordered. "I didn't authorize any such action."

I glanced at her. "Madam Ambassador," I said, "I'm within my rights to defend this ship and her crew—not to mention you."

"You're provoking them!" she hissed, strutting around the deck and gesturing in frustration. "You've convinced them we've come to conquer them."

"You were convinced an hour ago the system was dead. I'm only reacting to their hostile move."

She made a guttural sound of vexation. "I'm going to have to take over this mission, Sparhawk. It pains me, but—"

"It's too late for that," I said, brushing aside the computer scroll she thrust at me again. "We're in a combat situation. I'm now in charge of all tactical decisions."

"What? I thought the situation was clear. I'm empowered to take command of this—"

"Yes, under specific circumstances. I think it would aid you to read the document again. Under these conditions, I'm in charge of the expedition."

"This will go into my report, Sparhawk! Everything will be recorded and revealed at your court martial."

"Possibly, your scenario will come to pass—if we should be so lucky as to survive that long. In the meantime, I suggest you return to your quarters and strap-in. We're going to battle stations and our maneuvers are soon going to become harsh."

Apparently, she *had* read the entirety of the orders we were both following. She made no further effort to press her claims over tactical authority. She stormed off the deck and vanished into the passages behind me. I was glad to see her go. She was a distraction I couldn't afford right now.

The klaxons sounded to indicate we were switching into a combat configuration. All over the ship, crewmen rushed to their battle stations. Every spacer soon wore a pressure suit and helmet.

Armored ports rolled open to expose missiles, cannons and dozens of other engines of destruction. *Defiant's* weapons were revealed like fangs in the mouth of a predator.

"Shields are fully active, just in case," Zye said.

"Keep them at half-power until a specific threat is revealed," I ordered.

She made the adjustments without comment.

In space, combat can be tricky. One major element was a balancing act of power expenditures. There were many ways a commander could lose a fight before it even began. One sure way to hamstring a starship was to panic and turn on every defensive system too early. Shields, drones and the like tended to draw upon the same power sources that offensive weapons did. Turning them on too early was like firing your cannons before you were within effective range—a waste of energy that would cost you later.

On the other hand, if we went into combat thinking we had the situation perfectly mapped out, we might lose due to overconfidence. I'd put the shields up at half power to provide partial protection in case we were hit by surprise. This was, after all, an unknown enemy.

It was nice not to have my command staff second-guess my every decision. They were tense, but they displayed a certain confidence I felt gratified to see. I'd gained their trust.

Now, however, was the time to prove them right.

"The fighters are breaking wide. Three groups now, one starboard, one port and the third coming in low in an arc."

Tapping at my display, I examined this last group. "Mr. Durris," I said, "it's my opinion that the third group intends to flank and possibly come at us from the rear when we engage the other two squadrons. Do you concur?"

"The math supports your theory, sir. We can't let them hit us in the engines… but if we run with full shielding on every quadrant of the ship at once, we'll have nothing left for our main batteries."

I nodded. We were rapidly reaching the point at which there would be no options. We'd have to fire on them.

There was one more possible maneuver, a full retreat—but I felt that would be a mistake. These people weren't talking. They were hostile, and if their first experience with a ship from Earth was an easy victory, they might be emboldened.

"Open a hailing channel, Yamada. In the clear."

"Open, sir."

"Are they listening?

"As far as I can tell they are. They're not talking, just sucking in every word we transmit like sponges."

Nodding, I considered my words. I took in a deep breath. "To the indigenous people of this star system, we mean you no harm. However, you've seen fit to attack an Earth warship. We must defend ourselves. Pull your fighters back, or I will destroy your station."

Everyone looked at me in surprise. I ignored the lot of them.

"Tactical, lock in on the primary structure."

"Not the fighters, sir?" Durris asked.

I glanced at him. "You heard me. Target the facet that opened and released those fighters. Our main batteries will be within range in a few moments, if my reading of the data is correct."

"That's right sir," he said, all business again. "Firing solution computed and locked-in."

We waited tensely for nearly a minute. The fighter groups were all curving now, approaching us from three sides. Every heavy gun we had was targeting the main structure.

"Sir?" Durris asked.

I didn't look at him. They'd called my bluff. I wished things had gone differently—then I gave the orders I felt I must.

"Fire bank one. Destroy that launch bay. Try not to rupture the rest of the structure."

Durris met my eyes. "We're too far out for such precision. We don't know how thick their armor is, or whether or not they have shields."

"Destroy the launch bay."

With deliberate actions, he turned back to his boards and initiated the firing sequence.

Outside on *Defiant*'s hull, a blaze of energy flared into life. Millions of kilowatts were released. They leapt across space and several long seconds later touched upon the twirling, jewel-like station ahead of us.

-10-

As it turned out, the station did have shields. We lit them up, made them glow orange, and then punctured them—all within the span of seven seconds.

We watched as the triangular mouth that had spit out so many fighters in our direction melted. It sagged, buckled, and merged with the facets surrounding it. The entire region sank inward somewhat, and the station now looked as if it had been viciously kicked in the side.

"Cease-fire," I said.

"We haven't confirmed the complete destruction of the target yet, sir," Durris said.

"No, but I think they got the message."

On our long-range tactical displays, the fighters were now shifting course. They veered off in three separate directions.

Rumbold spun around and grinned at me. "That's Sparhawk-style diplomacy if I ever saw it, Captain!" he laughed, but no one else joined in. That had never phased Rumbold before, and he went on laughing.

"Captain…?" Yamada said suddenly.

Her tone was one of disbelief. I turned to look at her expectantly.

"They've opened a channel. They're talking, sir. I can't believe you did it."

I nodded as if I'd expected nothing less. In truth, I'd taken a gamble and made it pay off. There was no need to point that out to the crew, however.

"What are they speaking?" I asked.

"Terran standard. They have a slight accent, but any of us should be able to understand them."

"Pipe it through, please."

The speakers boomed with a loud, raspy voice.

"Vandals, marauders, fiends! We don't accept your authority here!"

There was no visual feed as yet. I signaled Yamada to allow me to respond.

"We are none of these things," I said. "Nor are we here to assert authority over you or your system. Please identify yourselves."

"We're the Chosen. The Remaining. The last of our kind."

My brow furrowed in thought. Their self-description wasn't as helpful as I'd hoped, but I didn't want to upset them any further.

"Tell me, Chosen Ones, did your kind come from Earth?"

"A vast time ago, there is evidence that we did. None alive remember such a time. We've lived through countless taxers and pirates such as yourselves. We will endure."

Yamada waved to me, and I muted our outgoing channel. "What is it, Commander?" I asked her.

"Analysis of the voice indicates it's being produced by a human throat. Maybe they've been cut off out here and abused for decades."

Her suggestion seemed to match the circumstances, and it gave me a direction in which to proceed.

"What is this place?" I asked. "Who am I speaking with?"

"This star system is known to us as Gi. We are also called the Gi. I myself have been appointed the Connatic."

"I'm not quite sure what a 'Connatic' is, sir," I said. "Can you describe your function?"

"I guide. I temporize. I defend and punish. I am the Connatic."

"I see. You're the leader, then, of your people?"

"That's a very simplistic description, but I will allow this conversation to proceed to other points for purposes of expediency. What is your position, creature?"

"I'm Captain William Sparhawk, of House Sparhawk. I command this battle cruiser, the *Defiant*."

"Ah-ha!" said the voice suddenly. "You command a ship of war? Your intentions are now clear. You talk to waste our time, all the while gliding closer to gut our beloved Tranquility Station. You'll not find the Gi who live here defenseless."

I rolled my eyes. "We're not here to destroy you. Getting closer would not aid us if that was our purpose. I would simply stand-off beyond your range and pound your station to slag."

"Violent words," he said. "Words of war mixed with words of peace. Arrogance extreme and malice immeasurable."

These colonists had a very odd way of expressing themselves. It was almost as if they were narrating their thoughts aloud. I was trying to get used to it, but it wasn't easy.

"Listen, Connatic. If we wanted to destroy you we would be doing it, not talking. I'm here to communicate with you and other splintered colonies like yours. Earth is back. We're rebuilding our network to our orphaned colonies. We intend to engage in trade and peaceful coexistence with anyone who will allow it."

There was a moment of silence, and when the Connatic came back on the line, his voice had changed. It now held a calculating note.

"I see. Rebuilding the Empire set asunder so long ago. All becomes clear. It's like a slice of sky free of gases and dust. You're here to ask us to yoke ourselves like idiot oxen."

Unable to help myself, I sighed loudly. "I suggest we stand down our weapons. We will close our gun-ports if you close yours. Withdraw your fighters, and we'll park ourselves in orbit around your station. Then, I'll come aboard with a few of my officers to meet you in person."

"Invasion?" demanded the voice incredulously. "Does it think we'd be so foolish as to allow ourselves to be boarded without firing a shot?"

The conversation went on in this vein for the next twenty minutes. In time, I managed to hammer out a plan of behaviors. They were paranoid in the extreme and would only agree to single steps at a time.

The first thing both sides did was sheathe our bared weapons. Our gun-ports, missile batteries and pellet-blasters were all closed and shunted into the guts of our respective vessels.

By the time we slowed and began to circle the station, the Connatic was in a more forgiving mood. Perhaps he was starting to trust me, just a little.

A full hour after the conversation began, I found myself marching down the central passage to my quarters. There, I donned a dress uniform, my smart-pistol and power saber. I tested the clasp at my neck, and momentarily my cloak blossomed into a personal shield.

A hundred strides later I found myself on the pinnace deck. *Defiant's* original design didn't have such a deck, but we'd altered one of the holds to allow small spacecraft to enter and exit. The ship now functioned more like a traditional Earth warship.

There, at the pinnace door, I met up with an unpleasant surprise. I could see through the hatchway, and there was no mistaking the distinctive form of Ambassador Grantholm.

"Are you flying this thing yourself, William?" she asked.

"No, madam. Zye here will serve as my pilot—"

Zye pressed past me and took her seat. She studiously ignored both of us. I was sure she was aware of our ongoing strife, but it didn't seem to interest her much.

"Well?" Grantholm called. "Climb aboard, Sparhawk. We don't have much time to waste. I let you prattle on and on with that Connatic fellow for nearly an hour. Imagine my trepidation and horror at every word. You almost started a war on three separate occasions, are you aware of that?"

"Madam," I said sternly, "the situation is volatile and may turn hostile again at any moment. No treaty exists between these people and Earth. They might intend to skewer us all the moment we arrive. Accordingly, I must ask that you stay here aboard *Defiant* until I declare the situation safe for civilians."

She cocked her head quizzically to one side and regarded me with narrowed eyes. "You'll not weasel out that way. The situation has progressed. You did an excellent job of gaining their trust after terrifying them. Honestly, I didn't think you had it in you to intimidate a lesser power like that. I stand happily corrected."

"Madam, I can't allow you to endanger yourself—" I began again, but she lifted her hand to stop me.

"Just give it up, Sparhawk. I know you too well. You're a man of truth and honor. Most importantly, you follow orders."

She snapped out the computer scroll again. This made me wince. She had a strong point.

"You've read this document," she said. "You know the truth. There's no room for odd interpretations, especially not for a rules-stickler like you. Now that hostilities have ceased, you must bend to my authority again. I'll be leading this diplomatic mission, as I'm the diplomat!"

We stared at one another, and both of us knew the truth of it. She had me.

Nodding my head, I reached up and grasped the hatch by the ring that served as a door handle.

"Very well, Ambassador Grantholm. I will await your return."

So saying, I slammed the hatch closed.

-11-

I managed to take a dozen angry steps across the hangar deck before the pinnace hatch creaked open behind me again.

"Sparhawk?" Grantholm called. "I haven't dismissed you. Please return and attend me immediately."

Halting in irritation, it took an effort of will to turn around and face her without shouting profanity.

It was one thing, after all, to accept her authority as a non-military official over what was essentially a military mission. To have her ordering me around like a cabin boy was something quite different.

All that aside, however, she *did* have the authority to command any diplomatic effort, which was what we were clearly embarked upon now.

Reluctantly, I returned to the pinnace and gave her a wry grimace.

"You can't abandon your role in this effort now," she said. "Is this a fit of pique? If so, it's quite unprofessional."

"Madam Ambassador, I'm returning to the command deck. Someone must prepare for any upcoming battle your visit may instigate."

She made a snorting sound. "Now who's insulting whom? Look William, let's cooperate. The people on this station spoke to you before, and you promised you would meet them in person. Why you did so is still beyond me—but that's done now. The point is they expect Captain Sparhawk to step onto their station."

"I will command the away-team," I said. "You must listen to me if things go badly. You can talk to their leaders after I introduce you. Agreed?"

She laughed. "The away-team? You mean yourself and this giantess? Fine. If things go badly, I would assume we'll all be swiftly killed anyway."

With ill-grace, I boarded the pinnace and moved forward to sit beside Zye.

The hangar was depressurized, and a blast shield rolled away to reveal a black rectangle of open space.

Off to the lower left the station was visible. Zye lofted the pinnace, and we glided out into the void. The view was magnificent. Up close, the station resembled a multi-faceted silver ornament. As it spun, the fire of the orange star nearby lit up the facets and sent brilliant flashes of color in every direction.

"There, see the damage you did?" Lady Grantholm exclaimed, pointing at a blackened facet that looked like a burnt out triangular hole in the hull.

"I do indeed," I said. "Recall that if I hadn't punctured their pretty station, they'd have attacked us with their fighters."

Her face twisted up in irritation. "Your crewmen are constantly telling me how smart you are. Perhaps in this case you were in the right, but you shouldn't let things like this go to your head, William. Speaking of the fighters... where are they now?"

"Following us cautiously. They have yet to return to the station."

"Perhaps they can't because you destroyed their launch deck."

I shrugged. "It's possible."

We said little else as we followed a landing signal toward the station. A section of the shield flickered out, and we entered the inner zone near the hull. At the last moment, when we were barely crawling, our guests finally saw fit to open another facet. The opening behind it was pitch-black.

Zye eased the craft into this massive region. Up close, the station was more impressive than I'd realized. Earth had never built anything so large. The station had to be the size of a small moon, at least five kilometers in diameter.

It felt as if we were being swallowed as we entered the station. The door slid shut behind us, and the chamber beyond lit up.

I'd been expecting to see a cargo hold. Instead, we landed on a large deck in the midst of a dozen spacecraft. There were shuttles, repair ships and several tugs. I assumed it was a small support fleet.

"These ships are damaged," Zye noted. It was the first time she'd spoken since we'd launched.

"How's that possible?" Grantholm demanded. "Sparhawk hasn't taken a shot at them yet."

"You're right," I said to Zye, ignoring the ambassador. "They are *all* damaged... That indicates this station has recently been in combat—but with whom?"

"Maybe they're paranoid for a reason," Zye suggested.

Together, we left the ship and stood waiting near its landing gear. A group of armored troops approached with rifles in their hands. We made no hostile moves.

"Captain Sparhawk?" inquired the lieutenant in charge.

"I'm Captain Sparhawk."

"Accompany me, sir."

We followed the guards, who closed ranks around us. They took our side arms, but left me my sword, assuming it was ceremonial in function.

Zye eyed them with distrust, but she gave up her pistol sullenly. The troops around us kept casting sidelong glances at her. They clearly found her worrisome.

The colonists weren't very tall people. They were all shorter than Zye and myself. Maybe they found our size intimidating, it was difficult to say.

We were ushered into a chamber deep within the station. The more levels we traversed inward, the more people seemed to join the party. I was impressed by their numbers, and by the apparent level of interest they had in us.

At last, we were marched into a sweeping chamber of unsurpassed beauty. The walls—they didn't look like walls. They were holographic projections, they had to be.

An apparent landscape of lush beauty and sunlight rolled in a curving arc for kilometers around. From our point of view, it looked like we were at the bottom of a bowl, with fields, trees and even gently rolling hills crawling upward in every direction around us.

The guards smiled at our reactions. Even Zye seemed taken aback.

"A false interior?" Zye asked. "An encapsulated atmosphere of such volume… this is an engineering marvel."

"Don't be daft, girl," Lady Grantholm said. "It's nothing but an illusion. Those walls are screens. They're probably less than a hundred meters off."

Frowning, I stopped to pluck a sunflower from a path strewn with white pebbles. I tilted my head up, until I looked directly overhead.

There, above us all, sat a bulbous contraption, much of which was shrouded in steam. It seemed to emit brilliant light from some angles and… was it possible?

Silvery rain fell. Droplets were falling from it, sheeting down toward us. As I watched, the rain came to sweep over us and sprinkle us with light droplets.

I turned to the captain of the Guard, enchanted. "I can't believe it," I told him. "This is marvelous. That's the core up there, isn't it? The core of the entire station. It's raining on us, and other spots are shining bright light as if you've captured your own personal sun."

"Yes, exactly," he said.

I couldn't help but note the pride in his voice.

"This is real?" demanded Lady Grantholm suddenly. "What a gross display of wealth—I like it. Powered by the sun outside, shining upon those countless solar collectors… yes, and don't think that I've missed the brilliance of this move diplomatically. How better to begin a negotiation than to impress your opponents so utterly?"

The guardsmen looked bemused.

"Truly marvelous," I said. "Is that what you've brought us here to see? To show us your engineering capabilities?"

"No, not exactly," the captain admitted. "But we are thoughtful people. Determined, yes. Harsh, some would say.

But we firmly believe the final moments of any being should be spent peacefully."

Frowning in concern, I took stock of the situation. We'd stopped marching. We were, indeed, at the end of the path of white pebbles we'd been following. A set of dark holes, freshly dug, could be seen here and there among the waving sunflowers.

Turning back toward the guardsmen, I nodded in understanding. My hand went to the clasp around my neck, which I touched with seemingly idle fingers.

"I get it," I said, "you mean to bury us here, don't you?"

"Yes," said the captain, brightening. "I hope you appreciate the gesture."

Grantholm froze. Her face displayed shock. Zye stood with her eyes cast low—I knew she was watching them all at once with her peripheral vision. Her bunched shoulders let me know she was ready for anything, despite her quiet demeanor.

My eyes returned to the Captain. "What gesture?"

"This is my personal plot. I volunteered this land for special service. Others had refused."

"Ah," I said. "Your generosity is to be commended."

Lady Grantholm's eyes slid to me. She clearly thought I was as insane as this farmer who so calmly discussed our murders.

"That can't be the entire story," I said. "Surely there's something in this for you."

The captain shrugged. "Well, I grow these sunflowers—I love the flavor of the seeds when they're soaked in brine. You'll feed them well, in my opinion. Also, I believe I can turn a better profit at the local market with the next crop by advertising they were fed by outsider fluids—even if they taste exactly the same."

"How enterprising," I said in a tone I hoped was perfectly calm.

Taking two strides toward the fields, I saw the squad around us become alert. They lifted their lance-like weapons. The tips were energy projectors. I wasn't sure yet whether they possessed range, or if they had to be applied directly to the body to kill. I figured I would most likely be enlightened on this point very soon.

"May I?" I asked the captain, reaching for a large bloom.

"Ah, of course," he said, stepping toward me and touching the plant I'd indicated. "They said you would be uncivilized, but clearly, you're a man of rare spirit."

As his hands left his weapon and touched the plant in question, I made my move.

-12-

My sword is anything but ceremonial.

To explain that reality requires some understanding of Earth's past. Dueling had been legalized on Earth nearly a century ago, during the period of relative lawlessness that followed the Cataclysm. Over time, dueling had come to be seen as a rational way to allow individuals to sort out disagreements among themselves.

By the time the Guard had restored order to the planet, the habit had become ingrained in the culture. Historians postulated that this change was nothing unusual. Throughout human history, the settlement of bitter disagreements had often been done through dueling. Ceremonial combat governed by rules of honor had provided countless societies a quick, cheap and final solution to arguments. They were actually quite effective when compared to, say, a civil lawsuit.

As a member of a Great House, I'd therefore been trained to handle a power-sword at a very young age. That process took decades, and it had started with the use of my sword as a utensil. As the duelists of centuries past had done, I'd been raised with my blade in my hand. I'd learned to use it as a pointing device, a tool, and even for eating at times. It had become an extension of my arm, and I felt more comfortable whenever it was within reach.

The guard captain believed his power-lance and the squad of troops backing him up meant we'd be easy to defeat—but he was taken by surprise.

As a rule, I don't like deception. I refused to practice it upon unsuspecting innocents. This man, however, had led us here under a false pretext. He was anything but honorable, farmer or not.

My rapier was in my hand after a brief rasping of steel and leather. In a single motion, I drew it and drove it between two ribs. He fell to his knees, his heart pierced. His hand went to the blade, but I drew it out quickly. The captain's severed thumb dropped to the turf a moment before the rest of him sagged beside it.

My other hand was at the clasp of my cloak, which served as a button to activate the garment. Some would say the cloak was an expensive rich man's toy, but I'd found it had served me well in any number of unexpected situations.

The cloak lit up, extending a personal shield around my person. To an outside observer, a series of angular planes of force surrounded my body. I resembled someone locked in clear ice. The effect moved with me, however, following my actions perfectly.

Surprised, the squad of soldiers only hesitated for a few seconds before they rushed me with their lance-tips glowing. As yet, none of them had been fired in my direction. I surmised immediately that the weapons killed by touch.

In their haste, the soldiers made a grave error. While rushing me, they'd turned their backs upon Zye and Lady Grantholm.

My aunt was elderly, but she was a mean old bird. I could have told them as much. She drew a hidden dagger and stabbed with it at the nearest man. He grabbed her wrist contemptuously—but then she caressed his arm with the blade. This caused a spark of power to erupt. The man slumped, his body wracked in spasms.

Zye was less subtle. She grabbed the heads of two of the smaller men, one skull cupped by each of her massive hands. Slamming them together, she sent up a spray of blood. The muffled crunch was awful to hear.

The last two men charged me and thrust. Their lances touched my shielding and a shower of sparks resulted. Finding my defenses impenetrable, they quickly backed away with their weapons held up in a defensive posture.

They were breathing hard, and their eyes were wide. Crushed sunflowers rustled under their boots as they backpedaled away from us.

The crowd of civilians that had quietly followed us to this spot, undoubtedly planning to enjoy our execution and burial, now melted away from the scene with shrieks and pounding feet.

"Don't let them live!" Grantholm shouted. "They'll bring a thousand more down on us!"

I glanced at her. "I'm in charge of this team's defense, remember?"

She bared her teeth and held her dagger like a trained fighter—which she was.

Turning back to the retreating soldiers, I lifted the man who my aunt had shocked into submission. He was groggy, but he slowly regained the use of his limbs as I talked to him.

"We must talk with your leader," I said. "Where is the Connatic? I demand to meet him!"

This seemed to get through to him. "You demand to see the Connatic?"

"I do. Summon him, or take me to him now. If you don't I'll kill you where you stand."

The guardsmen who'd been retreating had halted at a safe distance to watch and listen. They shifted uneasily on their feet, and I could tell they were considering another run for it.

"I've easily slain half your squad without a scratch," I pointed out. "If you don't obey, my ship will soon kill you all."

"What do you mean?" one of the wary guardsmen asked.

"Do you really think a marauding ship from Earth would allow you to kill her captain? They'll melt this shiny station down to a puddle of liquid steel."

They looked uncertain and fearful. I had to wonder, in that part of my mind that was still capable of reflecting on things coldly: how had these people degenerated to such a state? They appeared technological and capable, but there was an undeniable impression of the rube about them. They'd regressed in their knowledge of the behavior of others. Perhaps they'd even sunken into barbarism. I hoped the cosmos wasn't full of isolated colonists like these people.

One of the survivors finally swallowed. "I'll contact the Connatic. We must have guidance."

"Please hurry," I said. "My ship is expecting me to communicate soon. As per their orders, they'll proceed with the destruction of this station within the hour."

He nodded, licking his lips.

I'd bluffed him, but there had been some truth to my words. Left out of contact with me for long enough, First Officer Durris would assume command. He'd definitely consider damaging this structure. There would certainly be a great loss of life, whoever won the conflict.

The three of us were soon left to our own devices. Lady Grantholm turned to me and treated me to a very unfriendly expression.

"I've lived for over a century," she said. "And to think, after all that time, I'm going to end my days the victim of barbarians in this alien place. It's not fitting at all."

"You chose your path. We came as explorers. History is littered with any number of dead explorers."

"You're too clever for your own good, Sparhawk. You're arrogant, overconfident—just because you've won so often is no guarantee you'll win here today. These people have only to call for reinforcements. They'll pincushion us with arrows or encircle us with their powered lances and jab until we're dead."

I shrugged. "It may turn out the way you suggest."

"Why then are we here?" she demanded, her voice cracking in exasperation.

"We're on a diplomatic mission," I said. "What would you have said if I'd destroyed this station and all its inhabitants when they attacked instead of trying to come to terms?"

"I'd have called you a genocidal maniac," she admitted. "But you would have made the right decision if you'd struck. Now we're the weak ones in their power."

"I disagree. We're engaged in diplomacy of a sort. If we hope to make friends with savages, a certain degree of risk is to be expected."

She sniffed. "This world isn't at all what I expected. None of this is. My skills at negotiating have been negated by a pack of fools with lances. What did they think we would do? Climb into these graves and pull clods down over ourselves?"

The field moved in a soft wind. Somewhere, a chime tinkled. It was odd, standing among dead men in such a peaceful environment. Yes, it was artificial, but it didn't feel that way. Instead, it felt as if we were standing on a lovely alien world surrounded by lush growths.

"Perfectly simulated sunlight, rain and fertile soil," Zye said. "For all their faults, these people are industrious and artistic."

"They possess an appreciation for beauty and engineering," I agreed.

"Too bad they've fallen into a state of fear," continued Zye.

I turned to her thoughtfully. "Is that what you think? You might be right. Since we got here, they've been acting like we've come to abuse them. That would indicate they've been abused by others. We must try to get to the bottom of their story in order to more fully understand them."

"These people have clearly suffered much," she said. "They're so fearful they're dangerous—but they make terrible warriors."

In the midst of our discussion, a figure appeared. The figure was slight, and feminine. No one else accompanied her.

"Who are you?" I asked.

"I am the Connatic," she said. "I watch all, and all watch me. You have done much damage here."

Frowning, I looked around at the land. I sensed immediately how the scene must appear. We stood in a field of lovely trampled flowers with three dead men at our feet.

"Perhaps we can help," I said. "We can bury your dead. They will feed the flowers with their fluids."

The Connatic brightened. "Yes," she said. "That would be best."

Zye and Lady Grantholm exchanged baffled glances, and they both shrugged. While Grantholm stood well clear, Zye and I bent to the task. We dragged the bodies into the graves and placed them there as gently as we were able.

"Careful," the woman said, coming close and standing near to watch. "Make sure you bury them with their eyes open and their faces turned up to the sun. That is our way."

Zye glanced overhead, squinting at the brilliant glare in the center of the hollow station. I could tell she thought the Connatic might be mad, but she didn't let on.

After we'd buried them, I spoke to the Connatic gently. "You are the leader here?"

"I'm the Connatic."

"I heard your voice during our conversations—I thought it was male."

She shook her head. "We alter our transmissions to make ourselves sound more threatening. In this case, it appears that we failed."

I looked at her in concern. "Tell me, why do you fear us so? Since we've arrived, you've hidden, lied and attempted to trick us."

She looked at me thoughtfully. "I came here to offer my life in return for the lives of my people. Will you not accept this exchange?"

"What? I don't understand."

"You threatened to destroy our station. Was that report inaccurate?"

For some reason, I felt a pang at her words. She was a young woman, perhaps thirty years of age. She was pleasant to listen to and to look upon. She made me feel as if *I* were the barbarian, a monster bent upon disturbing the peace of her world.

In a way, I knew she was right if she held that opinion. Thus far, not a single member of my crew had died. In contrast, these people had suffered a number of losses and significant damage to their station.

"I must talk to my crew. They must know that I'm in good health."

"And if you don't, they'll kill two million peaceful souls, isn't that right?"

"Well..." I began uncertainly, "look, your soldiers said they would take us to meet you. Then when we arrived they took us instead to this field and told us we were to be executed. At that point *you* started the violence."

"Ah!" she said, shaking her head. She walked forward and knelt by the grave of the squad's captain. "Foolish Trent. That must have been his idea. It's too bad he failed so miserably. He was never a killer at heart, but he thought he should be."

"So..." I began, "these men didn't attempt to execute us because they were following your orders?"

"No. Trent took matters into his own hands. He's always felt protective of me. I'm sure he believed you would kill or abduct me if he led you into my presence."

Things were beginning to make sense at last. This woman—the Connatic—wasn't our arch nemesis. She was a calm leader, a queen of sorts. Her guardsmen had decided to protect her unilaterally.

"Well then!" boomed Lady Grantholm. She swept past me and interceded her body between myself and the Connatic. "I take great pleasure in making your acquaintance, Connatic. I'm an ambassador from Earth. We're here to open diplomatic negotiations."

The Connatic seemed bemused, but she allowed the older woman to take her arm and begin a very long speech about Earth's benevolence, our plentiful trade goods and our intentions of mutual defense.

I found myself, somewhat reluctantly, left behind in their wake with Zye as the two women walked toward a small village in the distance.

Zye observed me for a time and spoke at length.

"Why do you prefer the smallest of females?" she asked.

"Uh...she's nice enough, I guess."

"That wasn't my question."

"Zye, we've been over this before."

"And you've never given me a satisfactory response."

I looked at her. "We're not supposed to date, you and I. Guardsmen are forbidden to fraternize when one is in command of the other."

She tilted her head in a gesture of puzzlement. "Are you asking me to resign my commission so our relationship might advance?"

I heaved a sigh. "No, Zye. That isn't what I'm saying at all."

-13-

Over the next few hours many of our questions were answered. We were also allowed to communicate with *Defiant*. This contact was met with obvious relief by Durris.

"And things are going well, Captain?" he asked for a second time.

I ran my eyes over Grantholm and Zye. They both looked uncertain.

"Yes," I said at last. "We've met the Connatic. After a few misunderstandings, these people have turned out to be quite polite."

"All right, sir. I'll expect to hear from you again in one hour."

"You will."

Disconnecting, I managed to sum up a smile for the Connatic. She watched me warily. I had to give her credit, she was a brave one. She'd come alone and unarmed to speak with people who'd slaughtered a squad of her guards. We'd been provoked, yes, but she couldn't know if we were savages or not.

Noticing she was staring at me without speaking, I gave the Connatic a smile in return. Lady Grantholm cleared her throat.

"Originally, your people came from Japan sector, if I understand it," she said to the Connatic. "Is that correct?"

"Yes. I believe that was the name of the place."

"I take it you don't speak the old language?"

"Very few have any memory of it. We've taught our young only Standard for a century now."

"You know," Grantholm said, walking about the garden we found ourselves in. "This place is artfully done. Would it surprise you to know that there are places very much like this, back on Earth in Japan Sector?"

"I suppose it would only be logical," the Connatic said politely. She'd turned away from Grantholm and had planted her eyes back upon me again.

I found her frank scrutiny a little disturbing. So did Zye, I could tell.

Zye wasn't saying anything. She wasn't even frowning. But her unblinking gaze and slightly hunched shoulders told the tale to anyone who knew her well.

"Lady," Grantholm said, stepping closer to the Connatic and trying to wrest her attention from me.

"What is it?"

"We must discuss agreements. Earth has much to offer and would like to trade with you."

"As you wish, but we have little of value. Bandits regularly take it all."

Grantholm faltered, then continued. "Bandits? They come here often?"

"Yes. They demand tribute, slaves, resources… we fight them if we can."

Grantholm's tongue appeared and vanished again. "I see. Perhaps you need arms, then? That's a trade good you could use."

For the first time, the Connatic turned to her and gave the Ambassador her full attention.

"Earth would do that? Give arms for sunflowers, slaves and raw radioactive ore?"

I myself was taken aback. I didn't know what my aunt had been empowered to offer. Earth must want a trading partner pretty badly to hand out weapons in return for useless items.

"No slaves, please," Grantholm said, "but we'll take a few of your agricultural goods, if they're of quality. In return, we'll give you orbital platforms, missiles and detection systems."

The Connatic frowned. "We don't need more Earth troops or warships here. You fight well, but we must maintain our sovereignty."

"Of course! Of course!" Grantholm purred. "Are you interested?"

"I'd be a fool to pass up such an offer. It's so generous, however, I'm suspicious of your motives."

Grantholm nodded. "Let me enlighten you then. We need knowledge, Connatic. Earth is strong, but we've been cut off from our child colonies for so long we don't know them any longer. We need to know who is dangerous, who can be trusted, and how to find them."

"Ah…" the Connatic said in sudden understanding. "You need our maps. Our knowledge of the bridges and the systems beyond each of them."

"That's right."

The Connatic appeared to consider the matter carefully.

"We agree," she said suddenly after approximately a minute's deliberation.

"Just like that?" I asked. "You have that power? There's no council, no meetings of wise people to ponder the details?"

She looked at me as if I was unbalanced.

"I am the Connatic," she said simply. Her tone suggested this explained everything.

"All right then," Lady Grantholm said, clapping her hands together and giving the Connatic a beaming smile. She gave me a dour look that clearly suggested I should shut up.

"I hope you'll all meet me for a ceremonial dinner," the Connatic said.

"We certainly will," Grantholm assured her.

The leader of this strange colony then left us, and Lady Grantholm turned on me.

"William," she said, "please don't question the sanity of our hosts if they immediately agree to our terms!"

"Sorry about that. She surprised me."

"She surprised me as well…" Grantholm said, beginning to pace. "This deal is critical to Earth. I suggest you bed her tonight, after this dinner event of theirs. Don't be shy, be direct."

It was my turn to appear shocked. Zye was equally alarmed.

"What?" I demanded. "Why would I...?"

"Don't be naïve, boy. She fancies you, that's obvious. In primitive cultures, dashing men in ships have always held allure for a princess stuck on an island somewhere."

I didn't know what to say. "Madam, I have commitments back home."

"What? Are you refusing to do your duty out of loyalty to House Astra? Are you a Sparhawk or not?"

"I'm not sure what you mean, Lady, but I'm indeed a Sparhawk. Our House—"

"Your House is one of expediency. Your father would bed a crone to broker a deal, and your mother wouldn't do more than grit her teeth over it."

This statement bothered me, and it fascinated Zye. But I didn't protest. I couldn't. My aunt was right, and we both knew it. My parents were political animals. They'd long ago abandoned certain niceties in their quest for influence.

"Be ready in an hour," the ambassador said. "We'll eat with them and seal this deal. Once we have their star charts, we'll leave this abominable system. There has to be a better trading partner than this hell-hole out here in space somewhere."

So saying, my aunt left the room. I could feel Zye's stare upon me. I didn't face her.

"Are you going to do it?" she asked me quietly.

"I don't know," I said. "It's such a big opportunity for Earth. If we can get a list of ER bridges and the worlds connected—imagine the number of missteps that could be avoided. The risks would be drastically reduced. Our entire mission would benefit quite significantly as well."

"You like her, don't you? The Connatic?"

I didn't respond. I *did* like her. There was something exotic, intelligent, and innocent about her all at the same time. The truth was I'd had as much trouble keeping my eyes off her as she'd had with me.

"I don't see why she's so appealing."

"Zye, don't be jealous."

"Why not?"

"It's not constructive. It's not professional. Besides, there's no cause for it. You and I have never been involved."

She stepped in front of me, and I looked at her big face. "You saved me. Another would have slain me, or left me there to rot. You released me from my prison of years. I'd given up hope, you know."

I nodded. I'd suspected as much. When I'd first met Zye she'd been a forgotten prisoner, abandoned on *Defiant* by her own people. Only the fact that the cell had been automated to care for her had allowed her to live so long.

Putting out my hands, I took hers. "You're a dear and loyal friend. Can that endure? Can you overcome your feelings and stay at my side?"

"Yes," she said after a thoughtful pause. "But if you mate with this colonist, I'll dream of strangling her."

I chuckled. "I understand. You probably wouldn't be the only one."

We parted to clean ourselves in hot baths of still water in preparation for our political meal. I found myself thinking about Lady Astra, the woman who'd captured my heart nearly two years ago. We were lovers, but we weren't betrothed. We'd never made each other promise to be faithful during my long journeys. We were both realists—and now that relationship was at an end.

It was difficult for people of high station to remain monogamous, especially when one of them was obliged to travel the stars for weeks, months, or even years at a time. Lady Astra had moved on. I wondered if I should do the same.

What should I do if the Connatic made her intentions even more clear? What *would* I do? I wasn't sure.

Arriving at a set of ornamental gates, I offered my arm to Lady Grantholm. She took it, and we walked in together. Automatically, we moved with locked-step grace. We'd been to countless pageant-like gatherings of our own, and we felt at home among the silk-clad people who surrounded us.

Zye, on the other hand, looked very annoyed. She was a brooding figure. She hulked in one corner, eating and staring rudely at the colonists. The natives dodged out of her way whenever she approached the central buffet to fill her plate again, and she offered no apology for scaring them. She ate a lot, but I pretended not to notice.

The food itself was excellent. There were many dishes of an Earthly nature, such as kiwi-like fruits, chilled slices of spiced fish and rice with a peculiarly long grain. But there'd been several dishes I couldn't readily identify, such as a dark meat that tasted something like a cooked beet.

The Connatic finally made her appearance after everyone had eaten and engaged afterward in polite conversation for nearly an hour, awaiting her arrival. Apparently, coming to the party late was normal for the Connatic.

Her glorious entrance stopped my conversation at once. I could no longer recall what I'd been talking about.

She wasn't as she'd appeared before. Instead of simple, utilitarian clothing, she'd dressed in a blooming gown of white. The gown itself wasn't a flat fabric, but rather was made up of countless triangular wedges of cloth sewn together.

I realized instantly that she was wearing a costume that resembled the station we were dining within. It was an odd effect, almost something a primitive people of Earth might have done.

Whatever the intention and the origin of her clothing, the effect was stunning and her face was lovely. I stood up when the rest of the people did, and I felt myself entranced.

She made no lengthy speeches. She nodded to those who came close to greet her, and she eventually made her way to Lady Grantholm and I.

My aunt gave me an unsubtle nudge. I stepped forward and bowed low, sweeping my right hand almost to the floor as I'd seen the others do.

"My Lady," I said, "you look lovely tonight."

Those around us who were within earshot fell silent and froze. Instantly, I realized I'd committed an error, a breach of etiquette. Rather than apologize, I smiled broadly. Surely, these people must realize I didn't know their customs.

"I'm so sorry if my nephew offends," Lady Grantholm said quickly. "He's never been an easy one to train."

The Connatic slid her eyes to my aunt, then back to me where they locked in place.

"It is nothing," she said.

All around us, the others started breathing again. I did the same. I'd held my fixed smile throughout the moment, and I didn't let it slip now.

"Would you be so kind as to join us?" I asked.

"I will," she said.

Together, we circled around a low table with soft edges and firm pillows for seats. Zye watched this from perhaps ten meters away. She was alone, and she was consuming yet another plate of food.

The Connatic's dress didn't puff up and block her vision, as I'd thought it might. It had been cunningly designed to fold as she sat down, allowing her to appear at ease.

She nibbled a few choice items, then turned her gaze back up to us. "I didn't realize you were related."

"Oh," Lady Grantholm said. "Yes, we are. William's grandmother is my niece."

"I see," she said. "Such a relationship indicates either great age on your part, or great youth on William's. Which is it?"

It was our turn to be mildly offended. With the advent of longevity drugs, people's physical ages on Earth had been less easy to identify. It had, over time, become rude to bring up disparities such as the one she'd pointed out.

But as guests, we tried to hide our displeasure. Lady Grantholm leaned forward and whispered her answer, as if it was a distasteful topic.

"You have to understand, my dear, that on Earth people live very long, full lives."

The Connatic stared at her for a moment. "Just how old are you, Ambassador?"

My aunt licked her lips. Her eyes flashed, but she managed to hold onto her smile.

"I'm a hundred and seventy years young."

The Connatic made a tiny coughing sound. Her eyes widened to an almost comical degree.

"Really? How is this possible?"

I jumped in then, explaining that we'd developed Rejuv on Earth, and later on, even more powerful longevity drugs. She listened closely.

"So," she purred, "how old are you, William?"

"I'm still under thirty," I said, smiling. It was barely true, but I knew the answer was the right one, because she seemed relieved.

"Good."

Our conversation became lighter after that. The Connatic explained the origins of every dish at the feast. Some were alarming—such as the skull-sized spiders they'd learned to grow in their air shafts—to others which seemed perfectly normal to us.

By the end of the discussion on foodstuffs, I'd learned the station had regular trading partners as well as raiders. Since they'd never seen our ship before, they'd assumed we were the latter when we'd arrived.

After dinner was whisked away by a large group of servants that came in a rush and left in a flurry, we moved on to a new stage that involved drinking.

This was an unexpected development. I'd never seen anyone on the station drink, smoke, or otherwise engage in adult entertainment.

The clear liquid the Connatic poured into a tiny cup for me was quite potent. It tasted like pure ethanol, and I almost sneezed when I sniffed it.

Very quickly, the nature of the party shifted as we all sipped and relaxed. People became louder and less reserved.

I chanced to look in Zye's direction. She was still lurking in the corner. Alone and watching us, she refused the drink despite the attempts of multiple pourers.

Lady Grantholm soon noticed her as well. She leaned close to me and hissed in my ear so that no one else could hear. "You have to get control of your bodyguard. She's being extremely rude. Can't you send her back to the ship or something?"

"I think you misunderstand the nature of our relationship," I told my aunt.

She gave me a frown. "What? Are you bedding that big woman as well?"

"That's not what I meant," I said in irritation.

The Connatic giggled suddenly. We looked back up at her.

"You two are different," she said. "When we drink, we smile."

I forced a smile. I too, was being affected by the drink, but I had implants that were capable of chemically neutralizing the intoxicating effects if I wanted them to. That was a secret we'd yet to share with the Gi. It was good, I thought, to have such a strategic advantage over your negotiating partners.

"I'm sorry," I said. "We're large and accustomed to strong drink. I'll have another glass to improve my mood."

She poured again, and I choked it down. After that, I endeavored to appear at least slightly intoxicated.

"We must dance," the Connatic announced suddenly. She stood up, swaying very slightly.

I stood up with her. I'd been formally trained in a dozen types of dance, but as the music began and I joined her, I found it difficult to match her intricate steps. The situation wasn't helped by the fact I towered over her.

Still, she was impressed. "You can do it!" she said. "Many Gi take years to perfect even the basic steps."

"I've danced before," I said modestly.

She hugged up against me then, and I saw at least a dozen sets of eyes take notice. There were bodyguards in her party as well as Zye on my side. It was a thing I'd become accustomed to in my life.

"You must show me a dance from your world."

I began a slow waltz. She picked it up easily, despite her drunkenness. I found her touch and close movements as intoxicating as the strong drink had been.

At last, the music faded. Most of the party-goers began to exit the building.

With a flourish, I brushed the back of her tiny hand with my lips. She seemed fascinated with the gesture.

"It looks like the evening is at an end, my lady," I said. "I must take my leave."

She hesitated, then stepped close.

I dipped my head to her tiny mouth, and she whispered hotly in my ear.

"Won't you stay with me? For the night? Please?"

I froze. Here it was… the moment of decision.

-14-

A frozen second followed her proposal. During this short time, my mind traveled a dozen paths with lightning speed.

What does one do when asked to bed a princess?

During the evening of feasting and talking, I'd come to learn she fit the description of any princess throughout history. A hundred and fifty odd years ago, a colony ship known as the *Constellation* had left Earth. The vessel had been of an advanced design, for the times. The people aboard weren't poor refugees or outcasts. They were explorers determined to stake a claim among the stars and get rich by exploiting a system no one else could legitimately say was their own.

The Connatic had been born the great granddaughter of *Constellation's* original captain. As the colony had fallen on hard times almost immediately after leaving the Solar System, they'd never advanced to civilian control as most colonies did. The crew had remained in charge of the mission for a century and a half.

Over time, the ranks and positions had become hereditary, much as they had on Earth. Possibly, it was built deep in the psyche of human beings to follow a leader of royal blood when times became hard.

Others in the crew weren't related to the original individuals. There existed a social system of testing for aptitude and apprenticing that guided people into whatever role best suited them.

But that didn't hold true for the rank of Captain—or as it had morphed—the role of the Connatic. The Connatic's job was to watch out for his or her people. To guard them and guide them. They had an almost mystic reverence for her, and I knew I had to proceed carefully.

If I refused her, would it be a grand insult? Or, was it possibly a trap of sorts? Was she seeking freedom from her role and yearning to do something wild? In that case, a fling with a starship captain from Earth might be viewed negatively by her people.

I felt I could hardly ask the Connatic herself how the encounter she was proposing might affect our inter-system relations. She might take offense, which could blow the whole thing anyway.

At last, I decided to go with my heart. At our last meeting, Chloe and I hadn't been close. Before I'd left, she'd informed me it was over. Perhaps it was time to move on.

As my face was still close to hers, I turned my head to where her lips were hot and close to my ear, and I kissed them lightly.

This both shocked and pleased her. She almost shrieked with laughter and put her hand to her face.

Her bodyguards shifted uncomfortably, as did Zye. We ignored them all. Back home on Earth, I'd grown up being scrutinized by agents with private agendas of their own. One had to learn to ignore them or else having a personal life would be impossible.

The Connatic made a sudden gesture. She pin-wheeled one arm around, signaling the last guests and the bodyguards as well, apparently. They all rose and hurried out the door.

The very last to go was Zye. She stood up slowly, shoulders slumped, and stalked toward the exit.

Lady Grantholm stood in the opening, gesturing frantically for Zye to hurry. Zye didn't comply. Instead, she plodded out.

Finally, the door closed with a resounding boom.

"Are we alone?" I asked.

"At last. I've even demanded they turn off the cameras and stow the drones."

My eyes searched the corners of the room in alarm. This set the Connatic off into another fit of tinkling laughter.

She became most unladylike after that. She vaulted upon me, and I allowed myself to be borne to the floor.

There, on reed mats, lumpy pillows and spilt drinks we made love. It was desperate and hungry, at least on her part. I got the feeling she didn't allow herself to enjoy carnal pleasures often.

"You're a starship captain," she said when we'd separated and were lying side-by-side on the mats. "I'm the great granddaughter of the same. It's only right we should indulge in intimacy together."

I glanced at her. "You don't do this sort of thing often, I gather?"

"Almost never. The raiders ask, of course, but we have enough strength to deter them from risking the damage that forcing their will upon me would bring."

Frowning, I rolled up onto one elbow. "You mean these villains come here and ask to bed the Connatic as part of some kind of tribute?"

"Yes. Didn't it once work that way on Earth? I recall stories of Helen of Troy and Cleopatra of Egypt."

"Hmm," I said thoughtfully. "So, you've only lain with the captains of starships?"

"My people wouldn't allow anyone less for me. Even then, when a friendly man comes along, they're often unsavory. I've only met two suitable companions before you in my thirty-two standard years."

She'd reminded me that she wasn't younger than me, but older. Somehow, her demeanor and relative innocence had left me thinking she was younger than I was.

I corrected myself swiftly on the point of her innocence. The Connatic lived in a harsh galaxy. It might not be as full of byzantine intrigue as was old Earth, but it *was* full of pirates and conquerors.

She began touching me then, lightly upon my bare chest, tugging at my chest hair. I gathered she hadn't seen such a thing before, and I also got the message she wasn't satisfied yet.

We began a new round of love-making—but we never finished it.

Suddenly, a crashing sound interrupted our mood of pleasure. A hulking figure I knew too well had smashed her way into the room, bypassing the door entirely by breaking a window to gain entrance.

Zye stooped in, ducking her head low. Her boots crunched on broken glass. A brilliant light splashed onto us.

I've become wary over the years. Some might even say paranoid. My cloak and blade were never far from my reach these days.

Leaping to my feet, I lifted my blade in one hand. My other arm was wrapped around the Connatic's bare body. My cloak swirled around us both, and I switched it on. A series of gossamer planes of force enclosed the two of us.

"I'm sorry, Captain," Zye boomed. "There's no time. We must return to *Defiant*."

"What's the hurry?" I demanded between clenched teeth.

Zye had always been jealous of any other female that I'd encountered. She'd taken on the role of my bodyguard, but sometimes, she took that task too literally in my view.

"A squadron of raiders is approaching," she said, running her eyes over us. "Nine ships in all. They're out of range, but approaching fast. They're ignoring every call Durris sends to them. Lady Grantholm instructed me to locate you and escort you back to *Defiant*."

By this time, the Connatic's protectors had opened the front door and rushed inside. They stood with lances glowing blue in the dimness.

"Is this true?" the Connatic asked the leader of her guards, "...what the giant girl says? Are raiders approaching?"

The guard captain nodded. "Yes, Connatic. A squadron of pirate ships has arrived. They're led by the raiding ship *Blaze*."

"Captain Lorn from Dellamont has returned so soon?" she asked. "That bastard. He promised he'd hold off from visiting for three more years."

"Perhaps he left probes," Zye suggested. "Perhaps he spies on you in secret and when we arrived, he decided to drive us away."

The Connatic nodded. She was slipping on her clothes. She ordered everyone out, and they obeyed—even Zye.

I kissed the Connatic one last time, deeply. She and I shared smiles. We lingered but said nothing. Both of us knew it was time to leave our interlude behind and get back to work.

We were leaders of different peoples with different missions. Our private lives were minor details in the maelstrom of events.

We parted, and I ran to the elevators. Zye followed me. I heard her heavy footsteps, but she didn't say a word.

It took nearly half an hour to reach my ship, and in all that time I never stopped thinking about the Connatic's gentle touch.

When I stepped back aboard the command deck and strapped myself into my chair, I finally felt at home. The urgency of the moment drove any melancholy thoughts from my mind.

"Welcome back, Captain," Durris said with relief.

I looked at him, and it was clear he'd never left the command deck. His uniform was rumpled, and his hair was matted on one side. He'd probably slept in the command chair.

I frowned, thinking that the man should learn to pace himself. He was too much of a worrier, perhaps, to ever captain a starship of his own.

"Sir, the pirate leader is hailing us," Yamada said.

"Put the call on screen," I ordered.

The forward screen flared into life. I don't know what I'd expected—but what I saw wasn't it.

Rather than a surly pirate of earthly lore with colorful dress, a hoary beard and a toothless grin, I was met by an even more startling image.

Captain Lorn was a Stroj. That much was more than clear. His body was half-machine and half-human. The human pieces didn't match up, however. I could tell he'd taken trophies of flesh and plugged them haphazardly into his own mass.

Exposed metal poked through his central bio-mass, gleaming like wet bone. Most prominent of these revealed structures were his shoulders. They were shaped steel joints with cables that whirred and snaked when he leaned forward to look us over.

His arms looked fairly normal, but while the fingers of his right hand were pale flesh, those of his left hand were comprised of a web-work of steel rods. Each metal finger was as big around as a cigar.

The only thing about Captain Lorn that reminded me of a traditional pirate was his eyes. One eye was a black camera that swiveled independently to scan my crew. The other was a lidless marble of wet, fleshy blue. This eye soon fixated upon me, and there it stayed, staring.

-15-

Facing the Stroj again came as something of a shock for my crew. We'd battled them before in the defense of Earth, but we hadn't expected to encounter them so soon upon beginning to explore the colony worlds.

"Captain Sparhawk," the pirate said, speaking first. "I recognize you—you were highlighted in many reports after our failed mission to retake Earth."

"I'm afraid I don't recognize you," I said evenly. "I'm glad you apparently have a human brain, however."

"Is that meant as an insult?" Captain Lorn demanded, shifting uncomfortably in his chair. His shoulders whirred and clicked as he moved. "My mind works as well as the full-electrics, I'll have you know."

"No insult was intended, sir. I was merely noting that your manner of speech is more natural and fluid than your counterparts with artificial neurology."

"What of it?" snorted the pirate.

"I think it might be easier to deal with a being whose brain is at least made of flesh. I've dealt with a number of your kind, and I've found those with biological minds are more neuro-typical."

Lorn stared at me thoughtfully. I could tell he was surprised at my reactions. Rather than displaying fear and dismay, I was exhibiting personal knowledge of his people. I wanted him to know I could deal with and defeat his kind if necessary. In truth, my guts were roiling inside, but I hid all that and projected the utmost confidence.

"Hmmm," Lorn said after a pause. "It's as the nexus calculated. You're an existential danger to our plans. You must be countered—and if at all possible, excised. I'll make you a bargain, Captain."

"I'm always willing to listen to diplomatic offers."

At that moment, there was a ruckus behind me. Someone pushed past security and rushed to grip the command deck railing.

Lady Grantholm pointed a long finger at the screen. Her finger was shaking and slightly crooked.

"Again Sparhawk? How many ways will you seek to engage in diplomacy without my input?" she raged. "This can only be a plot."

I wheeled my chair to face her quizzically. "A plot?"

"Yes. You left me back on that station without consideration. I had to beg the Connatic for transport back to *Defiant*. Didn't you notice I wasn't there on the pinnace with you while you flew to the ship?"

She had me there. I *had* forgotten about her. The confrontation with Zye, the arrival of this pirate squadron—and most of all, my bittersweet dalliance with the Connatic—had driven all thoughts of my aunt from my mind.

It wouldn't do to admit this, however.

"I'm sorry, madam," I said. "My first duty is always to my ship. I rushed here to take up my battle station."

She stalked around the central deck, moving hand-over-hand along the railing.

"That's just it," she said, "you rush to battle, but no battle need occur! I'm here to perform my duty. To create peace where you would only deliver strife and destruction!"

My eyes turned back toward the pirate, who was still there, quietly leering at us from the forward screen. I could see he was following the conflict with intense interest. He wasn't even saying anything, just listening.

"Captain Lorn," Grantholm said, turning to the Stroj at last. "I'm Ambassador Grantholm, and I'm empowered to negotiate on Earth's behalf. I must apologize profusely for any problems Sparhawk may have caused. I would like to offer—"

"Apologies aren't good enough!" Lorn spat out. "You must concede your claims here. Leave this system, never to return."

My aunt seemed flustered. "That's an extreme position," she said. "We can negotiate—"

"No, we can't. Not until certain basic conditions are met."

"I don't understand your hostile attitude, Captain."

"Then let me spell it out for you, Ambassador Grantholm. Your fleets drove my people from the Solar System unfairly. It's our home just as much as it is yours. The system is large, and we could have been accepted as co-owners—but instead, we were attacked and exiled."

The Ambassador gave me a plaintive look, but I shrugged. I planned to sit back and watch her diplomatic skills in all their glory.

"You started off by infiltrating and attacking us," she said, returning her gaze to Lorn. "We responded in an act of self-defense."

"Nevertheless," Lorn said, "you're seen as the aggressor by the Stroj. You must therefore make concessions to regain our trust. Are you willing to entertain our proposals?"

My aunt licked her lips. She was rarely nervous, but the stakes were high today. She'd suddenly been thrust into a position that may trigger a fresh restart to a war everyone on Earth had hoped was over.

"Earth doesn't intend to invade this system," she said. "We won't occupy it, or attempt to drive the Stroj from it. Perhaps we should consider this to be neutral territory where both sides can trade with the Gi people as a go-between. It could be a first step toward normalizing relations."

"Normalizing relations?" Lorn asked incredulously. "For my people, normal relations are those manifest between any slave and their master. The only matter of importance is which of the two roles each side takes. No, if you want peace, you must flee right now."

Grantholm sucked in a deep breath, and then she gritted her teeth.

"All right," she said. "We'll withdraw to Earth. Give my best to your leader, and—"

"Hold on," said the pirate, leaning forward with predatory excitement. "I require a tribute as well. A trophy."

Grantholm frowned. "What kind of trophy?"

"It would award me high status if I was able to consume Earth's ambassador," Lorn mused, "but I don't relish adding weathered flesh such as yours to my person. Instead, I want Sparhawk. There's no more hated name among the Stroj."

Grantholm began to sputter. Zye stood up angrily. I had to admit, I was alarmed as well—but Lorn wasn't done with his list of demands yet.

"Further," he said, "I'll take the Connatic. I've brought many ships this time. Her fighters can't prevail."

"The Connatic?" I demanded. "You go too far even to suggest it."

Lorn looked back to me again. "I thought you were outranked, Sparhawk. Be silent and listen to your mistress."

"She has no authority to order me to my death. The same can be said of the Connatic."

"Ah, suddenly, I understand," the pirate said. "Of course, you favor the woman who commands this battered station. Yes, I watched the vids she broadcast to every citizen of this system. It's well-known the Connatic recently mated with you, Sparhawk, but I would urge you to overcome your protective emotions."

"Let's get back to the point," Grantholm interrupted. "Complete your list of demands for peace, Captain Lorn."

"Very well. I want them both. I want their flesh to merge with mine and adorn my body. There are spots on my person that are in need of replacement, they're beginning to leak and grow fetid. These new infamous shreds of meat will be grafted into those locations. I'll return to the High Court with a pair of trophies worthy of displaying to anyone!"

No one knew quite what to say—that is, no one other than myself.

"Zye," I said, "please escort Ambassador Grantholm to her cabin. Her work here is done."

Grantholm was grabbed rudely. She squawked and clutched at my chair as she was marched away.

I turned to watch her removal.

"This is a diplomatic crisis!" she insisted. "I'm still in command of this mission!"

"I would agree that we're in a crisis," I said, "but the matter has been removed from your hands. This pirate has physically threatened both myself and the Connatic. You should recall that you entered into a mutual defense treaty with her only yesterday."

"You'll not get away with standing on that thin thread!" she complained.

Zye applied fractionally more pressure to the elderly woman, and she was driven from the deck.

Spinning myself back around, I found the pirate had manufactured a sad face.

"A pity," he said, "you're likely to be destroyed before I can overcome your ship. I really wanted to merge with you, Sparhawk. There's no greater prize in the galaxy."

"My apologies, Lorn," I said, "but this discussion is at an end. You've chosen the path of war. The record will clearly show that for all time."

The hunched creature grinned. "We shall see if you're as good as they say you are, Sparhawk!"

The screen went dark, and the star field returned.

"They're accelerating Captain," Yamada said almost immediately. "The raider squadron has shifted into a wedge formation."

"Sound battle stations. Are the engines ready for battle-speed?"

"Yes sir."

"Then let's move out. Put some distance between us and the station. We'll try to get the Stroj to move between us so we can put them into a crossfire."

The ship began to lurch and heave under us. The power of *Defiant* was awe-inspiring at times like these. She was greater than she had been when she'd been commissioned by the Betas long ago. The best Earth technology had been applied to improve her. The resulting amalgam of tech from several worlds had created a ship that was unique in its capabilities.

The enemy quickly responded to my maneuvers. They changed course, shifting into an arc that would place my ship in range while staying outside the range of the station. My estimation of Captain Lorn's capacities rose.

"Captain," Durris said, "I think we should move around behind the station. Let it serve as a buffer between us and the enemy ships."

I looked at him, then slid my eyes back to the tactical screens. The Connatic had deployed her fighters in three groups, as she had before. They were wisely hugging up close to the station, no doubt watching the drama that was unfolding outside her walls.

"How quickly we consider throwing our new allies into peril when a serious enemy arrives on the scene," I commented.

Durris moved closer to my command chair and lowered his voice. "Sir, I urge you not to let your personal feelings interfere with the decisions you must make regarding the survival of this ship."

Becoming annoyed, I stood up and walked to the tactical planning tables in the back of the command deck. He followed me.

"First Officer Durris," I said, "have I done anything to suggest my judgment is compromised?"

"No, sir."

"Good. Now, please save such fears for a moment when I've earned them."

"Yes sir," he said, hanging his head. "I was in the wrong. Sorry, sir. The situation is intense."

"Exactly. That's when I need you on the top of your game. Now, let's figure out how best to destroy this force."

Over the next few minutes, I contacted the Connatic and requested support from her fighters, but she refused. She explained regretfully they were her only defense and she needed every one of them to protect her station. I couldn't argue in good conscience.

I wasn't surprised by her reaction in any case. The station was at a disadvantage in this scenario. That was generally the case with any fortification. The ships on both sides could move freely, while she was stuck in place. She couldn't take the initiative, she could only react.

We worked together on the tactical boards for twenty minutes, gaming out various strategies with the help of the planning computers. The situation was grim.

"We outrange them and outgun them ship-for-ship," I said. "But there's no denying the fact they outnumber us."

No matter how we set up the battle, the computer predicted defeat. Each time the pirates pulled us down like a bear encircled by a pack of wolves. We could take out several, but we could never take them all.

"There's only one solution, sir," Durris said. "We must flee."

I considered it, then rejected the idea. "There are factors at work here aside from the calculations. One of them is morale. These Stroj are humans—at least partly. If we can break their will, they'll run."

Striding back to the command chair, a deflated Commander Durris followed me.

"Helm, swing about," I ordered. "Take us closer to the Stroj forces until we reach maximum range. I want to snipe at them while retreating with our superior speed."

The ship made a gut-wrenching turn that lasted ten minutes or so. We'd built up enough velocity to transform a course-change into a long, drawn-out affair. The maneuver ended with us making a sunward pass, crossing the path of the pirate ships at an angle.

"Maximum effective range attained," Zye reported from the weapons board.

"Commence firing. Go easy, give the chambers plenty of time to cool between salvos. We might not hit much anyway."

She doubled up the timing on the cooling cycle, and the big guns began to release gouts of energy in the direction of the enemy. We were about two million kilometers out. At that range, the beams wouldn't hit with the same focused power they could muster when close. Still, it would make a good test case. I had no idea how armored the enemy was, or what kind of countermeasures they might possess.

The pirates sensed our fire when it struck one of the outside ships of the formation. They began weaving in a random pattern after that.

"Damage?" I asked Yamada, who was studying her sensor data closely.

"Not much. We have some dust and debris, mostly metallic. But the ship seems to be operating with no degradation of efficiency. It's difficult to measure damage precisely from this distance, sir."

I nodded and began to pace the deck, looking over people's shoulders. The whoosh and singing sound of our main guns kept going, every minute or so, as our batteries fired in a slow, rhythmic fashion. The sounds made by the big guns were impressive.

Defiant's primary armament consisted of three banks of heavy particle cannons. They'd been upgraded over the preceding year. We'd improved both the fire-control system and the punch the weapons could deliver. As a result, they created more heat, noise and even some recoil when fired.

In addition to firepower, we'd upgraded their operating options. I could now override safety systems and direct them to fire individually, or in unison. The original Beta-designed fire-control module had been simple and, like the Beta's themselves, more rigid in performance.

Durris waved me to his side, and I joined him at his planning tables.

"Captain, the enemy is releasing obscuring aerogels."

"A predictable countermeasure. What about incoming fire?"

"Nothing yet. I'd predict we're at twice their effective range, still."

"Doesn't do any good if we can't take them out. We've got them ducking, but they're still closing and not taking any—"

"Sir, we've got another hit," chimed in Yamada. "Same ship, but now she's leaking gas."

I rushed to her side. Durris was right behind me.

"That's gas all right," he said. "She's got a hull breach."

"That's excellent shooting, Zye," I said.

She flashed me a tiny smile.

Then, the enemy ship blew up. We sucked in our breaths.

"That changes everything," Durris said, moving back to his tactical planning boards. "Either we got lucky, or the enemy ships are more lightly armored than I'd assumed."

"Update your battle predictions."

"Uh... we'll take most of them now, before we're destroyed. Six at least, maybe as many as eight."

I frowned. I'd hoped for victory. "What's the turning point?"

He shrugged. "The moment they get within effective range. We can keep firing, getting closer every minute, blowing them down. If we can take them at this rate and a little faster, we'll get maybe three more—but then they'll be able to hit us in return. They'll outgun us and destroy us."

I knew math didn't lie, but I also knew that tactics could drastically change the math.

"Everyone get to their seats and harness-up," I ordered.

After a fraction of a second, they were all rushing to obey me. "Sound emergency maneuvers. Get everyone into a seat in thirty seconds."

All over the ship, klaxons sounded and lights spun. The crew buzzed in my ear as decks reported in. Some wanted to know what was going on, others were confirming that they'd complied.

I gave them their thirty seconds, then another ten. Finally, I figured they'd had all time I could spare.

"Zye," I said, turning to her. "If we black out, take over."

"Will do, Captain."

To the helmsman, I said: "Helm, hard about. Take us away from these pirates. Dive away from the plane of the ecliptic and don't look back. We're bugging out of this fight."

After that, the engines began to thrum, then roar, then scream. The ship shook, and the lights dimmed—or was that my vision going?

We plunged through space, using what was perhaps the greatest asset *Defiant* possessed—sheer speed.

-16-

We'd left the pirates with a difficult decision. They could continue to chase us, or they could turn away and bore in on the station. They chose as I'd hoped they would.

"They're going directly for the station, sir," Yamada said.

"All engines stop," I ordered. "Begin braking, gently, we're turning around again."

A few of the command staffers exchanged glances and shrugs. Maybe they thought their captain was crazy, but I didn't care.

Durris stood next to me, nodding. "Hit and run, sir?"

"What else can we do? We can't plow into them and die. If we keep harassing them, picking them off—"

"Sir," Yamada said, "the Connatic is calling."

I glanced at her in surprise. "I'll take it privately."

Stepping into my private conference room, I activated a much smaller screen. A distraught young woman faced me.

"I can't say that I blame you, but your retreat from battle has left us worse off than before, Captain Sparhawk."

"How so?"

"Normally, these pirates would only demand tribute. Now, after the wanton destruction of one of their vessels, they'll demand blood—literally. Rather than allow my entire people to suffer, I've opted to allow Captain Lorn to meld with my flesh and take what he will. I don't—"

"Hold on, Connatic," I said. "I'm not running, I'm maneuvering."

She cocked her head and stared at me. "We're watching closely. You are slowing down... why would you behave in this fashion?"

"It's called tactics. The enemy will shortly be between us. Please use your weapons. Make the best of this difficult situation."

She thought about it, then shook her head. "I cannot do that, as much as I'd like to. The Stroj are angry. They'll have to be appeased."

I stood up, becoming angry myself. "If you won't stand up for your own defense, you can hardly blame us for our tactics."

Her eyes stayed downcast. "I'm sorry," she said. "Think of me in your final moments. I promise to do the same."

The channel closed before I could come up with a suitable response. I slammed my fist on the desk, then stood and straightened my uniform. I walked out of the room with a forced smile.

"Any news, sir?" Durris asked.

"Yes. I suspect they'll help when they see we're winning. I'm sure no one expected anything else, did they?"

Their faces fell. My crew had been hoping the Connatic would cast her lot in with us immediately. That wasn't to be, but I tried to put the best possible spin on it.

"Are we closing again?" I asked.

"Yes sir, but at a slow rate. We're behind them now."

"Open fire, concentrating on the hindmost target as soon as we're within effective range."

The wait that followed was interminable. Space was a grim place in which to do battle. You could often detect your enemy, but you couldn't always do anything to him. Instead, one was forced to watch them maneuver and destroy things at great distances with nearly perfect visual and instrumental acuity.

It was maddening. The pirate ships were within range of the station's guns, but they didn't fire. Their fighters hid behind the station as well, like children gripping their mother's skirts.

Finally, we reached effective range. Our biggest guns spoke, and after several minutes, the hindmost ship of their formation was blown to atoms.

"There's a message incoming from the pirate leader, sir," Yamada said.

Smiling, I waved to her. "Put it on screen."

A mask of feral rage appeared. It was Lorn, and he'd clearly had better days.

"You're a jackal, Sparhawk," he said. "They didn't tell me that. You nip at my buttocks and run crying when I wheel upon you."

"Perhaps they didn't school you on basic tactics, Lorn," I said comfortably.

"You move me to take drastic action," he growled. "I'm giving you one more chance to comply with my wishes before I do something we'll both regret."

Frowning, I spoke as if barely interested. "Drastic action? Like what?"

"I'll have to destroy the station. Millions will die."

This did concern me, and I'd been worried he might try it. Fortunately, I had already decided how I was going to deal with this threat.

"It's about time," I said, shrugging. "Get on with it, by all means. We'll gladly destroy your ships one at a time while you waste your firepower on civilians."

"My threat doesn't end there," he said. "I must end you as well." He said this last with remorse. "I'd hoped you would see reason. I'd hoped you would allow me to feast upon you—but no, I can see now you're too stubborn and short-sighted for that."

The channel closed. My brow furrowed in irritation. Two people in a row had seen fit to end my conversations with them rudely.

That was my last thought, unfortunately, before disaster struck. I had an inkling of what was to come, but not enough of one.

"Captain!" shouted Yamada suddenly, "there's something wrong in the engine room. The heat levels—I'm getting a radiation spike."

"Get my engineer on the line."

O'Donnell had been replaced by a junior officer. I'd liked the new man the moment I met him, but it was possible that he was incompetent. There was no particular strain on the engines at this moment. No obvious reason why they should fail us now.

"I'm trying, sir," Yamada said. "No one in engineering is responding."

As I digested that statement, Zye wheeled around and reached toward me with a long, thick arm. She caught my spinning seat and forcibly spun me to face her. "Sir, they're dead."

"Who's dead?"

"The engineering crew. All of them. The core has been breached. Radiation and heat are flooding the ship. Captain... we're on fire."

Automated systems began going off, sounding the alarm. Damage control reported in, their teams were on the way, but they couldn't even get to the engine room.

Rumbold was acting chief of the damage crew when he wasn't running the helm. As he wasn't on the command deck now, I contacted him personally to see what was going on.

"It's awful, Captain!" he cried. "We've got burned bodies, and the air is sparkling. We can't even get close to engineering. Worse, it's spreading every minute. Sir, we might have to abandon ship!"

Stunned, I looked around me. Every crewman on the deck was in full panic-mode. Could this truly be the end?

And how had that pirate managed to reach out across a million kilometers and cripple my ship, anyway?

The moment I posed the question, I already knew the answer. O'Donnell and her crew of Stroj engineers had done more than blow apart a compartment and abandon ship, they'd left something else behind.

We'd searched. We'd done everything we could to find it, but we'd missed it. Now, the entire ship was in danger.

"Sir," Yamada said, "we're losing power. We're cruising but we're no longer capable of acceleration or making significant course changes. The main engines are dead, we're down to our steering jets."

She looked at me. I could tell she was frightened, but she maintained a professional attitude.

"What are the enemy doing, Durris?" I called.

My first officer looked worse for the wear. He was bent over the charting table, battling the planning computer.

"They've reversed course," he said. "They're not going after the station any longer."

I nodded, unsurprised. "How long until Lorn reaches us?"

"Six hours, sir, maybe less. I can only go by the speed they've mustered so far with their engines. They may have been holding back in previous engagements, but I doubt it."

"So, Captain Lorn will have his revenge in six hours. Time to earn our pay. Bring *Defiant* about and target *Blaze*—Lorn's flagship."

Durris shook his head. "That's not normal Star Guard policy, sir. If you kill the one man you have contact with, you don't have anyone to negotiate terms with when the battle comes to a conclusion."

I let out a bitter laugh. I didn't mean to, but I wasn't in the best mood right now.

"Lorn won't accept our surrender, and he won't offer his own. But if we can knock him out, the rest of his ships may suffer from the resulting confusion. Lock onto his ship and wait for him to come into effective range."

It would be several hours until the firing began again, so I got up and headed below decks. It was time for me to examine the damage personally and determine what, if anything, we could do about it.

From the start, the damage control people were less than encouraging.

"You can see the leak from here, sir," Rumbold said, standing next to me in a corridor that was full of flashing blue sparkles.

We wore radiation suits, but no one thought the protection could be one hundred percent effective. The leak was too significant.

"Flush the atmosphere on this deck out into space," I ordered.

"That's a lot of air we won't get back anytime soon," Rumbold cautioned.

I looked down at him. Sometimes, my crewmen were short-sighted.

"If we can't get past this leak, we aren't going to be needing an air supply."

Still, he hesitated. "Sir, if anyone's alive in there, needing help—"

"Flush the atmosphere now," I said in a hard voice. The odds were no one was alive, and even if they were, they couldn't be in good shape. Asphyxiating them now would be a mercy.

Without another word, he activated the hatches and pumps. In that moment, all hope of rescuing injured engineering people vanished.

The hard vacuum outside the ship effectively sucked all the air off the deck, and much of the radiation with it. The leak was still active, but without an easy gas medium to drift around on, the dust particles weren't as much of a problem.

We advanced to where the cooling jacket had ruptured. A shower of bluish steam still vented from the spot, but it froze into a crystalline mass almost as fast as it came out of the hole.

"The cold vacuum is working to contain the leak, at least temporarily," Rumbold commented. "That was probably a good call, sir."

"Let's go," I said wading through the shower of frosty particles and into the engine room beyond.

He looked startled, but he followed me quickly enough. A wary team in yellow hazmat suits followed us. Every one of them winced when they got near the frozen fountain of radioactive coolant, and I couldn't blame them for that. We'd all be eating potassium iodide tablets by the handful tonight—unless we died sooner.

When we reached the engine room we discovered a ghastly mess. Seven crew members had perished. They'd been burned and then frozen stiff when I'd opened the hatches. A few of them might have been alive, it was hard to tell. Their bulging eyes and bloody, frothing lips might have indicated death from any number of causes.

We pressed past the drifting dead and examined the engine core. This was the key to our survival—to the survival of *Defiant* herself.

It didn't look good. The engines had suffered a serious blast. Something had been placed under the core, possibly an explosive device, and it had gone off when Captain Lorn had commanded it to.

"The device can't have been very large," Rumbold commented, climbing underneath the cowling and grunting while he worked. "But it didn't have to be. It was placed with expert care. We didn't find it due to the shielding all around here—sir, I think this thing was planted very deliberately by experts."

"No kidding," I said. "A parting gift by O'Donnell and her crew, no doubt. The question is, can you fix it?"

"Fix it? Maybe, given half a year's time at a well-equipped dry-dock. This engine is dead, sir."

I heaved a sigh. The enemy had taken out Earth's first starship without hitting us with a single salvo.

"Do what you can. I need some kind of power. Anything, even just give me enough to maneuver."

"I might be able to do that," Rumbold muttered. He was already at work. Only his feet stuck out from beneath the cowling.

His nervous damage control crew filed in and began following his barking commands.

I left the engine room with a heavy heart and headed back up to the command deck. We had less than five hours before the enemy caught and destroyed us.

-17-

The enemy ships came into range three hours later. They'd adopted, by that time, what we considered to be unorthodox tactics.

"They've formed a column, sir," Durris said.

"A column?"

"Yes, they've lined up their ships. Only one of them is visible from our point of view."

I rubbed my chin briefly. "I see. They know now that we have superior range, and they've adapted. With only one ship in front of all the others, they hope to reduce the odds of our striking them."

"Exactly. Oh, and sir, the lead ship is not Captain Lorn's."

Chuckling, I found myself unsurprised. There was some humanity left in that Stroj after all. He wasn't interested in dying. He was going to let someone else do it for him. I had to wonder if he was in the very last ship in the line.

"All right," I said. "Hold your fire. I assume they're still dodging from side to side in a random pattern?"

"Yes, in perfect synchronicity."

"Right. Try to figure out their pattern and plot it, Durris."

He frowned. "Sir, I just said the pattern was random—"

I lifted a finger in his direction. "But it isn't. It can't be, really. They aren't coordinating with transmissions between the ships, are they?"

"No."

"Well then, they must be running a program that generates a seemingly random course adjustment after a predetermined length of time. That way, they're all able to stay in a perfect line."

"Hmm," he said, studying the data. After a few minutes, he returned with fresh hope in his eyes. "I think you're right, sir. They're shifting course about every eleven seconds. This is very consistent, and it matches your theory. They're all following a pattern."

"Exactly. Break the code, Durris. When you do, we'll strike."

We stayed almost motionless for the following ninety-one minutes. By that time, even I was doubting the rationality of my plan. I stood up and joined Durris at the planning table. Sweat dripped from his brow, despite the fact the command deck was heavily air-conditioned.

"We're in optimal range now," I said. "The enemy must think we're dead in space. No power, no weapons—nothing."

"Yes sir, I know sir."

"And while that does offer some strategic advantages," I continued, "I was hoping—"

"I'm sorry sir. There are three possibilities, and I just can't narrow it down from there."

I blinked. "Only three?"

"Yes sir. I've been stuck on this for the last half-hour. I just can't—"

My hand came up to rest heavily on his shoulder. "Give me your three solutions. I'll deal with it from here."

He complied, and I pondered them. I chose one at random and ordered Zye to unload all our cannons at once. We'd fire a full-burn barrage on one of the three possible positions the enemy might shift to.

Zye frowned at me. "The usual tactic is to spread out your fire so that—"

"We only have eleven seconds, Zye," I said. "Follow my orders, or I'll find someone who will."

Without another word, she engaged the algorithm. The cannons went live and after the next shift, they fired all at once.

The ship's response was remarkable. The deck shivered, and the lights dimmed. We were at our power limits, even with our engines dead and disengaged.

A tremendous gush of power traveled downrange at the speed of light. We were still several light-seconds distant from the enemy, so we didn't know instantly if we'd guessed right.

"Cycle the batteries," I said. "Fire them all again on the second solution in seven... six—"

"Sir, the cooling cycle hasn't completed yet."

"I'm well aware of that. Three... two... one... fire!"

The cannons unleashed their fury again.

"Retarget on the third—" I began.

"Sir!" Zye called out. "We've got a flame out on seven, twelve and nineteen. Taking them offline until—"

"Fire again on my mark! Seven... six..."

"Hold it!" Yamada shouted. "We've got a hit!"

"Confirmed?" I demanded.

"Yes sir, on screen at extreme visual range."

The forward screen lit up, and it was the most beautiful sight I'd seen so far today. A blossom of blue-white gas flared into existence. As soon as it faded, a second expanded into view behind it.

I began to grin. My plan had worked.

"Stand down the cannons. Send work crews to the roof to work on the failed units. Tell them to be prepared to duck in case we need to fire again."

"Crews dispatched."

Wheeling around to Yamada, I leaned forward anxiously. "How many did we get?"

"It's hard to interpret, given the enemy's placement," she said, staring into her instrumentation. "I think we burned through the first ship right into the second and probably a third, all at once."

She looked up at me. "That was your plan, wasn't it, sir? That's why you let them get close. So they'd be lined up for a single hard blow that would knock them all out at once?"

I shrugged. "They adapted, so I did the same."

"Genius," she muttered, turning back to her instruments.

It was Durris, however, who made the determination on how we'd scored.

"Three ships destroyed, sir, and a fourth badly damaged. They've broken up their formation and they're all widely dispersed now, weaving new and differing patterns."

I nodded, satisfied but not finished.

"Target the damaged ship. I assume it's not moving with the same alacrity as the others?"

He glanced at me. "No sir. But…"

I looked at him. "Has the damaged ship turned away?"

"No. They're continuing to close."

"First Officer Durris," I said. "I've fought the Stroj before. They're not easily dissuaded. In fact, in my experience, they have to suffer very heavy losses before they break off an attack. Fire on my mark."

Durris turned away without a word. The cannons hummed, then buzzed, then sang. Another ship was destroyed, unable to shift away fast enough. We'd made a good accounting of ourselves.

"Captain? Lorn is hailing us."

I looked at Yamada in surprise. I hadn't expected this. Parley in the midst of heated battle? Could it be a ruse?

"Open the channel, but keep up a random spread of predictive attacks. Maybe we can catch another of their ships before they get in close enough to shoot back."

While the cannons buzzed and sang periodically overhead, the forward screen lit up again.

"Sparhawk, you devil," the pirate said. He glared at me with a hate that was palpable.

"Captain," I said, "this is a surprise. Do you wish to discuss terms?"

"Yes," he said. "I have new demands. I'll accept only your person as a trophy. In turn, I'll let your ship escape, and I'll leave the station alone. Your beloved Connatic will live on, as will all her people. What do you say?"

"What changed your mind?" I asked curiously.

He snarled at me. We both knew my smashing blow to the enemy's snout had changed everything. He no longer had the clear upper hand.

"Do you accept my terms, or not?" he demanded.

I hesitated for a few seconds. It was a tempting offer in some ways. One life in trade for millions. Did I value my own skin so highly?

The trouble was, of course, I couldn't trust the Stroj to keep their word. Even if they did, they'd probably come back next year and do it all again.

"I have different terms in mind," I said. "Destroy your weapons, abandon your ships and set them adrift. If you do that, I'll stop firing. We'll pick you up, and I promise every Stroj who's still breathing now will continue to do so."

"That's your final word on the topic?" he marveled.

"It is."

"Truly, I expected no less from you. We'll make fine roommates in Hell, you and I, Sparhawk."

The channel closed.

"Continue firing," I said.

"But sir... they're breaking off."

I blinked at Yamada in surprise. "Hold fire then," I said.

Then I turned toward Durris and his planning table. I joined him at his boards.

"What's going on?" I demanded.

"They're turning to a new course, fleeing. This must be the reason."

Tiny new contacts were on the boards now. They were distant, but closing.

"Are those missiles?"

Durris smiled. "No, sir. They're fighters. The Connatic has finally committed herself."

I smiled back. "I knew she would," I said—but in truth, I'd known no such thing. It was technically a lie, but I had meant it to be morale-building, so it didn't trouble me much.

"Sir," Durris said a few minutes later, "I've figured out where the enemy is going—there's another ER bridge out there. They're heading for it."

Studying the data, I came to the same conclusion. It left me in a quandary. Should I let them go, or should I blast them until their last ship was destroyed?

-18-

In the end, I let the Stroj ships escape. It was probably a misguided act of mercy, but when an enemy is defeated and fleeing, any Star Guard officer would have trouble killing them as they ran.

After all, the Stroj had been human once. They'd warped away from Basics such as myself, their term for Earthmen, but perhaps they could be taught the concept of honor once again through example. It was a faint hope, but one that I refused to give up on.

The Connatic's fighters never caught the enemy ships as they fled, but they did return eventually to tow us back to their friendly port.

Our second visit to Tranquility Station was much more pleasant and cordial than the first had been. The Gi people welcomed all my crewmen this time with open arms. We were more than their allies now, we were their saviors.

The station's mechanics became wholly focused on repairing *Defiant*'s significant damage. Ambassador Grantholm quickly took to showing exaggerated interest in anything to do with Gi fashion, culture or cuisine. There is no doubt that boasting of her familiarity of alien subtleties would cause her to be the envy of all the Great Houses of Earth.

The Connatic was particularly accommodating. She and I shared each other's company nightly. This fact never failed to put Zye into a bad mood, but I overcame her sullen glares.

After a month, our vessel was ready to fly again. During that time, the Gi people had impressed upon us one single fact: the Stroj were not done with this system. They would return to seek vengeance at some point. This didn't concern me too much, as they'd sworn vengeance upon Earth as well. Perhaps if I kept beating them in battle, they'd have a long list of systems they wished to destroy, and the inhabitants would band together to bring them down once and for all.

When our engines were fully operational again, I called a conference aboard *Defiant*. My top commanders gathered, and we discussed our next move.

Ambassador Grantholm barged in when we were in a heated debate. Durris and Yamada wanted to press ahead and explore more systems, while I wanted to head home and share what we'd learned with Earth.

All of us looked up at the ambassador in surprise as she entered. Her brows were knit together, forming a potent glare as she swept the group with her eyes.

"So... you three again," she said. "Does a day go by during which you don't seek to undermine my authority?"

"I'm not sure what you're talking about, Ambassador," I said.

"Of course not... You've already forgotten the division of authority on this ship? Is that it? I'm in charge when we aren't in battle. This mission is mine to command when there's no danger. I'm asserting that authority now."

She stepped in and sat down across the table from me. Her aged fingers folded together into a wrinkled lattice, and she stared at me over the top of them.

"Very well," I said. "We were just discussing our next destination. I wish to return to Earth, as we now have a great deal of data. We can transmit that data the moment we enter the Solar System, inquiring then where they think we should explore next."

Grantholm chewed that over. It was a sound proposal. Surely, even she could see that.

"No," she said at last. "We'll press on. We'll follow the Stroj. You should have destroyed those ships when you had the chance."

"Is that what this is about, a difference in tactics?"

"Not at all. I simply wish to see where they went before they get away completely."

"I can tell you that," said Zye.

We all looked past the Ambassador. Zye had appeared in the doorway, behind the older woman. I frowned at this development. Zye often managed to horn her way into these events. She didn't seem to care if she'd been invited or not.

"Zye, why are you here?" Grantholm asked pointedly.

She shrugged. "I know more about the Stroj than any of you. Will you not allow my input?"

Heaving a sigh, Ambassador Grantholm waved for her to enter and be seated.

That was another thing that irked me. Grantholm had demanded mission command again on the basis that we weren't in a combat situation. I had no choice but to give it to her, but the point was contestable. At any moment we might be attacked again, which to me indicated we were indeed still in danger.

Holding my peace with difficulty, I sat quietly while Zye sat down and looked at the Ambassador.

"The bridge the Stroj took goes to Beta," she said. "I've managed to interpret the maps that the Connatic shared with us. They were encoded oddly, with a different coordinate system, but the results are clear."

"Beta?" I asked. "That's odd. Why would they do that? Surely your people's navy would destroy them."

She looked at me, and I saw a sadness in her eyes. "They would if they were able. But since the Stroj chose that route, I can only assume they can't stop the pirates."

"Grim news," Grantholm said. "Beta was counted as a possible ally of Earth's. I hope you're wrong."

"Me too," Zye said.

We continued the discussion, but in the end, Grantholm prevailed. She was technically in command of the mission overall, and in the current situation I couldn't convince even myself we were under immediate threat.

As far as I could tell, she only wanted to press on in order to return home with a more dramatic series of accomplishments. I railed against her orders, but it was hopeless. Unless I was willing to toss my own aunt into the brig and declare myself a mutineer, I had no choice but to accept her directives.

We adjourned and moved to our posts on the command deck. The ship thrummed and the repaired engines pushed us gently away from the station.

The Connatic wished me well on the main screen, and I returned her salute. I was keenly aware of a few smirks shared by my crewmen, but I pretended not to notice. Let them think what they may, she and I were both doing what we thought was best for our commands.

We gathered speed without incident as we crossed the star system until we reached the point where the Stroj ships had vanished. By that time, I'd carefully reviewed the information Zye had decoded. If this bridge did lead to the Beta home system, the implications were both clear and alarming.

We entered hyperspace smoothly, wondering what we'd find beyond.

A few hundred hours later, we found our way out of the maze of hyperspace. The star maps given to us by the Connatic helped with the mapping process, but as hyperspace was typically unstable, they weren't perfect. This time, the intervening region seemed to be in flux. The points we'd left behind us varied greatly, and we were a full twenty-nine degrees off our original course when we managed to solve the curve and find our way out.

At last, we located the exit. It was with some relief we found ourselves in a new region of normal space. Prolonged periods spent in hyperspace—or nonexistence, as some physicists insisted was the case—never allowed a crew to rest easy. The accounts from the past explorers of Earth had been very clear on that point. There'd even been recorded stories of crews becoming hopelessly lost and going mad with fear and grief before escaping through the end-point of a bridge. When such lost souls finally wended their way back to our part of the universe, the survivors were never able to serve effectively again.

Such thoughts also led to the ominous knowledge that many exploratory missions were never heard from again. Fully fourteen percent of "blue-jumps", as they were called, never returned home.

Even some of the jumps directly out of Earth had been labeled as deadly, and no one had ever figured out exactly where they led. They were like the blank regions on ancient maps, the equivalent of seafaring cartography that imagined a sharp edge to the world, with ravenous monsters waiting just beyond.

With some trepidation, we examined our surroundings.

"Gravimetrics?" I demanded.

"Good readings so far," Yamada said cautiously. "There's no black hole, no high-radiation giant. Looks like we'll survive our first hour, sir."

I turned to Durris, who was working up a closer analysis of the data. He wasn't looking for planetary bodies or stellar ones, he was looking for ships, mines and missiles.

"First Officer, will we survive?"

"As far as I can tell, sir," he said.

Sighs of relief swept the command deck.

"We've come out pretty far from the central sun," Durris continued. "We'll have to fly a long time to get to the rocky inner planets—assuming that's where we're headed."

"First, tell me if the star charts the Connatic provided us with are correct. Is this the Beta home system, or not?"

Durris hesitated, going over the data and comparing measurements to our past records.

Zye wasn't so reluctant to make her declaration. "This *is* Beta, sir. I can recognize my own sun and the circling litter of planets. It's strange being home again."

I eyed her thoughtfully. She was showing emotion in a way that was rare for her. Rather than a face of stone, or a mask of anger, she was looking wistful. Her eyes were glued to the forward screens, which displayed the central sun in all its glory.

"Welcome home, Zye," Rumbold said. "Every spacer knows the feeling well, but I've never been away so long as you have."

It was a poignant moment, but there was one individual on the command deck who seemed not to notice.

"Sparhawk?" Lady Grantholm asked. "Why are we sitting out here on the rim of the system? Take us in closer, man."

I gave her a glance, then nodded to Durris who plotted a course.

"Nothing on the scopes," Zye said, turning back to her work. "No known enemies appear to be waiting for us. There's nothing out here but comets and asteroids, sir—this system is full of them."

The Beta home system was younger than the Solar System and lacked a gas giant of sufficient mass such as Jupiter to clean out all the outer system debris. That was part of what made her home planet so inhospitable. In addition to nasty life forms, a high gravitational pull and raging tides, the planet was frequently bombarded by chunks of matter from space.

"Have you located Beta?" I asked Durris.

"Yes sir. Course plotted."

"Helm, let's get underway."

Smoothly, we powered away from our entry point and approached the inner planets. The central star blazed and twinkled, being a little less stable than Sol. It wasn't a flare-throwing inferno like Gliese-32, but it wasn't a perfectly steady burner, either.

As we approached over the following day, I came to appreciate how perfect Earth was at providing a stable platform for life. We'd been spoiled by eons of minor storms, balanced temperatures and only the rarest collisions with errant chunks of ice.

After some twenty hours of steady flight, we were challenged by an incoming message.

"Unknown ship… you must turn back."

The message came in without visuals, but in a way, they weren't necessary.

Everyone on the command deck looked at Zye. The voice speaking to us was her voice. There was absolutely no difference in cadence, tone or inflection—which is to say, there was no inflection at all.

Zye looked back at us for a moment, uncomprehendingly. "You must answer promptly," she said. "Or they will fire a missile barrage."

Lady Grantholm cleared her throat. "Yamada," she said, "put me in touch with these ruffians."

"Transmitting."

"Greetings, kind souls of the planet Beta. We are from Earth. We're on a peaceful mission, and we only wish to explore your system."

"Spies are not permitted," the response came back several long minutes later. We were pretty far out, and each exchange took quite a while to reach the other speaker.

"But Betas," Grantholm pressed, "please listen. I'm an Ambassador from Earth. I'm empowered to offer you treaties, including trade between our planets and military assistance."

The reply came back somewhat faster this time, as we were approaching them at great speed.

"There are no Earth ships. Even if there were, we would not agree to any of your proposals. We have no need of military assistance. We have even less desire to trade trinkets with vagabonds."

Grantholm looked surprised and annoyed. She summed up her next pitch in her mind, took in a deep breath and—

Before she could say anything, the Betas talked to us again.

"We've analyzed your ship in detail. We're shocked to recognize it. As we initially believed, you are a band of pirates. You've stolen our ship, and no doubt killed her crew. Prepare to be destroyed."

Grantholm made a squawking sound. "Please, listen to me," she begged. "I can explain everything. Don't start an interplanetary incident without cause. We're here in the name of peace."

"They've fired a barrage," Zye said calmly.

"She's right, sir," Yamada said. "Your orders?"

She was looking at me. They all were.

I was back in command of my ship, but under the circumstances, that didn't please me at all.

"Get them talking again!" my aunt demanded. She staggered toward Yamada angrily. "I can stop this."

Yamada shook her head. "They've closed the channel. They're not accepting our hails. We can't talk if they don't want to listen."

Yamada turned back to me while Grantholm breathed in whistling gasps. For once, the older woman was speechless.

"Orders, sir?" Yamada asked me.

"How long have we got?"

"Until impact? Several hours, sir."

"Good. Time enough to think."

Putting on a confident expression, I began reviewing the data.

-19-

My aunt walked up to me and put a claw-like hand on my bicep. She whispered in my ear in a harsh tone. "You can't believe you're going to get away with this. Not again!"

I turned to her and nodded. "Unfortunately, it looks like diplomacy has failed this time, Lady."

"And you relish that fact, don't you?" she asked bitterly.

"Hardly," I said. "I've got no more wish to die than you do. Possibly less."

Moving back to the planning tables, I considered my next move. The situation had turned deadly remarkably fast. Before coming to this system, we'd naturally considered the idea that the Betas might not be happy with the fact we were cruising into their system with one of their own lost starships. But we'd always assumed we could talk them out of an immediate attack. Such had proven not to be the case.

Durris and I put our heads together and crunched numbers. We essentially had two options. We could fight, or we could run. Given that we were supposedly on a diplomatic mission, I decided to take the latter course of action.

"Let's run the numbers on a race back to our point of entry," I said.

"Already done, sir. We can't make it. We're headed in the wrong direction. Reducing speed, turning around and heading back will take too long."

"I see. Where else can we retreat?"

"I've been scanning the system and examining the star charts the Connatic provided us. There are several bridges that lead out of this system that we could reach in time."

"Are the destinations known?"

"No. Two, in fact, are listed as terminal—meaning no one has ever come back from them alive. The third goes to a system that the Stroj allegedly occupy."

I pondered the options briefly. "What if we ride out their missiles?"

"That's not advisable, captain," Zye interrupted from behind me. I turned to find her standing nearby.

"Why not?" I demanded. "We've suffered strikes before. *Defiant's* hull is tougher than any earth-built ship in history."

"That's true, sir," she said. "But Beta missiles are built for precisely this kind of thing. They'll have fired hundreds of them, not all of which we can even see yet. They'll converge and destroy this vessel with gigatons of applied force."

Nodding, I went back to the planning table. I tapped the hyperspace bridge Durris had selected.

"Let's run for this one. Select the course of your choice and relay it to the helm. I'd suggest you give the widest berth possible to the Beta homeworld."

Durris hurried to obey. Wearing a grim expression, I listened while my flight crew performed their duties flawlessly.

They were doing the work, but I'd been tasked with the hard decisions. Knowing we may all live or die based on the path I'd chosen wasn't easy, but in this case I didn't see any other viable options. We couldn't stop their missiles, much less do battle with the naval forces they were no doubt deploying even now.

Flying obliquely, we cut a huge arc across the system. This way we didn't have to stop, turn around and build up momentum again. The missiles tracked us, predicting our path and moving to intercept. We were safe, however, unless something changed. They wouldn't have enough time to catch us before we reached our escape point and exited the system.

After the next dozen hours, some of the tension left me. No new threats had appeared. The deadly birds in our wake were now almost directly behind us. They were still gaining, but slowly.

"Four hours to go, sir," Yamada said. "Permission to be relieved until we hit the breach into hyperspace again."

I nodded to her. "Good idea. We'll all take a break. Durris, begin rotating the command crew."

Leaving the command deck with Yamada at my side, we made our way directly to the mess hall, where we found the remains of a cold dinner waiting for us. We ate in a brooding quiet.

"It's not your fault, sir," Yamada said after a time. "No one could have done any better."

"That's impossible to know for sure, but I appreciate your vote of confidence."

She put her fork down with a clatter and pushed her dish away. "You're too hard on yourself, William. You're the best. The smartest captain I've ever served under. You've always done amazing things with practically no support, no clear path to success."

I put up my hand to stop her. "You're biased. Anyway, we should be getting to our bunks for some rest."

She looked me over, and right then for the first time on this mission, I thought she might be entertaining some unsanctioned ideas.

I cleared my throat and yawned. "Aren't you tired?"

"No," she said. "In fact, I was wondering if you might want some companionship."

There it was, out in the open. She wasn't meeting my eye, but I knew immediately what was going on. I'd been stalked before, even by Yamada. She'd clearly seen my carnal interest in the Connatic, a small woman not so different from herself. Perhaps she figured out I'd given up on Chloe back home, and saw this as an opportunity.

For a moment, I was tempted, and I didn't respond right away. After a man gives in once to temptation, the second time was twice as easy, they say.

Finally, I shook my head sadly. "It wouldn't be right," I said, "we've got a ship to run. This mission must be executed with the utmost professionalism."

"What wouldn't be right, sir?" she asked.

Her lips were pinched tightly together, and her eyes were angry. *Great.*

"Nothing," I said quickly, and I got to my feet. I put a gentle hand on her shoulder. "I'll see you back on station in two hours."

I walked out of the mess hall. I could feel her eyes on me, but I never glanced back.

Reaching my cabin, I flopped onto my bunk and stared at the ceiling, thinking about women, Betas and missiles.

Moments later, or so it seemed, I heard a buzzing sound in my ear. It was my implant.

"Sir, we have a problem," Durris' voice said.

"On my way."

Springing out of the bunk, I staggered to my feet. I was half way across the cabin before I was fully awake. I paused to splash water into my face and then headed out into the main passage.

I'd planned on a shower and an aspirin before returning to duty, but I could tell that wasn't going to happen.

The command deck was humming with activity by the time I got there. I frowned at my first officer.

"You let me sleep? What's the nature of the emergency?"

"Sorry sir—the danger wasn't obvious at first. We thought it was only a blip, a mining ship, maybe. There are so many asteroids and ice chunks out here... It could have been anything."

"*What* could have been anything?"

He put his hands on his screens and caused a projection to spring up in three dimensions. It hovered over the planning table like an ugly wedge-shaped rock.

I knew that outline immediately. It matched *Defiant*—almost. The configuration of the weapons was different, as were the aft sensor arrays.

"Another Beta battle cruiser," I observed. "Where is it?"

"She's moving to intercept, sir. She must have been on deep patrol out here. She's matched our speed already, and soon our courses will fully converge. I'd hoped we might be able to outrun her—but it's not happening."

"Of course not," I said. "The ships are the same. If she's closer to the hyperspace bridge than we are, then she'll intercept us."

"No sir," he said quickly. "That's not what I meant. We're ahead, and we'll get there first. But she's on the same course that we are, and she's showing no signs of steering away. It's my belief that she intends to penetrate the barrier and enter the bridge. After that, she'll attempt to catch us—in hyperspace."

I looked at him with wide eyes. "You're telling me the Betas plan to fight a battle in hyperspace? Are there any precedents?"

"Not in Earth history. There were a few recorded run-ins with pirates in the old logs, but nothing like two capital ships engaged in an all-out struggle."

"Hmm... another first for this ship and her crew. Someday we'll be asked to give lectures on this situation at the Academy—provided we live, of course."

The next hour went by quickly, despite our tension. We'd found a way to escape their missiles, which didn't have the tech to follow us into hyperspace. The Beta battle cruiser was a different matter entirely.

Lieutenant Commander Yamada made an appearance as we neared the bridge. She looked disheveled. She glanced at me, but then cast her eyes down to the deck. She hurried to her post and began working the boards.

"Hail that ship, Yamada," I said. "And keep hailing it. Maybe they'll change their minds at some point."

"Will do, sir."

I watched her for a moment. Her body language was uncomfortable. Right there, I knew I'd made the correct decision. She was flustered about the results of her flirtation, and so was I. How could two commanding officers do their best work when they were distracted by thoughts of sex? The fact that I'd rejected her had done damage enough.

Turning away from her with an effort of will, I took my command chair again and waited out the final minutes.

The bridge entry point loomed. It was invisible to the naked eye, but our instruments identified it and outlined it with a luminescent bluish glow on our screens. The opening had a diameter the size of a small moon. It was a weak point in normal space that constantly shifted its exact shape and dimensions. It was a theoretical spheroid of nothingness—but a different sort of nothingness.

When we punched through at last, I felt a now-familiar sense of exhilaration.

Were the star charts right? Was this route safe? Would we be able to navigate to the other end faster than our pursuers, even though they'd probably traveled this way before many times?

Self-doubts, thoughts of Yamada, the Connatic, Chloe—even of Zye... all of these twisted in my mind during the dreamlike moment when I passed between states of existence.

Time paused when we went through. That was a known, measurable fact. We lost about six minutes in what seemed to all those aboard to be a single flashing moment.

What happened during those six minutes? Did we cease to exist, or were we frozen like statues? No one knew the answers, although theories abounded among theoretical physicists. Each was certain he was right, as had been every other physicist throughout the history of science before him.

Whoever was right about the details of passing that barrier, when we came to life again, the universe was six minutes older.

And we were somewhere else entirely.

-20-

My crew quickly began probing our new reality, attempting to take stock of our surroundings.

This time, hyperspace was different. There were objects in here with us. Debris of some kind.

"Captain!" shouted Yamada, "I'm picking up small objects, regularly placed—"

"Zye," I interrupted her, "shields to maximum power. Helm, hit the braking jets hard."

Zye turned to me. "The shields are coming up, sir. But it will take time to ramp up to a full charge. It'll be eighty seconds at least."

I bared my teeth in a grimace. We'd again run into an age-old problem. Every ship had only so much power to go around. While running, we'd dropped our weapons power to near zero, flowed every watt of juice we had to the engines and lowered the shields to half-strength. Now, we needed the shields more than our weapons or our engines.

Shields were standard equipment on any high-speed modern spacecraft. One of the biggest dangers any ship had to deal with was the risk of running into a stationary object at great speed. At ten percent of the speed of light, even a rock the size of a marble could punch through any normal ship's hull and every crewman's body in between with ease.

Defiant, like all large interstellar vessels, had several defensive systems to prevent accidental destruction from such mundane causes. The first of these systems was a specially treated hull. It was laced with fullerene tubes. Much as lead stopped radiation, the dense layers of *Defiant's* hull served to protect her against smaller grains of errant matter.

But while that had proven to be enough to stop sand-sized objects, it didn't stop bullet-sized ones. Electro-magnetic shields had been developed to repel obstacles that couldn't be absorbed or deflected by a tough hull alone.

Over time, shield technology had been refined and improved to the point where it was capable of stopping more than just grit. Our shields could stop incoming fire as well.

This was a good thing, as I strongly suspected the objects we were about to plunge into were, in fact, mines. They'd doubtlessly been laid here in hyperspace to catch the unwary. They might be easy to avoid for pilots who knew their pattern of dispersal. Unfortunately, we didn't have such knowledge.

"Unidentified object directly ahead," Zye said calmly.

Rumbold worked his boards like a devil, and the deck heaved under us—I could tell by the screens it was too late.

"Impact in four... three... two..." Zye said, but she must have missed something, because she never made it to the count of "one".

A terrific flash bloomed directly under our bow. The ship bucked, and we went into a spin.

"That one hit us in the belly!" Rumbold called from the pilot's chair.

"Get us back onto an even keel, Rumbold."

"I'm working on it, sir!" He fought the controls, and we soon stopped our sickening spin.

"Have we got more mines in front of us?"

"It doesn't look like it at the moment," Yamada said. "I'm not tracking any."

"Good. Damage, Zye?"

"We're okay. Forward shields were knocked down to fifteen percent, but they held."

"Proceed with caution, helm."

Zye got my attention again. "Sir, the Beta ship will be right behind us. We have to accelerate."

I returned her intense gaze with a calm glance of my own. "We aren't going to run any further. This minefield will do their work for them if we try."

"What are your orders then, sir?"

"Helm, turn this ship around. Keep braking. We'll do a little ambushing of our own when the Beta ship crashes through."

Zye's face became tight with concern, but she turned back to her station. She worked the controls with mechanical efficiency, but I could tell she was thinking very hard.

I couldn't blame her if she was feeling distress. She'd thrown her lot in with Earthlings because her own people had rejected her. She'd killed a number of her own kind over the last year due to this switch in allegiance. But still, preparing to ambush a ship crewed entirely by her twin sisters had to be difficult for her.

"Zye," I said, "do you wish to be relieved from duty?"

She looked at me quizzically. "Why, sir? Have I made an error?"

"No," I said gently. "But this battle might become grim in nature. If you don't want to be part of it, I'd understand fully."

She looked around at the rest of the crew, who were watching the exchange.

"You've shamed me with that suggestion, Captain," she said. "I don't feel I deserve to be dishonored in this way."

"That wasn't my intention... very well. You're to man your post until this action has been concluded."

"Thank you, Captain," she said, refusing to meet my eye again.

Fine. That made two of them. Both Yamada and Zye were miffed with me. I thought that perhaps, if I survived long enough, I could piss off Rumbold as well. Managing that would hardly be a challenge. He was usually the most oversensitive of the lot.

Before the Beta ship broke through the barrier, we'd turned and come to a full stop. We trained our weapons on the region of space where the ship should appear and waited. I felt like a hunter in a blind.

Guilt touched my mind now and again. The Beta ship wasn't our real enemy. They were, from their perspective, pursuing pirates who'd captured one of their ships and dared to return with it to the scene of the crime. I was certain that every member of that crew was fully convinced that they were in the right, and from their point of view, they were.

That cast me in the role of the bandit. We were the interlopers, the intruders. We were supposed to be a force for peaceful meetings, but it hadn't yet worked out that way.

"She's here," Yamada said suddenly. "Down low—not where we expected."

"Weapons free," Durris said. "Lock on and fire at will."

"Belay that order!" I boomed.

The crew looked at me in surprise.

"We're not firing first," I said.

Durris slapped at his boards, and red lights were converted to glowing yellow. Every gun we had was hot, but it wasn't releasing a deadly payload yet.

"Sir," Zye said, "I feel I must point out that you're endangering this ship by hesitating. I assure you, my sisters will not show you the same courtesy."

"I believe you," I said, "but I'm not going to have it recorded in any ship's log that we coldly ambushed a Beta vessel without being fired on first."

The crew fell silent, but I knew some of them were thinking that I was mad. Support came from an unexpected source.

"Good play, William," my aunt said, laying a gentle hand on my shoulder. "The bravest man is one who dares to risk it all for peace."

I glanced at her in surprise. I hadn't even known she'd returned to the command deck. She'd been unexpectedly quiet during the tense moments preceding this critical predicament.

"Yamada," I said, "keep trying to hail them."

"I am, sir. No response."

Lady Grantholm put her lips near my ear. "Why don't you have the Beta try it? They are her people, after all."

I considered the suggestion. Zye wasn't doing anything else at the moment.

"The Beta ship's shields are coming up," Durris said. "She's braking, turning—she's spotted us, sir. She's pinging us with active sensors."

"Zye," I said, wheeling to face her. "I want you to try to hail them. Give them the secret Beta handshake, or something."

"Excuse me?"

"Convince them you're in earnest. That you're a sanctioned crewmember on this ship."

"Ah, right sir."

Yamada transferred the com control over to her with a shrug. She leaned back and crossed her arms.

Zye looked uncomfortable, but she squared her shoulders and began to transmit.

"This is Beta unit Epsilon-Phi-Tria-Zeta, crewmember of Battle Cruiser S-11—"

"Her gun ports are opening, Captain," Durris said urgently. "Do I have permission to fire?"

"Permission denied. Keep talking, Zye. You can convince any Beta of anything, remember?"

She glanced at me, and a secret smile played on her lips. "I'm a surviving member of Eleven's crew," she broadcast. "We were attacked by Stroj, but they were repelled. I—"

"She's firing, sir," Durris said in defeat.

"Full power to the forward shields."

Before I could get those words completely out of my mouth, the ship was struck by powerful beams. They raked our bow, and our shields buckled. A few thin wisps of vapor puffed from *Defiant's* hull where finger-like lines were drawn across her.

"I repeat," Zye said, "this is Epsilon-Phi-Tria-Zeta. You're firing on a sister ship."

Finally, the screen lit up. I looked up in amazement. Zye had done it!

A twin sister of Zye's stared at us. Her eyes were cold, intelligent and dispassionate.

"Basic humans," she said. "I should have known. Zye, you are known to us. You are a Rogue, a pathological liar. That's why you were imprisoned. Not everyone else on your crew died—the few survivors were thoroughly debriefed—I was one of them."

Zye stared at her sister. "They gave you another command?" she asked. "After you lost your first one?"

"I'm an Alpha, Zye," the captain said. "We are born to rule. Others are born to toil, or to be expunged."

"I don't understand," I said to Zye. "You know this Beta?"

"Do not insult her, Captain. She's an Alpha, not a Beta. She is known as Okto. She was the captain of this ship once. Now, she commands another."

"Captain Okto," I said, "I'm Captain William Sparhawk. Please talk to us. We haven't fired on your ship. We found this battle cruiser—Eleven, I believe you called her. She was derelict and adrift. We repaired her and—"

Okto made a waving motion as if my words hurt her ears.

"Stop that bleating," she demanded. "You humiliate yourself, Earthman, with your lies and omissions. I doubt in fact that you are an Earthman. You're almost certainly a Stroj draped in the flesh of a Basic."

"That's not true. Allow me to prove—"

"I will not," Okto said. "I will give you two options: surrender, or die."

Everyone aboard stared at me. I couldn't think of another path out of this, so I accepted Okto's ultimatum.

"So be it," I said. "Earth sees the Beta people as allies. Therefore, destroying your ship will be a stain upon my honor. I hope that historians will at least recall that your ship fired the first shot."

-21-

My heart pounded as our two ships squared off. Already, the battle was unprecedented in nature. We were fighting in abnormal space at close range. Worse, my ship couldn't maneuver without risking a mine strike.

We were thus limited to a confined region. Both ships were very similar in capabilities. This was going to be a duel of two titans trapped in what amounted to a pocket universe.

The Beta ship immediately accelerated, using her most significant advantage over us. Knowing where the mines were located, she didn't have to sit still and wait for our weapons to lance into her hull.

My diplomatic entreaties had bought us one small gain. Our shields had been given time to recharge after taking a hit from the minefield. They were at ninety percent when Okto's beams reached out for us again.

"She's circling around us, sir," Rumbold said, working the helm controls. "She's going to try to hit us in the butt."

Our aft shielding was less formidable for obvious reasons. I couldn't allow the enemy to strike at our relatively unprotected stern.

"Turn with her, Rumbold," I said. "Keep her in front of us."

Our ship began to rotate using steering jets, keeping our forward shields and armor aimed at the enemy.

"If you get a shot at her flank shields, take it Durris," I said.

"Firing… now!"

Beams leapt out, momentarily connecting our two vessels—but nothing happened.

"We missed," Zye said. "No more than a hundred meters aft of her."

"Dammit," Durris said. "This space is heavily warped. Computing and adjusting."

"Durris," I said, jumping up and joining him at his station. "Let's not hit them with everything we have. Fire our three main batteries in sequence. Adjust for warping errors each time until we get a lock."

Another set of beams crashed into us a moment later. Firing freely now, Okto's ship connected again and again while we kept spinning in place to face her. Not all her beams struck home, but she was having better luck than we were. As a stationary target, I supposed we were easier to hit in warped space.

Finally, we landed a punch on her flank. Okto's starboard shield buzzed and flared orange.

"We drew a few lines on her hull that time," Yamada said excitedly. "But I'm not reading any debris or venting. We didn't punch through."

"Keep trying," I said. "Work the math, people. We need a firing equation that's reliable."

Seeing that we weren't going to let her get around us for a stern rake, the enemy switched tactics. They came about hard and flew right at us.

"Hold your fire!" I ordered. "When they get in close, our odds of hitting will grow due to proximity. We'll hit them hard as they pass by."

Beams lanced toward us, flashing past in most cases. It was nerve-wracking to have an enemy ship charging directly toward us, firing as they came. It was difficult to hold back our own cannon shots. But my crew was well-trained, and they managed it.

At the last moment the enemy closed, and they hit us square-on. But that wasn't the worst of it.

"They've released their missiles, sir," Yamada said. "Point-blank."

"Fire all passive-defense systems. Release countermeasures. Time to punch them in the belly—on my mark... Mark!"

All three of our cannon banks gushed power at once. The snap and thrum was deafening. The enemy shields were struck dead-on, and they flickered out. I saw bright blue-white fire as our beams dug into the thick hull beneath, leaving scorch marks and deep furrows in the ship's skin.

"Direct hit, sir," Zye said.

"She's venting," Yamada called.

"Bring us about, Rumbold," I ordered.

"Hold on!" Durris shouted. "Those missiles, sir—they'll ram right up our tailpipe if we turn our backs on them."

"I'm well aware of that. Helm, proceed."

Rumbold did as I ordered with sickening speed. We watched as the enemy ship limped away, trailing burning metals and gases.

"Cycle our cannons," I ordered, "hit them in the stern before they can get away."

"Weapons charging—I'll fire the moment they go green."

"Fire them on yellow, Zye," I said. "We can't wait for them to get more distance. We'll start missing again."

Our cannons began firing again, erratically. They were cycling and firing as soon as they could without overheating. Each cycle, however, increased the chance we'd overload them and turn any given cannon into a heap of slag by firing it too early.

Long before that could happen, however, the Beta missiles slammed home into our own stern. Our shields were thinnest there, and they went down quickly. They got inside our guard and hit us with more than half the energy of eight close-range, ship-to-ship torpedoes.

The deck lurched under me, and everyone was thrown against their harnesses. The running lights flickered and then dimmed to a deep red.

As I'd been standing, I'd been dashed to the deck. I climbed back to my feet and helped Durris to stand up. He clutched the planning table like a man holding onto a life raft. Blood had filled his mouth, but he barely seemed to notice.

"Damage report, Durris?" I demanded over the clamor.

"Our engines are damaged, but they're still providing thirty percent of normal thrust. Shields are gone, all quadrants. The aft hold has been breached, and we've lost a number of missiles stored there. We've lost a fuel cell too, but that didn't cause an explosion. None of the decks have experienced major decompression—overall, I'd say we were lucky. There are only six reported casualties so far."

My jaws clenched. Six more were dead due to my decisions. I tried not to think about that part of the game. If we didn't do this right, we would all be frozen corpses soon—floating in hyperspace.

"Zye, keep hitting their stern," I ordered. "Give chase, and don't let up. Stay on their tail."

I watched the action this time on the forward screen and caught the critical details as they occurred. Three of our beams converged and penetrated the enemy defenses. There, the armor was thin and their vulnerable engines were exposed.

The enemy exhaust port array suffered a direct hit. Our beams dug into the ship's bowels, and something ignited inside.

"Engine failure!" Durris shouted jubilantly. "We stuck the fork in them that time! I'm surprised they didn't breach and explode."

Rumbold spun around to look at me. "They're dead in the void, sir. Helpless. What are your orders?"

I glanced at him, and our eyes met. He and I had worked together for most of my career in Star Guard. I knew what he was asking me: should he steer in for the kill, or not?

"Stand down, Rumbold. Keep our distance, stay on Okto's stern. We've got them where we want them. Zye, cease fire. Durris, have we got those lower deck fires under control?"

"Huh? Oh, yes sir... I just can't believe we beat them. That was excellent maneuvering, Captain. They'll be impressed back at CENTCOM when they review these logs."

I chuckled, suddenly feeling an excellent mood overtake me. I leaned back in my chair and breathed deeply for the first time in two days. "We'll have to live long enough to reach home for that, XO," I said.

Turning to Zye and Yamada, I nodded to them. "Zye, try to talk some sense into them. I see them turning around slowly. They've got nothing but steering jets. They must know they're beaten."

Zye shook her head. "I probably can't, sir. Okto is an Alpha while I'm a Rogue. My words will never impress her."

We stared at one another for a few seconds. "You mean they won't surrender? They'll keep fighting until we're forced to destroy their ship utterly?"

"That's the most probable outcome now," she said. "If they'd been damaged badly, but their engines were still operable, they might have run. In this case we've crippled them, but left them with fangs. Under these circumstances, they'll turn like a cornered beast and do what they can to hurt us."

My good mood evaporated. Earth captains knew when they were beaten. Any of them would have surrendered honorably. This battle should be over. I'd miscalculated concerning Beta psychology.

"All right," I said. "We're left with two choices: we can pull Okto's fangs, destroying her weapons and circling her at short range. Or, we can move to a safe distance."

"Retreat?" Durris asked incredulously. "But we just won the day!"

"True enough, to our way of thinking. But destroying Okto's ship and killing her isn't going to gain us anything. If we stay in range and try to disarm her, she might get lucky with a punch of her own."

As if to make my point for me, the enemy cannons struck another hard blow to our forward shields. The Beta captain was letting me know she was still in this, and she wasn't quitting.

"Your orders, sir?" Durris asked sullenly.

I stood up and walked around the command deck, checking screens. "Get us out of here, Rumbold. Circumvent that minefield and move us beyond Okto's reach. Zye, hold your fire on all weapons systems."

A few minutes later, we slipped away from the enemy. They still fired, of course, as we were within easy reach. But in hyperspace, our effective ranges had been greatly reduced. Their repeated salvos missed.

Finally, an unexpected development occurred.

"Sir," Yamada said, "Captain Okto is hailing us."

I shrugged. "Maybe she's come to her senses. Put her on the main screen."

An image of destruction flashed into existence. The enemy command deck was more or less identical to ours, but it was in a state of severe disarray. There were two bodies in evidence, smoke hung in the air, and Okto herself had one eye closed due to a gash across her face.

Her expression wasn't a happy one. She glared at us with her good eye, generating such a gaze of hatred it was like a force of nature.

"Sparhawk," she said, "you're a vicious fighter, but you lack honor."

"We came on a peaceful mission of exploration and trade," I said. "We didn't steal this ship, we salvaged her. You attacked us, so we defended ourselves. Where in this series of events have I acted dishonorably?"

"You're leaving us here to die in hyperspace. You lack the decency to come back to us and finish what you started."

I heaved a sigh. "I'm sure another Beta ship will come along sooner or later. We'll release emergency supplies in our wake. Find them and you'll keep breathing until your sister ships can come to help."

She sneered. "Charity? From a Basic? You further stain my honor."

"Do as you see fit," I said, "but every captain's first duty is to her ship and her crew. Put yours back together again. Live to fight another day. Remember Captain: the true enemy is the Stroj. They attack us both, and they'll never show you any mercy. If we come back this way another time, please talk to us before attacking."

Her expression was still as malevolent as ever as she stabbed the disconnection button, and we were cut off.

My Aunt Grantholm came forward and nodded to me with pursed lips. She'd been hanging back during the battle, content to let me execute my plans while she watched from a crash seat.

"Not bad," she said. "It wasn't effective, but I doubt anyone could have turned that woman into an ally with mere words. I'm impressed, William. I didn't know you had the heart of a diplomat beating in your chest in addition to the cold logic of a spacer captain."

"Thank you, aunt—if that was meant as a compliment."

"It was," she said, then she smiled and retreated below decks.

I sat back down in my command chair and watched as the image of Okto's ship shrank steadily down to size of a credit coin, then disappeared entirely.

We'd escaped the Betas, but we had no idea where we were heading next. Still, it was hard to count today's action as anything less than a victory.

As we tried to find a way out of hyperspace, we found our star charts were useless here. The Connatic had provided us with a list of ER bridges and where they led to, but most of the itemized breach points were connected to the Gliese-32 system directly. There were only a few jumps listed in the Beta system, all of which were apparently major trade routes.

I realized after studying them at length that the Connatic's knowledge was useful only in her local area. The farther we got from her system, the less useful they'd become.

"If only we'd been given the time to take one of the known routes," Durris complained. "We wouldn't be in this situation."

"How's the math to determine our exit point going?"

"Miserably," he said. "This chunk of hyperspace seems to be more warped than usual."

Rubbing my chin, I considered his numbers. "What about all the firing and targeting data from our battle?"

He looked at me quizzically.

"We recorded every hit and miss, right? The angle of projection, the final landing point of each plasma beam? If you patch all that into the computer as raw data, then begin extrapolating to number-crunch out a formula—"

He grabbed my arm and grinned. "You're right!" he shouted. "I'm a fool. We've got reams of raw data just waiting to be analyzed. I'll come up with a pattern-detection algorithm right away. Good thinking, sir."

I nodded tiredly as he rushed to talk to the data people. The man was practically unstoppable. I'd found the battle had left me drained, but he was fresh, despite the streaks of dried blood on his face.

Taking my leave of the command deck, I headed down the main passages toward my cabin. It was my intention to take that shower I'd been cheated of hours ago.

To my surprise, I heard heavy footsteps in my wake.

"Zye? What is it, Lieutenant?"

"I wanted to thank you, sir," she said.

I cocked my head thoughtfully. "For what, exactly?"

"For sparing Okto's ship. I know that was a difficult decision, but I'm grateful. All Betas are."

Narrowing my eyes in confusion, I nodded slowly. I wasn't sure what she was getting at, but thanks and gratitude were rare things in Zye. I was more than willing to take them whenever I could get them.

"There was no need to take more lives," I said, "the entire battle was unfortunate."

"No, Captain!" she boomed. There was a strange gleam in her eye. "The battle was *glorious*. Don't let anyone take that from you. *Defiant* won victory even though we started out with a huge disadvantage. No Alpha will look at Earthmen with contempt ever again."

I wasn't entirely sure that was a good thing, as Okto's overconfidence had helped me win, but I nodded encouragement.

"Why, exactly..." I asked, "do you believe the decision was so difficult for me?"

She huffed. "Well... it was a dishonorable finish. Any Beta would have blasted a crippled opponent to atoms with glee. Instead, you ran like a kicked dog the moment you could."

"You really think that's how the Betas will see this action?"

"How else could it be viewed?"

"As a reluctance to kill. As an attempt to make an ally out of an enemy."

She shook her head. "That would never occur to any of my sisters, especially not an Alpha. They're all about winning at any cost. If you'd beaten Okto and destroyed her—"

"I *did* defeat her," I pointed out.

"No, not really. That impression was erased by your reluctance to finish the task. You showed weakness in the final moments. Your hand trembled, and you felt fear overtake you as you wavered. Imagine… fearing to deliver a deathblow, even upon a helpless enemy… That fear—that's what will be remembered by my people."

I sucked in a deep breath and let it out again as a sigh. "I did it because our sense of honor is different. Slaying a helpless foe is dishonorable to an Earthling."

She looked at me quizzically. "That would explain a lot."

"Well, in the future, perhaps we'll come to fully understand one another."

"No sir," Zye said confidently. "The Alphas know all they need to know about you now. They'll adjust their tactics accordingly."

This whole conversation was beginning to make me very tired. Nodding, I turned to go. I took my shower in a disquieted mood. Could it really be the way Zye had described it? Were the Betas so bloodthirsty they couldn't even fathom a man who wasn't?

She'd thanked me for sparing the Beta ship, but at the same time informed me that I'd doomed myself to the role of a coward in the eyes of her people. The truth was, we still didn't entirely understand one another. Our cultures were too different.

After my shower, I passed out on my bunk again. My dreams were troubled affairs. They were full of warped, moving volumes of space and madwomen hell-bent on my destruction.

-22-

The following day I learned Durris had found a way out of this slice of hyperspace. The angle was sharp, but we adjusted our course and found the exit a mere fifty hours of having entered here.

The exit point was still some distance away, but at least we now had a goal firmly in sight. That fact alone allowed everyone aboard to rest easier.

I thought about the six crewmen we'd lost. I considered performing the funeral and jettisoning them out of the ship, as was our tradition, but I passed on the idea. Old superstitions bothered me. They frowned upon leaving a crewman in hyperspace—even a dead one. Since I had the option to wait until we reached normal space, I took it.

Why did people fear these strange places? Perhaps it was because people still wondered about the journey of the soul after death. For those uncertain of a soul's destination, beyond a shadow of doubt, the loss of a life in space evoked a terrible respect for both the living and the dead. If you joined that with the incomprehensible magnitude of hyperspace, the usual protocol wasn't going to lead to a good night's sleep for any of us. In short, nobody wanted anything to do with dumping our dead peers into limbo.

Another negative to hyperspace burials was the extreme finality of the act. If jettisoned into space anywhere near a star, a corpse had at least some possibility of falling into the fusion furnace at the center of that system. Eventually, the star would collapse and oftentimes explode, seeding new stars with the matter expelled.

Every human being contains within their body elements which had long ago formed in the center of stars. From those raging infernos came the forged heavy bits of matter required to make any known life form function.

In a way, every living thing that died could be recycled into new life. Some part of us was therefore immortal. But, to leave them out here in the nonexistence of hyperspace, a theoretical void that could never support life or even a single star—that was a true punishment. No bit of matter could ever hope to escape.

So we held onto our dead. We froze them—a simple matter on a spacecraft—and carried them with us for burial in a more hospitable place.

Instead of holding a funeral, I decided to hold a celebration instead. Despite Zye's gloomy opinions, I thought I'd done rather well against Okto. I called my officers to my private table for a formal dinner in compensation.

The only bad thing about my plans was the automatic inclusion of my intractable aunt. I couldn't very well leave the most important personage aboard out of the party, so I invited her with gritted teeth. In preparation for possible difficulties, I ordered that a double-ration of wine be served. As part of the final course, three bottles of brandy from my private reserve were uncorked and poured with unusual liberalness.

Everyone was already smiling by the time the brandy came out. Even Aunt Grantholm, bless her soul, seemed to be enjoying herself.

"I propose a toast!" Rumbold announced loudly, rising to his feet.

"Another?" Durris demanded. "What's your excuse this time, old man?"

Rumbold hushed us with a hand. "To a fine ship, the loveliest vessel in Earth's navy." He leered at my aunt pointedly. "And the *Defiant* ain't so bad herself!"

He finished his toast, squeezing off a deliberate wink toward my aunt. His face displayed a broad, self-satisfied grin.

He lifted the glass, and the rest of us, eyes wide, lifted ours as well.

Everyone was glancing at Lady Grantholm to see how she was taking Rumbold's boisterousness. There was a moment of tension, during which she eyed the assembly thoughtfully.

At last, she smiled and raised her glass to join the rest. Everyone sighed in relief. We clinked and gulped. The brandy burned all the way down.

I'd yet to turn on my implant to metabolize the alcohol at an increased rate. To do so would remove my heady glow—but more importantly, it seemed like a crime. What was the point of celebrating with fine drink if one immediately erased the effects in the name of duty?

So, I let my head swim, and I let my mind wander. Lieutenant Commander Yamada sat to my left side. She'd grabbed that spot when she'd shown up ten minutes early.

"Rumbold is making his move!" she hissed to me in delight.

I looked across the table, and it was true. The old buzzard had his arm draped casually around the back of my aunt's chair. He was talking to her animatedly, and she was eyeing him in amusement.

"Now, that's a sight," I said, chuckling. "I don't recall seeing my aunt locked in flirtation for years—maybe it hasn't happened in my lifetime."

"She's not married?"

"No," I said. "She's outlived three husbands. Rejuv only takes one so far, and not everyone reacts the same way to it."

"How old do you think she is?" Yamada asked. "I mean, *really*."

I glanced at her. She grinned conspiratorially in return. We were all getting drunk, I realized, and having a good time. I couldn't blame any of my crew. We'd had precious little to celebrate on this long journey thus far.

"She confesses to one-seventy," I said, "but some whisper it's more like two hundred."

"Wow," Yamada said, sipping her drink, "like it makes a difference!" She sprayed a fine mist of red wine and merriment through pursed lips, but quickly recovered herself.

I smirked at her, realizing that she was adorable.

"Two hundred years, maybe...?" she said, staring at my aunt again. "She looks pretty good, I guess. It's to her advantage that birth records were lost in the purges after the Cataclysm. No one will ever know for sure. I mean, what would Rumbold say if he knew he was chasing a significantly older woman?"

"I don't think he cares, to be honest with you."

We watched the courtship continue. I began to suspect my aunt had switched on her metabolic implants at some point, sharpening her mind. I was just as certain that Rumbold had elected *not* to do likewise. I supposed it was for the best on both counts.

In time, the guests began leaving the party. Soon, it was down to myself, Yamada, Rumbold, my aunt—and Zye.

My aunt declared first. She rose, putting the back of her hand to her forehead.

"I think the wine has gone to my head," she fibbed. "Will you escort me to my cabin, helmsman?"

"Certainly," Rumbold said, springing to his feet like he was a century younger.

The two left almost arm-in-arm.

The moment the door swished shut behind them, Yamada put her face against my shoulder and giggled like a girl. "Did you see that? So cute!"

Zye looked baffled and suspicious. "What was cute?"

"The two of them—so old, but still flirting and having a good night. Gives us all hope, doesn't it? Or at least it should?"

Zye stared at her flatly. "Are you suggesting they'll have sex now?"

Both of us recoiled slightly. Zye was always one to be too direct at moments like this.

"Let's hope so," I said, "if their health permits."

For some reason, this sent Yamada off into another fit of laughter. Zye eyed her in distaste. She stood up stiffly and nodded to me.

"I'll be going now," she said, pointedly. "As there is no one here to escort me anywhere."

She left, and I looked after her with a frown. Yamada got up, walked to my bed, and flopped onto her back on the sheets.

"I'm yours tonight, Captain!" she sighed, eyes closed and smiling.

Eyebrows raised, I walked near and gazed at her. She was attractive, but not as much so as my Chloe, or the Connatic. She was an earthy girl. A woman of a practical nature. I'd always liked her.

Things might have advanced, but then I heard a very soft, rhythmic purring sound. Yamada was snoring.

I chuckled. Taking a final slug of brandy, I straightened up. It wasn't in me to take advantage of a lady.

Walking to the door, I opened it.

Zye was standing there, no more than a foot from my face. She was glowering and her hands were balled up into fists.

"Zye," I said mildly. "I'd like to walk you back to your cabin, if you don't mind."

She blinked and her bad mood evaporated. She nodded once, and I took her arm.

Walking together down the long passage, we passed various couples flirting in doorways and holding private parties of their own. Somehow, my celebratory mood seemed to have swept the ship. It was odd to think that even when off-duty, an entire ship's complement could take their cue from their captain almost without thought.

When we reached the door, Zye stepped inside and glanced back.

"Would you like to come in?" she asked. "William?"

I looked down then at my hands. I had a bottle of brandy in the left. I hadn't recalled bringing that along…

"Yes," I said, and I followed her into her cabin.

She seemed stunned and almost nervous. She sat down on the bed and stared at me.

"Zye, if you want me to leave—"

"No," she said quickly.

"You seem nervous."

"You've never entered my cabin before. No one has ever visited my cabin."

I looked around. There was little in the way of furnishing or decoration. There was an isometric weight set attached to one wall, with all the settings switched to maximum. Her bed was perfectly made. It looked as if her sheets were boards, rather than soft fabric.

"Very nice," I said. "Would you like a drink?"

I offered her the brandy. She took the bottle, up-ended it, and consumed nearly half the contents with loud, gulping swallows.

She handed it back, eyes watering and gasping for a breath. I took a dainty swallow myself.

"Zye," I asked, "are you a virgin?"

"Yes sir."

"Please don't call me that. Not now."

"Yes... William."

I shook my head. "You've been on Earth for nearly a year. Anyone could get lucky in that timespan if they truly wanted to."

She shrugged. "I didn't know how to go about it. People I approached were intimidated or disinterested. I discovered that some people pay for intimacy—but that seemed too undignified."

Sighing, I sat next to her. I suspected she had another problem: she was in love with me. What should I do? This woman wasn't going to conveniently pass out and let me escape her cabin. I figured I'd probably lose any contest in drunkenness if we both continued drinking, unless I used my implant.

At some point, while I thought about what to do, I touched her. I'm not sure how it started. My hand was on the bed, then it was at her knee. I might have suspected that she'd placed it there herself if I hadn't known better.

Before I knew what was happening, we were making out and eventually making love. It was the strangest sexual encounter of my lifetime.

But it *was* enjoyable. She was a strong girl. Her muscles were unlike those of other women. She could apply pressure wherever she wanted to, and the results were quite pleasing.

-23-

We punched through the ER bridge exit with minimal velocity this time. We had little idea what we were going to encounter on the far side.

When we finally got there, I was struck by the beauty of the place.

"Three Earth-like jewels," Yamada said, enchanted. "Sir, we've got no record of this system in our logs. The colonists must have discovered it on their own."

The worlds were indeed lovely. The planet closest to the star had reddish landmasses and blue oceans that flowed like cool lava over a quarter of her surface. The second was a green planet that was vibrant with thick jungles and a steamy canopy of clouds.

The last inhabitable world captured my heart at first sight. Farther from the sun than Earth was, it was cooler than my home planet, but not frozen entirely. My eyes roved over sharp peaks, frosty slate oceans and green valleys like emeralds that dotted the equator. It was easily the most beautiful of the three.

We proceeded with great caution. Using only gentle power from our engines, we didn't charge in, nor did we announce our presence via communications broadcasts. This time, I wanted to know what I was in for before I gave any possible enemies my address.

"Sensors are listening in full-passive mode," Yamada said. "It would help if we could release a few probes and steer them on gentle arcs toward the inner planets."

"No," I said immediately.

She looked annoyed. "Sir, we need multiple points of reference for triangulation."

I considered. "Dump them out one at a time as we drift closer. Don't power them up. No transmissions of any kind. No engine signatures."

She rolled her eyes at me. That was my confirmation that getting drunk with her the night before had been a mistake. Always, in these situations, people became more familiar with their superior officers after intimacy. We hadn't had sex, but we'd certainly shared a few private moments.

Zye... I hadn't dared meet her eyes yet.

How had *that* happened? I'd managed to evade Yamada, a woman who was at least from Earth. If I'd gone to bed with her, all would have been relatively well. She was a grown-up, an adult about sexual issues, as far as I could tell. I truly believed that we could have shrugged off a moment in the night, had we shared one.

But Zye? She was none of these things. I had no idea how she was going to react to the natural emotions everyone felt the day after they lost their virginity. Worse, she might have fallen in love with me. She'd already been devoted—I thought I might have made the situation worse.

It was the brandy. What a mistake. Even then, I could have switched on my implant and drained the effects from my system rather quickly.

But using the implant was always difficult. It was like swearing off the next drink. Easily done early-on, but after a dozen drinks, the thirteenth seems to have a mind of its own.

That's how it was with the implant. Hell, I should have turned it on the moment Zye and I had retired to her cabin.

Giving my head a shake, I concentrated on the here and now again.

Yamada was eyeing me strangely. I suspected she'd asked me something, and I hadn't responded.

"All right," I said. "You can drop off probes, and after we've drifted a hundred thousand kilometers or so, give them a fast booster to push them sunward. We'll manage."

"Okay," she said, "I can work with that."

I felt I'd dodged a bullet. Things went smoothly for the next hour, until my aunt stepped onto the deck.

She was in a good mood today. That I could see immediately. I hastened to avoid thinking of possible reasons why—but I couldn't stop myself from envisioning Rumbold and Lady Grantholm together.

Suppressing a visible reaction, I smiled at my aunt. "Hello, Lady. I trust you are well today?"

"Very well, thank you."

"What brings you up here this morning?" I asked. "Perhaps you wish to see these three lovely worlds for yourself?"

She was looking at the forward screen, but at my words, she eyed me coldly. "They are lovely. Are they inhabited?"

"We don't know yet. We're drifting quietly, investigating and listening."

She frowned. "How long will that take?"

"It's difficult to say. We'll map the system completely within the hour. But to detect technological presences takes a little longer. They don't all announce themselves openly. These systems are dangerous and—"

"I want to play the recording," she said decisively. "Yamada, begin the broadcast immediately."

"Madam—" I began.

She turned on me. "Nephew, you're a masterful warrior. A gifted tactical genius, I'm beginning to believe. But let's face facts, it takes risk to explore and entreat with new colonies. Try to put yourself in their shoes. Here we are, sneaking into this system like thieves."

"I only want a few hours, Ambassador. I need to know if there are any fortifications to avoid—that sort of thing."

"Have you found anything like that yet?" she asked.

"No, but—"

"You won't. Any thinking colony would have placed sensors out here. I suspect they're already observing us, sizing us up."

"Pardon me, but that's pure conjecture."

She continued on as if I hadn't spoken. "As the mission commander, I've decided to allow you six more hours. After that, we're going to start broadcasting our recorded greeting.

Let's hope these people aren't as anti-social as our previous hosts were."

She swept off the deck leaving me standing in her wake. I gritted my teeth and vowed that the next time I went on such a mission I would be in command of my own ship without such constant interference.

"Well Captain?" Yamada asked. "Do I drop the probes or not?"

"Yes," I said. "In fact, they give me an idea."

The hours passed quickly. Before half of them had gone by, we'd learned that the system didn't have any regular, normal traffic.

There were a few signals here and there. They knocked and twittered with unknown codes, and packets flying about. We couldn't understand them, but they all seemed to be automated transmissions. The sort of things that satellites and communications systems relayed to one another when there was no other traffic to be had.

"I think this star system is dead," Yamada said after a time. "I don't understand it. These worlds were definitely colonized. There are a dozen signatures indicating that fact. We've spotted purified elements, indicating space mining. There are asteroids that are half-gone, in fact."

"What about the planets?" I asked, going over the close-ups we'd managed to get from space. "Cities? Lights?"

"Nothing that grand. There are settlements, but they're dark and quiet. It's as if the colonists left these worlds and all their equipment behind. That's what's chirping in the background. Their computer systems, weather-predicative satellites and the like. But there's no one here. No one I can detect, sir."

Durris moved to my side. "There's another possibility, besides the exodus of the colonists."

"Yes?"

"They may have been exterminated, Captain. We can't deny that possibility."

I nodded. Secretly, I thought that was the more likely scenario. What colonist would abandon three planets, each more perfect than the last?

Sucking in a deep breath and letting it out slowly, I shrugged. "Activate the most distant probe," I told Yamada. "The one we dropped first. Have it broadcast our message of peace and love. I doubt there's anyone here to hear it, but you never know."

She did as I asked. Sometime later when the ambassador returned to enforce her will, she was pleased to find we were already broadcasting her canned diplomatic words.

"Any response yet?" she asked.

I quickly enlightened her as to the nature of the system, and its mysteriously abandoned state.

Her disappointment was palpable. "Such lovely worlds," she said wistfully. "If they're all dead, then I'll take the opportunity to name them."

She looked around at me. "Unless you've already taken that liberty?"

"No madam. Do the honors."

She eyed them. "The first one, the red one that boils close to the star—that's Ruby. The second, the jungle-choked eye of green—that's Jade."

Everyone's eyes fell upon the third world. The cool, blue marble shrouded in fluffy white clouds.

"That one is Sapphire," she said decisively.

"Excellent names, Lady," I said.

"I'm glad you approve. Now, fire up our main engines and take me to Sapphire, I want to stand on the surface of it and breathe that fresh, clean air. It is breathable, isn't it?"

She turned to Yamada, who nodded.

"Aunt," I said carefully. "Your request is a romantic one, but I must point out someone or something destroyed these colonies. We can't do what you suggest safely."

"Destroyed?" she asked, staring at Sapphire. "Are there blackened buildings? Broken towers? Crashed ships? Bodies frozen in the ice?"

"Not that we've seen so far, but that doesn't mean—"

"Take me there, William. At least let us survey the place from near orbit. Don't you want to investigate the situation?"

She had me there. I wanted to go almost as badly as she seemed to.

We'd all been in space for some time. We'd visited Tranquility Station and been chased away from Beta. To stand on an unknown world… so far, that delight had been denied to all of us. The artificial station had been wondrous, but nothing like a truly wild planet of alien beauty.

"All right, Ambassador," I said, quelling my better judgment. "We'll fly closer, and see if we can find a safe place to land. I must insist you stay aboard *Defiant*, however, until we're sure there's no threat."

"Fair enough, I suppose," she said, relenting at last.

She smiled at me then, and I felt good about my decision. She was different today in that she hadn't yet attempted to order me around like a puppet. She'd asked for my permission, even my approval. For some reason, that had made me want to give it.

I sincerely hoped it wouldn't turn out to be a grave error.

-24-

As we got closer to the three inner planets, now dubbed Sapphire, Jade and sweltering Ruby, our disquiet grew.

Things were not as they should be. There had indeed been a civilization here, a small fledgling set of colonies. All three of these Earth-like worlds had been colonized.

There were settlements dotting the choicest regions of each planet. On Sapphire, the towns formed a thin belt around the equator where the climate was most temperate.

On Jade, they'd chosen offshore islands near the major continents. On those islands the jungles weren't as thick, and the native animals were less fierce.

On Ruby, the hottest world, tiny towns had been placed in the cool zones around the poles. From space, they resembled dark pebbles embedded in the planetary surface.

All of this made sense—but what didn't add up was the condition of the settlements. They were all empty, devoid of human life.

There were other things living on the worlds: animals, fish, insects... These planets fairly teemed with creatures we'd never seen before but which were somehow hauntingly familiar. Bird-like beasts that flapped wings underwater occasionally breached the surface of the seas on Jade. Living air-bladders that resembled jellyfish drifted in the skies over Ruby—but there were no humans in evidence anywhere.

"Sir," Yamada said, looking up from her scopes, "I'm not finding anything. No colonists, anyway. They must have pulled up stakes and left."

"Are there signs of battle?" I asked.

"Nothing obvious. Here and there, buildings are burned or collapsed. But that could have happened naturally if the colonists left many years ago."

Stepping around the railing to the forward screens, I looked up at them. They were of such high resolution, it seemed as if I could reach out and touch the scene depicted. Right now, we were looking at a town along the equatorial belt of Sapphire. Nestled in a jewel-like valley of intense green, it was sheltered from the driving snows and winds of the towering peaks around it.

I touched the town on the screen. It magnified, but optics could only take our vision so far. The atmosphere of Sapphire was turbulent and full of streaky clouds. Even with AI interpolation techniques, I knew I couldn't see the true state of affairs from space.

"We'll land here," I said. "Prepare a pinnace, Rumbold."

He gawked at me.

"Me sir?" he asked. "I thought I was too—"

"You're coming along. I know you can handle a pinnace like no other. Even if it breaks down—you'll fix it."

"Very well, Captain," he said, swallowing hard. "Who else is going along on this… adventure?"

I turned to look at each of them in turn. "First Officer Durris, you'll stay here and command the ship."

"As my first act," he said, "I'll log my disapproval of this idea. It's entirely too dangerous."

I gave him a flickering smile. "Yes, that's true. But it must be done. I have to know what happened down there. Did you think that exploring the colonies was going to be safe and relaxing?"

"It's proven to be anything but," he said ruefully.

"Zye," I said, turning to her last, "you can come along as well."

She stood up promptly. "I'll see that the ship is prepared."

She left, and I caught myself staring after her. It was hard to tell what she was thinking. Maybe to a Beta, the night before had been nothing but a bit of harmless fun. But I doubted that.

Rumbold hurried after her. "She'll fill the entire ship with weapons if I don't get down there to keep her in check!" he complained.

Next, I looked at Yamada. "I think you'd do best up here helping Durris."

She cast her eyes downward. "I thought you might say that."

I frowned. Was she jealous? Perhaps upset about last night? How much did she know about what had happened between Zye and myself?

Giving my head a little shake, I did my best to erase these thoughts. I turned back to Durris.

"I'll take along Marine Commander Morris as well. Have him choose two of his troops and send him down to meet us on the hangar deck in their full kit."

"Will do, sir. Good luck."

"Thank you."

I exited the command deck and soon afterward, the ship itself. Like all starships, *Defiant* wasn't built to land on planetary surfaces. We flew the pinnace down into the atmosphere.

As we plummeted like a whistling bomb from space, I told myself repeatedly that this was the best possible course of action. In order to really explore these worlds, we had to perform our investigations in person. We'd move as quickly as we could and then fly back up into the relative safety of space.

We landed in a gush of vapor and dust on the main street of the abandoned town I'd chosen. My three marines were the first to disembark, rushing to either side and seeking any possible enemies. They found none, but they stood tensely in their body-shells. Their automated cannons swiveled this way and that, tracking everything that moved.

I stepped out of the ship next and walked down the ramp more slowly.

"All clear on the plague factor, Captain," stated Morris, looking up from a device designed to detect biological pathogens.

I nodded and opened my helmet.

Sapphire was a bright world. The air was clean and thin. It was also shockingly cold. After being trapped in ships breathing stale, recycled gases, it felt good to suck fresh oxygen into my lungs.

"Taste that air," I said. "It's glorious."

Zye stepped down after me and stood at my side. She looked at me quizzically. "You like the air? It seems thin and cold to me."

"Exactly. It's frosty. I haven't experienced anything like this since the last time I visited Lady Astra."

Zye reacted with a flinch. I immediately regretted my words. After last night, she obviously didn't want to hear about any other women I'd recently been visiting. I spoke up again to quickly cover any signs of embarrassment for both of us.

"Any life-readings?" I asked Marine Commander Morris.

He examined his detection equipment speculatively. "Nah. Nothing to speak of. A few odd birds in the trees, a dog or two. Nothing else on the scope—nothing human, anyway."

"Dogs?" I asked. "You've found dogs on the tracking systems?"

Morris nodded and showed me the tiny screen of his handheld tracker. It listed identified contacts and displayed their descriptions in tiny print. The icons said it all—there were two, medium-sized dogs in the trees behind the pinnace.

I walked around the ship and surveyed the land on that side. If they *were* dogs, they were hiding well, and remarkably quiet. They certainly had no interest in barking at us.

"Over there," Morris said, following me with his instrument in hand. "Between those two freaky trees."

The streets were overgrown with twisted roots from the towering trees that grew in the region. The growths were indeed odd-looking, as he'd suggested. They were gnarly and uneven in every dimension. The trunks themselves seemed to lean randomly like drunken men staggering out of a bar.

The streets were equally strange. Why would there be dogs, of all things, somewhere in the middle of those trees...?

"Let's check it out," I said, and began walking toward the distorted trees.

"Whoa, hold on, Captain!" Morris cried, hurrying after me. "It's not safe to leave the pinnace. We haven't secured the area yet."

I snorted at him. "We haven't got all day. If you like, you can aim your chest cannons at the dogs in case they bark."

Frowning, he marched beside me without further complaints. Zye and the marines walked cautiously in our wake. Rumbold stayed quietly in the pinnace's pilot seat, and I let him.

I was the only member of the group who wasn't heavily armed. I had my sidearm, a smart-pistol that had served me well over the years, and I openly wore my power-saber. But I'd left behind the body-shell and heavy, swiveling chest-cannon. After all, this was supposedly an exploratory mission. If we did meet colonists, appearing to be armed to the teeth probably wasn't the best way to earn their confidence.

Stepping into the cold gloom under the trees, I suppressed a shiver. This world wasn't warm and inviting. I still liked it, but it would take some getting used to.

The dogs converged on me suddenly, silently. They'd been hiding in the undergrowth watching us. Neither of them barked—they didn't even whine.

Instead they stared, and as they got closer, they sniffed.

With a frown of concern, I extended a hand toward each of the dogs.

"Careful, sir," Morris said. "They might be starving."

"I doubt it. Look at their coats, their paws, their red lolling tongues. These animals are well cared-for."

The dogs snuffled my fingers at length then withdrew as silently as they'd come.

Abruptly, a patch of leaves and sticks pushed up from the ground nearby. A man's dirty, unkempt head appeared. Their foxholes had been camouflaged in the brush, I realized immediately.

All around us, more men did the same. They held weapons: Crossbows, worn rifles and a plasma blaster or two.

My hands lifted into the air. My marines circled around me. Their cannons swiveled automatically, aiming at one target after another like the beaks of nervous birds.

"Careful," I said to the marines. "Remember why we're here, gentlemen. Stand down."

With obvious reluctance, the three marines directed their weapons skyward. Zye scowled fiercely, but she didn't say a word or draw her gun.

"Hello colonists," I said, "we're human explorers from a neighboring system. We've come to talk to you, to trade with you."

"We know who you are, Sparhawk," said the leader, a man with a shock of red hair and a torn shirt of woven flax. "We heard your transmissions. Did you notice we made no response? What we want to know is why you won't leave us alone?"

I smiled. "You certainly have taken great pains to hide yourselves," I said. "We thought this planet was abandoned."

"You can't claim Sapphire," the red-headed leader said quickly. "It's ours. Nothing here is for sale, either. Not our women, or our dogs—not even our children. You'd best pack up your trade goods and go back to your ship while you can."

His words surprised me. Not because he was so unfriendly, but because he'd referred to this planet as Sapphire. It had been my impression, up until that moment, that Lady Grantholm had recently named these worlds upon seeing them for the first time.

It made me wonder about her motivations. Had I been duped into coming here? What was she really up to? For all I knew, she was misbehaving aboard *Defiant* right now, perhaps sending further unauthorized transmissions.

That was a mystery for another time, however. At the moment, I had other considerations to contend with.

"We're here to talk," I said. "If you have nothing physical to trade, we might as well share information. That's free."

He looked me up and down speculatively. "All right. We can't stay here, though. This place isn't safe."

"Perhaps you can take us to your living quarters," I said.

"We'll go somewhere secure. Follow us into the tunnels."

Bracing myself, I did as he asked. The troops behind me grumbled, but they didn't openly object.

As we moved through what amounted to cramped, dirty holes, I soon learned the colonists were a tough, primitive lot. They were highly suspicious as well. Their leader was named Jkal, and I found that I liked the man, despite his faults.

"Jkal," I said, "you haven't yet explained to me why your people are hiding underground."

"You're the visitor. You will explain things first, Earthman."

Nodding, I had to admit there was a certain logic to that statement. I followed Jkal and his group farther and farther from the source of gray sunlight behind us, I found the tunnels oppressive. Worse, they became muddy as we passed under the village and continued onward.

At last, several hundred meters along, the tunnels opened out into a more wholesome region of thick concrete pipe.

"This must be their sewer system," Morris said to me. "But they don't seem to use it that way now."

Looking down, I saw a trickle of dark water that looked like melting ice from the surface. Morris was right, there was no sewage here. My nose wasn't as happy as it had been on the surface, but it wasn't rebelling, either.

"Tell me, Jkal," I called. "Why haven't you taken our weapons?"

Jkal stopped and turned. He had a startled look on his face.

"Would you have allowed such a thing?"

"No," I admitted, "probably not."

"Good," he said. "I'm relieved to hear you're sane."

"What do you mean?"

"No sane warrior would give another his weapon. Not without dying first. Even then, a death grip can be hard to dislodge."

"I see."

We pressed onward. When we reached a major junction in the sewer system, I expected to find some sort of habitation.

Instead, we were turned in another direction and headed down a longer, darker tunnel.

"Hold on," I said. "Where are you taking us?"

"To our village," Jkal said. "You asked to go there."

"Yes, but… aren't we already underneath your village?"

"What? The buildings? We don't live in buildings! We did once, of course, but that was before even my parents were born."

I was beginning to catch on.

"Who raids your planet?" I asked.

He looked at me with narrowed eyes. "What?"

"Someone comes and captures your people, right? That's why you hide like rats under the ground."

Jkal looked suspicious. "What's a rat?"

"A noble animal," Morris said over my shoulder, grinning.

I didn't chide him for lying. After all, it was for a good cause.

"We'll talk when we reach our destination," Jkal said.

At length, we were led to a natural cavern. I had the feeling we were under one of the peaks that circled the valley. That meant we were entombed beneath a thousand meters of rock—the very thought was oppressive.

Heading upward through winding, natural passages, the cavern eventually opened at last to a yawning mouth. I was quite relieved to feel the sting of Sapphire's breath in my lungs again.

Jkal walked some steps ahead, peering intently into the distance for long moments.

We could see the sky again. From underneath a thick overhang of granite, I could see the valley sloping away. There was a tremendous amount of cover provided by trees. The terrain was rough and covered with scrubby brush. The village itself must have been hidden by the strangely twisted trees.

"Hmm…" I said, looking around. There was no encampment here in the cave mouth. There were only a few ash heaps, indicating people had burned campfires and eaten game.

Jkal came to me. "You must stay here," he said. "I'm going to get our leader. You must wait. You may start a fire if you like."

Shrugging, we did as he asked. The group of villagers left us and stealthily crept out of the cavern and into the open.

Sitting down on a rock, I noted that Zye was looking agitated.

"What's wrong, Zye?" I asked.

"I don't trust these men," she said. "They're carrion-feeders."

"I wouldn't go that far," Morris said, stepping into the conversation. "Sure, they've had a rough time of it. They're failures in comparison to your civilization. But not all colonies were destined to be successful. Especially not after they were cut off from Earth. These folks just got the short end of the stick, that's all."

I frowned, thinking about Zye's concerns. She was standing, not sitting. She was near the edge of the cavern mouth, staring outside.

Darkness was falling fast. The local sun had dropped behind a craggy peak, and the light was fading rapidly, as it always did in the mountains.

Standing up and walking to the edge of the cavern mouth, I decided to communicate with *Defiant*. I hadn't done so for quite some time, as we'd been trapped underground.

"Captain," Durris said when I contacted him. "There's something wrong. We're picking up an audio signal from your location. A repeated pinging sound, too high in pitch for human ears to pick up. Are you transmitting something?"

Puzzled, I assured him we weren't. I immediately set my team to searching the area.

We found the source of the noise just as the darkness became total. A silver box with a crude speaker attached to it sat just above the cave mouth. I put my hand on it, and I felt a tiny vibration, but I couldn't hear anything.

I yanked the cord out, and it stopped vibrating.

"That little red-headed bastard," Morris said when he saw the contraption. "What kind of a trick is this? He set this up deliberately, that's for sure. I'm going to have some words with him when he gets back here."

"He's not coming back," Zye said.

There was certainty in her voice, and I had to agree with her.

The first thing I did was try to contact Rumbold. There was no response from the pinnace.

I growled in frustration. We were faced with a difficult decision. Should we march back down to our pinnace? Or should we search for Jkal?

"I vote we hunt that skinny frigger down and burn some holes in his legs until he explains himself," Morris suggested.

"Certainly not," I said. "This is an exploratory expedition, after all. The locals may have played a trick on us, but they've done nothing overtly hostile yet."

"Always do the unexpected," Zye said in the tone of one quoting a proverb.

Glancing at her, I put up my hands. "What would that be, in this case?"

"I don't know, but we shouldn't stand around in this cave any longer."

She was right, of course. For all we knew the transmitter could have been a homing device marking our location for some kind of primitive missile.

"Let's head back toward the ship," I said. "They might be back there now, breaking into it."

Hurrying this time, we used our compasses to draw a line through the forest. The terrain was rough, and we were breathing hard before we were halfway there. This planet had no moon. The darkness was nearly complete. We had to use the infrared systems in our helmets, and the light boosters in our implants to see where we were going.

The first warning we had was a tremendous crashing sound.

"What was that?" demanded one of the marines.

"A tree went down," Morris said, "I'm sure of it."

"Keep moving," I said, drawing my pistol and saber.

Zye had her weapon out now as well. No one was calm, but we weren't running in a panic. Not yet.

Another tree went down. The sound was unmistakable. In spite of our hasty pace, it seemed to come from closer behind us than the first one.

"Something's coming," Zye said. "Something big. I've been stalked before by megafauna on Beta. They come like this, sometimes—the largest of them."

That was it. We'd been jogging, but now we broke into a run.

A thumping sound came from behind us. A series of cracking sounds joined it. There was something big on our tails. And it was gaining.

When the third tree crashed down, closer than ever, I ordered a halt.

"We've got nearly a kilometer to go," I said. "We can't make it. We should consider hiding and ambushing it."

Nodding, Morris and his troops spread out. Zye stayed with me. We chose a boulder that was big enough for the two of us and crouched in the frosty darkness.

While we waited, and the thing crashed closer and closer, Zye reached out a big arm and gave me a squeeze. I looked at her in surprise. She met my eyes.

"We'll be fine," I said. "If it can die—we'll kill it."

She flashed me a smile that I could see by the lights inside her faceplate—and then something waded through the trees and paused right on top of us.

I knew in an instant that we'd miscalculated. The alien creature was *huge*. Above us, where there had been branches and stars a moment earlier, there was now nothing but blackness. I tried not to breathe, and for a moment, the beast seemed to have lost us.

"Permission to fire, sir!" Morris' voice hissed inside my helmet.

"Hold," I transmitted back.

We were conversing using our helmet radios. The creature shouldn't be able to hear us, not unless it had—

But the beast reacted. Twisting and looking this way and that, I saw the shadowy monster searching for our voices. Fortunately, Morris had shut up. I thought of the high-pitched sound Jkal had used to summon this monster—it only made sense that it would have excellent hearing. Many predators did.

One of my marines didn't follow my orders to hold his fire, however. He broke from his hiding spot and opened up with his chest-cannon, ripping the air with flashes and a crackling spray of plasma.

The creature attacked immediately. A long curving shape dipped out of the sky and lifted again, taking the man and his weapon away.

Jaws? Had I seen, in a brief flash of gunfire, the drooling jaws of a bizarre monstrosity?

To me, it resembled something like the toothy head of a barracuda on a long, sinewy neck. But instead of scales or smooth skin, the beast was shaggy with matted fur.

The neck convulsed, and the teeth crunched down. After a few tries, it choked down the marine, swallowing the body-shell armor, gun and all.

"That's it!" I shouted. "Light this thing up!"

All of us began to fire then. We concentrated our weapons on the head, which was hopefully a weak point.

Releasing a thunderous howl, the head dipped and tried to get Morris. He rolled away and came up firing in a new position.

Deciding my own pistol was useless, I drew my saber. Switching it on, I found it lit the region in a reddish glow like a torch.

The monster stopped trying to eat Morris and turned toward me instead. The light of my power saber, rippling with force, had made me its target of choice.

There was nowhere to run. I was between two tree-like legs—of which it had at least six. The neck coiled and then lengthened again, reminding me of a striking snake.

I knelt, activated my personal shield, and thrust my blade toward the gaping mouth.

The blade touched the creature's tongue before those teeth reached me. There was a snapping sound, and the smell of burnt meat filled the forest.

Bellowing, the creature reared up, then struck again, enraged. I stared in the dark, hoping it had weakened.

Was it weakening? Yes—a rolling shiver convulsed through the assemblage of its massive form and it paused. The pounding fire of two rifles, peppering the neck, body and skull with burn marks, had taken a toll.

The second strike came then, and I was snatched up in those vast jaws. A sickening sensation filled me, and I realized I was being hoisted aloft. The teeth were crushing down, but they weren't penetrating my shield as yet.

Forming a ball with my body, I endeavored to thrust and cut the inside of the monsters' mouth. It convulsed around me, and I recognized the unmistakable signs.

I was about to be swallowed whole.

-25-

The monster's throat gaped, and I almost slid down into the acid-bath churning in its stomach. I knew my only possible move was a single thrust up into the monster's brain, and I went for it.

I couldn't brace my feet, as I was riding the rolling, burnt chunk of meat that served the creature for a tongue.

Taking my best shot, I stabbed upward. My thrust never reached the creature's brain, but it did quite a bit of damage to its olfactory region. What saved me, I think, was lacerating the sinuses.

Choking and coughing, it spat me back out. I crashed to the ground with jarring force and lay there with the wind knocked out of me, coated in disgusting fluids.

The monster, snorting and shaking its head, ran off into the forest. It crashed through the trees and trumpeted in rage and pain as it went.

I remained where I'd fallen until Zye came and helped me to my feet.

"Are you injured?" she asked, running her hands over me.

"Stunned, but alive," I said. I rolled to my knees so I could begin wringing slime from my clothes and wiping it on the turf.

"Captain!" Morris shouted. "This way!"

Not knowing what the trouble was, I envisioned a full herd of additional monsters. Zye and I rushed toward his voice.

We broke through a copse of brush to find Morris standing over Jkal and two of his compatriots. He had his rifle leveled in their faces.

"Here they are," the Marine Commander said. "They came back to gloat. To watch us die."

I walked unsteadily toward Jkal and put the tip of my glimmering blade near his throat. He watched the power sword with naked fear.

"Don't kill," he said. "Humans don't kill humans. It's forbidden."

"Really?" I asked. "But it's acceptable to lure your fellow man into a cave and summon a monstrous beast to devour him, is that it?"

"The serpent was hungry. We fed it. Better you than one of us."

I nodded. "Very logical. Now, it's time for you to start talking to us, Jkal. Or I'm going to have to damage you."

"Don't kill. It's—"

"Yes, yes, I heard that part. But I won't kill you. A brush with the tip of this weapon usually isn't fatal. It isn't pleasant, however."

Zye came up and squatted near us, watching. She didn't turn away. She didn't seem squeamish at all. Betas were a stoic people. They neither relished giving pain, nor avoided dispensing it when effective or appropriate.

"The Beta," Jkal said. "That's why we did it. You're in league with them. We know it."

I glanced at Zye. "You know about Betas?"

"Of course. We're not fools. We've been trapped here for generations, but there are a few old ones who still teach us of the neighboring colonies."

"Where's your leader?" I demanded. "The one you were going to take me to."

Jkal licked his lips, then shrugged. "I'm the only leader here. These few are all that survived in this town. All the other nearby towns are empty."

"What about the women and children you mentioned?" I asked. "Where are they?"

He shook his head. "Not anywhere near here. Maybe some live on the far side of Sapphire. The Stroj took all of them from our village. They come every year in the summer heat for a hunt. Those who are slowest, the weakest—they don't survive."

I lowered my sword and switched it off.

"You believe me?" Jkal asked.

"To a point," I said. "The Stroj did come through this system. We saw their ships exit hyperspace here. We were following them until we lost them in this system."

Jkal licked his lips again and got up into a crouch. I sensed he wanted to run, and I barely had the heart to stop him if he did.

I believed he was telling the truth about the Stroj. They were hunting humans on these worlds, taking them like trophies. That explained a lot.

What I knew of the Stroj led me to think these worlds would be attractive to them. They'd found fast-running prey full of tricks. I suspected immediately that Jkal and his crew had been left behind to provide further entertainment. Perhaps the Stroj allowed them to run free here. There were probably knots of survivors on all three of these worlds. The Stroj liked to track wild game. They would enjoy nothing better than a pack of feral humans who could be hunted and used as a source of fresh body parts to adorn themselves.

"Hmm," I said, "can you tell us exactly when the Stroj are due to come back?"

"Any time now," he said. "This is high summer. We watch the skies every day."

Looking around, I felt a chill in the night air, but said nothing. I suspected that on Sapphire, summertime was a relative thing.

"Jkal, have you ever heard of a Captain Lorn?" I asked.

His face paled. "Are you in an alliance with that devil? Is that why you came here, to sell us to the—"

"No, no," I said. "I'm merely asking the question. When I said we'd followed a Stroj pirate to this system, I'd meant Lorn."

Jkal looked more frightened and worried than he had when I'd put the tip of my sword to his throat.

"We know Lorn. He's worse than the Gi. Don't trust any promise he makes you."

I smiled grimly. "Don't worry. Obviously, he's come here before. How often?"

"I have to get back to my camp now."

"Not so fast," Morris said, prodding him with the barrel of his weapon. "Answer the Captain's question."

"Let him go," I said, standing up straight and stretching my back painfully. "I doubt he can be any more help."

"One moment with him first, sir?" Morris asked.

Glancing at him, I nodded.

Morris grabbed the man up and dragged him to a collection of stones where one of the marines lay, crushed and mangled.

"This isn't all fun and games to me, Jkal," he said. "If I get my way, I'll kill the lot of you for this. Now, run off before the Captain changes his mind."

Jkal and his companions vanished into the dark forest with pounding feet.

With a heavy heart, I helped Morris carry the body of our fallen comrade. After a ten minute hike, we reached the pinnace.

The tiny ship's door yawned open. Rumbold was gone.

"They ransacked the ship," Morris said. "I bet they ate Rumbold or something."

"He'd be a tough old bird," I said. Straightening and looking up and down the abandoned streets, I called loudly for Rumbold.

After a few echoing shouts, a figure appeared.

"Sorry Captain," he said. "They surprised me. I opened the hatch when they said you were injured. Their leader—"

"Yes, I know," I said. "He's quite persuasive."

"I slipped away while they were busy taking our foodstuffs and our gear."

"Are you hurt?" I asked him.

"Only my pride, sir."

"Very well. Let's lift off from this accursed planet."

Moments later we soared up into the high thin layers of the atmosphere. The entire experience had been sobering, but in a way, it was also understandable.

The degenerate people who still clung to life on this world weren't a friendly bunch. Maybe half of what Jkal had told me was a lie. Probably, there *were* women and children somewhere, but he didn't want to reveal their location. I couldn't blame him for that.

They'd survived decades of Stroj hunts. What kind of a man could keep breathing under such circumstances? Only the meanest of men. A rodent on two legs.

Trying to forgive them for their trickery and thefts, I thought about what had been visited upon them—the suffering they'd undergone. That was the true evil.

The more I thought about it, the more I came to blame Captain Lorn and his band. They were the ones who had to be dealt with harshly.

In my mind, a plan began to take form.

-26-

When we reached *Defiant*, I ordered my helmsman to take us out of orbit. After one last look at the blue-white beauty of the world, we left Sapphire behind.

"Where to, sir?" Durris asked from navigation.

"Find the closest bridge entry point," I said. "I don't care where it leads."

Durris frowned, but he did as I asked. "This one," he said, tapping at a glowing point on the screens. "We can exit the system here."

"Set a course for that bridge. Get underway, helmsman."

Durris got up and approached my chair. "Sir, that bridge leads to an undetermined endpoint. It might be terminal. There are a few others, much further out, that are on the Connatic's star charts. They lead to known systems—places with markets to trade, colonists we can talk to."

"No," I said. "We're not done with this star system yet. Set the course."

Confused, he returned to his boards and did as I asked. Soon, the ship's powerful engines rumbled, and we were pulling away toward the distant breach point. As it would take a full day's flight to reach it, I got up and left the command deck.

I was in a sullen mood when a knock came at my office door.

"Enter," I said.

Lady Grantholm stood revealed when the door swished aside. Her brow was stormy.

"Where are we going?" she demanded.

"Nowhere."

"What kind of nonsense is this, William? I know you suffered a death on the planet, but that isn't any—"

"No," I said, "that's not why I'm brooding. I've got a plan, and I'm executing it right now."

She came inside fully, sat in the chair opposite mine, and stared at me expectantly.

I said nothing in response.

"Well?" she demanded. "What is this vaunted plan of yours? Why should I approve of it?"

"We're not in a diplomatic situation," I told her. "We're soon going to engage in combat. That places me in command."

"Really?" she demanded. "I don't see it that way. There are no enemy ships nearby. There are only a few pathetic colonists, huddling on these forgotten worlds. There's never been a more obvious diplomatic situation on this mission. I demand that you turn around and allow me to talk to the people you've made contact with."

"No," I said flatly.

Her face flushed with anger. "Listen, William Sparhawk. There will be a full court of inquiry when we return if you persist in these power struggles. Our orders are clear. Must I read them aloud to you?"

She pulled out a computer scroll and began tapping at it.

Leaning forward over my desk, I plucked it from her fingers. After glancing at it I dropped it on my desk.

"What is the meaning of this?" she demanded. "What's gotten into you, William?"

"Aunt," I said, "I want the answer to a question of my own. How did you know the true names of these planets before we got here?"

That stopped her for a moment. The anger on her face faded, and she scowled at me.

"I hardly see how that—"

"Sapphire, Jade, and the burning ember named Ruby? What a coincidence it must be that you knew them all."

She eyed me with a pursed mouth and furrowed brow, but said nothing.

"These three worlds weren't named by you," I told her. "They were named a century or more ago by the people who landed here. But I've scoured our databanks. There's no record of these planets. No record of these colonists. I demand that you explain how you knew the names of these worlds, and what else you might be holding back."

She sat back, glaring at me. After a moment, her face softened a little.

"Let's put our cards on the table," she said. "Why are we flying toward a system exit point now? Why would we dare to enter an unknown bridge? And why do you claim we're in a combat situation?"

"We're moving toward an exit point because it's my belief there are Stroj hiding in this star system. I'm trying to flush them out. Now, answer my questions."

Pursing her lips even more tightly, she nodded. "All right. I accept your explanation, although I see no evidence of these Stroj."

"The enemy ships are self-described pirates. They're deceptive and stealthy. They also know we can beat them in a fight. They're hiding here, somewhere. The colonists told me Lorn comes here regularly at this time of year. I believe they're waiting for us to leave."

She leaned forward and put her hands on the table between us. "You actually spoke to these colonists? Some of them have definitely survived?"

"Yes."

"What else did they say?" she demanded.

"I'll make a full report after you tell me what you know of this place."

She flopped back again. "You always were a difficult child. When you first stood up, do you know that you didn't want to sit back down again? You gripped a table fiercely for over an hour until your mother finally dragged you away from it."

Rolling my eyes, I gestured for her to get on with her story.

"Very well," she said stiffly. "As you may know, I'm what they call an oldster. I'm not as young as I look."

"Really?" I said, doing my best to hold back any hint of sarcasm. She was correct in that most people believed her to be no more than a century old, while the family knew her to be twice that.

"There's no need to be rude," she said. "But it's true. The records of my birth were lost in the Cataclysm, and I never share the true date. Let me assure you, people would be shocked if they knew the truth."

That part I did believe. I nodded and waited.

"There were many colonists coming and going in the old days," she said wistfully.

I could tell she was looking down through many decades of life.

"Many young people followed the colony reports closely, some of us even made it a pastime. News came back, oftentimes secondhand, of new planets and worlds being discovered and inhabited. When I first saw this place, I recalled the names of these worlds. The planets are so beautiful, just as they'd been described to me so very long ago."

"All right," I said after a pause, "I believe that part."

"You should. It's the truth."

"Very well. But what I'm more interested in goes deeper than that. Some people on Earth knew of these places, even after the Cataclysm. Why didn't Earth reestablish her connection with these lonely outposts? Why did we wait so long? Why did we sleep for a century and a half?"

"That's harder to answer," she said. "The Cataclysm disrupted everything. After we rebuilt our homeworld, there was a natural tendency to retreat from the stars.
People blamed our explorations—rationally or not—for our hardships. There was no longer an appetite for expenditures of any kind in space."

That rang true to me as well. There had been, throughout history, pauses in humanity's natural urge to expand and explore. The Chinese, for example, had sent out huge ships to discover Africa before Christopher Columbus had even been born. But they'd quickly tired of the expensive practice.

Similarly, after a few missions that led people to set foot on the Moon, the United States had failed to follow through. It had taken a full century after those early forays for anyone to push into space with vigor again.

"There's more to it than that," I accused, "isn't there?"

"Well, yes," she said. "The Great Houses of Earth had little appetite for exploration. Rediscovering the colonies might give people... ideas."

Nodding, I smiled tightly. "Right. The ruling class might not survive exposure to democratic ideas echoing back from the colonies. Wasn't that the main reason for ignoring the stars?"

She shrugged noncommittally.

I stood up and paced, gesturing with my hands in anger. "In the meantime," I said, "worlds like these were abandoned—places that you'd personally heard about when they were first discovered. Don't you think we're at least partly to blame for the mess we've found out here, Lady?"

"Perhaps," she said, "but we didn't know what had happened to them."

"I think that you did. You and the rest of them, those of our family who've held power over the last century. You had to know in your heart what was going on out here. Barbarism. Genocide."

"Why do you think I volunteered to come on this mission?" she demanded suddenly. "I'm old, nephew, but I remember these places from my youth. It's strange to see them in person—and sad, I'll admit it. But the best we can do is explore, reconnect, offer trade and diplomatic discourse."

I shook my head. "No," I said. "We owe them more than that. They're our abandoned children. We must establish order out here if we can."

She heaved a sigh. "That's an expensive, painful task to undertake. You may not realize what you're getting yourself into, William."

"Maybe not," I said. "But I'm through hiding from our past and shirking Earth's duty. We're going to end the Stroj hunts in this system for starters."

Moving decisively, I walked out of my office. She called after me, but I ignored her and headed for the command deck.

My mood was dark, and I felt the outraged betrayal of all the souls who'd died on these worlds as if it had happened to me personally.

We'd abandoned our own, forgotten about them. It was unconscionable. How could my own relatives be responsible for such misery?

-27-

After streaking across the system, we broke through the membrane between two forms of existence and entered hyperspace.

Normally, at this point, we'd immediately begin seeking a way out. But this time I had different ideas.

"First Officer Durris, drop the first probe now."

He looked surprised. "We just crossed into hyperspace, sir. We need to gain some distance so we have two points of reference—"

"I know all that, Durris. Drop the probe, but don't bother to drop any more of them. I'm working a strategy, here."

He did as I ordered. My staff exchanged glances and shrugs, but they obeyed.

I'd yet to take them all into my confidence. I suspected some of them might object to my plan, so I waited to inform them of its nature.

After flying for several hours, I did the unexpected again. I ordered the helm to reverse course and head back toward the initial probe.

This baffled everyone. "But sir, we're moving at speed. We'll have to counter all our inertia and come to a full stop before we can even begin to backtrack—"

"I'm well aware of the procedure, Durris," I said. "Please follow orders."

My crew did as I'd ordered, and ten hours later we were crawling back toward the bridge point we'd crossed the first time.

I took the time to sleep in my cabin. I hadn't had a good sleep for days. The horrors of the colonists, both current and past, haunted my dreams. My mind was full of massive unseen monsters, villagers being slaughtered, and lovely vistas seen from mountain peaks.

It was the second or third chime at my door that awakened me at last. Suspecting there must be a systems problem, I staggered to the entrance and touched the wall.

It dissolved to reveal an unexpected figure. Zye stood there. She wore an uncharacteristic expression of concern. Her pupils were dilated and her breathing deliberate.

"What is it, Zye?" I asked. "Is there trouble with the ship?"

"Not that I know of," she said.

"Well then, what—oh…"

She let her tunic slide open and revealed herself. "I thought this might be a good time," she said. "If you're not too tired, that is—"

"Come in here before someone sees you in the passage," I urged.

She stepped into my cabin and shed her clothing. Without a stitch on, or any hint of embarrassment, she walked over and sat on my bunk, looking at me expectantly.

My eyes roved over her imposing breasts. They were faultless. But, since she was a statuesque woman, they were somewhat astonishing.

"Is something wrong?" she asked.

"No," I said, "I'm surprised that's all."

"It was my understanding that males are always ready for a spontaneous sexual encounter."

I laughed. "Well, there's some truth to that," I said, "but we can still be taken by surprise. We have to be ready—in the mood."

"I'm in the mood now," she said.

For some reason, her brutal honesty and nakedness was daunting to me. I realized then I'd made a mistake when I'd started this whole thing between the two of us. We were so different. We had different expectations. Additionally, we were breaking unwritten rules. In Star Guard, fraternization wasn't forbidden, but it was frowned upon.

"You do not desire me?" Zye asked.

"What? No, not at all. You're perfect, in fact."

"But overwhelming? Threatening?"

She was right, but I knew I couldn't let her know that. She was already picking up on my hesitancy.

"Zye, we have to talk," I said.

There it was. The classic beginning of a break-up conversation. Unfortunately, Zye didn't even recognize the signs. She'd never had a break-up before.

"We are talking," she said flatly.

Suddenly, the magnitude of the error I'd made by bedding Zye some days earlier was crashing down upon me. She might be devastated. I might have screwed up what was an otherwise excellent working relationship.

"Right…" I began, sitting on the bunk next to her, "what I mean is that I don't think we're compatible in the long term. We had a moment, and—"

"I'm unappealing to you," she said, standing abruptly. "I suspected this might be the case. I've studied the human ideals in female anatomy. My height of two meters falls well outside the usual parameters indicated by my research."

My hands came up defensively. "You aren't unappealing. You're actually perfectly proportioned. Large, yes, but that's something many men can overcome."

"Hmm…" she said thoughtfully. "That's what Norrick said. His word-choice was almost identical. Did you confer with him on this topic?"

Blinking, I shook my head. "Are you talking about Ensign Norrick? The new man in the life support module?"

"Yes. He's the only Norrick aboard, I believe."

"Of course… how did this topic come up with him?"

"During our sexual event last night, I asked him if he was pleased with me. He insisted I was perfectly proportioned, as you just did."

I was my turn to stare in shock and confusion. "You slept with him? Last night?"

"I'm sorry if you're offended," she said. She reached out a hand and patted mine in what I took to be a clumsy effort to be comforting.

"I'm not—well—this is unexpected. You've slept with another man so soon?"

"You were unavailable. You spend most of your time on the command deck, you know. After our first encounter, I found I couldn't stop thinking about the next. Eventually, I grew tired of waiting and sought out companionship elsewhere."

My mouth was hanging open. I closed it with an effort.

"Right..." I said, grasping the situation at last. "Well, I'm happy for you Zye. I want you to enjoy yourself with Norrick. He's a fine young man."

"He's a year older than you are, actually."

I sighed. She wasn't the best at tact. "What I mean is we had a nice time once, and we've moved on. That's all right with me."

"You've moved on? Meaning, you have a new partner?"

"No," I said. "Not yet. As you said, I've been busy."

She frowned. "I'm glad you helped me get over my initial reluctance and fear of rejection. After we finally mated, I felt much less tense about subsequent encounters."

I was pretty sure she meant she was no longer hung up on me. That could only be a good thing.

Smiling, we stood up, and I gave her a hug. Our contact lingered. She was close, and nude, and the tension and worries of the day had faded from my mind. As her touch began to get my undivided attention, we separated. I fully expected her to put on her clothes and leave.

Instead, she headed to my tiny liquor cabinet and brought out a bottle and two shot glasses. She poured without asking.

"Zye..." I said, "I thought we were breaking up."

"I didn't come here to break up."

"What about Norrick?"

She shrugged. "Let's forget about him and drink one glass to our newfound understanding."

What could I do? I drank the shot. Then we had another. By the fourth, we were back on my bunk, and by the fifth—well, it was all over.

Lying next to Zye an hour later, confused and amused at the same time, I fell asleep.

* * *

When I strode back onto the command deck, the ship was less than an hour away from the breach. Looking over the ship's speed and course, I frowned.

"First Officer Durris!" I boomed.

He stepped in my direction. He had a look on his face, one that told me the tale.

"Yes, sir?"

"Are you the one who altered our plan of attack?"

"Not at all, sir. I simply reduced our speed to normal breakthrough levels."

"Could you see me in my office—immediately?"

I turned and left him standing there. He had no choice but to follow me.

Taking deep breaths, I tried to calm myself. Durris hadn't been down there on Sapphire. He hadn't seen what our colonists had become. He hadn't realized, either, that my own family members bore some level of responsibility for the situation.

"Sir?" he asked, standing in the doorway. "I can explain."

I waved for him enter then touched my desk, causing the door to coalesce behind him.

"You were saying?" I prompted. "Why are we traveling more slowly than I ordered?"

"High-speed breaching is dangerous, sir. I know that you briefed us yesterday on the possibility of pirate Stroj hiding in the system somewhere, but I—"

"My orders weren't followed while I was off-duty," I said. "That's unacceptable."

"Captain, you briefed us yesterday on your plan. I know you want to break through into the system again at high speed.

Using only inertia, we'll glide back toward the target worlds, looking for the enemy without drawing attention to ourselves by using our engines."

In space, a ship's engines were like beacons in the night. A large starship could produce a trail of exhaust and radiation resembling that of a comet and was therefore easily identified. Gliding without thrust, however, made any ship fairly stealthy and difficult to detect.

"Why are you obstructing my goals?" I asked him.

His mouth worked for a second. He squirmed visibly. "I'm sorry sir. This situation is impossible. I don't know who this ship's master is. I'm sorry."

I stared at him for a second. "Lady Grantholm…? Let me guess: she came to you, and she changed my orders while I was off the deck."

"I did *not* tell you that, sir," he said quickly, looking down.

"No, you didn't," I said. "I figured it out for myself."

Walking to the far wall, I swept my hand over it. A portal opened. It was frosted and heavily shielded with lead. Beyond the glass itself, electromagnetic shells of force protected my eyes—but it was still an actual window onto space itself.

Hyperspace was outside. There was nothing else.

"So bleak," I said. "Hyperspace makes normal space look bright, cheery and full of objects."

"Really sir, I couldn't do anything. Why did CENTCOM put us in this situation? Why didn't they simply trust you with full command?"

It was a good question, and I thought I knew the answer.

"Did you know my aunt—excuse me, the Ambassador—recognized this star system the moment she saw it?"

Durris looked at me. "No sir… how's that possible?"

"Because she was alive when the news came of this system's discovery. I think of it—a woman among us who is so ancient she recalls watching the colony ships lift off with her own eyes…"

"That's an amazing concept, sir," Durris said. "I didn't know any of the oldsters who are still around dated back that far."

I continued to stare out the window at nothing. Gamma particles sparked now and then, striking the ship at tremendous speeds. Even though hyperspace was empty, there were radiation belts now and then. Possibly, they were echoes of the exhaust of past ships that had crossed this lonely bridge.

"I should have known the second I saw the course corrections that it was her doing," I told Durris. "Get back out there and fix this. Dismissed."

He left. Once he was gone, I summoned my aunt.

She was in a bad mood from the moment she entered my office—but I no longer cared about her mood.

"Aunt Helen," I said to her, still staring into the endless dark, "please sit down."

She did so, but she muttered something behind my back.

I turned to fix her with angry eyes.

"Yes, yes," she said. "I adjusted your plan of attack. I'm *so* sorry. But unless we're in combat, Star Guard put me in command. It was my prerogative."

"That's debatable," I said, "but in any case, *why* did you do it?"

She leaned forward. "William, I'm here to make contact. I'm here to open diplomatic channels. Blasting apart colonist ships—*any* colonist ships—is not part of my stated mission."

It took me a second to get it.

"Star Guard wishes to open diplomatic relations with the Stroj? Is that it?"

"Yes, of course. It's not a popular idea back home, but it's necessary. You're flying a starship—you really should try to grow up."

"By 'growing up', I take it you mean I should turn a blind eye to pain and suffering? That I should sell out these colonists as hunting trophies if it buys Earth some years of peace?"

"Exactly," she said in a patient tone. "Earth is weak right now. We've begun to expand our military budgets, but it can't all be done in a year or two. We need to talk with the Stroj, to put them at ease until we can rebuild our fleets."

I shook my head. "I know the Stroj better than most. It won't work. They can't be dissuaded that way. In fact, showing weakness will only encourage them. They must fear us, Lady, or we are lost."

"Defending your ship is one thing, but the Stroj ran and they got away. Let them be, William. I'm pleading with you."

I gave her a dark and silent glare.

She frowned fiercely in return. "I can see by your attitude you don't agree," she said. "Therefore, you're forced my hand. I hereby forbid you to attack the Stroj!"

"Under what authority?"

"You read our orders."

"Yes, I did," I said. "I read it very carefully. You're in overall command, and when we're *not* in combat, that's clear. But this is a combat situation. I've deemed it so, and I've logged the supporting data."

She stood up. "What! You can't just decide that arbitrarily."

"Wrong," I said, pushing a computer scroll of my own toward her with the orders printed on them. "You should read the seventh paragraph—the determination of immediate danger is mine to make. I've made it."

She didn't bother to read the document. She shoved it back toward me instead, with such force that it flew onto the floor.

"They said you'd be unmanageable, but I truly had no idea. Very well, William. We'll let Star Guard decide your fate when we return home."

She left then, in a huff. I didn't watch her go. Instead, I turned back to the portal and watched hyperspace slide by until we were close to the breach.

I could feel the G forces building all the while. Durris had gone back to the bridge and begun a heavy acceleration curve, getting us back up to speed.

In the final minutes, I stepped out of my office and took my spot in the command chair. Calmly, avoiding eye contact with my confused staffers, I stared straight ahead until we hit the barrier and passed through it.

-28-

Back in normal space, I felt relieved to see stars again. There was something oppressive and unnatural about hyperspace. It felt as if you were dreaming—but still awake.

"No obstacles, sir," Durris reported immediately. "Everything is smooth and quiet."

"All engines are stopped? No transmissions?"

"We're running silent, sir, as ordered."

Finally satisfied, I leaned back in my chair and watched the screens. Everyone on the deck was doing the same.

Now and then, I couldn't help but glance over my shoulder toward the main passage. People came and went. Most of them were powder-monkeys—an old naval term we still used for crewmen running errands.

None of them turned out to be my aunt, and for that, I was grateful.

I'd pulled my final card with her. She was now on notice. There wasn't going to be any more rolling over and taking orders unless the situation was appropriate.

It occurred to me that I probably should have pulled this right from the start of the mission. Declaring that the entire length of the mission was hazardous and therefore placing myself in full command on the first day would have saved a lot of headaches.

But then again… I kept glancing back at the hatchway. Another powder-monkey rushed in, delivering coffee to the navigational team.

Turning back to the screens, I sighed. I had my aunt corralled, but how long would that last?

Hours passed. During that time, we plunged at an oblique angle back toward the inner planets. Our course was less than ideal. When coming out of hyperspace, it wasn't possible to measure with precision where you would be headed when you got there.

As a result, Jade was the closest to our current projections. Sapphire was slowly sliding away from us, slipping around to the far side of the star. I thought about using our steering jets, but I didn't dare. We didn't want to scare our pirates.

Six long hours passed. I took meals in my chair and I became slowly more annoyed with everyone as each minute crept by.

"We'll come around the star and fall into an uneven orbit soon, sir," Durris informed me. "At that point, we'll begin to slow down due to her gravitational tug."

I didn't respond.

"That orbit will decay, sir, within thirty-two days."

I finally looked at him. "We're not going to be gliding around here for thirty-two days. Don't worry."

"Good to know, sir."

A new worry had begun to set in. Every instrument we had, every measuring device aboard, was telling us the Crown System was as dead as it had ever been. When we'd first arrived here, we'd done so with a blazing arc of deceleration. Maybe the Stroj had seen us and hidden.

Or maybe, they'd never been here at all.

Four more hours passed. Each minute, I checked every instrument. I was no longer watching the hatch behind me like a nervous rookie. I was past that. As a consequence, when my aunt finally did pay me a visit, I was taken unaware.

"So," she purred next to me, "how's it going, William?"

"Perfectly," I said.

"I can see that… It looks to me like we're in the heat of battle. Oh, by the way, where are these enemies we're stalking?"

I glanced at her. "You'll be the first to know when we find them."

"See that I am," she said, and she left the deck again.

In a sour mood, I took a break to eat and piss. I was bursting from inactivity by this time, but any second I figured might be the moment of truth.

It was, in fact, when I was in the head relieving myself that everything changed.

The ship lurched. Steering jets had been fired. Right away, my mind leapt to the only possible conclusion: my aunt had ordered a course change.

After wetting my shoes and cursing, I trotted back to the command deck. The woman was a witch. She must have watched me, or paid someone off to tell her when I was off the deck.

Bursting through the hatchway, I found my Aunt standing beside my empty command chair, just as I'd expected.

"Dammit, Ambassador," I said. "I thought we had an understanding."

She looked at me. "We did," she admitted in an uncharacteristically quiet voice.

"You weren't going to give orders on this deck any longer."

She looked at me, and I realized for the first time that there was touch of contrition in her eyes.

"It's all yours, William. You were right this time. They've spotted us. They're lifting off to meet us in battle." She stepped to one side, looking annoyed and defeated.

I ran my eyes over the instruments. Durris was putting us onto a new course.

"They came up off Ruby, sir," he said. "We might have missed their heat signatures as they've been disguised all this time by the warm world. There are a few oceans there, too. They might have been sitting in water—we just don't know."

"It's all right," I said. "The Stroj are nothing if not deceptive."

A hand grabbed my arm, and I looked down to see it was my aunt. She looked up at me intensely.

"How did you know, William?" she asked. "How did you know they'd be here?"

"Just a hunch. The Stroj don't like to retreat. They don't like to give ground. They'll run if they must—but only as far as they must."

She nodded. "I guess they chose the right man for this job. I tried hailing them, but they're ignoring us."

She left the deck then, and I took my seat again. Reports began flooding in.

"I'm sorry, sir," Yamada said when my aunt had left. "The Ambassador refused to let us buzz your implant when we detected the enemy. She wanted to confirm the ships really were Stroj pirates first."

"And are they?"

"The signatures match, sir. These are Lorn's ships."

My heart was pounding, but not with fear. I had a grin on my face, I realized. With an effort of will, I suppressed my emotions. Now was the time to win a battle, not to gloat.

"Range, Durris?"

"We're still pretty far out. About twenty million kilometers."

"Enemy count?"

"Seven ships. The same seven we let slip away before, sir."

I gave him a sharp glance. He looked back at me blankly. Was he needling me for having allowed the Stroj to survive our previous engagement?

Perhaps he was, and I had to admit, he was right to do so. These beings were abominations. It was hard not to think of them as rough humans when talking to them, but I had to remind myself that they'd gone so far in self-alterations that they were no longer like us. They were only partly human at best, and they had to be destroyed.

"For the blood of all the colonists who've died at their hands in the Crown System—and probably countless others—we're going to take them out as soon as we're in range."

Durris smiled tightly and nodded. "They know they can't run this time, sir. We've got too much speed built up, and they're still within Ruby's gravity-well. They're moving into attack formation."

"That's just what I wanted to hear. Vector in on their position—and Yamada, I want you to begin recording and transmitting this battle from our point of view with a twenty minute delay. Hit all the colony worlds with the vid. Jkal told me they were monitoring us passively on Sapphire, at least."

"Recording. Transmission will begin in twenty minutes."

Durris came up to my chair and leaned close.

"What if we get our asses kicked up here, sir?" he asked quietly.

"Win or lose, I want them to know Earth's doing battle in their system on their behalf. Let them see the truth."

He shrugged and moved back to his station. He may not have been entirely convinced I was doing the wisest thing, but I didn't care. I wanted to give these people hope again, if nothing else. Let them watch a battle cruiser from Earth fight for them in real time. I suspected the sight would be unique and unforgettable for them. It was the least I could do after centuries of neglect.

-29-

The pirates came up from Ruby's gravity-well as fast as they were able. They were racing to square-off with us and do battle.

That was another advantage of my scheme. They would be hindered by their nearness to a planet. Fighting within the pull of a gravity field was like fighting with your legs in water—every maneuver was constrained.

"Commence slow, steady fire when we reach maximum range," I ordered. "Target the hindmost ship—that will probably be Lorn's vessel."

Battles in space were strange. They were both long and short, depending on your point of view. If you were getting hit, they might last only seconds. But if you were approaching an enemy fleet at a considerable distance it was like charging across a vast, empty plain toward an army that similarly charged toward you.

The difference was the charging took hours or even days to complete. We watched them grow steadily for three solid hours.

When we got in close enough to take our first shots, my heart began to pound. Unfortunately, they knew from our previous engagement how far our heaviest guns could reach. They began to dodge and weave as soon as they were in range.

"Firing bank one, sir," Zye said.

I felt the ship shudder. There was a singing sound and then the hiss of escaping gases as the big guns paused and readied themselves again. The chambers were being cooled for the next salvo even before we knew if we'd hit or not with the last.

The second and third banks fired as well before we got visual confirmation of the results.

"We grazed target six," Zye said. "No appreciable damage noted by the AI analysis."

I frowned and wheeled on Durris and Zye.

"Not really a surprise," Durris added quickly. "We're at maximum range. We can't expect to cripple them on the first shot."

"That's not what concerns me," I said. "Why are we hitting ship six? I ordered you to attack the hindmost ship."

"Ship six dodged into the path of the beam and took the hit, sir."

I stared at Zye for a second, then laughed. "So, Lorn is a coward, is he? Why am I not surprised?"

Zye shrugged. "Most Alphas from my world would do the same. The commander is obviously more important than the crews of her supporting vessels."

"Really? What if she's a poor commander?"

Zye looked confused by the concept. Alphas were always better at command than Betas.

"Never mind," I said. "Second salvo is blazing away. Report."

"No hits. We even missed ship six this time. They've put up an aerogel screen to hide behind."

"Let's do the same. Diffuse the beam to burn away the gel."

"Adjusting the apertures…"

The battle, such as it was, continued. Things didn't get interesting until we got closer—then, suddenly, three of the ships vanished. One of the ships that disappeared was the one hiding in the rear.

"Where'd they go?" I demanded. "Yamada?"

"I don't know, sir. Running a sensor diagnostic—everything checks out."

"What's my target, sir?" Durris asked.

I looked at him. He had an I-told-you-so look on his face.

"Keep firing at the ship in front of Captain Lorn."

"That ship is now off-track, sir," he said.

Frowning, I made a growling sound. We were just moving from long to medium range. Our odds of a solid hit were growing steadily.

"Lay down a pattern where they were a moment before," I said. "Let's see what they do about that."

Shrugging, Durris did as I ordered. The big guns sang and hissed. We waited tensely, then—

"Hit!" Yamada shouted. "We hit something, Captain. We hit it hard. I've got debris, radiation, explosive gases—even lateral motion. I think we nailed one of them and it's spinning out of control."

"Excellent," I said. "New target, use the last known coordinates of one of the vanished vessels."

"Input complete," Zye said, "canon bank traversing... ready."

"Fire, and keep firing on that line of attack."

Durris left his planning table and came up to stand at my side.

"All right," he said. "I have to know, sir, how did you accomplish that bit of wizardry?"

"Logic, First Officer. There were only a few explanations as to why the enemy vanished. Either the enemy moved somewhere else so quickly that we couldn't even track them, or they've managed to render themselves invisible. I reasoned that the latter was more likely."

"All right," he said, nodding. "But—"

"Another hit!" Yamada shouted. "We're on to them now, sir!"

We turned our attention back to the forward screens. This time, the vessel we'd connected with blew apart. It was strange to watch. At first, there'd been nothing there. Then our beams hit something invisible and it became visible again in a brief sheet of flame and spinning chunks of metal.

Daring to grin, I turned back to Durris. "You were saying?"

He shook his head. "Okay, they're stealthed somehow. Why are they suddenly easier to hit?"

"That's a mystery," I admitted.

"No..." Durris said, looking intensely at the screens. "I have it. It must cost them a lot of power to stealth. Maybe they don't have the power to alter their course as quickly while they're in that state. Maybe they don't have shields, either.

"We're locking onto the third ship that vanished," Zye said. "At least, where she was when she disappeared. Firing."

We waited, excitement building. But ten seconds later, there was nothing. We'd hit empty space.

"No-joy," Durris said.

Frowning, I nodded in thought. "That third one had time to get away from the spot where it vanished."

"Presumably."

"All right," I said, "Zye lock onto one of the ships we can see and continue shooting at it."

She looked confused. "But sir—they've all stealthed now."

I stood up and examined the tactical maps. I'd been zoomed in on my personal screen, looking at the narrow region we were targeting each time we fired. I'd missed the bigger picture.

"Damn," I said quietly. "Switch to the last known visible target. Lock onto the coordinates where it was and unload. Fire on yellow this time."

She worked the boards swiftly. The cannons hummed and sang. "Failure on bank two, cannon seven. Overheated, sir."

"Let it clear out, send up a crew."

We waited, watching the region of space where I'd taken my best guess. Nothing happened for too long.

"A clean miss," I admitted at last.

"Looks that way," Durris agreed.

"Target, sir?" Zye asked, spinning her chair to look at me.

"We don't have one. Hold your fire. Prep our missiles for a proximity launch. We'll have to guess where they are, and move the missiles up slowly to intercept them when they come out of stealth mode."

"*If* they have to do that in order to fire," Durris added. "We don't know their full capabilities."

I eyed him. "Let's pray that they have to show themselves to engage us."

The waiting began again, but this time it was infinitely more tense. We were being stalked—boxed in by invisible enemies. It appeared that their maneuvering was very limited when they were stealthed, but that didn't help us much.

"Keep tracking their likely positions," I ordered. "Fire a barrage now and then at the predicted coordinates every few minutes. Maybe we'll get lucky."

Durris and I glanced at one another. We both knew the math was against us and getting worse every moment. They could be anywhere in a widening cone of probability. Hitting a ship at this distance when you couldn't track it—well, the odds were extreme.

We played back the vids, looking closely at each second of data. We examined the split-second during which they'd vanished in minute detail.

When the moment came, it was as if the ship's image had been erased. From the top to the bottom, it vanished. It was as if a shade had been pulled down, hiding it from view. Instead of a metallic vessel, we saw the stars behind each hidden enemy ship.

"I can see why we couldn't find them during all those system scans," I said. "They were clearly hiding on Ruby, cloaked."

"But they had to uncloak to fly up out of the gravity well," Durris said. "That further indicates the cloaking system is using a lot of power. They can barely maneuver while it's operating."

"That seems to match the facts as we know them."

"But what I don't get is why they didn't pull this trick before, back in the Gliese system?" he asked. "They were retreating toward a bridge, and they could have blinked out then."

I shrugged. "Maybe the shield only works when approaching the enemy head-on. Or maybe the Gliese system was too full of solar flares, dust and debris."

"Or maybe they only equipped the cloaking systems when they reached Ruby," Durris added. "Who knows?"

"Okay, let's deal with the cards we've been dealt. How long until we're in range of their guns?"

Durris pointed toward a timer he'd set up on his main boards.

Frowning, I shook my head. "T minus zero?"

"Right. We're already in range. They stealthed just as they came close enough to take pot-shots at us. Now, however, they're presumably closing in every moment."

I returned to my command chair. "Everyone, strap in," I ordered over the PA system. "We're in for some harsh maneuvering."

The klaxons sounded. Yellow flashers spun. All over the ship, the crew scrambled to get into a crash seat and enclose themselves in webbing.

After a full minute passed, I ordered Zye to take over the helm controls and unleash the full power of our vessel.

"Sir," Durris gasped from his seat a few moments later, "I get why you're doing this. But are you sure it's your best option? We can outrun them, but we can't—"

He broke off as a terrific explosion lit up the forward shield.

"We're hit," Yamada said unnecessarily. "Forward shield is down. Hull fractured at the bow. We're losing pressure on decks, five, two—"

"Was that a nuclear missile?" I demanded.

She looked at me, her face contorted by the G-forces Zye was exerting upon us.

"No sir—one of those invisible bastards rammed our ship!"

We broke off and began to run. Without being able to see or target the enemy, it was time to put some distance between them and our vulnerable hull.

Realizing our intent, all of the remaining stealthed ships revealed themselves. There were four of them left. They began pursuit, firing away at our hindquarters.

We took hits, but they didn't knock out our engines. That was the only true danger in this situation. We could outrun them, and we could outgun them. The only advantage they had left was their stealth. But, if we wouldn't let them sneak up on us, they couldn't use that ability effectively.

-30-

Once revealed, the enemy didn't stealth again. Instead, they turned to run away when we were beyond their effective range.

"Sir, the pirates are breaking off," Yamada said.

"Ease down on the throttle, Zye. We're clear. Yamada, get a medical team to check every crewmen aboard for internal bleeding."

Extreme bouts of high-G acceleration had grim effects on human spacers in particular. I had a sudden thought concerning my aunt. How had she fared during yet another rough ride?

"Durris, take command," I said. "Follow the Stroj. If you get close enough, light up their sterns."

He shook his head. "Not likely, sir," he said. "Our courses are diverging, and there's a lot of inertia to overcome. By the time we get fully turned around, they'll be out of range for days.

"Right, but if they change their minds and engage again, call me back to the command deck."

I left and headed down toward my aunt's cabin. I had a sick feeling… we'd endured hard maneuvers before, but I knew she was four to six times the age of most crew members aboard. It would be a shame if she'd died alone with a crushed ribcage.

On the fourth chime, the door finally dissolved. I'd never been in my aunt's quarters. They weren't what I'd expected.

Rather than an ostentatious and out-of-place display of wealth, she'd opted to keep the room spare and functional. There was no sign of the old lady herself—at least not at first.

"Aunt Helen?" I called.

An egg-shaped capsule stood near the far wall. Something stirred within it. I'd thought the capsule was a chair at first—but it was something else entirely.

The capsule spiraled in my direction and split open. Purplish goop spilled out on the floor—along with my ancient aunt.

"What is it?" she rasped. "Haven't you done enough to these old bones today?"

"I'm sorry," I said. "I came to check on you."

She was on the floor in the midst of the foamy mess that had spilt out of the egg-thing. She looked up at me, and I realized as the foam evaporated she was nude. I turned away.

"Hand me a towel, damn you."

I found a towel and handed it to her. I did so with my eyes directed toward her desk.

She laughed and covered herself. "Are you embarrassed? Or disgusted?"

"I'm a gentleman," I said.

"Good. Good answer."

She put on clothes and flopped in a chair behind her desk. She let out a long sigh.

"This trip will be the death of me. Did we kill any pirates? I can't see much inside that egg. There's audio input from the ship's feed, but that's about it."

I examined the contraption. "This is some kind of survival system, isn't it?"

"Built to withstand atmospheric reentry, if necessary. It can take more newtons of force than your skull can without cracking, that much I assure you."

Pinching up some of the purple foam, I worked it between my fingers. It disintegrated quickly into a slippery film.

"Pressure-absorbing foam? Complete submersion?"

"My doctors recommended it. Overpriced quacks—but they were right this time. This ship could kill someone as weak as myself without serious protection."

Nodding, I turned to face her again. She'd dressed herself in a gown of black. Her hair still looked as if she'd shampooed it without a rinse.

"I had no idea you had such a useful survival system in your cabin," I remarked.

"I didn't reach my two hundredth birthday and pass it by without taking care of my health."

My eyes did a slow blink. *Two centuries.* I'd guessed her age could be that extreme… but now she'd openly admitted it. Deciding it would be impolite to press further on the subject, I moved on.

"We destroyed three of the pirates," I said. "The others have run off."

"Hmmm," she said, looking over recordings of the action on her desk. "It appears the last one almost took us out. If they'd been able to build up more kinetic force before ramming us—"

"Yes, I know. We'd have all perished."

"Well? What are you going to do now, Captain Sparhawk?"

I thought about it for a moment. There was really only one answer.

"I'm going to chase them down and destroy them all."

She nodded slowly. "I'm not surprised. Nor do I think now that I could do much to stop you. You *are* like your father, no matter what anyone else back on Earth says. They only look at the uniform and sneer. But I see a ruthless man. A man of honor—but someone who is determined to achieve his goals."

"Thank you."

"That was not a compliment."

"Nevertheless, I feel uplifted by your words."

She glared at me for several long seconds. At last she sighed.

"All right," she said. "You're going to chase these Stroj and wipe them out. What if they arrive at a breach point before we can catch them?"

"Then I'll follow them into hyperspace."

She played with her computer scroll. "What if they're heading into a breach marked as terminal? Something no one has found their way out of alive?"

After thinking for a second, I made my choice. "I'd have to follow them."

She fooled with the scroll, letting it tip and bounce on the desk.

"Why?" she asked sincerely.

"Because Captain Lorn has proven to me, on multiple occasions, that he very much cares about his personal skin. Each time it's threatened he runs or deflects. He'll kill any and all of his underlings for the privilege to keep breathing. Therefore, he'd never take us on a blind jump he couldn't escape."

She nodded. "For the record, I agree with your predictions. Even better, we're about to get a chance to put this theory to the test. As we speak, the pirates are heading for a blind jump into a bridge that's been marked terminal by your little friend, the Connatic."

I snatched the scroll from her. Somehow, it displayed the command deck. Tapping at it, I was able to view the crew from any angle. I could even pull up displays of our instruments and weapons systems. It wasn't a control system, but there was no data it didn't seem to have access to.

I tossed the scroll back on her desk. "Cameras?"

She nodded.

"How'd you get them to do it?"

"Star Guard?" she asked mildly. "I'm supposed to be in command of this mission, remember? That was the condition I made when they begged me to take this role. In order to perform my duties, I needed aids."

"Like this survival egg? And a spying app depicting my command staff in every detail? This is why whenever I leave the helm alterations are made to my orders, correct?"

"I've only done that on rare occasions."

Angry, I began to pace. "Why did Star Guard put me in command of this ship if they didn't trust me?"

She laughed. "They don't trust anyone. Especially not after the Stroj ate half their commanders. That wasn't so long ago, William, and they very much remember it. They sent me out here to provide adult supervision. If I remember correctly, those were Halsey's precise words."

I glared at her. "Halsey. I should have known. He promotes me, praises me, but doesn't trust me when it comes down to it."

"Judging by your behavior thus far on this voyage, I believe he was right all along."

"No, he wasn't," I said. "I've made the right choices. I've explored three systems and fought off several deadly attacks."

"You've made *choices*… that's true. Whether they were the right ones or not, well, that remains to be seen. Now, if you don't mind, I think I'll clean up a bit. Will you be having dinner with me?"

"No thank you, Lady."

I stormed out. I could hear the old warhorse chuckling behind me.

-31-

When I got back to the command deck, Durris was the first one to incur my wrath.

"Why didn't you tell me?" I asked him.

He gave me a blank look. "Tell you what, Captain?"

"That the ambassador has been spying on our activities."

"Oh… that. I honestly thought you knew. It's your ship, sir."

I felt a red heat rising around my neck. "She came up here and reversed my instructions on several occasions. Is that right?"

"Yes, sir… and I really feel I must lodge a complaint at this point."

"How's that?" I demanded.

"It's difficult to keep two conflicting sets of orders straight, especially when from day to day I don't know who's in command."

I bared my teeth momentarily, but I controlled myself. "It's Star Guard's fault, not yours. It's been too long, I think, since Earth's met a serious adversary. We're out of practice. There can only be one captain on a ship. That's a basic rule of every navy throughout time. This fiddling from CENTCOM amounts to a social experiment, and it's been a dismal failure."

"I would applaud a return to the old principles," my first officer said.

We eyed one another for a moment. I could see how Durris was in a tight spot. He was only trying to follow orders—but whose orders were legitimate? Halsey had really screwed things up for me on this mission.

"Let's put that aside for the moment," I told him. "Where are the pirates headed? Can we catch them?"

"They're headed for this bridge entry point, here," Durris said, directing me to one of the red links on the screen.

"Hmm, one that goes nowhere," I said in concern, "at least, according to the Connatic's charts."

"Interesting," Durris said. "The question becomes whether or not we believe Lorn is the suicidal type. Personally, I don't think he is."

"Neither do I. Let's follow him."

Durris followed me to the helmsman, where we laid in our coordinates and felt the *Defiant* shift course under our feet.

"To answer your second question, Captain," Durris said, "we can't catch up. At least, not until the enemy reaches the breach point and enters hyperspace."

Durris eyed me. He wasn't sure what I'd say next.

"Follow him anyway," I repeated decisively.

Returning to my seat, I slouched in an uncharacteristic fashion. I'd felt somewhat betrayed by Durris about the surveillance, but I hadn't let him know that. He was, after all, trying to follow orders. As this was only our second mission together, I guess he hadn't seen fit to inform me concerning what was going on during my absences.

Rotating my chair around slowly, I fixed Yamada with a stare. She noticed in time and looked back questioningly.

"Let's talk," I said to her.

I led her out, and we walked the passages toward the lower decks. I didn't feel like going to my office or my cabin. For all I knew, they were bugged as well.

"What's this all about, Captain?" she asked.

"I'm trying to find somewhere private—perhaps the gym. There's no one there at the moment, I believe."

She gave me a strange look, but she followed along without comment. When we found the gym, it was indeed empty. PT was a required regimen for all aboard, but it was only done in shifts which usually occurred at the beginning of the morning and evening watch periods.

We had no weight sets in the gym, of course. Instead there were intelligent machines that varied stress-loads on various muscle groups according to the ship's angle of flight, G-forces and the individual history of the participant.

Yamada looked around in confusion. "You call this private?"

"We're alone, aren't we?"

She searched my eyes and shook her head. "Well... all right. Wait!"

I'd been sitting down on a bench-press machine and settling in to do a few repetitions. Her sudden change of tone caught my attention.

"What?"

"Are you crazy?" she asked. "I'm not going to do it on a sweaty weight-lifting machine. You can forget about that."

"Forget about what...?" I asked. Suddenly realizing what the misunderstanding was, my mouth sagged. "Lieutenant," I said sternly. "That wasn't my intention at all."

She crossed her arms and shifted her weight onto her left hip. Her eyes narrowed to regard me suspiciously. "Well, as you seem to be working your way through all the women on this ship, I naturally—"

"That's an unfair and inaccurate description of my behavior," I protested. I began pumping the machine, which felt good. Cracking my muscles against the increasing squeeze of the machine gave me a satisfying release of tension.

"Really?" she asked. "What about the Connatic?"

"She's not aboard this ship. She never was a member of the crew."

"A technicality. What about Zye?"

Her words made me pause. I looked at her, and she stared back.

"You heard about that, did you?"

"She's telling everyone—all the women, that is. She starts off by asking weird questions about our sexual habits and partners. Eventually, she gets around to asking if we've slept with you while informing us that she has. Then she asks who else we think might oppose her."

"Oppose her?" I asked in confusion. "What does that mean?"

"It means she's warning us off."

"I see," I said. "I was under the impression she didn't have any strings attached to our moments together. She seemed very casual about it."

"You might be feeling casual, but I think she's taking things more seriously."

"Great. Is that your entire list of my crimes? On this basis I've become a philanderer in your eyes, apt to do anything? Half this ship is involved in some kind of relationship. I think it's a natural hazard during such a long mission."

Inwardly, I was concerned. Had I started a disintegration of discipline? Long-term voyages with both sexes aboard had always been problematic, and Star Guard's policies had become lax over the decades.

She thought about my words seriously. "We're pair-bonding," she said. "You're right. We've been out here for many weeks, and we're so far from home we can't even see our own star at night. We're looking for mates. I hadn't thought about it like that."

"It's a threat to discipline. This must be why the old colony ships only allowed family units to board. Even then, there were problems."

She nodded. "What about Suzy?" she asked me suddenly.

"Who?"

"That brassy ensign Suzy Gelb. She works the nav table with Durris."

"I barely recall such a person," I said defensively. In truth, the girl was quite attractive, and my eye had lingered on her from time to time.

"Every male on the ship has his eye on her. The word in the passages is that you've slept with her as well."

"That's worse than a rumor. It's a lie. A fabrication."

She sighed and uncrossed her arms. "All right then. I'm truly sorry, Captain. I got carried away, and I've embarrassed us both."

"It's quite all right," I said. "Now, if you'll kindly remove your clothing and climb aboard this machine…"

I met her shocked expression, and I laughed. "Sorry, I just couldn't resist."

She moved as if to strike me, then remembered who we were and laughed instead. We'd worked together in tight quarters for years on ships much smaller than this one.

"Remember *Cutlass*?" she asked wistfully. "I think of that rust-bucket every day."

"So do I," I said. "I felt an attachment to that vessel I'm only just beginning to build for this one."

"There wasn't much room for an affair aboard *Cutlass*."

"Not unless you wanted a dozen eyes to watch."

My first command had been a pinnace that worked as an escort ship for the destroyer *Altair*. A tiny ship with a tiny crew, I'd learned how to lead and keep a ship from falling apart while commanding her.

"Anyway," I said, "I'm glad you're giving me some inside information on what everyone else aboard is thinking. Why have I been left in the dark about these things?"

"Well... there's a certain natural distance. You're in command of a starship. That's a lofty position. Aboard *Cutlass*, we all seemed like a family."

"Right... Add to that the distraction of Lady Grantholm's antics, and I'm all business most of the time. I'm missing out on the psychological mood swings. I need to track the morale of the crew better."

"I can fill you in on that point. The crew is very impressed. We're still alive, and we're going after the pirates. The only act that's thought of as a mistake involves Lorn. Most of them believe you should have tried harder to kill him when you had the chance. We're glad you're correcting that mistake now."

"I agree," I nodded. "That was a mistake."

"Is that what you wanted to talk to me about, Captain?" she asked.

"Yes. I wanted to establish a rapport," I said. "Also, I want you to tell me if my aunt tries to undermine my authority again."

"But sir... that would place me in-between the highest ranking people aboard."

"Exactly. Will you do it? For me?"

She stared at me for a moment, then nodded.

"Yes. For you."

I fell back onto the bench press again, but before I could squeeze together my pectoral muscles, she darted in and kissed my cheek.

Watching her leave, I began a vigorous workout. My muscles burned afterward, and it felt good.

-32-

Two days later we arrived at the breach. To us, it appeared as a sinister and uncertain region of space. It was invisible, but still somehow oppressively dangerous in our minds.

The pirate ships had left us well behind by this time. They'd crossed the barrier nearly seventeen hours earlier. We had no idea what they'd been doing during that interval. They could have traveled far toward the exit—or perhaps they'd prepared a trap for us.

The problem was they were undetectable on the far side of the bridge. It was my opinion they were setting up an ambush in there. Waiting for us to crash through, so they could light us up with every weapon they had at close range.

Yamada said something as I pondered the approaching bridge.

"What was that, Commander?" I asked.

"Sir, I'm getting trace tritium readings," she said more loudly.

"There's nothing odd about that," I said. "Standard fuel traces left behind by—"

"Captain!" she interrupted, now sounding alarmed. "I don't understand it, but I'm picking up these readings from *beyond* the barrier. The traces lead to either side of it."

My mind froze as I registered what she was saying. My eyes darted to the timer—we had one minute twenty-nine seconds to the breach point.

"Emergency evasive action!" I shouted. "Turn away from the breach! Get us out of here, Rumbold."

His bulging eyes were like those of frog. "We can't now, sir—"

"Do it!"

He attacked his controls, unlocking the course they were set for. We lurched, feeling the tearing of our insides as G-forces were applied without mercy.

Despite his efforts, we were still heading into the breach. At significant speeds, it's hard to make a sudden turn.

Rumbold was talking, but the rising roar of the engines obliterated his words.

"Zye," I grunted out, "take over if anyone passes out."

As if I were a prophet, we lost two of the command crew in the next few seconds. Durris, down in the navigational pit, slipped and slammed his head into the metal tableau. Suzy Gelb was leaning over him—at least she seemed unharmed.

As I watched, another ensign came through the main hatch—a powder-monkey—and she did a flip right over the railing, unable to stop herself.

Zye got up on steady feet in the midst of this chaos. Taking six careful and decisive steps, she reached Rumbold. She pushed him out of his chair unceremoniously and took the helm. He rolled away, limp and unconscious.

I wanted to shout orders, but I could no longer make intelligent sounds. My vision was dimming. I could see the blood vessels in my eyes, it seemed.

Then slowly, things came back to normal.

"We've avoided the breach, captain," Zye said from above me.

Her round face filled my vision.

"Good," I said.

"May I ask why that was necessary?"

"It was a trap," I said, sitting up and having a coughing fit.

"A trap? I don't understand."

Around me, half the crew was unconscious. A few others stirred weakly.

"The tritium trail… the Stroj never entered the breach. They stealthed at the last second, and they slipped to the side.

From a distance, from our point of view, it looked like they'd vanished into hyperspace."

"Ah..." she said, intrigued. "The Stroj are tricky. I have to give them that. Beta ships often fall for such deceptions."

"You mean you knew they might pull something like this?"

"It was a possibility."

"Then why the hell didn't you warn me?"

She looked puzzled. "You're the captain," she said. "No captain wants to hear that they've made a mistake."

"Well, Zye, I do. Next time, please enlighten us earlier if you suspect there's a danger to the ship."

Her eyes drifted toward the forward screens.

"Sir, I believe we're in danger."

I followed her eyes, and I saw the last four pirates converging on our flanks.

They were coming out of stealth and firing all at once.

"Battle stations!" I shouted, stabbing the PA button and trying not to cough. "Zye, continue evasive action!"

I had no idea how many of my crew were still functional after the last high-G swerve, but anyone who was still on their feet had to perform now.

The battle alert status flashed up on our screens, and klaxons sounded. At least someone was still listening to me.

Yamada crawled back into her chair. Her hand had reached up from the floor and initiated the alarm.

"You don't look so good," I said, noting the blood matting her hair and her tunic.

"I'm fine, sir. Just had the wind knocked out of me."

"Good. Call our backup helmsman to man the helm. Rumbold is out cold."

"On it."

"Zye, get confirmation from the gun crews. We need them online immediately."

"No response, sir," she said. "Our shields are down, too."

Alarmed, I looked at her, then the panels. "The power couplings are all wrong. Durris? Are you still with us?"

"I'm here, sir."

I couldn't see him, but by leaning forward I found him lying on his back on the floor where he'd fallen near the nav table.

"Get up and get into action. I need you."

"Sorry sir—I think I have a spinal injury."

It was then I noted the odd cant of his neck.

"Dammit," I breathed. "Ensign Gelb, take over navigation."

Suzy nodded and stood over Durris, working the big table. I was impressed that she was able to stand despite the ship's lurching about. Her taut body clung to the table and she looked very fit and shapely. I could see right away why Durris had chosen her to be his aide. She was as attractive as she was competent.

Forcing myself to my feet, I walked forward and worked Zye's tactical boards. Zye was still at the helm, and we couldn't afford to be left flying blind.

In the meantime, the ship continued to swerve and bounce. We were taking incoming fire and dodging all at the same time.

A rainstorm of sound began to ring on the outer hull. It sounded like rocks hitting a steel roof.

Reaching Zye's station, I managed to get the shields going by diverting power from the engines. At least the shield capacitors were still operating. All the weapons banks were blinking yellow, unable to fire.

"What's wrong with our cannons?"

"We're moving with violent course changes," Durris said painfully from the floor. He was rolling around now and then, and I could only imagine what that felt like with a broken neck. "The cannons won't deploy if the lateral Gs are too high. They'd be damaged."

"Where's the override?"

"Captain, I don't recommend—" Durris began.

Using my fingers like claws, I hugged the console. I turned to Zye.

"Zye, how do I override all the safety systems and open the gun ports?"

"The selection is in the menus under attack options," she said calmly.

Cursing, I finally found it. I stabbed my finger on the screen option repeatedly until the cannons were forced to display a green ready-symbol.

"Nearest ship... lock," I said. I fired the second the control system allowed it without another override. The big guns sang, and one of the pirates disintegrated.

Grinning with bloody teeth, I tapped at the console furiously. The cannons swung around and began to track the next target. I lost my lock almost immediately.

"Damn, what's wrong now?"

"They're breaking off, sir," Zye said.

"Cowardly bastards. Hit us, hurt us, and run. That's their game."

Zye swung us around to follow the fleeing enemy, and our violent maneuvers stopped. We were now the hunters again, rather than the hunted.

One by one the pirates winked out, turning on their stealth systems. I wasn't able to target them any longer, but instead allowed Zye to work the tactical boards. She tried to predict their positions and fired more barrages—but we hit nothing.

Medical people reached the command deck about five minutes later. Durris was still on the floor, breathing shallowly, but conscious. They went to work on him immediately, as his injuries were among the worst we'd suffered.

When they had him on a grav-stretcher and through the hatch, the leader of the medical team faced me. "The command deck is clear, sir," said the corpsman.

"Good," I said, but as he passed my chair I snaked out a hand and caught his arm. "How about Durris?" I asked. "What's the prognosis there?"

"I'm not a doctor, Captain, but I think he's going to live."

"I know that! Will he walk again? Will he be paralyzed?"

The corpsman shrugged helplessly. "He's paralyzed now. But the disconnection isn't total. I don't know how it will go, Captain. The auto-doc boxes can work miracles... sometimes."

I let him return to his duties. Staring at the big forward screen, I rubbed my chin and muttered dark curses meant for my Stroj enemy.

-33-

First Officer Durris was absent from my next command meeting.

"Let's discuss what we've learned," I said. "The enemy—"

"Is running rings around us," interjected Lady Grantholm.

"That's an unhelpful statement, Ambassador," I said sternly.

"But an accurate one. That last attack almost finished us—but the real threat was the trap. They almost got us all without firing a shot."

"There's some truth to what you say," I admitted. "But they failed. As a result, we took some hull damage and they lost a ship."

"We did lose six more crewmembers," Yamada chimed in. "Not all are fatalities, but they can't serve. That's a serious blow."

I gave her an irritated glance. "I can see how this is going to go," I said, looking around the group. "You've all lost heart, haven't you? You've decided we can't catch the Stroj, and that we should turn around while we can."

"That pretty much sums it up," Rumbold said reluctantly, from behind a pair of shockingly bloodshot eyes.

"Well, on this ship, there's only one Captain. We're in hot pursuit, and I'm planning on finishing this conflict."

They looked baffled.

"How, sir?" Rumbold asked. He spread his hands wide. "The enemy is out there—but their ships are invisible."

I smiled. "No, not entirely. We're following their tritium trails. That's how we spotted their change of course away from the trapped breach in the first place."

Everyone looked at Yamada. She shrugged.

"It's true. We can tell where they've flown. After adjusting the instrumentation, it's like following jet contrails."

"What?!" demanded Rumbold. "Why haven't you fired on them, girl? We should hit them hard before they figure out that we know where they are."

"It's not that simple," Yamada said. "The trail is somewhat intermittent, and predicting their exact coordinates from such limited data is almost impossible."

"In short," I said, "we can generally tell where they're going, but our information isn't good enough to use for targeting data."

Rumbold sat back with a growl of frustration, crossing his arms over his ample belly.

"Captain, the group has elected me to voice our concerns."

At that point, I ran my eyes around the assembled crew and my aunt. They were all listening, but no one seemed surprised. That meant they'd talked privately among themselves.

I felt my temper rising. This mission had suffered setbacks, yes, but—

A beeping came from Yamada's communications cuff. She had an implant, but as our communications officer it was extended by a cuff to connect to the ship's systems.

"Check it," I said.

She did as I asked, sliding her fingers over the section of the conference table that was in front of her. She reacted in surprise.

"I think you should look at this, Captain," she said.

She tapped again, and a three-dimensional image rose up from the table to spin slowly between us. The image was the ugly form of Lorn's head.

"The Stroj are trying to contact us?" I demanded.

"Yes."

"Don't open the channel, not yet. See if you can get a fix on their location."

She shook her head. "I did that immediately. They must have dropped a probe behind them and just activated it to transmit this message."

Nodding, I leaned back. My index finger made a spinning motion in the air.

"Play it."

She gestured, and the head began to speak.

"Earthmen," Lorn said. "I commend you on your hunting skills. It does the heart of a Stroj good to see that the Basic stock of humanity hasn't been watered down to the point of oblivion. Unfortunately, this game is now at an end."

As the message was a recording, not a live interview, we couldn't interact with it—at least not yet. Sometimes these messages had a basic AI to them.

"We've left the system by the time you will have received this message. It's a pity, but I'm required at this point to retreat and report. My orders are no less strict than are yours, I'd imagine."

"What the hell is he talking about?" I demanded. "Can they have exited the system?"

Yamada shrugged helplessly. "We don't know all the breach points. Maybe they found one and took it."

Growling in frustration, I had her rewind the message several seconds and play it again. We'd missed something.

"Due to your persistent hostility, and the loss of the majority of my ships, protocol has forced my hand. I'm returning to my homeworld to report your actions. You should be apprised that a formal state of war will exist between the Stroj and Earth once I make my report."

My heart sank. My officers were white-faced. Sure, we'd all known that the pirates weren't in love with us. But a formal declaration of war? That was the exact opposite of our reasons for coming out here in the first place.

The head spun around, leering at us in turn. It was an alarming effect, because even though I knew the AI running the apparition couldn't really see us, it felt as if it could.

"You've fired on our ships," the vile head continued. "Aggression upon meeting is to be expected. We get that from many local powers. But you've gone far beyond that acceptable action. You've violated our hunting grounds and pursued us over multiple star systems. Those details, once reported to the High Council, will automatically result in a general declaration of war. Now, you may ask this program questions. It is capable of limited responses."

It was such a malevolent apparition that I was tempted to shut it off. My hand reached out to do so.

"Wait!" Ambassador Grantholm said.

The head spun around to face her. My hand paused, then lowered to the table.

"Why would you attack us over this small conflict?" she asked.

"Stroj follow an algorithm," the head explained. "We find it very successful. When we attack, if we are defeated, we rebuild and come back later. But, if we ourselves are successfully assaulted and driven from our claimed territory, we gather as would any angry nest and destroy the intruder. Following this simple series of steps has led to our domination of many colony worlds."

"Lorn," I said, "why are you telling us this?"

The head turned to me. Did it recognize me? I wasn't sure, but the effect made my skin crawl.

"You may ask why I'm telling you this," the head responded, clearly reacting to my words with a prerecorded script. "Why should I provide you with a warning?" Suddenly, the head took on a feral grin. "This is a self-indulgence, I admit. I want you to water your suits with your bowels! You're all going to die for the trouble you've caused me, and I wanted you to be the first to know this. Fear me in your bones! Prepare yourselves to be skinned and—"

My finger swiped the cut-off, and the apparition faded away.

"Why'd you turn it off, Captain?" Yamada demanded. "It might have given us more valuable intel."

"No," Zye said, "it was only meant to torment us."

I took in a deep breath. "Well, you heard Lorn in his own words."

They looked at me expectantly, and I shrugged.

"We have no choice. His ships must never reach the Stroj homeworld. If they do, we'll be at war."

The group looked glum.

"But Captain," Rumbold said, "how do we catch him?"

Turning to Yamada, I stood up suddenly and gestured for her to follow me. "Come, sensor op. We have work to do."

Once back on the command deck, my crew went to work. We traced the tritium to the very last molecules. This took time, but we managed it by the end of the next watch.

"It has to be here, sir," Yamada said. "But there's nothing on the Connatic's star charts. Not even one of those 'beyond this point there be dragons' type warnings."

I had to agree, as I'd looked carefully at the charts for hours.

"Do a full scan. Use active sensors. Use everything we've got."

"But sir," she protested. "If we do that, and the enemy are nearby, they'll see us for sure."

I scoffed. "They jumped us before. If they were planning an ambush, I'm sure they'd have sprung it by now."

"Possibly, but in order to scan for a breach we don't know about, I'll have to fully drop our shields. We'll have zero protection."

I suddenly got her point. Maybe this was all just another trick. Maybe the head, the message, the dead trail of their engines had all been left to get us to lower our shields. The enemy could then reappear and slam us like sitting ducks.

On the other hand, the enemy was escaping us every minute, every hour. If we waited any longer, we might never catch them.

"Do it," I said. "Zye, warm up the cannons and get us into motion. Hit the accelerator the second you see any hint of Stroj ships."

We began the scan. Several tense minutes passed. At last, a hundred thousand kilometers off, a breach glimmered on our sensors. It was an unstable one. The rim of it shifted and roiled.

"That's the smallest, most squirmy breach I've ever seen," Yamada said. "It could be another trap, sir."

"Is it drifting?" I asked.

"Yes, a little."

"Plot its position several hours back. Give me a projection over time."

She did so, and the results were impressive. The tritium trails merged with the breach point—or at least they had done so some hours earlier.

"They did their best to hide their tracks," I said. "Still, they left behind that message. Why would Lorn leave such a thing behind to taunt us?"

"Maybe it's just as he said," Rumbold suggested. "Maybe he's just a bastard, and he wanted us to squirm."

"It's possible," I said, examining the twisting breach. It looked like the head of a snake on my screens.

"Let's do it," I said. "We'll see if the enemy has left us a trail on the other side."

Zye immediately laid in the course, and Rumbold steered us toward it.

Yamada licked her lips. "Captain? I'm concerned. Are you sure you want to charge through another unknown breach?"

Smiling, I gave her a confident chuckle. "Of course I do. Put up our shields in the meantime. We don't need to use our most sensitive detection equipment any longer."

"What if they aren't there?" she asked me.

"Then I'll turn around and take us home, that's what."

She looked relieved. Maybe she'd thought I'd say that I'd follow the damned Stroj to the ends of the cosmos.

The truth was I did feel that way—but it wouldn't do to let the crew in on my state of mind.

-34-

Breaking through the unstable breach was possibly the most daring act of the mission thus far.

After the Stroj vanished, I could have called it quits and headed for home. There was even an argument to be made that I *should* do exactly that because it was more important that I reach Earth and warn her than it was that I hunt down our elusive enemy.

But I didn't turn tail and run. Instead, I followed my instincts, and plunged my ship into the breach. I watched the universe waver around me with a terrifying flicker.

In what seemed like a brief moment later, we were in a different place. Sometimes after explorers returned, they'd found hours or even days had passed since they'd left. I had no idea yet if time had shifted on us on this occasion.

I told myself it didn't matter. We were committed now. We'd reached hyperspace once again. Since we weren't dead yet, I allowed myself to start breathing easily. All around me on the ship's command deck, people released similar sighs of relief.

We'd taken a dark road, a path that was unknown to us. Most bridges connected two points in the universe, each of which floated near a region of considerable mass. But a large percentage of them led to useless spots, such as dead star systems with suns that had long ago expired. Others led to the center of a swirling dust cloud. A small percentage became useful trade routes between two inhabitable star systems.

The worst of the bridges went to places unknown. No one had ever returned from these, robot or human, and they'd been marked as dead links to nowhere on every existing map.

This bridge had never been mapped at all, to my knowledge. A significant part of our mission was to explore. Perhaps today I'd be able to extend humanity's knowledge of the cosmos one more single tick. Either that, or I'd killed us all.

"What have we got, Ensign Gelb?" I asked.

The woman I'd called upon looked over her shoulder at me. Suzy Gelb was blonde and wore her hair a fraction longer than was regulation. No one had called her on that infraction yet.

She was Durris' replacement. The second best astronavigator aboard.

"I don't know," she said with a slight European accent. "I've never seen anything like this."

I moved to her side. The map did look strange. Normally, hyperspace was broad and empty. No data would come back, unless there was another ship or dropped probe present.

This time the feedback from our sensors was vastly different. It was reporting large objects in every direction—masses that should have torn our ship apart with gravitational force.

"All engines halt!" I ordered.

The thrumming sound of our drives deepened and faded.

Watching the map, I frowned. The objects surrounding us were swelling as our active sensors reported back contacts from farther and farther away.

"This is so strange," Ensign Gelb said. "What do we do, Captain? Should we turn and run out?"

"No," I said. "We'll wait until the picture is complete."

"But these masses around us—we'll be crushed."

"Yamada," I called over my shoulder. "Do a full diagnostic on these sensory readings. What are we looking at? Can this be real?"

"I've already done that, sir. They check out. We're surrounded by large formations. Objects the size of stars—it's almost like we're *inside* a star."

Rumbold left the helm and came to look over our table. He'd recovered nicely from his earlier injuries, I noticed. Modern medicine was automated and highly effective.

"Sir, I think I know what we're looking at," he said, staring at the looming walls around us. Every second, more was sketched in. The mass of objects surrounding us was nearly complete.

"What is this?" I demanded. "Are we inside some kind of cave between titanic objects?"

"Can't be," Rumbold explained. "First of all, if these contacts had mass, they'd generate so much gravitational force they'd tear us apart. They'd also light up and become fusion-driven suns on their own—maybe even a black hole."

"What are we looking at, then?"

"We're in a small universe, sir. A pocket. That's what hyperspace is, you know. A region of space in-between the fabric of normal space. A void between voids. What we're looking at are the walls of this universe. They're very close, and if I don't miss my guess, they're shifting as we watch."

Staring at the screen, I touched Ensign Gelb's shoulder. "Can you program this system to change colors over time? Brighten and darken regions as they shift and fade?"

She worked the controls for a full minute. At last, the effect I wanted began to appear. Not everything was in motion, but there were zones that were receding, while others loomed closer to our ship.

"This is fantastic," she said. "I think I've read about this type of phenomena. It's rare, but it's not unknown."

Rumbold's big eyes stared. "If this is a small, unstable bridge, it's very dangerous. Spacers have reported that this type of passage might shrink to cover the exit or the entrance. Then, it might take a thousand years to reveal itself again."

"Well then," I said, "we'd better get moving. Yamada, feed us data on the tritium trails, if any."

Glittering streaks overlaid the map before us. They were faint, but undeniable.

"Our stealthy friends have shown us the path. Follow them. Give us one gravity of acceleration."

Rumbold licked his lips and returned to his station. Soon, we were underway again.

"Is this wise, sir?" Gelb asked me quietly. "They know this route, we don't. Perhaps they've timed it so we'll run into a shifting wall of this sub-universe."

"What could such a wall be made of, anyway?" I asked.

She shook her head. "I don't know. If they ever figured it out in Earth's past, they aren't teaching us about it now in the Academy."

"Right," I said, looking as unconcerned as I could manage under the circumstances. "Steady on, we'll follow them to the exit long before these walls converge."

"If you say so, Captain."

"I do."

I left Gelb to ponder her navigating table. When I returned to my seat, I found Zye was standing there beside it, waiting.

"How is she?" Zye asked.

"Who? Durris' replacement? Ensign Gelb is doing her job, I guess. She's new, but she studied under his direction for months. She should work out until his neck heals."

Zye was staring at Gelb. I got the definite feeling she didn't approve of her.

"Is there a problem, Zye?" I asked.

"No Captain. Not yet."

Zye returned to her station. I considered saying something, but I held my tongue. She was paranoid, that's all. Arguing with her about it would only inflame her suspicions even more.

We followed the tritium trail for a solid day. Believing my crew had the matter well in hand, and with strict orders to wake me if anything went wrong, I ordered a watch change and left the deck.

After a quick meal, I headed for my cabin. There, I found someone was already inside waiting for me.

"Zye?" I asked in the darkened room. "I need to get some rest. This isn't the time or the place—"

"I'm not Zye, Captain," Ensign Gelb murmured softly. She stepped out of the shadows and tilted her head coyly.

"How did you get in here?" I asked. "I didn't give you my code."

She laughed gently. "Lots of people have it. There are universal codes as well, used by the cabin stewards."

"Right... well, how can I accommodate you?" I asked pointlessly.

"Could you close the door, Captain?"

I was acutely aware of her. She seemed even more attractive in my cabin than she had in formal settings. She was quite different when compared to other women I'd been acquainted with. She had a Nordic face with naturally sleepy eyes, an impressive chest and swelling hips. She wore her uniform cinched up tightly—and that hair. It was very feminine. I could see now why she'd gotten away with it. No one had the heart to order her to cut it.

"You still haven't told me—" I began sternly, but then she reached up with her hands and touched the releases on her uniform.

As her clothing was tightly wrapped around her person in the first place, it sprang loose easily when she touched the releases. She stood comfortably before me, nude and smiling.

My jaw dropped in surprise, then I heard footsteps out in the passages. She nodded toward the door, and I leapt up to close it.

It wouldn't do at all to have this woman spotted in my cabin. The worst case was that Zye was lurking out there. I wouldn't have been surprised at all if she was.

I had to give it to Zye, she'd read the signs, while I hadn't. She'd suspected from the start this young officer had designs upon me. I'd missed that somehow.

"Ensign Gelb..."

"Call me Suzy," she said smoothly.

"Ensign Gelb," I repeated. "I must protest. This behavior is entirely inappropriate."

She stopped her advance and pouted.

My eyes ran over her, up and down twice, despite my attempts to be professional.

"You don't like me?" she sulked. "I thought you were interested after the way you touched me at the navigational table."

Ensign Gelb was very attractive and aggressive. I could see how she'd gained her reputation. Even Yamada had asked about her... how could I have missed her interest so utterly?

"It's not that I don't like you—it's that barely know you!"

"I felt certain that you'd given me a clear signal, and I've heard stories about your conquests."

Huffy now, she pulled up her clothes and fought to get them to stretch back over her body. The clothes were not winning this fight. Two tiny clasps of elastic, slipping from her fingers, shot over her shoulders and fell down her back.

"Let me help you," I said, stepping forward.

I attempted to lift a strap and stretch it over her back, but she shifted and my hand ran up along her ribs instead.

She squirmed. "You're tickling me!" she said. "You did that on purpose, didn't you? Is that how you want things to go? Does everything have to appear accidental? Is that it?"

She was close, warm and vibrant. I looked into her eyes. Our lips were almost touching. I realized I was losing control of my actions. The temptation she represented was too great.

But I saw something there, in her eyes. Something I would never have suspected until that moment.

Once, a year earlier, I'd stared into the robotic eyes of an imitation of Chloe. That woman, like this one, had been ravishingly beautiful.

But the eyes—they hadn't been right. The human eye was too complex to mimic. Every capillary, every tiny discoloration of the iris—humans looked their most human when you looked into their eyes up close.

To cover my shock, I kissed Ensign Susan Gelb.

But I knew, without any sense of doubt, that she was a Stroj agent.

-35-

Stroj mimics had become infinitely more sophisticated since the first crude robots they'd planted among us. Nano-fiber musculature was now used over polymer bones in the newer models. These materials were difficult to detect without a full body-scan. They also served to give the Stroj a more human appearance.

This creature, Suzy, was a pinnacle achievement. I realized the engineers that had abandoned our ship must have been of a similar technological level.

Her hands, so soft and feminine a moment before, became like polymer claws. Her right hand grabbed onto my uniform, jerking me back toward her. Her left snaked around my neck and pulled me toward her mouth.

I decided to play along and stopped resisting. If we could capture this thing alive, we could study it. Accordingly, I kissed her back. Then I activated my implant and called for security.

I was surprised when my message failed to transmit. It was jammed. People often used jammers for privacy when in their sleeping quarters. I'd never used one as I needed to be in touch with my crew at a moment's notice. But Suzy must have turned one on for our little engagement—I was on my own.

With her body locked around me like a python, she planted her mouth aggressively on mine. She pushed her bare breasts against me, and I could feel the sheer strength of her artificial muscles as she struggled with me. Was she as strong as I was? Possibly. Her muscles flexed and bulged with effort.

The door opened behind us then. I would have closed it, but the Stroj had me in a death grip. Her hands weren't caressing, they were wound up tightly in my hair. Her lips weren't just kissing me, they were applying suction, and her tongue wormed its way into my mouth.

My hands came up to push her away, but she quickly gripped my wrist, guiding me to handle her full breasts. They felt as real as any I'd ever had the privilege to touch. In fact, they felt so real that I lost myself for a moment.

"I see that I'm interrupting," Zye's voice said behind me in a cold tone. "Excuse me, Captain."

Embarrassed, I considered calling out to her, but passed on the idea. I would handle this particular monster on my own.

Biting down hard, I crushed the cyborg's tongue. She recoiled and spat blood.

"Don't do that again," she slurred, "or I'll kill you instantly."

"Isn't that your intention?" I asked. I was glad to learn that a Stroj could feel something in the way of pain. The Stroj were known to disconnect such nerve circuits, finding them distracting in combat.

"Don't worry, I'll get around to killing you," she said, smiling with perfect, blood-stained teeth. "But I'm going to have sex with you, first."

"Ah, I understand. You've been conditioned to like sex, haven't you? How better to play the role of seductress and get people to give you the assignment you want, the code to the captain's cabin, or whatever else you need."

"That's right," she said, "I do enjoy it, and you shouldn't complain. Isn't this way better than a foul death full of nothing but pain? At least you'll get some pleasure first."

I considered it. If I did give in to the creature's demands, I would be buying time. I could use a little time to think—if one *could* think clearly while making love to a killer cyborg.

My arms came up as if to embrace her. She smiled and seemed genuinely pleased. How many others had she strangled while she entwined her tight body with theirs?

"Wait a second," I said, putting up a hand. "You're the one who broke Durris' neck, weren't you? I saw you at the navigational table at that moment, even though it wasn't your shift."

She flashed me a grin. "I had to get closer. One step closer to you. Now, are you going to let all this go to waste?" She ran her hands over her own taut body.

I let my eyes appreciate her once more and moved in. She let me put my hands on her, and we stepped toward my bunk. As we moved to sit down upon it, I made my move, lying on my side in just the right spot.

When on the command deck, I generally didn't wear my power-sword. I left it in my cabin instead. But where to place it? Reasoning long ago that the most likely location I'd require use of it was when I was lying on my bunk, I'd placed it between the mattress and the lip of the bed that surrounded the padding.

With a natural move, I settled back and put my hand on the bed, as if to support myself as I leaned back on pillows. I maintained eye-contact with Suzy the entire time.

The lustful she-creature came down on top of me. She didn't weigh much, no more than what any young woman weighed, but her strong hands never left my body.

Deciding I didn't want to tip her off, I let her push me down flat on the bed. She ripped at my clothes, and soon I was exposed. She moved sinuously, and I found myself enjoying the experience. I almost forgot that I was in mortal danger.

With an effort of will, I forced myself to act. I felt somewhat guilty doing it. I knew this creature wasn't a normal human girl. Her flesh was like rubber and her mind was an evil, twisted thing. I had to remind myself that she was going to kill me when her physical lust was satisfied.

Before I could entertain second thoughts, I skewered her with a flick of my wrist. The sword rose in my hand I drove it into her arching back all at once.

She made a hissing sound, and she clenched down on me. I felt a terrific pain. She wasn't dying, however. She was transfixed on my sword, but her hands were still free, groping for my throat.

I had no choice. I switched on the sword, and a jolt of power electrocuted the monster that was trying to kill me even in her death throes.

Fortunately, I hadn't slid the selector to the continuous "on" position, but simply pressed the activating stud long enough to cause the sword to ignite briefly.

Even so, there were enough conductive materials in the Stroj to cause me to get a jolt as well. My mind blanked.

We were still coupled, even though the monster was stone dead.

I was aware of vomiting and passing out. My thumb slipped away from the switch on the hilt, and the full weight of the creature slumped over me on my bunk.

-36-

Someone shook me awake a few minutes later. I groaned, unable to open my eyes for a moment.

"So," Zye's voice asked somberly. "This is your secret desire? How can you derive pleasure from such an act? Is this sort of thing even legal on Earth?"

Blinking, I fought to force my body to obey me. My jaws were sore and stiff.

"She's a Stroj, Zye," I said. "She tried to kill me. Get her off me."

Zye pulled at the corpse, which was stiff and arching still. I howled in pain, but managed to untangle myself from what had so recently been known as Suzy.

Zye looked at the staring eyes doubtfully. "She looks human."

"Yes, she's quite convincing. That's how she joined the ship's crew undetected. She also managed to work her way close to me, as I was her assassination target. She's the best Stroj mimic I've seen yet."

"You're bleeding," she said.

Cursing, I gathered my uniform and headed for the infirmary.

After making sure the Stroj was well and truly dead, even going so far as to give her a farewell kick in the side, Zye joined me in the passageway.

"When did you know she was a Stroj?" Zye questioned.

"When? When she started trying to kill me, that's when."

"Were you engaged in a sex act at that point?"

"No. She appeared in my cabin, uninvited. She kissed me and went for my throat right after I realized what she was. That was when you stepped in the first time. By the way, you have to stop doing that."

"If I hadn't come back, you might have died."

"Well, next time someone is trying to kill me, please knock first."

She walked next to me in brooding silence for a while.

"I think I understand," she said at last. "I've been reading online articles about Earth males. Your kind requires a large personal region."

"You mean personal space?"

"Yes, that's it."

I gazed at her in disbelief. "I told you not to read those things. Without any perspective, you'll only get confused. This isn't about my need for personal space. I was attacked by a sex-bot that worked its way to my cabin and tried to kill me."

We reached the medical bay and the doctors there went to work on me, clucking their tongues and eyeing Zye in disdain. I got the feeling they thought she'd abused me. I didn't bother to explain.

"Why didn't this Stroj take drastic action earlier?" Zye asked.

"What do you mean?"

"It replaced Durris to get closer to you, then it attempted to seduce you. That seems too complicated. Why not just show up on any given night in your cabin after one of your shifts? Surely, you would have coupled with it."

I laughed. "How little faith you have in Earthmen," I said. "Apparently, she enjoyed having sex before a kill. She flirted with her targets to gain their attention, and then she pounced when the time was right. I think that's why she came to my cabin tonight. She must have sensed an opportunity"

"Ah," Zye said nodding. "I sensed the attraction. I saw you run your hands over her unnecessarily. That's a sure sign of sexual intent."

Oddly enough, I was embarrassed. What I'd done had come naturally to me, but hearing it from Zye, I could tell it had been inappropriate.

"I suppose you're right," I admitted. "I hadn't intended on anything happening. All I did was touch her lightly when showing her how to use the system."

"Would you have touched Durris that way while training him?"

"No," I admitted.

"You were sabotaged by your instincts. Very clever, these Stroj. Her beauty and overtly sexual nature helped her seduce you. No wonder she was programmed that way. I wonder how many more Stroj are aboard."

That thought alarmed me. "We don't really know, do we?" I asked. "The newer models pass for human so easily… I thought our tests were foolproof, but clearly they aren't."

"Perhaps you should take the entire crew to bed," Zye said wryly. "The ones that try to kill you are probably Stroj."

"That approach wouldn't be practical," I said, smiling.

She shrugged and stood up. "I'll be going. Looks like you'll need time to recover."

"Right. But I'll be back on the command deck before we find our way out of this pocket of hyperspace."

She left me there to wince and growl as the medical bots were applied. They patched my wounds with fresh skin cells then sealed the mess with tiny applications of self-dissolving glue.

* * *

The following day, we found our way out of the tiny hyperspace region. We had to change course several times to avoid exiting the region early—which the theoretical physicists among my crew said might prove to be fatal. What appeared to be walls surrounding us were indeed the limits of the sub-universe, but to leave this slice of space in any way other than the two bridge-points would probably result in an unfathomable disaster.

Some postulated that we'd end up back where we started, or in normal space near our destination. But most insisted that to exit elsewhere would cause our existence to come to a dramatic, instantaneous finish.

Following the tritium trail, we finally discovered the exit point. It was clear the pirates knew where it was, as they'd been heading directly for it from the start.

"Fire at the exit point," I directed. "We know they have to travel through it, and in this ER bridge it's unusually small. We might get lucky."

Durris had returned to the command deck, but he was unable to stand. He floated in a hovering chair and worked the controls with loose fingers and a lolling head. Still, with his understudy gone, he was the best navigator we had.

"Point marked in the battle computer, sir," he said, slurring slightly.

I frowned, wondering if I should relieve him and man the post myself. Deciding I would give him a chance, I nodded to Zye.

"Fire at the First Officer's coordinates."

Reluctantly, Zye turned to her boards and the big cannons spoke again. They fired in a predetermined grid, peppering the target region with particles.

"Report, Yamada?"

"Nothing, sir. The tritium trails for two of the ships have ended."

"Adjust, fire on yellow," I ordered quickly.

Zye worked the controls, and the guns went off again. I saw one blink red, overheated.

We waited quietly until a flare of light appeared.

"Contact!" Yamada said excitedly.

I got up and moved to her sensor array display. The data presented there was complex. Her job was to sort through it with the help of an AI system and present her analysis to the rest of us.

"I think we got one, sir. The hit registered catastrophic venting. But it vanished immediately after we struck the vessel."

"Are you sure it was a fatal blow?"

"That's my interpretation of the data."

Nodding, I moved to Durris, who was groping at his nav table.

"Durris, I need a course to follow that wounded pirate. There's blood in the water."

"Already figured that," he said. "The course has been sent to the helm."

Rumbold took the course and applied it. We veered slightly, and raced after the wounded ship.

While the breach loomed closer, I had a few seconds to talk to Durris.

"You're doing well, despite your injuries," I told him. "But if we're caught up in open combat, I'm going to have to relieve you. Your spine needs time to heal."

"I understand, sir," Durris said.

"How are the replacement vertebrae?" I asked.

"A little gritty when I turn my head. I think they're just printed copies of the originals, after all."

I narrowed my eyes, cringing sympathetically. I knew he was in pain.

"Here, why don't you retire to your bunk? I can take it from this point."

He slewed his eyes around to look at me without moving his neck more than a fraction. He gave me a tiny, wincing headshake. "Please don't relieve me yet, sir. I need to witness more of our revenge on these Stroj devils."

"When Ensign Gelb worked with you," I said, "did you ever suspect what she really was?"

"No sir, she had me completely sucked in."

"I see," I said, nodding. I thought it might have been a poor choice of words on his part, but I didn't comment.

"She kicked your legs out from under you right here," I said, tapping on his nav table. "At this very workstation. Such cunning and ruthless behavior."

"The Stroj are nothing if not cunning and ruthless."

"What did you think? When she kicked you?"

"We were in combat, so I thought she'd slipped, and I believed it was an accident. It seemed plausible at the time."

"All right, carry on. We'll be reaching the breach point soon."

Returning to my seat, I noticed Zye lingering nearby, listening and watching.

"Yes, Lieutenant…?"

"I watched you closely. During that entire interchange, despite the fact that Durris is your friend and injured, you never saw fit to make physical contact."

"No, I didn't."

"In such a situation, even two Betas might have touched one another comfortingly."

"Zye, I know I shouldn't have put my hands on Ensign Gelb. We've already been over this."

She nodded. "I just wanted to make sure the lesson had been understood."

I frowned at her back as she returned to her chair, then I shook my head and chuckled. Zye was very predictable in her own odd way.

-37-

When we passed through the barrier at the far end of the unstable bridge, it felt different somehow. The instant we'd made the transition, I learned why.

"Sir, we're in the middle of an artificial structure!" Yamada shouted. "Sensors are showing a metallic web-work around us of gigantic proportions.

"Helm, prepare for evasive actions," I said. "Get the shields open and show us where we are, Yamada."

The visual screens activated, and we could see the web-work, as she'd described it, surrounding us.

"I see a conical exit point, head that way, Rumbold."

He'd been braking heavily to prevent a collision, but now he slewed the ship around, and we did a power-arc toward the only visible open space.

That's when the guns began to fire. Tracking the incoming beams and hurled pellets back to their source points, the battle-computer showed graphically that we were under attack from the wiry structure itself.

Hundreds of beams lashed the hull. The projectiles were slower, and they progressed steadily on every screen toward our position.

"Shields up on all sides. Hit the gas, Rumbold."

To his credit, my helmsman had improved dramatically in his skills during the voyage. He served on the bridge regularly now, unless we were in a particularly dull stretch of space. Under such conditions I ordered him to go off-duty and rest.

The shields were up and fully energized just in time for a storm of pellet fire to land on them.

"Analyze this incoming flak," I told Yamada.

"It's depleted uranium slugs, sir. Each one about a centimeter in diameter. Not all that dangerous unless it's encountered while moving fast, unshielded."

The pellets disintegrated against our shields for the most part. Those that managed to overwhelm the shields and penetrate to the hull made thousands of pockmarks. The sound was like that of hearing gravel dropped onto the roof of a house.

"Damage report?" I shouted over the din.

"The fire is heavy, but uncoordinated. We're getting some hull erosion, but it's not critical yet."

"Hull stats."

"Seventy percent integrity. Forward shield at fifty percent, flanks just over forty."

I found her numbers alarming, but I took them in stride.

"Any sign of the pirate vessels? They obviously set us up by leading us here."

"Sir... I've lost them. The beams and pellets—there's too much interference to sort out a trace of the enemy engines."

Suddenly, Lorn's plan was crystal-clear to me. He'd led me here, while stealthed, knowing this ambush would occur. Perhaps the entire point hadn't been to destroy my ship, but rather to provide him the cover he needed to escape.

We powered our way out of the web-work of struts and automated guns into open space. This system seemed monumentally hostile already, and I hadn't even laid eyes on the stars and planets yet.

We were in a binary star system, with two central suns. The primary was a white, F-class star that had a smaller red companion. There were planets, but they were pretty far away from us. Over ten AU distant.

"Once we're clear of that flak, drop the forward and flank shields. Crank the sensors up to maximal sensitivity. We need to pick up their trail again."

The crew carried out my orders efficiently. Within twenty minutes, we were listening for the enemy in relative silence.

After pinging away for a full ten minutes, I became frustrated.

"Nothing?" I demanded, hovering over Yamada's station. "You're telling me you've got nothing?"

She shook her head. "I don't see any tritium trails, and no energy signatures anywhere close."

"Could they have coasted out directly from the entry point," I said, pacing behind Yamada's chair.

Durris waved for my attention, and I rushed to his side.

"Have you got something?" I demanded, running my eyes over his nav table hungrily.

"Just an idea."

I straightened in disappointment.

"Let's hear it."

"We should follow our best guess of where they went, looking for their trail. If we are lucky enough to get close, they'll probably drop stealth and run in fear."

My face twisted into a frown. "That's it? A gambling man, eh?"

He gestured weakly toward his table. "I've been working with the battle-computer since we entered this star system. I've channeled all our known contacts with the enemy and our best guess concerning their course into the computer. Here's what it's showing us."

He displayed a three-D image that included the web-work structure, the bridge entry point and even the central stars.

"See this lavender line? That's our best guess concerning their course. They can't change it much without leaving a trace behind. If they continue on this line, they'll eventually be caught up in the gravitational influence of the larger of the two stars. We'll end up somewhere near the inner, rocky planets we've discovered."

I stared at his work, unable to hide my skepticism.

"What if they diverted their course while they were in that hailstorm of fire inside the structure?"

"Unlikely," said Durris, tapping a finger on his table. "The exit point was small, and the automated guns might have sensed them and fired on them if they'd used their engines."

"I don't know... What do you think that structure was, anyway?"

He looked surprised. "Don't you know, sir?"

"I said as much."

"It's an artificial bridge projector. They always were theoretically possible, but I think we've seen our first one in reality."

His words stunned me. "I recall such a thing from the Academy," I said, "but I didn't know any of them existed."

"They don't—or at least, they didn't until now. They were theory, but that structure we passed through matches the designs Earth engineers developed nearly two centuries ago down to the last detail. Which proves two things."

"Please continue," I prompted him.

Internally, I was still trying to absorb the idea that the bridge had been created artificially. That meant whatever beings controlled this system had advanced technology. Earth had never managed to do more than draw up blueprints of something like this.

"First," Durris said with the air of one delivering a lecture, "this colony was founded by humans. No alien race would invent a system that looked identical to examples in our textbooks."

"What's the second item on your list, professor?"

Durris' strained to look at me sideways, his ear touching his shoulder.

"Just that they've managed to create a link with a single open unit on one end of the bridge. That's an amazing improvement to known designs."

"Hmm, right..." I said. "Otherwise, we'd have seen a matching webwork of metal in the last star system. The idea is fantastic, you know. Such freedom and power... To build a bridge to go anywhere you want..."

"Exactly."

I leaned against his nav table and studied his data closely. It all added up, as far as I could see. The implication was that the Stroj were even more technically advanced than we'd given them credit for.

We followed his plan to search for the missing pirates. After seven hours of looking and listening, I began to quietly despair.

I could see the same emotion reflected on the face of every crewmember present. They'd been hopeful at first, but none of them were fools. With each passing hour, our odds of finding our invisible friends was dropping.

After crunching numbers on my own, I decided to make a change.

"Let's pull up," I said. "Let's begin decelerating, coasting—even braking."

"But we haven't caught up with them yet, sir," Yamada said.

"Haven't we?" I asked, turning on her. "How do we know that? It's difficult to determine an enemy's exact speed without direct sensory data. What if we've sailed right past them? What if we're right on top of them now? They had several minutes to make adjustments before we broke through the barrier on their tails."

Durris shook his head, then winced and stopped himself. He rubbed at his neck with closed eyes, in obvious pain.

"I don't think so, sir. The automated weapons system would have turned on them instead of us if it knew they were there. They had to use stealth to get past the structure."

"We don't know that," I said. "All engines, halt. Rumbold, begin gently braking. Go to full-active pinging."

Like an ancient destroyer searching for a submarine, we slowed and began a thorough scan of our immediate environment.

My hunch quickly proved correct. One of the pirate ships was flushed out, convinced we'd spotted it somehow.

But, in typical Stroj fashion, it didn't run. It attacked us at point-blank range.

Twin disrupters fired and we took a hit in the belly. Deck four was damaged, and reports of casualties and pressure leaks flowed in.

For once, my predatory mood was such that I hardly cared about the injury they'd inflicted.

"Lock on all banks," I ordered. "Fire at will."

The plasma cannons, along with our smaller secondary batteries, all fired at once. A lethal mixture of beams, particles, radiation and pellets struck the pirate, tearing her apart.

Her last salvos rocked our ship, flickering the lights and making everyone grab their armrests and railings for support. But the ship was blown apart.

"And now, crew," I said, "there's only one Stroj ship left."

-38-

Our prideful sense of accomplishment only lasted about fifteen minutes. During that brief period we kept searching for that last ship, pinging and focusing our sensor arrays on small regions of local space, figuring that bastard had to be close.

"We're going to find him, sir," Durris said, his head tilted oddly to one side. "I feel it. He's right here close."

"We're not seeing any tritium traces any longer," I pointed out. "We could be a million kilometers off."

Durris shook his head, slightly and painfully. "No. The ship is running silent. That means he can't do anything—not even change course. He is right here."

Unconvinced but intrigued, I moved to Yamada's station and hovered over her for a time.

"Anything?" I asked.

"We've got every array focused on the nearest ten thousand kilometers of space. I'm not picking up a damned thing. A couple of times I thought I had something, but it always turned out to be background radiation from the last ship's explosion."

"Let's widen it out a little. And turn one array toward the central planets. Maybe we'll pick up a response to an S.O.S."

She looked at me quizzically. "How so?"

"The enemy ship is stealthed, but it might have a way of reaching out for help. Are you getting any transmissions from that structure at the breach point?"

"Yes, quite a bit of packet traffic. All encrypted of course."

"Well, they came in before we did. If I'd been given even one minute of time on this side of the breach alone, I would have transmitted my situation in the clear, then gone silent again when my pursuers came through."

She nodded. "I'll take a look in that direction."

Turning around and heading back to Zye and Rumbold, I'd intended to discuss our damage repair status—but Yamada swiftly called me back.

"Sir, we have a contact."

"Where?"

"Inner planets—something big. It's coming toward us now."

That wasn't what I'd expected. My eyes raced over the raw data. The contact was several AU out, and we didn't have a visual yet. But there was no doubt it was coming, and it was transmitting its own pings toward us. We could tell it was large because its engine signature showed a heavy output of energy.

"A warship," I said. "Whoever runs this system, they've sent out a warship to deal with us."

Yamada nodded, meeting my eyes briefly. I could see fear in her face. It only made sense that if Lorn had called for help, he would have been specific about what he was up against. That meant the enemy would have dispatched a warship they felt could deal with us effectively.

"All right, listen up everyone. We're going to have company in—Yamada?"

"The acceleration curve is steep, even though the enemy is coming at us up out of the gravity-well of the local star... Ten hours, I'd say. They'll be in extreme range by then."

"Durris, do the math. Give me a confirmation on that. I also want navigational options."

"In case we have to run, sir?" he asked.

"Exactly."

Just like that, our good moods evaporated. The enemy pirate was still hidden—but we weren't. We'd made ourselves the biggest, fattest target in the system by using every active sensor we had. That tactic had flushed out one of the pirates, but it might have doomed us at the same time.

Moving to Durris' table, I looked on as he worked his projections. Two ballooning spheroids had appeared on his nav table. They were different colors, and they showed how events may possibly unfold over the next few hours. Our balloon was green, and the unknown warship's balloon was red. The two spheroids splashed together in the middle, creating a vast area of possible contact where they could intercept us and commence firing.

"What's the word, First Officer?" I asked.

"The big picture is this: we only have about another forty minutes to hunt for the pirate before we're locked into a battle with the approaching ship."

"Your recommendation."

He looked tortured for a moment, then made a hissing sound of vexation. "I think we should withdraw, sir. Let the pirate go, as much as it pains me to say that. We can't risk this entire vessel in a battle against an unfamiliar warship just to run down one Stroj pirate—even if Lorn is likely aboard."

I nodded thoughtfully. "I agree," I said. "We've got forty minutes to find this bastard, then we have to veer off and head for the nearest breach out of this system."

"There's a problem with that approach as well, Captain."

"What else do I need to know?"

"The breaches here—this entire system—we're off our charts. This star system isn't listed or recognized by the computer. I can't find it on the Connatic's maps, either."

"Meaning that any bridge we use to exit this system might be a deadly one?"

"Exactly."

Troubled, I moved to Zye's station. She was, after all, in charge of tactical operations. In most cases that amounted to following my orders concerning when and where to fire *Defiant's* armament. But technically, she was supposed to help draw up our battle plans.

"Zye," I said, "tell me how we can flush out this rabbit."

She looked at me quizzically for a moment. "Rabbit? Oh, you must be talking about the Stroj pirate. He won't appear, sir. He'll hide now, as you implied, like a small prey-animal in a hole. Only when we, the predator, have left the vicinity will the vermin emerge again."

Snapping my fingers, I gave her shoulder a gentle squeeze. She flashed her eyes up from my fingers to make eye contact with her brows raised slightly. She appeared alarmed, but not upset. Remembering our previous conversation, I took my hand away again immediately. We needed at least one more discussion on work-ethics versus our personal lives.

"That's a good idea," I said. "Helm, give us a ninety degree turn to port. Pull away from here at six gravities—and turn on the inertial dampeners so we aren't all crushed."

"On it, Captain!" Rumbold beamed. He was more than happy to put some distance between us and any possible threat.

"Captain," Zye said. "I don't understand your actions."

"You will. Yamada, switch our sensor arrays into passive mode and focus them on the region we're leaving behind. Look for tritium trails."

"Ah," Zye said, "you're trying to flush the enemy out by appearing disinterested. When they show themselves again, we'll pounce—is that it?"

"Exactly, Zye. Now, all we have to do is wait."

The wait began—and it ran too long. After twenty minutes of nothing, I became frustrated again. I was hovering over Yamada's chair and gripping the back of it with a claw-like hand.

"Damn that Lorn," I said, "he's too clever. He's going to wait until we're gone before he stirs again."

"Looks that way," Lieutenant Yamada said.

Checking with my officers in turn, I asked for more ideas. None of them gave me much I could work with.

At Durris' nav table, the projected spheroids of possible action had shifted dramatically. There was now a larger region of non-conflict. We were moving out of harm's way.

About ten minutes later, things changed again.

"Contact!" Yamada shouted triumphantly. "The pirate is back, Captain."

"You found his tritium trail?"

"No sir, not just that. See for yourself."

She patched the feed onto the forward screens, and we all watched, grinding our teeth.

The last pirate ship had become visible. Its engines had flared white, and it wasn't bothering to stealth or dampen emissions. They were running for it, in the exact opposite direction we were headed.

"We flushed him, but it's too late," Zye said. "We're just out of range."

"Prepare a spread of missiles," I said.

Durris waved for my attention.

"What is it, man?" I demanded.

"Sir, we have a limited supply of warheads. If we fire them after the pirate, we won't have them for any later battles. It's my job to warn you of this."

"Damn it," I breathed. "Stand down the missiles."

I felt defeated, even though I had no real reason to be. We'd destroyed nearly all of the enemy ships. Letting one get away wasn't a disaster. Still, it pained me to allow it.

"Captain," Yamada said, listening to her headset. "The Stroj pirate is trying to open a channel to talk to us."

I stared at her for a moment. I felt my face tighten.

"Put him on screen."

She did so, and we all learned the truth together.

-39-

The Stroj pirate leered at us. It was indeed Captain Lorn. As I'd always believed, he'd sacrificed the lives of every underling he could to stay alive himself.

"Greetings, pathetic Earthmen," he said effusively. "I must say, I've never seen you run from a fight like this, Sparhawk."

"Is that why you called, Lorn? To gloat? Perhaps on the Stroj homeworld, losing every ship under your command save for the one you're in can be described as a victory."

His face darkened. "This isn't over yet, Sparhawk. You've outgunned and abused my forces for a long time. But that is about to end. I'll return to my home system with your skin melded into mine yet."

"Ah, thanks for that valuable intel," I said.

"What?"

"You just informed me that this isn't the Stroj home system. We weren't sure, but some of my officers believed it was. It's very helpful to have confirmation on this critical point. Our star maps will be much more complete when we return due to your helpful efforts."

I was needling him, and it was working. His face had fallen from affable to angry.

"You won't be returning anywhere. There's no way out of this system for an Earth ship. You've signed your own death warrants by coming here."

The channel closed.

Frowning, I turned to my sensory data. "Yamada, I want you to stop focusing on the enemy vessels. Examine the outer regions of the system. What breaches have you found?"

"None yet, sir," she said. "We had everything beaming our local region of space to find the pirate."

"Of course. Now, be so kind as to find me an exit out of here."

She began to work her controls, but she quickly became concerned.

"I'm not seeing anything, sir," she said.

"Nothing?"

"No breaches—other than the one we came through to get here."

I moved to Durris and examined the situation. As we'd turned away from that region of space, the escape path was no longer a viable option. The enemy vessel coming at us from the inner planets—whatever it was—would catch us long before we could return to our original point of entry into the star system.

"So that's what he meant," Durris said. "Could this all be an elaborate trap, sir?"

I shrugged. "Only in the sense that we followed Lorn here. Maybe he meant it to be a trap. What are our options?"

"Well, we can continue circumnavigating the system, swinging around the two central stars. Maybe we'll find another exit."

"Maybe. What else do you have?"

"We could turn and fight. Right now. If we keep running around, maybe another warship will come for us. One on one, we win or lose, then we retrace our steps back to Earth."

Beginning to pace, I was keenly aware of the passing minutes and the passing opportunities they represented.

"Let's use logic," I said. "The Stroj had to come here somehow, right?"

"That stands to reason, sir."

"So if they didn't use the path we just traveled by to reach this system, they must have used another route. There has to be another bridge somewhere."

"Possibly so," Durris admitted. "But what if we find it? The odds are fairly good it will lead us back to the Stroj home system. Or at least, to another Stroj base. We'll be out of the frying pan and into the fire."

I nodded and continued to pace. "All right then. We'll have to try something drastic. How much acceleration can our crew live through? For a period of, say, four hours?"

Durris blinked at me. So did the other crewmen who overheard my question. No one looked happy that I'd asked it.

"Two or so Gs, maybe, past the rating of the inertial dampeners. We could take up to thirty Gs for very short periods of a minute or so, but even with our suits fighting the pooling of blood with smart-mesh and other adjustments, we'd pass out or suffer tissue damage if we tried anything like that for hours."

"Right," I said, "so let's do the math. We'll spin around, and punch it past the enemy ship in bursts. Say, no more than three minutes at a time."

He shook his head. "That's too much, sir."

"We only have to get past the approaching enemy ship in a short burst. We need to give the enemy as small a window to shoot at us as possible."

He returned to his boards and his math, working the nav computer and simulations. After ten precious minutes, he had an answer for me.

"We might be able to do it," he said. "We'll brake hard, then thrust back the way we came—I'm assuming you just want to get past the enemy warship and exit through the bridge that brought us here, right?"

"No," I said, "I want to skirt the enemy ship, then run down Lorn's ship. We've still got a fix on him, don't we?"

"Absolutely," Yamada called. "I've got him on scope. He's cruising around to the far side of the bigger star right now."

"We could try it…" Durris said. "We'll be in their range for a short time at least, though. We'll have to expect to take some fire."

"Zye, you'll be at the helm. Rumbold, you're relieved. Find a couch and fill it with support foam. Tell everyone below to start doing the same. They should pack themselves up like melons in crates."

"Got it sir!" Rumbold said, and he jumped out of his seat and practically ran off the deck.

I'd never seen anyone so relieved to be relieved of duty. Zye smoothly moved from her station to Rumbold's.

"Before you leave tactical ops," I told her, program our shields to divert all power to the flank and belly shielding. We might be taking a few hits from that direction."

She did as I asked wordlessly.

When everything was ready, we spun the ship around and slammed the throttle down. The powerful engines thrummed and sang.

We shook, we drooled, and most of us blacked out over a period of fourteen harrowing minutes.

During that time, I hazily recalled taking hits. Yamada said something about a shield buckling, but I couldn't turn my head far enough to look at the data. I did consider that if we were forced to do battle any time soon, my crew wasn't going to be in the best of shape.

Watching Zye struggle through it all stoically, I began to wish I'd had a hundred of her kind on board rather than just one. But that might have caused as many problems as it solved.

When the ordeal was over at last, we'd slowed and begun to recover. Our bodies were more damaged than the ship itself.

"We did almost forty-nine gravities," Durris whistled from the floor. His neck was back in a brace again, and medical people were gently trying to pull a computer scroll out of his shaking fingers.

"Forty-nine gravities," he said. "That's a record, as far as I know. The dampeners halved that, of course, but no Earth ship has ever performed such a stunt under fire."

"This isn't an Earth ship," Zye said proudly. "There is no comparison."

"Truly said," Durris replied as they loaded his prostrate form onto a gurney and gently bore him off the deck toward medical. "No engineer on Earth would be mad enough to build something like *Defiant*."

He was gone then, and I wished him well.

Rubbing at numb extremities, I asked Yamada to give me an ETA. "When are we going to catch Lorn and his fleeing ship?"

"Maybe never, sir," she said a moment later. "He must have seen what we were doing. He's vanished."

Cursing, I lurched to her station and almost slumped over it. "Look for his trail. It will point the way."

After a few tense minutes, she picked it up. "Here—tritium traces. But sir, I can't be sure that's—"

"It's him," I said, interrupting. "Get after him. Mark his course. We'll intercept—here."

We laid in the course and eventually Rumbold staggered back to the helm. He had his head wrapped in a bladder of rubber and one of his eyes had swollen shut.

"Can you fly like that, Rumbold?" I asked.

"Sure. I've had worse."

"Liar."

He chuckled and returned to his chair. He flopped into it and winced.

"Captain Sparhawk? Could you answer me one question?"

"Certainly, Rumbold."

He swiveled around and fixed me with his one good, working eye.

"Why the hell did you nearly kill us to run down Lorn? Is this a simple matter of vengeance?"

"Not entirely," I said. "Think, man. There has to be another way out of this system. Who do you think knows where that might be?"

He looked at me for a frozen second, then he grinned—his square teeth rimed in blood.

"Captain Lorn would know, wouldn't he? He's a pirate, so he must know every bridge and system by heart."

"Exactly, Rumbold. Now, you're going to help me run him down and capture him."

"Will do, sir!"

-40-

Finding the last pirate ship turned out to be easier than we'd imagined.

Seeing us make a screaming pass by his friends, and quickly realizing he could never outrun us, Lorn went into silent-running mode again.

The mistake he made was leaving a very straight line of tritium in his wake.

"There," I said, leaning over Zye's shoulder. "Lead him. Fire ahead of where you think he is."

"Why not run a missile right up his tailpipe?" Zye asked.

I glanced at her. She'd been picking up old-fashioned idioms from Rumbold. One element of longevity that I'd never gotten completely used to was the way that oldsters sometimes expressed themselves. It was almost like talking to someone from Elizabethan times, when they lapsed into the slang of their youth.

"Because we want to force him to capitulate," I explained, "not destroy him."

She shook her head. "He's Stroj. He won't surrender. Even if he does, he'll only do so to harm us in some way. He'll never cooperate."

"Leave that up to me, Zye. Fire as I've directed."

The missiles zoomed ahead moments later. Twin vapor trails followed them. The engines quickly dwindled to tiny points of light like stars, then vanished completely into the eternal night which we called space.

About sixty seconds after we launched the weapons, they ignited in a single brilliant puff of energy. I studied the data.

"That was too close. Zye...?"

She shrugged. "I struck directly ahead of the enemy craft," she said, wearing her best poker face.

Growling in frustration, I moved to Yamada's side.

"Any sign of debris? Zye decided to play one of her tricks."

"We've got venting," Yamada said, her voice rising in excitement. "Gas traces, residual radiation, but the ship isn't visible."

"Open a general hailing channel," I said.

"Ready to transmit."

Engaging my implant, I spoke into the void, hoping the damaged enemy could still hear me.

"Captain Lorn," I said. "We know where you are. We've penetrated your stealth technology. If you don't heave-to and prepare to be boarded, we'll fire again. This time, we'll hit your ship directly and take it out."

We listened for a full minute, but there was only crackling static in return.

"Maybe they can't hear us," Yamada suggested.

"Or maybe," Zye said, "they don't care. They'll play dead until we get close, then strike without—"

That was as far as she got with her prediction before it came true. The enemy appeared directly in front of us and unloaded all its remaining armament.

"All decks, brace for impact!" I shouted.

The missiles were so close we could see them. The forward shields were up, fortunately, but at this range—

I barely made it back to my command chair before the ship began to shudder with the strikes. The energies released buckled our shield and slammed into the hull so hard it would have destroyed a lesser ship.

But *Defiant* was nothing if not tough. She was thicker-skinned than anything Earthmen had ever built. In that moment, I was very glad the Betas were a paranoid people.

The nav table flickered and went out. The starboard side of the ship had lost power, including portions of the command deck. Emergency power kicked in and took over automatically. Red lights glowed dimly and the air smelled of ozone.

Hurriedly, I lowered my faceplate. There was no telling if there had been radiation contamination. We'd been hit hard and there were cracks in the tough hull.

A dozen voices were talking all at once. I cut through them all with my own booming shout.

"Damage report!"

"Decks three, two and one—our deck, Captain—all suffered serious damage. Two casualties reported, one killed, one seriously wounded."

"What about our weapons? Zye?"

"We've got one bank of plasma cannons online. Our missile ports are not responding."

I looked at her. "Not responding? Send a crew down there to get a visual."

"On it, sir. Shall I fire our remaining plasma cannons?"

For a long second, I regarded the ship hanging in space in front of me. It was mocking us. Damaged but unwilling to surrender, the Stroj vessel had turned about and was now lashing our hull with her thin beams. If they had any more missiles, I had no doubt her crew was racing to load them into their tubes.

My fist came down on the arm of my chair. "Damn it, yes. Destroy her."

Zye let a quiet grin play on her lips as she spun back around to her boards. She must have had every gun target locked and ready. The beams sang, and at this range, we could hardly miss.

The pirate ship was cut apart. We couldn't see the beams themselves, of course, but we watched as they drew lines of explosive heat across the hull, striking amidships. They dug and dug deeper, releasing billows of pressurized vapor and burning sparks of metal. The internal vessel was compromised, life-giving gases and fuel escaping into vacuum. The gases were ignited by the intense heat, creating a series of flashing explosions that quickly died out, swallowed by the hard vacuum.

Then, after we'd cut her almost in half, the pirate's engine core was breached and the whole thing blew up in our faces. I blinked and squinted, such was the level of that momentary brilliance.

Zye turned back around to me. "I told you. The Stroj would never let us capture their ship."

I nodded in defeat. I thought of reprimanding her for what I suspected was shaving down the range on our missile strike, but I realized that there was little point to it now. She'd been right, after all. The enemy hadn't allowed us to capture their ship. Destroying her was the only true option we'd had all along.

"Sir, I'm picking up something else," Yamada said.

"Specify."

"Small objects—relatively small. There are three of them drifting away from the debris."

"Scan them for life signs."

"I've got nothing. Nothing on any of them."

"They could be mines," Zye suggested.

"Yes, or records of the battle," I said. "Target the nearest and destroy it, Zye."

Happily, she turned back to her work. A single cannon fired, and the first of the canisters vanished in a puff of heat and gas.

"Doesn't look like it was a mine, anyway," I said, examining the spectroscope readout. "Fire on the second."

The second was disintegrated without incident. It didn't even explode.

"Sir, the third is moving away from us," Yamada reported in surprise, "under its own power."

"Interesting. Weapons-lock, Zye?"

"I have a firing solution."

"Don't fire," I said quickly. "Yamada, try to hail that canister."

She listened for a second, then smiled. She piped the input to the forward screen.

A very angry image of Captain Lorn appeared. He looked the worse for wear. His body was scorched in places and most of his hair had been burned away. His metal and polymer parts were exposed like scorched bone all along his right side. I wondered briefly how he'd evaded our sensors, but then decided it hardly mattered.

A huge grin expanded over my face.

"Captain Lorn!" I boomed. "I'm so glad you survived this misunderstanding."

"The feeling isn't mutual, Sparhawk," he growled.

"Don't be a poor sport, man," I said. "We won, you lost. That's how it goes in battle."

"Why do you contact me? To torment me before you deal the deathblow? In that case, I'm done with this conversation."

He reached up to switch off the comm system, but I raised my hand toward the screen to stop him.

"Hold on, Lorn. Let's talk seriously."

"Speak, don't prolong this."

"I'll get to the point. You seem like a thinking man. A man who values his existence more than your average Stroj."

He stared at me for a moment. He was breathing heavily, as if injured. Curls of smoke twisted above his head. I wasn't sure of the source, but it might have been his scorched body.

"You insult me. I'm Stroj. I think only of service to my people."

"Of course," I said smoothly, "but think: a man can't be much help to his people when he's dead."

"Again you call me a man. You must stop with these insults or I'll terminate this conversation."

I found it interesting he objected to being called human. Insinuating that Earth Basics, such as myself, could be considered in any way equivalent to a Stroj was insulting to him.

"Captain Lorn," I said, "I would like to meet and discuss matters with you personally. I'm offering you your life as a prisoner of war."

He eyed me thoughtfully. "Such a thing is unknown to us. You wish to dissect me."

I gave him an airy wave of the hand. "There are countless Stroj bodies drifting around in space due to our efforts. It's not your anatomy that I'm interested in."

"What then?"

274

"Come aboard as my guest—under guard, of course—and we'll discuss it."

His haggard eyes took on a calculating aspect. "You mean we'll discuss this in person? Face to face?"

"I wouldn't have it any other way."

He rubbed at torn, blackened lips with a hand that was missing a finger or two. "All right. I'll come aboard. But remember, you said we'd talk face-to-face."

"We'll talk," I said, "rest assured on that point."

The channel closed, and Zye looked at me as if I'd gone mad.

"Many times you've met with the Stroj," she said with a mixture of anger and disbelief. "And still you would invite one aboard our ship? To sit and talk with it?"

"Relax, Zye," I said. "I know what I'm doing."

Her face smoothed out, and I was surprised to realize she was actually making a serious effort to do as I'd instructed.

-41-

Letting a Stroj commander board *Defiant* was a big step. I did it with trepidation, but also with haste. The enemy warship, which we'd only caught a glimpse of when we'd buzzed by her hours earlier, was still in dogged pursuit.

The enemy ship couldn't catch us with sheer speed, but she clearly outclassed us. Resembling a barrel bristling with weapons, I went over the imagery we'd gotten during our fly-by.

"That, sir," Zye had declared, "is a Stroj dreadnought. She's probably tasked with security for this system, which is obviously some kind of advanced base for the enemy."

I nodded, having come to much the same conclusion. The enemy warship displaced twice the amount of mass that we did. Maybe, if the truth were to be told, she was even a bit bigger than that.

"Well," I said, "she hasn't caught up with us yet. We have time to talk to our guest."

Zye's thick arm came up to bar my passage. I pushed it away, and she looked down.

"Sorry sir," she said. "I would just like to point out that Captain Lorn can have only one purpose for allowing us to capture him."

"Which is?"

"He wants to kill you. Probably through self-demolition. Remember the Stroj agent back at House Astra?"

"Yes, of course," I said. "I have no intention of allowing Lorn to injure me. Rumbold? Where's Rumbold?"

"Here sir," he said.

His voice was muffled, and I realized he was one of the three techs standing in blast gear at the back of the group. I gave him a twisted-lip stare.

"I take it you're prepared to withstand a bomb?"

"Just in case the enemy slips one past us, Captain. I'm sure you understand. Not meant to be an offense in any way, shape or form," came his muted response.

"None taken," I said, and I led the way to the landing bay.

All vehicles and cargo had been cleared from the deck. The small Stroj craft came tumbling in, having been dragged into *Defiant's* belly by grav-beams.

When the pod stopped rolling, we approached it diffidently.

"Looks hot, sir," Rumbold said when the craft had come to a full halt against the back wall of the hangar.

"It's smoking like a meteor," I said. "Is that because of the grav-beams?"

He nodded his head. "This only happens if the craft battles the beam. The life pod was probably flying on automatic. Maybe that's why Captain Lorn gave in—maybe he didn't really have any choice."

Shrugging, I directed two crewmen to set up a stasis field around the pod. They did so, and the field swiftly deployed. It felt like a cobweb was being dragged over my face and entire body. The field was visible only as a slightly shimmering dome in the air. The air itself felt full of static charges. Every movement made my uniform crackle and flash with tiny discharges.

"Open the pod," I directed.

The two crewmen did so fearfully, despite the fact they were suited up in what amounted to blast-proof armor. Rumbold stood well back and supervised.

Almost immediately, a hideous head popped out of the pod.

"You took long enough," Lorn complained. "If I were you, I'd punish these crewmen for their slow performance, Sparhawk."

"Thanks for the advice," I said. "Now, if you would be so good as to shed all your weapons on the deck, we'll take you into protective custody."

"Protective custody?" he asked, laughing. "Absurd. This is a hijacking—false imprisonment. If our two empires don't go to war immediately, this event will soon push the matter over the edge."

I gestured toward the deck. Lorn hesitated.

"What's to stop me from taking you all, right here?" he asked.

I'd been expecting that question. Stroj rarely respected anything other than superior force. I drew my saber and powered it.

"I'll cut you down myself if I must."

Lorn loosed a hollow, ringing guffaw and shook his head. He climbed out of the tight pod with some difficulty, but soon he stood before us on the deck. He looked around the group again, obviously sizing us up.

At last, he nodded affirmatively. "I can take you. All five of you. You're not even carrying guns."

He lifted both his artificial limbs and black tubes extended from his wrists.

I took a half step forward in response, lifting my sword.

A spray of dark spheres, about the size of beetles, sprayed out of those tubes. They showered all of us. The crewmen, including Rumbold, backpedaled reflexively.

"Steady on," I said, "stay within the dome."

Rumbold and his men stopped retreating. The black balls bounced off of our bodies and rolled all over the deck. A few made it past the protected limits of the stasis dome. Flashes immediately occurred when they exited the dome.

"Bomblets?" I asked. "Crude, but probably effective under some circumstances."

Lorn looked confused and annoyed. He took two steps closer and put his fists on his hips.

"What's this then? Some kind of field? That's very unsportsmanlike of you, Sparhawk."

With the tip of my blade, I scooped up one of the bomblets and bounced it off his chest. He winced reflexively.

"It's far more sophisticated than your clumsy attack."

"That was just a personal defense system," he said, waving his hand at the bomblets dismissively. "I just wanted to test your resolve."

"I see. Now, Captain Lorn, if you would be so good as to comply with my orders. Remove your weapons and drop them on the deck."

"My entire body is lethal," Lorn said. "You can't truly disarm me."

"We'll start with those black tubes that dispensed the bomblets."

The process took several minutes and countless threats, but we finally got him to shed a variety of needlers, energy projectors and bomblets as well as other, less easily identified items.

At last I was satisfied. Directing Rumbold and his team to pick up the stasis generator and follow, I turned to lead the way into the ship.

Lorn balked in annoyance. "We're taking that contraption with us?" he demanded.

"Of course. Every moment during your stay aboard *Defiant*, you'll be in close proximity to a stasis generator. You won't be able to blow yourself up or commit some other combustible crime of large scope."

"Bah!" he bellowed. "Then I'll have to end it here."

He charged me then. I had to admit, I was somewhat surprised. My hand reached up to the clasp on my personal shielding—but of course, that didn't work. No major energy release would.

Zye moved to intercede, stepping between my person and Lorn. He reached her, and the two struggled.

Under less threatening circumstances, the battle would have been fascinating. Zye was a clone, genetically selected for size and strength with powerful arms born from the rigors of life on a high-gravity world. Lorn was a hybrid of flesh and machine with polymer substitutes for muscle and bone.

My impression was that both were surprised by the strength and ferocity of the other. Zye locked arms with the Stroj captain, but he quickly swept her feet out from under her with a thick leg.

She held onto his arms and pulled him down with her, rolling him over her head so he landed flat on his back. She sprang up, as did he, and they charged one another again.

It was my sword that ended the conflict at that juncture. I thrust it between Lorn's legs, taking one of them off just below the knee. He went down and tumbled onto his face on the deck.

Zye fell upon his back and held him down. The Stroj heaved and bucked under her, but was unable to dislodge her weight.

"That was unnecessary," she said, breathing hard, "but thank you."

"You're bleeding," I said, looking over her forearms where Lorn had gripped her.

"It's nothing."

In the end, we had to chain Captain Lorn with thick force-bonds and frog-march him to a cell in the brig. The stasis-generator stayed outside his cell, just out of reach. He glowered at us, angry and soundly humiliated.

As a peace offering, I brought his lower leg to the bars and passed it through. He grabbed it.

"Here," I said, offering him a set of basic tools.

He took the tools and hopped to the back of his cell. There, he began to reattach the limb.

"Why did you take me aboard, Sparhawk?"

"Because I wanted to exchange valuable information."

He snorted. "What, in your fevered dreams, do you expect to extract from me? Surely, even a foolish Basic such as yourself must know I'll do everything I can to slay you."

"You've made that abundantly clear, yes," I agreed. "But I still hold out hope for an exchange of value to both of us."

"You're a dreamer. You should listen to that pet Beta of yours. She knows my kind all too well—as I know hers. I've killed no less than six of her sisters personally, you know."

"Perhaps it would be best if you didn't share *that* information," I suggested.

"Get to the point then, man. You're wasting what little lifetime I have left."

I cocked my head curiously. "Why are you so sure it's limited?"

"Because of that dreadnought out there. Surely, you've noticed her? She's a predator. A shark where your ship and mine were only minnows. She'll come for us, and catch us, and mangle us in time."

"You've struck upon an area in which we might be able to cooperate," I said, "privately, of course."

He looked at me quizzically. His expression was one of irritation mixed with curiosity.

"I get it. You want a way out of this system. I led you here as part of a trap—but you know that, don't you?"

"I figured it out eventually. But you're trapped as well."

He shrugged and snorted. "What of it? I'm screwed regardless. For a Stroj who's been defeated, the only final act that makes any sense is to damage or kill the enemy who bested him. Now, you've denied me even that small pleasure."

"What if I offer you survival?" I asked.

"In exchange for what?"

"There must be a way out of this system. A way to redirect the artificial bridge, for example."

He shook his head. "No, not that one. It's been shut down. You sent a probe through to check, didn't you?"

We hadn't of course. After a brief pause during which I considered lying to him, he shouted with laughter.

"You didn't know, did you?" he demanded. "You had no idea you couldn't go back the way you came!"

One of our viable options *had* been to circumnavigate the central binary stars and come around to escape through the same portal where we'd entered the system. Lorn had just dashed that hope.

"Listen, Sparhawk," he cackled. "Before this is over, you're going to wish you'd let me blow us both up. That would have been a kindness. You're going to watch your entire crew die, knowing that afterward scraps of their flesh will be hunted for within the wreckage by a thousand greedy Stroj spacers from that dreadnought."

"We're still alive now," I told him. "You and I both. I repeat: let's come to an understanding."

He approached the bars, carrying his severed foot. "Really? Am I detecting a craven side of you I hadn't suspected? You'd perform a treasonous act to save your skin?"

"That's not how I'd describe it. What I'm proposing is that you help this ship exit the system, and I'll drop you off in your lifepod there, or wherever you might want to be released on our return journey to Earth."

His eyes were calculating. I could see he was interested, but he was probably also trying to figure out how to screw me in the bargain.

"All right," he said. "Free me from this cage. I'll accompany you to the command deck and direct you to the exit from there."

Shaking my head, I chuckled. "I'm a gullible man," I said, "but there are limits. You will give us the data we need and we'll check it out. If we escape with your help, I'll honor my bargain and free you."

He made a dismissive gesture and returned to a small stool at the back of the cell. He sat on it and tinkered with his damaged leg.

"No, I'll pass," he said.

"Really? There's no other way either of us will survive. You said so yourself."

He shrugged. "No matter. I was willing to die to take you with me just an hour ago. Or have you forgotten?"

"Fine," I said, walking toward the guards. "Attendant, it's time to flush this cell. Are the evacuation hatches in working order?"

The man looked surprised, but he nodded.

"Good. Let's clear the chamber and—"

"Hold a moment," Lorn said behind me.

I ignored him. "We'll have to secure the stasis unit to the deck first," I told the guard. "I wouldn't want to lose it when we space the cells."

"Sparhawk!"

Slowly, I turned toward him. "Is there something you wish to say, Lorn?"

He was breathing hard and his face was pressed against the bars. I could see he'd been reaching, straining to touch the stasis unit. But I'd made sure it was beyond any hope of retrieval.

"Are you a man of your word?" he asked, eyes rolling toward me.

"Yes, I am, actually."

He nodded. "I thought as much. Only a true fool would have picked me up at all. Fine. I'll tell you how to get out of this system—but you're not going to like it."

Curious, I approached the bars again.

-42-

As it turned out, Lorn was correct. I didn't like the method of escape he described to me.

"You're sure there's no other way?" I asked him.

"Positive. We'll both live, but only if you follow my instructions explicitly."

"This doesn't seem quite above-board," I observed. "Why would you agree to harm your own people this way? I thought a Stroj was down for the cause with his life. That he would sacrifice anything and everything for his homeworld and brethren."

Lorn laughed at that. "How greatly you misunderstand us. We're not mindless soldiers. Robots march in a perfect hive-mind—not the Stroj. We're quite the opposite, in fact. We are individualistic to a fault."

Honestly curious, I pressed him further. "I've always wondered about the philosophy and psychology of your culture," I admitted. "What keeps you together if not a sense of devotion to a cause?"

"We are devoted to a cause—ourselves!" he explained. "You see, it's all about status. It's rather like being a committed capitalist. Think, what drives a narcissist?"

"Self-aggrandizement?"

"Yes," he said. "We Stroj like to one-up each other. Nothing makes us feel better than that—to know we've dominated a rival. Among our own people, this takes the form of being promoted over one another. If one commands a ship, that captain takes great pride in the trophies he has carried home with it."

"What about a Stroj who commands a mop?"

"That's even more clear. We're all concerned with our status among our peers. A man with a mop wants to put all other mop-men to shame. Perhaps even to rise above all others utilizing that very mop."

"I see," I said, "you're individual warriors, rather than soldiers in formation."

"Exactly. Cheating is therefore acceptable, as long as that cheating is never discovered. Since you're a man of honor, I can be assured you'll never tell another of my people. I'm free to invent whatever story I want about my daring escape. Your silence will support my case, and my status will be elevated."

I could tell he was salivating at the deal. He'd been assured of a defeat, but now, he thought he had a way out.

"I still don't understand one thing, however," I said, "why were you so willing to die to kill me?"

"Again, you have to understand our perspective is different than your own. We fight like wolves, but when we see our final moments are upon us, we stretch our minds to find the best way possible to die. Killing one last enemy is often the best choice that can be made—particularly if it's an exceptional kill."

Nodding slowly, I was reminded of the nihilistic culture of the Vikings. They, too, would rather die with a sword in their hands, fighting to the death. Any other way out was disgraceful.

"All right then," I said, "as strange as it may seem, we've struck a bargain. How shall we proceed?"

He began to tell me, and it got worse as the discussion progressed. Before we got to the end of it, the cellblock hatchway opened.

I frowned at the guard. "I gave explicit instructions we weren't to be interrupted."

"I'm sorry, sir," he said sheepishly. "Her excellency refused to be put off."

My aunt slipped past him, appearing far more hunched than usual. She hobbled toward me with a cane rapping loudly on the floor and looking quite angry.

"Have you been injured Aunt Helen?" I asked.

"Don't 'Aunt Helen' me, William," she said. "As if you care about my health. That last stunt you pulled, zipping by the dreadnought, that nearly killed me!"

"I'm sorry to hear that. Oh, by the way, this is Captain—"

"I know who he is! Do I understand correctly that you've been conducting unsanctioned negotiations down here with this creature?"

"I'd hardly describe them as negotiations. Our discussions have been of a personal nature."

"What?" she demanded. "Are you going to marry this monster?"

Captain Lorn laughed then. "Sparhawk! You've been holding out on me. Such a ravishing beauty. She's full of fire and spunk, too."

She turned each of us a baleful eye. I noted that one of her eyes wasn't opening properly. It was bloodshot and weeping. I thought that was probably a side effect of our violent maneuvering earlier. High-G accelerations took a toll on oldsters, but she was still kicking.

"This fiend is *my* responsibility now," Lady Grantholm insisted. "I'll handle all further negotiations."

I threw up my hands. "Fine, but I suggest you don't get too close to the bars."

She watched me leave.

"Kind Lady," Lorn said, "would you be so considerate as to switch off that abominable box? It's making it hot in here, and I'm very uncomfortable."

My Aunt leered at him. "Don't take me for a fool. Stroj," she said. "I've been talking to monsters like you since before your planet was discovered."

This seemed to surprise and amuse Lorn. I left the two of them together. Their personalities were more alike than they were different, after all.

"Command staff, report," I ordered when I stepped onto the command deck.

Durris lurched up from my seat with a painful jerk. I could tell his broken neck was still bothering him.

"No major changes, sir," he said.

"How's that spine of yours?" I asked, trying to hide my dismay at his odd appearance.

He seemed surprised at my question. "It's not bothering me much right now. I've got neural pain-clamps and nano-strings holding together the vertebrae—thanks for inquiring, sir."

Modern medicine allowed spacers to walk away from injuries that would have taken months or years to heal in the past, but there were always alarming side effects. It was disconcerting to watch his head loll and twist, despite the fact I knew the artificial fibers in his vertebrae were strong enough to keep him from further damaging his spinal cord.

"Excellent," I said, trying not to wince as I looked at him. "Now, proceed to these coordinates."

I handed him a computer scroll. Frowning, he unrolled it and tapped at the data he found there. He looked up at me in alarm.

"Captain...? This will take us to their base—to the spot where we first spotted the dreadnought."

"Exactly. That's the only way out."

I explained in detail, leaving out any mention of my bargain with Lorn. He already thought I was a madman for following this scheme, there wasn't any point to confirming his suspicions.

After several baffled looks, he moved to his nav table and tapped in the data. "Here," he said, "there's a small nickel-iron moon around the second planet in the system. It'll be hot and highly radioactive."

Nodding, I examined what little data we had on the region. We had more than when we first entered the star system, but it still wasn't much.

"Surface temperature around the boiling point of water," I said. "Atmosphere made up primarily of carbon dioxide mixed with nitrogen and other trace elements. Upper cloud layer is sulfuric acid, and it rains acid on a daily basis. Sounds like a vacation spot."

"Yeah," he said. "You think the Stroj really live on that burning rock?"

"I don't think they're here for the gardening, but that's where the majority of them are—on that moon."

Durris shrugged. "We can get there, but the dreadnought will gain on us. We'll only have a few hours' time to spare before we'll have to get underway again. Otherwise, she'll catch up to us and pound us with her big guns."

"All right. Set the course and give it to Rumbold. I need to go talk to Lieutenant Morris."

He watched me leave with a strange look on his face. I thought maybe he suspected—not much got past Durris.

When I explained the situation to Morris and described his role in the scheme, he expressed disbelief.

"You've got to be fucking kidding me, Captain!"

"Sadly, I'm not."

He strutted around the room, waving his arms and shouting at the walls.

"We can't do it. The mere suggestion is crazy. You expect us to raid an enemy base—after they watch us fly right into their teeth? When we get down there we're to capture some kind of computer code key and escape? It would take ten thousand commandos, not a handful of marines."

"I'll bolster your ranks with regular spacers," I suggested.

"No, no, no," he said, waving away my offer. "Don't screw me further with baggage. We'll have to move fast. We'll have to get in and get out within ten hours."

Sucking in a deep breath, I told him the rest of it. "We don't have ten hours over the site. We've got three and a half—tops. After that, the dreadnought will be all over us."

"You can't be serious. Captain, I can't land a force, run across a dozen craters, then penetrate a defended base—"

"You won't have to do all that," I told him. "We're taking the pinnace. Lorn will get us down by spoofing their friend-or-foe recognition system. Then we'll steal the key and run for it."

His eyes narrowed. "We?"

"Lorn and I will be coming along. He has to identify and secure the code-key, after all."

He stared at me. "You trust Lorn?"

"Certainly not."

"He'll bolt the first chance he gets. He'll give us away—something like that."

"He may try to go off-script. But he has a strong reason for not doing so: he wants to live and collect trophies."

Morris shook his head. "Trophies? What trophies?"

I told him, and he was even more incredulous than before.

But also, he was somewhat intrigued.

-43-

Reaching the moon was simple enough. We swooped down out of deep space, took up a position in orbit near and began bombarding it. They had defensive batteries, but they were nothing that could stand up to a battle cruiser.

The pinnace was our sole landing transport. We hadn't anticipated needing a flotilla of small invasion craft for this duty. As a result, I was forced to make do with what we had and wait until we'd been ejected directly over the target. The *Defiant* was our only cover fire, but I wasn't complaining.

As time was of the essence, we launched the pinnace the moment we were on the far side of the moon. Then when *Defiant* swung around again, the defenders had their attention diverted. They were too busy trying to survive to concern themselves much with the pinnace that zoomed down and unloaded its tiny complement of marines onto the rocky, airless surface.

We landed in a crater about two kilometers from the main enemy base. It wasn't far, but far enough to avoid their anti-space weaponry due to the sharp curvature of the small moon.

Deploying a landing vehicle, we rolled forward on spinning balloon tires. The wheels were laced with magnets and hooked spikes so they could cling to the surface of a low-gravity planetoid like this one.

A few minutes later we found ourselves at the base of an escarpment.

"Okay," Morris said, "on the far side of this ridge is the enemy base. It's in a crater, and this rise in the land is where the enemy fire might find us. The plan is to scramble over the edge and rush down while they're still firing up at *Defiant*."

Lorn shook his head and laughed. "You're a fool if that's your plan."

"What have you got, pirate?" Morris asked angrily.

"Brains," he said, limping up to the top of the crater and then hunkering down at the lip. He peered over the side, absorbed.

Morris and I scrambled up the shifting rocks and dust to join him.

"See that?" he asked, indicating a hexagonal structure. "That's a defensive bunker. A pillbox. The domes beyond it comprise the base itself."

Morris stared, aghast. "Defensive bunkers? You never mentioned anything of the kind."

Lorn shrugged. "Any commander worthy of the title would have assumed this base would be defended."

"Never mind," I said, cutting off Morris' incoming tirade. "How do we get past their defenses?"

"We jog around the crater to the other side, that's what," Morris suggested.

"A waste of time," Lorn said. "There are six of these pillboxes located in prime positions all around the base."

Heaving a sigh, I gestured for him to continue.

"*Defiant* must continue her bombardment—but she has to come in closer to engage the gun mounts in the bunkers. They can only be taken out with multiple direct hits, or an attack that gets under their shields. If we rush the operators while they're engaged with your ship, they might not even see us coming. We'll take them out and enter the base beyond."

"Ah-ha!" shouted Morris. "Now I know how you really intend to collect your scalps on this rock. You want us to die, then you'll pick up *our* scraps."

Lorn's strange eyes glittered. "You bring up an excellent suggestion," he said, "sadly, some of your people are likely to survive. I'll stick with the original proposal."

He eyed me, and I nodded.

"You'll have your trophies," I said. "Get on with it."

Morris' men were well-disciplined, but clearly they were worried by their assigned task. They gathered up in a line hidden by the ridge surrounding the crater. On Morris' signal, they were to rise up as one and charge once cover-fire commenced.

Being on a tiny world with very little gravity helped. They would take great bounds as they rushed the pillbox. Usually, their powerful leaps would have taken them right off the moon's surface and off into space. It was easy to gain escape velocity and launch yourself into orbit if you weren't careful.

But my marines had some specialized gear. Automated jets of gas puffed upward from their shoulders, pressing the spacers firmly down on the ground.

After calling in the change of plan to *Defiant*, we waited for the ship to descend. It did so rapidly. Durris seemed eager to engage the Stroj base directly. I knew Zye was operating the ship's weapons, and it was a terrifying sight to behold.

A rain of fire began lighting up shielding and rocky armor all over the moon base.

"That's it!" Lorn shouted. "Now, rush in there and take out that bunker!"

He stayed crouched on the lip of the crater and looked at us expectantly. I stepped close to him, waving for Morris to hold on.

"You first, Lorn," I said.

"What? Are you mad? Stroj commanders go *last*, Sparhawk. I'll go when you do."

Nodding, I accepted his challenge. "Follow me then," I said, and rose from hiding.

Heart pounding, I began a skidding, stumbling run downslope and quickly picked up speed. I turned down the pressure on my stabilizer jets and took bigger leaps as I ran. Covering ten meters or more with every bound, I knew I was getting too high and was therefore too visible, but sometimes speed of attack was more important than stealth.

Behind me, the Stroj Captain reluctantly followed. Morris' men surrounded him and ran with him, making sure he didn't try anything treacherous.

The bunker's primary armament, a Gatling gun of tremendous size, pumped thousands of rounds up into the sky. A shower of sparks rang off *Defiant* in the distance, where she paraded and presented an obvious target. From all around the crater, similar streams of fire converged and blazed away at the ship.

Any battle cruiser worth talking about could have pulverized this base, naturally. But we weren't here to destroy the place—at least not until we had the code-keys we needed.

With surprising rapidity, I found my charge coming to an end. The bunker loomed, and seemed much larger close-up.

It wasn't until my final, bounding steps were taken that the troops crewing the Gatling gun noticed what was happening. They slewed their gun down and around in an arc. Blazing fire flashed over my head, silent in the vacuum of space, but still deadly in the extreme.

Ducking, I found I was underneath their arc of fire. The turret hadn't been built to shoot at something so close and low.

My marines, however, weren't so fortunate. The rippling wave of pellets swept across their ragged line. Seven went down, shredded by a line of deadly orange sparks. The dusty surface of the moon behind them was churned into a gray cloud of dust, and their blood boiled away in the blazing heat of the moon's surface. Each fallen figure was shrouded in a dark, bejeweled mist.

Running into the bunker's shields, I pushed doggedly through them. The feeling of cobwebs crawled over my skin, even through my helmet and suit.

Coughing, rasping and choking from exertion, my troops soon joined me. We were all sweating now, our suit air-conditioners unable to keep up with the blistering radiation of the nearby twin suns.

We hugged the base of the rocky foundation under the bunker, relishing the shade and letting ourselves slowly cool down. Morris stepped up to me. I was glad to see he'd survived.

"You stay here, sir," he said. "My marines will take out this gun nest—what's left of it."

He said this last with a dark glance toward Lorn, who seemed not to notice. Like most Stroj I'd met, he wasn't an empathetic creature.

While Morris' men unloaded equipment from their backpacks and began climbing up the sheer wall with spiked gauntlets, I watched Lorn. He seemed excited and pleased.

"Surprised we got this far?" I asked him.

"Not at all. You Earthmen are weak and gullible, but you're competent in the essentials of warfare. How else could you have spawned the likes of us?"

There was an explosion above us. We couldn't hear it, except as a muffled vibration coming up through our boots, but we could see the glare of the blast. A cloud of dust formed around the bunker.

A tumbling figure fell from the upper part of the turret. I ran, ready to grab hold of the fallen marine, who bounced off the hard rock and spun up into the air again. With his stabilizers shut down, I was worried he might drift away into space.

When I pressed his body down into the dark moon dust, he stayed there, motionless. His vitals were in the yellow, but he was alive and stable. I turned to look over my shoulder at the bunker.

The bunker had been destroyed by an explosive charge. Morris and his men were leaping away from it, whooping in my headphones about a job well done.

But when my eyes fell from them to the base of the tower, they froze there.

Lorn had vanished.

-44-

"Morris!" I boomed. "Where's Lorn?"

"I thought you had him, sir."

"So I did," I said after a difficult moment of self-recrimination. "I've got one of yours out of action over here, he's stable."

Morris trotted to my position, and he checked the fallen marine. "Peterson. He'll live. He's damned close to unkillable. You did the right thing, sir, helping him out."

He clapped me on the shoulder. Together, we carried Peterson to the base of the bunker and laid him out flat. Morris watched me closely.

"Is this mission still a go, sir?"

"Yes," I said. "We're going to find that weasel, Lorn, and we're going to get the code-key."

"Have you considered that this code-key might not exist, sir?" Morris asked gently.

"Of course I have. But as far as I can tell, there's no other way out of this system. We can't outrun that dreadnought forever, so if Lorn evades us here, we'll return to the extraction point and nuke this base until it glows. Lorn knows that. He can't escape any more than we can."

"Maybe he doesn't want to escape. Maybe he came down here to lure you into some kind of deathtrap. That's what the Stroj do when there's no way out, you know. They kill themselves and take as many of their enemies with them as they can. Maybe this fellow is just a hair smarter than the average Stroj."

I got up and dusted myself off. Heading around the foot of the pillbox toward the interior of the base, I saw the other guns were still blazing up at *Defiant*.

"Let's go," I said, "before they move against us."

Morris grabbed my shoulder.

"Are you sure, Captain? In my opinion, this is a trap, sir. We should bug out right now. In fact, we should never have come."

Shrugging him off, I started trotting toward the inner domes. "If you want out, Morris, the edge of the crater is behind us."

Cursing, Morris followed me, as did his men. They weren't happy, but they hadn't lost heart yet.

Looking down, I soon saw what I was looking for—a series of widely-spaced footprints in the dust. According to Yamada's analysis, this moon had a constant drifting fall of ash over most of its surface and footprints didn't stay for decades or years. They were usually covered up in a matter of days. For that reason, I knew they were Lorn's.

"This way," I called. "I'm on his trail."

We crossed an open region with our teeth clenched. If any of the pillboxes rotated around and saw us—

"Incoming!" roared Morris.

I was the first to reach the domes. I slammed into an airlock, but realized it was sealed shut. There wasn't time to figure out the code to open it, so I drew my blade.

One of the advantages of a power sword was the lack of need for an atmosphere to operate it. Swords also never ran out of ammo. As long as the tiny fusion-cell that powered it wasn't depleted the weapon would still work.

Drawing it now, I slashed the side of the dome. Behind me, I could tell there were puffs of dust and debris rising, but I didn't have time to glance back. Two strokes opened up an "X" in the side of the dome, and I punched my way inside.

A gush of escaping pressure tried to force me back, but it soon subsided. With one leg inside the building, I saw two Stroj on the ground, writhing and grabbing their throats. The pressure inside their bodies was causing their blood to boil in their veins.

A third Stroj had an emergency mask over his face. He ran toward me with what appeared to be a repair torch.

My blade met his charge, and the low gravity caused his body to settle gently to the floor.

Morris was shoving me aside a moment later. With their breath puffing over their microphones, my last handful of survivors entered the dome behind us.

We gaped at our surroundings. I'd expected equipment, sheer walls and life support systems. Instead, I saw the floor was made of—resin.

That wasn't the strange part, however. What made us all stare in shock were the faces in that resin. They were buried—or purposefully entombed. There were motionless Stroj all around us.

Peering down into the floor below my boots, I saw layers and layers of them, stacked like bricks and locked in poses. Their eyes were shut, but their hands were up as if they'd met their fate willingly, but without pleasure.

"The deck… these are suspended troops. Hundreds of them."

"Yes, Captain," Morris agreed. "The Stroj must be storing them for later. I guess they don't eat as much when used as a building material."

"Such a strange people…"

"Captain," he puffed, "we're never going to get out of here alive. The pillboxes have all spun around. They know we're in here."

Before I could say anything else, the Stroj made a fateful decision. They unleashed their guns on the dome we were standing within.

Throwing ourselves down and crawling toward an open stairway that was built with bodies in resin blocks, I fell over the edge and down into the lower levels of the station. The bricks packed with suspended Stroj all around us began to crack and chip as more impacts were scored everywhere. The thinner dome over the shelter was shredded.

Morris and the rest of the team pressed deeper, seeking any refuge from the hail of gunfire above. It was strange, taking cover among what appeared to be a thousand sleeping Stroj.

The guns tore the building apart above us. As the structure hadn't been all that substantial to begin with, we could now see directly into space.

The planet this moon orbited filled the sky like a glaring red eye. The heat of it could be felt right through my suit, we were so close to the central star. All around us, the resin blocks began to warp and crackle.

"Movement over that way, sir," Morris said.

I ran after him, gulping for a breath. Everything had gone wrong. A clandestine mission had turned into an open fight, then transformed into a struggle to merely stay alive. Our attack had not yet failed—but it might as well have. We had no idea where the code-key was, or if it even existed.

"Stop," I said, grabbing Morris and swinging him around.

"But that could be Lorn, Captain!"

I nodded. "Yes, it probably is. But if so, he's just leading us further into these resin bricks. He'll lead the rest of us to our deaths. I'm going to have to talk to him instead of chasing him."

Morris looked at me like I was crazy, and I couldn't blame him for that. His men took up firing positions at the exits, and I set my helmet to broadcast in the clear.

"Lorn, this is Captain Sparhawk," I said in a voice I hoped conveyed confidence and control. "Answer me please, I have an offer for you."

There was no response. I waited a few seconds before speaking again.

"Lorn, I understand your fear and plight. You've been terrified by our attack. Let me assure you, we don't intend harm when "

"What's this?" demanded Lorn angrily. "*You* are the ones who are terrified! You're surrounded by Stroj and cut off inside our base. Fools—you're dead fools!"

Morris grinned at me, his face sweating visibly inside his helmet. "You got his goat, sir," he said. "He can't have the other Stroj thinking he's some kind of coward."

Nodding, I put up a hand to stop Morris from speaking further.

"Lorn," I said, "glad you can hear me. Listen, I have a proposal: *Defiant* will let you live if you return to us and complete your bargain. If you don't—you're dead. Every Stroj on this rock will be dead as well."

"Nonsense," Lorn said. "I know your cowardly kind. You'll do anything to live."

"Really? Where do you think that instinct for self-sacrifice comes from, my rebel colonist friend? What are you, other than a reflection of some magnified element of my kind? We're the Basics, remember. By definition, we're capable of making any choice that you are."

"Nonsense. You won't blow yourselves up. I know cowards when I see them."

Sucking in a deep breath, I added *Defiant* to my open channel.

"First Officer Durris," I said, "can you hear me?"

"Yes, Captain. We can see the fireworks going on down there, but we can't extract for at least half an hour. We took out two of the pillboxes, in addition to the one you destroyed. But there are still three, and they'd shred the pinnace."

"I'm not calling for a rescue, Durris. I'm giving you an order. If I don't countermand this order over the following twenty minutes, you're to carry it out. Are we clear?"

"Clear, sir."

Morris was staring at me now. His eyes were big, and his mouth was open. I think he, of all of them, suspected where I was going with this—and he didn't like it.

"You're to bombard this base, and this entire moon, with nuclear weaponry. Once everything registers as dead on Yamada's scanners, pull out of orbit and retreat from the dreadnought. At that point, you'll be in command. Are there any questions?"

Durris was quiet for a moment. "Are you sure about this, sir?"

"I am."

"You know that I'll have no choice other than to carry out your orders. Once we go past zero-twenty minutes, I'm going to unleash hell right on top of you."

"I know you will," I said. "That's precisely why I wanted you to be my first officer."

"Orders acknowledged, Captain. The timer is ticking."

"Excellent. In the meantime, you should—"

Someone tapped me on my shoulder at that point. Annoyed, I waved Morris off.

The tapping came again, and I turned in irritation. My eyes widened in surprise.

The man tapping on my shoulder was none other than Captain Lorn.

His spacesuit was dirty, scratched up and scorched. Inside his helmet, his eyes blazed at me with an intense hatred. It warmed my heart to see this.

I smiled in greeting. "Good to see you've rejoined us, Lorn."

"Shove your good cheer up your ass, Sparhawk. Call down that extraction."

"And why should I do that?"

"Because I've got the code-key!"

He lifted a small white-metal object. It was oddly designed with a diamond-shaped tip that reminded me of an arrowhead.

"How do I know it works?" I asked.

Lorn jerked his thumb back toward the passageway through which he'd entered the room. I saw a great deal of movement down there.

"Better call now, Sparhawk," he said.

"Enemy troops incoming, sir," Morris said.

"Hold them."

My last five marines circled our end of the passage. Two knelt, one lay prone, while two stood tall. They fired together, knocking a Stroj attacker off his feet and onto his back. He tried to crawl away, but more fire tore him apart until he stopped.

"They're coming for us," Lorn said. "They're not happy I stole the key."

"Where'd you get it?" I demanded, still unconvinced.

He lifted up something he'd been dragging behind him. I hadn't noticed it in the excitement. Pulling, he lifted up a head and torso by the hair. The lower half of the body had been sheared away by some calamity.

"See this man's chest-plate? He commanded this base. When I heard your terms, I cut him down and brought him—along with the key he had around his neck."

Morris nodded to me. "He's telling the truth about that, sir. I don't know if that key does anything, but he did kill his own man and race up here while you were talking to Durris. We almost cut him down, but he put up his hands and dangled that key—and that corpse."

Glancing from the corpse to the key, then to Lorn's bloody face, I nodded.

"All right. Durris, send down the pinnace to the extraction point."

"Am I to consider your previous order countermanded, sir?"

"No," I said. "Not until I'm standing beside you on the command deck."

"That'll be cutting it pretty close, sir," Morris said.

"Then we'd better get moving."

The marines fired their weapons, knocking down two more Stroj as they charged toward us.

"Lorn," croaked one from the floor on an open channel. "Your treachery will be known. You'll die a thousand times with your pain receptors sewn into different bodies."

Lorn gritted his teeth and looked at me. "Are you still a man of your word, Sparhawk?"

"I am—within reason."

"Then get me off this rock with you. After that—don't countermand your order to your ship. Pulverize this moon."

I nodded slowly. I could see no loss for me in his proposal.

As we exited the rubble down a shallow culvert toward the crater's edge, I noted that Lorn was still dragging the badly damaged corpse of the base commander with him.

"You can drop him now," I said.

"Him? Never! He's my trophy. I counted six bodies melded into his. Some of them are impressive kills. I intend to subsume them. I'll be admired by every female on Earth."

Shrugging, I decided not to tell him he was operating under a misconception concerning women on Earth. Everyone needed a goal to goad them into doing their best work, after all.

-45-

Half an hour later, I stood on *Defiant's* command deck. The moon below us was a cauldron of released energies. Nuclear strikes had obliterated the base where we'd been fighting only minutes before.

"What did you do with Lorn?" Durris asked, looking me over in concern.

"I put him back in the brig. Surprisingly, he's glad to be there now."

"He's requested surgical equipment," Yamada said. "I asked if he wanted medical aid, and he refused it. What should I do, sir?"

I glanced at her. "Give him the equipment."

She turned away, and Morris stepped closer. "He still has that corpse with him, doesn't he?"

I nodded. "Yes. He's got a good bit of work to do, and as the body will decompose in our pressurized ship, he probably wants to get to it right away."

Morris gave a disgusted shudder. "Such an animal. We should space him."

"We have a bargain to keep," I reminded him, "and he might still be useful."

"How so?"

I lifted the key and held it up between us. "Do you know how to use this thing to get an artificial bridge to form?"

"No," he admitted. "But that freak might not know, either. He's been full of shit at every turn."

"Sort of, but not entirely. He made a bargain, and he kept it, despite several attempts to twist out of the deal."

"He hasn't got us home yet. We're still trapped in this system. Everything he promised might be a big pack of lies."

I had no answer for that charge as it was quite possibly true. Although Lorn frequently told the truth, it was invariably woven with as many or more lies. In fact, the true parts were completely optional in his mind. I'd gone out on a limb with him, but only because I hadn't seen any other viable option.

"Durris," I said, calling to my XO. He was now standing at his nav table again. His neck seemed a bit straighter than before.

"Captain?"

"Plot a course to circumnavigate the star. We'll swing around in a wide loop and end up at the artificial breach point again."

"Already plotted, sir," he said. "I had quite a bit of time to come up with contingencies while you were down there on that moon base."

"How long will we have at the breach to figure out the code-key?" I asked.

He shook his head. "No time, at all. The problem is one of relative velocities. If we slow down long enough to board that structure and look around, the enemy will catch up to us."

Frowning, I turned away, then back again.

"How long until we arrive at the breach?"

"Less than a day."

Walking briskly, I moved down several decks to the brig. There, I found Lorn in the midst of a horrifying procedure.

"Ah, there you are!" he said, smiling at me. He lifted the severed head of the moon base commander and shook it at me like a puppet. "This fellow has quite a tale to tell."

"How's that?" I asked. "He's dead."

"Dead? To you, maybe. But his exploits live on in the form of these symbolic emblems of flesh. Look here, you see his lips? Fuller than they should be, aren't they? And his eyes are artificial—that's a dead giveaway."

"How so?"

"Isn't it obvious? They're from the Faustian Chain. Oh, yes—I forget how provincial you Basics are. You don't even know one type of colonist from another."

"We know the Betas and the Stroj well enough."

He chuckled darkly. "I guess you must by now."

I watched him work from a safe distance. Various offensive odors made my nose twitch, but I didn't comment.

"What part of this person do you plan to pilfer?" I asked.

"That's an insulting accusation. I'm not stealing anything. I claimed this kill, fair and square. If a man can't keep hold on his life against an enemy—well, he's not fit to live anyway. But to answer your question—I only need his left ear and one finger."

He showed me the parts, lifting them for my inspection.

"Are these of special significance?"

"They are to me. The finger was mine, once, years ago. I want it back. The ear was part of the original man. He has many trophies grafted on, but I don't want his hand-me-downs. I want my property back, plus part of him. None shall ever say again that I was bested by this loser."

Suddenly, I grasped more of Lorn motivation. If he'd had a previous and personal feud going with the moon base commander, it made more sense that he'd go to such great lengths to acquire parts of him.

"What did you have against the man?" I asked. "I take it he wronged you in some way?"

"Yes, he did. He's the reason I'm a pirate. You see, in order to advance as a commander, we Stroj engage in ritual combat. That doesn't mean a fight to the death, but the victor is permitted a small trophy from the loser. We fought because we both wanted to command this system, to build this breach point and coordinate the invasion of all the local stars."

"So, I take it he won the combat that decided which of you should get that job?"

"Exactly. He won nearly a decade ago, and he took my ring-finger as a trophy. I've always hated him for that."

While he talked, he lifted the severed head and examined it closely. He treated it as if the dead man was able to hear us. With a sudden movement, he slashed away the ear and hurled the rest of the head away. It struck the back wall of the cell, fell to the floor with a horrid squelching sound and rolling to a stop. It left a ghastly stain where it had landed.

Lorn then removed his own ear and replaced it with the dead man's appendage. The process didn't seem to pain him, but it made me uncomfortable.

"There's a problem Lorn," I said. "We may not be able to escape the system."

"A problem? Explain."

"The code-key—can it be used remotely? We're going to have to do a fly-by of the breach point. We can't afford to slow down, or your dreadnought will catch up."

"Ah, now I understand why you're here," he said. "Not to gloat or brag, but to beg for my aid yet again."

"You won't get to enjoy those trophies—no member of your race will ever know you got them, in fact—if you don't help me find a solution."

Lorn didn't answer me right away. He was busy sawing at a finger now. It came off with a bit of work.

"See here?" he said, holding the digit aloft. "The tendons were connected with wires. You can see that, can't you?"

"I suppose."

"That proves this digit was stolen from someone else. From me, in fact. That's why I never replaced that finger. I wanted the original back. Because of you, Sparhawk, I've got it."

"I'm glad you're pleased. Back to our problem—"

"*Your* problem," Lorn corrected me. "I've achieved my aims. I'm now prepared to die with dignity."

Standing up swiftly, I turned to go. I could feel his eyes on my back as I headed for the exit.

"That's it?" he called after me. "You're giving up?"

Pausing, I glanced over my shoulder and shrugged. "The Stroj willingness for self-sacrifice is legendary."

"That's true of course, but—"

"I know that no amount of begging, threatening or cajoling will change your mind. Please feel free to commit suicide. That scalpel should make the task a trivial one. When you're done, we'll space the whole mess out of the cell block and figure our way out of this situation by ourselves."

I took two more steps toward the exit. Lorn jumped to his feet and moved quickly to the bars. He rattled them in a sudden fury.

"Sparhawk!" he roared. "All right, you win! You called my bluff. We'll work on this together."

Just for my own personal enjoyment, I hesitated indecisively at the exit. Finally, I returned to the cell and stared at him.

"I have questions," I said.

"I'll answer them—within reason."

"What were those Stroj bodies encapsulated in resin?"

"What? The invasion force? That's what you want to know about?"

"I said as much."

He shrugged. "Fully thawed, they're grunts. Heavy shock troops. They don't have much brain power, but they strike very hard when armed and directed toward an enemy. Their blood has been drained and edited for long term survival in suspension."

"We saw evidence of thousands of them."

"At least. Probably, I'd place the number in the low millions. A good portion of the crater was packed with them right under the upper layer of crust."

For some reason, this thought pained me. They weren't exactly alive, but they could have been brought back to life. Had I really killed a million enemy troops without realizing it? The thought was disturbing—but these details seemed not to bother Lorn at all.

"And how were these troops to be used?" I asked.

"As I said, they were here to invade neighboring worlds. The artificial bridges were to be created to provide access to neighboring star systems."

"I see. Speaking of the artificial bridges, how do we use the code-key to change the destination of that device?"

He looked at me suspiciously. "I want assurances before I answer that. I want you to swear, right here and now, that if I give you that information you'll release me and allow me to return to my people."

"So you can gloat over slaying your rival?"

"Why else? What better flavor is there in life than the grieving of your enemy's comrades?"

"What else indeed... All right. When we get out of this system, I'll release you with the pinnace to escape."

He moved closer to the bars and grasped them. I noticed that one of his fingers didn't curl with the rest.

"You swear this? By Earth, Star Guard, and your family's House?"

"I do so swear."

He nodded and released a sigh of relief. Then he promptly returned to his work. He was soon engaged in sewing loops of thread into his reattached digit.

"I must say, Sparhawk," he said conversationally, "I'm glad you're a man of your word. I wouldn't be able to deal with you like this if I wasn't confident in your reliability."

"Yes, yes," I said impatiently. "Now, out with it. What do we have to do to get the code-key to work?"

"Why, nothing at all," he said. "You simply fly through the breach. Every ship captain has one. They're distributed on the basis of need. It will detect that key and direct you accordingly."

Blinking in astonishment, I wasn't sure if I should be angry or not.

"I see that I've been played," I said.

"Not so. I procured the key for you, and now I've instructed you upon its proper use. Both these services are invaluable to you and your crew."

He was right, of course, but I still found his trickery galling. He'd managed to bargain from a weak position, gaining his own freedom in the deal.

Sighing heavily, I told myself I should look at the deeper side of things. If this worked, I'd have saved my ship. What difference did it make that I could have done it more easily if I'd known the truth? The fact was that I *hadn't* known the truth. As Lorn had pointed out, he'd done me an invaluable service.

Leaving him to his grisly chores, I left the brig.

Just as the hatch door sealed shut, I thought I heard a sonorous chuckle breaking out behind me.

-46-

Taking the Stroj at his word—because we really didn't have any other choice—we flew toward the web-like structure. The only breach point in the system we could detect existed at the same point we'd arrived at.

"We're just going to fly right into that thing?" Rumbold demanded yet again.

"Yes, exactly," I said. "Slow down steadily, we don't really know what we'll find on the far side."

"We're not going to go back to the same place we came from when we entered this system?" he asked with growing alarm.

I quickly explained to him what Lorn had told me about the artificial bridges. That the gateway would transport us to wherever the code-key had been preprogrammed to send ships.

He chewed that over for a minute, then asked another question. "Will those guns fire on us again?"

"No. Not according to Lorn. But we'll leave our shields up just in case."

"Seems like we're trusting that Stroj more than we should," Rumbold muttered.

"Captain," Zye said, spinning her chair around and joining the conversation. I got the feeling she'd been listening in and trying to stay quiet, but she'd finally lost her cool.

"I must protest again," she said. "You can't trust any Stroj to do something that isn't in its best interest."

"I agree," I said. "But getting this ship destroyed and all aboard her killed won't help Lorn."

"You can't know that," she said. "Not with certainty. The Stroj are a very odd people. They don't think in a fashion that would seem linear and logical to you and I. Death might be exactly what Lorn is seeking now."

I had to admit that she had a point there. The trouble was, I was out of options.

"Are you suggesting we turn and face our pursuer?" I asked. "Do you think we can take on a dreadnought singlehandedly?"

"No... that would be suicide."

"I agree. So, what would you do instead?"

She thought about this for a few seconds. I stared at her, and everyone else serving on the command deck joined me.

"We could deploy the pinnace," she said. "We could send it through the breach with the code-key aboard. I'll pilot the ship if you like. If I don't return by the time *Defiant* circumnavigates the system again, we'll know Lorn set up a trap somehow."

I threw up my arms. "And what would we do if you never return? Or if you do returned and explain this is all a grand trick?"

"Then we'll fight the dreadnought and die well."

Nodding, I understood at last. Zye didn't want her last act to be a futile one. I, on the other hand, was only interested in playing the best odds I could. I'd take any scheme that might save my ship and crew.

"I'd rather take my risks now, with you aboard *Defiant*," I said. "We're flying through the breach in seventeen hours."

Turning, I raised my voice and addressed the rest of the crew. "Get some rest everyone. We don't know what we'll find when we reach the far side."

Taking my own advice, I'd made it halfway back to my cabin before I noticed I was being shadowed. Zye stalked after me like an angry panther, a dozen steps behind.

When I opened my cabin door, I waved her inside. She hesitated, but then accepted the invitation.

"Captain," she said, "I don't wish to make this personal between us, but I have reasons why I don't want you to follow this plan."

My eyebrows raised high. "So... I gather than you *are* making it personal?"

"Yes. It's come to my attention that other women aboard this ship believe our relationship is abusive."

"How so?" I asked.

"You're my direct commander. Therefore, any sexual favors I provide for you aren't entirely consensual on my part."

"I'm taking advantage of you?!" I rolled my eyes.

"That facial gesture is also considered offensive to Earth women," she informed me, pointing at my eyes.

Sighing, I took a seat behind my desk and leaned back in it. I pulled a bottle out of the bottom drawer and poured myself a double.

"Would you like to join me?" I asked her.

Her frown intensified. "There—that's another example of abuse. You've plied me with drink to gain sexual access before."

"Zye," I said, "I know you're upset, but I think our first sexual encounter was your idea, remember?"

"Hmm... that's true," she said quietly after thinking about it for a moment.

"Have you paused to consider that the women who've made these suggestions to you either don't know what they're talking about, or that they may have agendas of their own? Anyway, how does this affect my decision to pass through the breach?"

She looked at me with her arms crossed for a moment. Then, she relaxed.

"I'd like to have a beverage after all," she said at last.

I poured her one, and she sat down. We sipped them together.

"I've come to a decision," she said when she'd finished her drink.

"About what?"

"You may not be aware of this," she said, "but I've been seeking sex with you for a long time."

"You don't say?"

"It's true. That's what troubles me now—because we must end that part of our relationship."

Tilting my head, I looked at her seriously. "That's it? We're through?"

"Yes."

"Because of the opinions of others?"

"Partly. But the biggest problem is that it's causing me more distraction and worry than it's worth."

"I see," I said. Internally, I felt relieved, but I was smart enough not to show it. I tried to look injured but thoughtful.

"Have I hurt your mind?" she asked.

"You mean my feelings?"

"Yes."

"I'll be okay, Zye. I enjoyed it, and I hope you did too."

"Yes, I did," she said.

She poured herself a second glass, threw it down her throat and stood up suddenly.

"What's the hurry?" I asked.

"I have a date with the one called Andrew in engineering. I only have sixteen hours left to live before we hit the breach. Therefore, haste is necessary."

"I see. That's why you don't want me to follow my plan. It was all a matter of timing?"

She nodded.

"Well then, good luck with your date."

She left, and I chuckled bemusedly when she'd gone. I poured one more to "dying well." Privately, I thought that if we lived, Zye was going to have a very interesting sex life due to her pragmatic attitude.

* * *

After everyone had time to eat, sleep and make their peace with the unknown, we reached the artificial breach again.

The bridge entrance grew on our screens, and we soon drew close enough to make out details. This time around it looked like the finger bones of a reaching metal hand.

"The guns, sir," Rumbold said in a hushed voice. "They're tracking us, but they aren't firing. That code-key must be doing something."

Swallowing hard, I gave the order to make the final approach. We flew toward the spidery network of metal and into it. A moment later, we left the system and found ourselves somewhere new.

This time, the boundaries of hyperspace were cramped and grey—suffocating us like a blanket.

"All engines, reverse!" I shouted.

The crew was already in panic-mode, bringing us around and firing every thruster we had to slow us down.

"Yamada, how close is the nearest wall?" I demanded. "Will we make contact with it?"

On the screen, it looked like we were driving right into a fog bank. The surface of it roiled and pulsed.

"A second ago, yes—but now we're green. The variables seem to be dynamic and changing."

I looked at her. "You mean because we're braking hard?"

She shook her head and gave me a look of confusion and wonder. "No sir, the walls are retreating from us. This region of hyperspace is still forming, still unstable. It's... *expanding*, Captain."

Nodding slowly, I thought I understood. The artificial bridge system didn't just allow entry into a breach, it had *created* the breach we were in now.

I looked at the ballooning walls, which were now clearly in retreat, shaking my head in amazement.

"This is impressive technology," I said. "The Stroj are going to be even more dangerous opponents than I'd previously believed."

"I must correct you on that point," said a voice behind me. It was my aunt, the venerable Lady Grantholm.

"Madam," I said, "I didn't know you were coming to the command deck."

"I've lived a very long time," she said. "I've earned the right to watch you extinguish my existence."

"Thanks for that vote of confidence," I said, making a sweeping gesture toward the screens, "but I think your prediction is premature. We're still very much alive and well."

"For now," she said. "We're in a newly hatched slice of hyperspace without a paddle, as they used to say."

Her reference was lost on me, but not her attitude. I turned away to go over what little data we had so far.

We were in a small pocket of hyperspace—the smallest I'd ever even read about. It was expanding however, and it already encompassed a region about an AU in diameter. But the rate of expansion was falling fast and my techs estimated it would stabilize completely within a few minutes.

"So," Lady Grantholm said as she followed me to the nav table. "Where are you taking us this time?"

"To the other side of this breach," I said. "We can't be sure where it leads."

She released a long sigh of exasperation. "Exploration is one thing, William. Wandering around lost in the woods is quite another. I'm hereby ordering you—you would agree we're not under immediate threat, wouldn't you?"

I glanced at her. "Perhaps the pursuing dreadnought will come after us and change things," I said.

She made an exasperated sound. "Until they do, I insist you relinquish command."

At last I nodded. "There's no immediate danger," I admitted.

"Good. At least you're still honest. What I want you to do is take us home *now*. We've seen enough of these worlds and peoples. We've made contact with several colonies, and it's time we reported home."

I nodded thoughtfully. I assumed that meeting a Stroj dreadnought had taken some of the spirit of adventure out of my aunt.

Unfortunately, I had no idea how to get us home right now. I was simply glad not to be running in circles away from a killer enemy warship.

But I said none of this. I didn't lie to her, of course, I simply gave her a tight smile.

"As soon as we can get our bearings, Ambassador, we'll head home."

"Excellent," she said, and she left the deck.

Rumbold eyed me strangely. "Captain," he whispered loudly, "we have no damned idea where we are."

"Yes, I know. But when we figure it out we'll head home—as per the Ambassador's instructions."

He chuckled and went back to his duties.

A powder-monkey came up to the deck after an hour of cruising, exploring the bridge and dropping probes. We'd found the region to be quite unstable. The probes had distributed themselves in a broad series of undulating curves, despite the fact we'd been flying in a straight line from our point of view.

"What is it?" I asked the girl who'd come to speak to me.

"That thing in the brig—Captain Lorn—he demands to talk to you. The guards ignored him at first, but he's become obnoxious."

"He always was obnoxious," I pointed out. After making sure the command center was running smoothly I went down to talk to Lorn.

"About damned time you showed up!" he roared from inside his cell.

His appearance, always disturbing, was now hideous. He'd grafted on extra digits on each hand, among other things. The digits were curled and useless-looking.

He must have seen me eying them, because he lifted them with a grin.

"You're admiring my new fingers, aren't you?" he asked proudly. "Don't bother to deny it! I couldn't resist just a few more. And don't worry, they'll start working soon. Right now, they're dead flesh. But they'll revive with enough resprayings of nu-skin and nanite paste."

"I'm sure they will. What do you want?"

"I want you to keep to your bargain."

"How so?"

"Let me out of this ship! Give me the pinnace and dump me out—right here."

This demand took me by surprise. "Right in the middle of hyperspace? How will you get out of here? A pinnace can't breach out of this new pocket of space."

"It won't have to. You've opened a new path. Other Stroj ships will follow in time."

"You mean the dreadnought?"

"Possibly."

I considered. Every second I spent doing this seemed to irritate Lorn. He shuffled his feet, then glared, then shook the bars with his hands. His fingers clenched into fists, both the living and the numb, dead ones.

"Sparhawk, you're reneging, aren't you?" he demanded after a time.

"No," I said, "but I am trying to figure out why you don't want to wait until we exit this universe."

"What? Are you trying to say I'm playing a trick? A helpless man in a cell? No… that's not it, is it? What you're up to is far more sinister."

"Calculating the motives of a proven enemy is not sinister."

"Nonsense. You're trying to weasel out of our agreement. I got you out of that star system. I wanted my freedom in return. What do you call it when one man keeps his end of a bargain and the other immediately begins to hedge when it comes time to pay up?"

"I'm not—"

"Dishonesty, that's what it is! Skullduggery. Bait-and-switch. Go ahead, confess your vile intentions. I've been tricked and played for a fool, haven't I?"

Heaving a sigh, I decided he was right. There was no going back on the deal now. If I couldn't keep a simple agreement with a Stroj—the first one ever made, to my knowledge between our two peoples—how could I expect them to ever trust us?

"All right," I said. "Take the pinnace. Guards, take him there. Keep him chained. Free him remotely, only when he's been ejected from the ship and our shields are back up."

I turned away from Lorn and left. I hoped never to have to meet up with him again.

Less than an hour later, the pinnace puffed out into space. Shortly thereafter, the engines sparked, and it pulled away from us. It soon drifted in our wake, lurking near one of our probes.

"That creature is a monster," Rumbold said when I returned to the command deck. "A ghoul without a soul."

"True enough," I agreed, "but I'm not. We struck a bargain, and he kept up his part of it."

"Maybe, or maybe we'll come out of this breach right into a supernova."

"It could be, but why would the base commander of a Stroj outpost possess a code-key that leads to a deathtrap?"

"I don't know," he admitted. "But I still smell a rat, sir."

"That's rotting flesh," I commented.

Rumbold shuddered and turned back to his duties.

We sailed on at a gentle pace for three more hours before anything happened. I was about to retire when a klaxon sounded.

Everyone turned toward Yamada, as the sensor-arrays had triggered the alarm.

"Do we have an exit point calculated?" I asked hopefully.

She shook her head slowly, her face bathed in blue light as she studied her instruments.

"I'm afraid not, sir. The computer is warning us that we're being pursued."

She reached for the screen activation, and she piped her data to the forward screens. I saw a speck, and red lettering appeared beside it, identifying the contact.

"Are you sure about this?"

"Yes, Captain. The enemy dreadnought has followed us somehow. It's pretty far back still, but it never had to brake like we did when we first entered and discovered the tightness of this newly formed bridge. It's moving at full velocity."

"Helm," I said, "increase power. Give us two Gs of acceleration."

Almost immediately, I was staggered. My weight had dramatically increased. With great effort, I made it back to Yamada and sat heavily beside her, studying her raw data.

"Can we make it out of here before the dreadnought catches up?" I asked.

"Only if we find the exit very soon."

Slowly, I turned my head back toward the forward screen. I nodded thoughtfully. This was why Lorn was so adamant about getting off my ship out into hyperspace. He hadn't wanted to be around when his friends caught up to *Defiant*.

-47-

Studying the situation behind us with interest, I watched the dreadnought approach. It was overtaking us.

Periodically, I swung the optics to locate and study the pinnace I'd given Lorn. His situation was also of interest. He wasn't heading for the dreadnought—in fact, he appeared to be running away from it. He was already lingering near the billowing walls of this hyperspace pocket, staying as far from us and the dreadnought as possible.

Yamada took note of what I was doing.

"That bastard looks like a fly on a curtain, doesn't he?" she asked. "The dreadnought is pinging him in the clear. They know he's there."

"Any hint that they may pause to swat our pesky fly?" I asked.

"Negative, unfortunately. Why do you think he's running from them, sir?"

"I recall that the base commander told Lorn his treachery would be broadcast far and wide. I can only assume the crew of this warship knows that patchwork traitor gave us a code-key to escape the system."

"I see…" she said. "In that case, they'll get him."

"Unfortunately, it appears their priority is to run us down and swat us first."

She nodded glumly and returned to her duties.

Moving to the nav table alongside Durris, I gave him a nod in greeting. He returned the gesture, but winced when he did so.

"Sir, we're going to be overtaken. We'll have to turn and fight."

"We have options, Durris."

He looked at the nav table with me, baffled. At last he shook his head. "All I can think of is to slow them down with missiles and mines, but we expended every warhead we had destroying the moon base. We don't even have a pinnace anymore."

I thought he might have let a twinge of accusation enter his voice at that point, but I chose not to respond to it.

Reaching over the table, I tapped time controls and spun the scene backward. Once it showed the walls of our fledgling wormhole at the first moment we entered, I used two hands to magnify the zone ahead of us.

"When we first entered hyperspace, this is what the region looked like," I said. "Space narrowed at the far end of the hyperspace bridge. It's since expanded outward, but the far end is still identifiable."

I circled this region, which in the old vid files resembled a blunt tapered point in the distance.

"The breach must be here," I said. "It's the only thing that makes sense."

Durris stared at the table, dumbfounded. "Aim for the blurry spot? Have you got any evidence to back up this theory?" he demanded.

"Only logic—and a careful analysis of our previous passage through an artificial bridge. Let's review those files."

After working with the table for a time, Durris displayed the first artificial breach we'd discovered. The pattern was again clear. There was a large region off to one end of the universe that was elongated. As time progressed in flickering motion on the displayed scene, the hyperspace expanded and billowed into a new configuration.

"I'll be damned," Durris said. "When the new bridge is formed, you really can tell where the way out must be. It's a large area—but much smaller than our previous guesses have been."

"Exactly. I propose that we increase our speed, locking down in our crash seats and pushing our luck. We'll slam into the far end of this tiny existence—or shoot right through the breach and back into normal space."

He stared at me thoughtfully. "We've got no chance to take out this monster on our trail, sir?"

"She displaces more mass than we do by two to one. Logically, she'll out range us with the main cannons by at least fifty percent. That means we'll have to absorb six to ten volleys before we can return one of our own."

He looked over my equations grimly. "Battle in space is even more susceptible to mathematical realities than combat on a planetary surface. We can't even hide behind a tree and jump out in ambush. I have to agree with your assessment, sir."

"I'm glad you see it my way. Begin implementing our escape plan."

He left the table and began making the rounds to the other stations. The helm, sensors, life support and crew safety officers were all informed. Alarmed, they took up battle stations and sounded alarms all over the ship. We were about to take a drastic risk.

Soon, the engines were thrumming deeply, the pitch rose steadily until it vibrated the teeth in my head.

"Ready, sir," Durris said, casting me a reluctant glance.

I gave the order, and we were all pressed back into our seats even more firmly than before. The effect was a painful one, and it made the skin pull away from my skeleton as if it were elastic.

"Primary engine chamber overheating," Zye said calmly. "Secondary chamber coming online."

"Maintain course and speed," I said, determined to ride it out.

Watching through blurred eyes, I saw the computer update our positions steadily. The increased speed was now projected to cause us to reach the exit point before the enemy dreadnought could catch us—provided that the exit was where I hoped it was. Where it *had* to be.

The following hours were both painful and stressful. We watched with bleary eyes as the end of the line approached. Only with the greatest effort could we rise to drag our bodies around the deck, exhausting ourselves quickly.

Few of us even spoke as the probable breach point loomed at last. We weren't exultant, or relieved to know the ordeal would soon be over one way or another. We were too bone-weary for that. We just wanted the ride to end.

When at last we approached the proposed breach-point, I thought I could see it. They had a certain shimmer, an amorphous outline when you knew what to look for. But I couldn't really be sure I was witnessing this with a clear mind.

"Captain," I heard a faint, weary voice call to me. "Captain…"

"Rumbold? What is it?"

"Permission to nudge our course, sir."

"Why?"

He stirred in his chair, but his head didn't turn to face me. Perhaps he couldn't manage it.

"The coordinates are off… I can see it. I can *feel* it."

I stared at the forward screen. With an effort of will, I rotated my chair and saw that Yamada had slumped over her boards. She was out, either sleeping from exhaustion or unconscious due to the force being exerted on her body.

Our suits were built to inflate at the extremities, exerting pressure at the feet and stiffening over other vulnerable spots to prevent blood from pooling and soft tissue from tearing. Although helping to prevent death, there were still many unpleasant side-effects when we were under long term G-forces.

"Permission to ease down," I said. "We've got a window of six minutes."

Rumbold needed no more encouragement than that. He immediately eased off the thrust and everyone aboard sighed in relief. Within ninety seconds, Yamada was breathing easily again, and I saw her escorted off the deck to the medical bay.

Zye was the only one on the deck who seemed displeased with my decision. While I stood unsteadily over Rumbold, going over our projections, she stood behind me ominously.

"Zye, not now," I said without looking over my shoulder.

"The Stroj are not to be taken lightly, Captain," she said. "We should either run as hard as we can, or turn and fight to the death right now. There can be no middle ground with them."

"Return to your post, Lieutenant."

She did so, her usually stoic face betraying her disquiet.

"Now, Rumbold—can you breathe, man?"

"Yes, Captain."

"Can you tell me what you're talking about?"

"No time, Captain. Either trust me, or overrule me. Decide now."

Our eyes met. Rumbold and I had been serving together for a long time. There was a certain something I respected about this veteran spacer. He'd survived where hundreds of younger men had perished. Often, people took him for a fool. Some said I had a soft spot for a man in his declining years.

But I felt differently. "The helm is yours, helmsman. Don't drive us into the rocks."

He gave me a flickering smile. Reaching down, he took out a silver flask I didn't know he had on him. He downed some kind of rotgut narcodrink that released a powerful vapor.

Putting his hands on the controls, he made a series of fine adjustments. He didn't type in numbers, but rather he actually nudged the touch controls. I felt somewhat alarmed—but I'd given him permission and I didn't want to reverse myself now.

At last, he sat back with a heavy sigh of satisfaction.

"Well," he said, "if we die now at least we'll know a man's hand was on the tiller to the last."

"Yes, well thank you, helmsman…" I took my seat again, and I tried to find comfort in his words. Somehow, I failed to do so.

I'd passed through several breaches over the preceding months, but this passage was the worst of them. Looking back, I realized that I'd never know whether Rumbold's final adjustments saved us or nearly doomed us. There was simply no way to tell the truth.

We'd flown through the knife-edge, the rim of a breach. Each one was like a bull's-eye in space, a relatively tiny hole in the vast fabric of the universe that was weaker than the rest. It was a pore between one state of existence and the next that a gnat-sized object like our ship could wriggle through.

The ship shivered and groaned, as if part of her had encountered an infinitesimal resistance to her passage. At these speeds any unevenly distributed force could easily be fatal—but we survived.

"By God," Rumbold breathed, "we just about shaved our tails off that time!"

"Status, Yamada?" I asked.

She didn't respond right away. Her face was glued to her scopes.

Frowning, I turned toward Durris. "First Officer—where are we?"

He turned slowly, giving me an odd look. He shook his head.

"I don't understand it, sir," he said.

"You don't understand what?" I demanded, moving to join him next to the nav table.

"Look for yourself."

I did, and the truth dawned on me slowly. We were in a system with eight planets quietly circling a single yellow-white class G star with a steady output. There was a significant Kuiper Belt, a swirling field of frozen debris beyond the eighth planet…

"This looks like the Solar System," I said, staring.

"It *is* the Solar System," he said simply.

Yamada turned away from her instruments at last. "It's no mistake, Captain. We're in home space."

-48-

The revelations of the past few minutes left us briefly euphoric—but the sensation quickly changed to one of cold fear.

"This means the enemy has been preparing to strike," I said. "That ship behind us—the masses of suspended troops on that moon…"

Durris nodded slowly. "It's the only possible conclusion, sir," he said. "The Stroj have been preparing to invade. That huge ship was going to transport an invasion force. One that would surprise Earth by coming through an artificial breach and striking at our heart."

"At least we destroyed their troops," I said. "That must have put a kink their plans."

Rumbold cleared his throat loudly. He often did that, but this time I sensed he had a different intent.

"What's on your mind, Helmsman?" I asked.

"Well sir, if you don't mind my speaking out of turn among the command line officers…"

"Not at all. Tell me what you've thought of."

He licked his cracked lips and his eyes rolled from side to side. "That ship sir—she's got no more reason to wait."

"What do you mean?"

"She'll follow us. She'll attack Earth right now."

Thinking it over, I had to nod in agreement. "You may be right. Yamada, are you watching the breach behind us?"

"Like a hawk, Captain."

"Good. How long until the enemy comes through—assuming she hasn't changed course or velocity?"

"She'll hit the breach within twenty minutes—thirty if the pilot is cautious about an ambush."

I shook my head. "I doubt her captain is thinking about caution now. Their cover is blown. They've lost their ground forces and the element of surprise—unless they strike right now, that is. Yamada, hail Central Command. I must talk to Star Guard."

We were pretty far out, just past Neptune. That meant any signal we sent would take over four hours to reach Earth.

While Yamada made the arrangements for a long-distance beam to Earth, I considered what my report should say. We'd hardly accomplished our primary mission. We'd established no trade routes and forged zero treaties.

We had, however, made numerous discoveries. We'd mapped out our local bridges and discovered a dangerous enemy force on our doorstep. We'd even discovered some new technologies with alarming ramifications.

But, despite all our accomplishments, we were quite possibly bringing doom home to our planet. The dreadnought would not be the last of her kind, even if she could be stopped today. We'd have to build a war fleet of unprecedented power to meet this implacable enemy.

Sighing quietly, I began recording the message I must send to Central. While I spoke, the rest of the crew stayed quiet. They were white-faced, and they spoke only in whispers if at all.

At last, after I'd hammered out all the details in a succinct fashion, my finger hovered over the transmit button.

That's when the rear hatch of the command deck opened. An irate figure stood there. She was hunched-over, and framed by the dim lit passage behind her.

"Lady Grantholm," I said. "How good of you to join us. Have you heard? We've returned to our home—"

"I know where we are, Sparhawk!" she said in a rising tone of voice. "Why didn't you alert me immediately?"

"I'm merely reporting to CENTCOM, as any captain must upon returning home."

She hobbled forward quickly, but painfully. "Don't transmit anything!" she said.

"Why not?"

"Because, I must approve it first," she said. "I had to nearly kill myself to get out of my cocoon and down here in time."

I noticed then there were wisps of lavender foam in her hair and clinging to her clothing. The smart clothes writhed over her body, as if they'd been very hastily applied.

"Approve it? This is my report to make. My ship, my report. That's the way we do things in Star Guard."

She slapped at my hand, and I almost stabbed my finger down on the transmit button. I thought I could easily pretend to have made a mistake. She wouldn't believe it, of course, but the deed would be done.

Reluctantly, I withdrew my hand.

Hunching over the boards, she brought up the recording and listened to my simple, truthful statements closely. During this process she clucked her tongue, gasped infrequently, and in the end tapped the delete key.

"What are you doing?" I demanded.

"I'm going to make the report. Have the brains to sit there and stay quiet!"

She began to speak, and I had to admit, I was impressed. The import of her words was more or less the same, but they were much less plainly delivered.

She started off by listing our accomplishments in detail. She spent the majority of the next ten minutes ticking off discoveries, inserting still images and vids. The message became an audio-visual feast as she melded it all into a smooth presentation.

I realized her report would play much better on the news nets. There was no question about that.

Finally, as she reached the ending, she mentioned the dreadnought that pursued us in deadly earnest. It was as if this fact were of merely passing interest. A footnote in an otherwise glowing story of accomplishment.

Then, she did something more drastic. She reached up and edited the list of receiving entities at the top of the message. She also removed the encryption option.

"What are you doing?" I demanded. "Sending this in the clear? That's a violation of military protocol—"

"So what if it is?" she demanded, slapping away my hand again, as I reached to change back her alterations. "Sparhawk, who's going to hear anything out here anyway?"

"There may be enemies lying in wait in the system. Enemies that don't yet realize we've discovered their invasion plans."

"So what if there are?" she asked. "The second that big battlewagon sails through the breach after us, it will activate these bogeys anyway—if they exist."

I had to admit she was probably right about that. But it did bother me to breach protocol in such a basic manner.

"It's not just CENTCOM that will hear this," I said. "The whole planet will. The news organizations—everyone."

She jabbed a finger at me and nodded. "Exactly. That's why I'm doing it this way. I'm saving Earth."

Before I could stop her, that same finger darted down and touched the transmit button. The message was gone. There was no way to get it back, no way to retrieve it now. At the speed of light, it was heading toward every receiver on Earth, or in space, that might be listening.

Leaning back, I attempted to relax. "Let me see if I understand your reasoning," I said. "Instead of a report to CENTCOM, you just made a deliberate leak of data to the entire world. The news people aren't stupid. They'll see through your carefully couched wording. They'll report that doom stalks the skies."

"Exactly," she said. "And then a low-level public panic will begin. There's nothing that will get a planet's military moving faster than a public fervor. The politicians—including your father—will be forced to act decisively. They'll have Earth barricaded before we get home."

"All right," I said, "I still don't like breaching protocol… but this may have been for an excellent cause."

She patted me on the arm as she retreated.

"You're learning, nephew," she said. "You're definitely learning."

No sooner had she left than the enemy ship appeared at the breach. Everyone on the command deck fell silent when they saw this engine of destruction.

We'd never seen her so close. She gleamed, having a surface of unpainted metal. There were no adornments, no identifying insignia. Unlike the Stroj themselves, their vessels were very utilitarian. They only decorated their own bodies, not their warships.

The enemy engine was blazing. They hadn't stopped accelerating at all. The only answer to this was they must have known exactly where the breach was. They'd had it all mapped out, all pre-planned.

"All ahead full plus fifty percent," I said. "Engage in one hundred seconds. We'll give the crew a heads-up first."

In truth, I was thinking of my aunt. She'd made the right call, I realized now. It was better to warn all of Earth, not just the military. Acknowledging her wisdom had made me reluctant to crush her body with excessive G-forces—at least, not without a warning.

Klaxons sounded and recorded messages played. All over the ship, the crew groaned aloud then scrambled for a berth and strapped themselves in.

-49-

The following hours were as grueling as any I'd spent on this voyage. We were outdistancing the enemy ship—but only barely.

"Captain," Zye said, rousing me from a fitful slumber in the command chair.

I came awake gasping for breath. The weight on my chest—it was too much. Many of the crew were delirious. They had forced-air breathing systems and oxygen monitors that puffed extra life-giving gasses when they sensed the need—but it was still too much to be borne.

"I'm awake," I said, shaking myself painfully.

Lying in any chair for long hours always gave me aches and pains in my limbs, but when under heavy acceleration it was infinitely worse.

Zye shadowed me, and looked me over with a critical eye.

"My leg's gone numb," I told her. "Help me up."

She lifted me and set me on my feet. I took a deep breath and checked my monitors. They were mostly green—but a few were dipping into the yellow.

"We must eat, and we must rest."

"It's not time yet," Zye said, looking at me in concern. "The schedule calls for four full hours of—"

"Damn the schedule. Ease off the throttle."

Rumbold was nearly comatose. Zye gently removed his hand from the boards and touched the release on the throttle. The engines groaned with a sound like that of dying fans.

Feeling a great relief, I swung my arms and stamped my feet until I could walk straight again.

"How far is the dreadnought behind us?"

"About twenty million kilometers," she said.

It sounded like a lot, but I knew it wasn't. A few hours at these speeds would close the distance.

The enemy dreadnought reminded me of a relentless shark. It had little in the way of cunning but was seemingly unstoppable. As we rested, it pressed ahead. Stroj were built to take more gravity than Basics were, that was clear. Either that, or they didn't feel the pain.

"Any response from Star Guard yet?" I asked Yamada, who was awake and rubbing her neck.

"I've got a terrible cramp," she said.

"We all do. Check your boards."

"Sorry Captain… no response yet. It won't get here for about thirty more minutes, and that's assuming they responded immediately upon receiving our transmission."

I chuckled at that. "Be assured, they'll respond fast. We'll probably hear from a great many interested parties. Have you been sending steady updates on the enemy ship?"

"Yes, Captain. We've forwarded every bit of intel on the dreadnought we have. It isn't much, as we haven't yet faced her in open battle."

To my mind, that moment would probably be our last in this universe, but I kept those thoughts to myself.

Half an hour later, the responses to our initial report began coming in. At first, we got a simple automated acknowledgement from CENTCOM. It was from Admiral Halsey himself.

"Captain Sparhawk!" the recording said, "I've just been informed you've returned to Sol. I'll check on the rest of your report just as soon as I'm able. Congratulations on what I'm sure has been a successful voyage."

The canned response was almost amusing. I knew he must have recorded it months ago, ready to transmit the moment we reported our return into home space.

It wasn't long after that, however, that the tone changed. My next transmission surprised me: it was from my father.

Rather than coming through regular channels, it buzzed its way into my head via my implant. I decided to take it privately, since it had been transmitted with that intent.

"William," my father said, looking as if he'd been dragged from bed and hastily placed in front of a vid pickup. "I've heard that you're on your way back to Earth. There's some confusion about your status. The Star Guard people are buzzing about it. I just wanted to warn you. Rest assured that our House is behind you. Sparhawk out."

His message didn't surprise me. My father often got official communiques even before I did despite the fact he wasn't always on the list to receive them. Members of the permanent ruling class of Earth had privileges.

The next message was from Halsey again. He looked different this time. His service cap was gone, as was his dress-uniform. Instead of smiles, he regarded me with a glum expression.

"Sparhawk? What's this about you bringing home an enemy warship?" he demanded. "I can't believe you're responsible for such a gross lack of judgment. Maybe the joint chiefs were wrong about you... 'the best,' they said. 'Wise beyond his years,' they said. Now, it looks like you've embarrassed us all."

That was it. Short, to the point, and irritating. I turned to Yamada.

"He's clearly not yet had time to view the files depicting the dreadnought's displacement or our firepower estimates."

"It's the middle of the night, and it's a weekend," she said. "They're going to freak out when they realize what we've brought home."

"Yes... as they should."

Cautiously, I waited for five more minutes.

Long distance communications in space were problematic. They were more like holo-mail correspondences than conversations, as the back-forth messages couldn't be responded to quickly.

As each new message came in, the picture grew more grim. Star Guard was beginning to panic.

"Official request from Central Command," said the next message. I directed Yamada to put it on the primary screen.

The face of a middle-aged rear admiral filled the forward bulkhead. She was very serious in her demeanor, and her uniform was perfectly crisp despite the late hour on Earth.

"Captain Sparhawk," she said severely. "You're hereby ordered *not* to lead that enemy vessel to Earth. Get it off-track any way you can."

Shrugging, I thought the idea wasn't a bad one. I doubted if I could pull it off, however.

"Helm?" I asked.

Rumbold snorted awake. "Ready!"

"Shift course toward our base on Ceres. Let's see if they follow us."

Rumbold laid in the course and we felt ourselves gently slewing to starboard for several long minutes.

"Captain," Yamada said. "The Stroj ship is still heading for Earth. They've made no effort to alter their angle of flight."

Nodding, I sipped a cup of hot caf and weighed my options. Really, there weren't many.

"Come about," I said. "Rumbold, turn back toward Earth. Let's see what a parallel course does to impress them."

"Nothing, sir," Durris said. "They're not reacting at all."

About a minute later Durris walked up and approached my command chair. "Many might take you as disobeying a direct order from CENTCOM, William," he said quietly.

"You can relieve me if you think you have the grounds," I said.

He shook his head and crossed his arms. "I only want to hear a justification."

"I was ordered to distract them from their course. My first effort failed. Turning back to pace them isn't disobedience. Quite the contrary. I'm considering other options."

We studied the boards in silence for a few minutes. At last, he sucked in a breath and nodded.

"You're right. They're ignoring us. What else can we do?"

"I'm open to suggestions," I said, "but I really know of only one other maneuver."

"Which is?"

"To turn and fight."

"That's suicide."

"Probably," I admitted. "That's why I haven't given the order yet."

At that point some ten minutes had passed since we'd made our course corrections and been ignored by the Stroj ship. The communications light blinked again.

"Put the transmission on-screen," I said.

It was Admiral Halsey again. He was now standing in Star Guard's War Room. He was dressed but bedraggled. The female rear admiral was nowhere to be seen.

"Sparhawk?" Halsey boomed. "I want you to ignore that last order transmitted by our idiot standby crew. You're to stay between Earth and that monster at all costs. And most importantly, *do not* engage with them. Not yet. We're gathering the support you're going to need—if we're going to pull this off, we'll need time to do it."

Relieved, I sat back in my chair. Durris approached again, shaking his head.

"Halsey figured out we're the biggest line of defense between Earth and this monster ship. He doesn't want us wandering off. You knew they'd see the light, didn't you?"

"I certainly hoped that they would."

He studied the data. "We've got nearly a day's flight to Earth. I'll warn you if anything changes."

"Are you suggesting I should retire, XO?"

"I am indeed, sir. We need your fine mind operating at peak capacity as we approach Earth. At that point, there won't be any second chances."

Taking his advice, I heaved myself up and headed for the showers. Even before I got there, I felt the ship slow down. We were nearly weightless. The helmsman had orders to match the enemy course and speed. Clearly, they were slowing down to meet Earth in her locked circular orbit around Sol.

The thought was chilling in a way. The dreadnought was implacable, methodical, and deadly. Those aboard her were going to park in orbit above Earth, doubtlessly intending to take their time while delivering destruction onto our cities.

In the meantime, *Defiant* was to be ignored. Probably, they thought of us as negligible. Like a small, barking dog that couldn't stop a prowler, we could only irritate them.

Crashing onto my bunk, I passed out into what seemed to me a dreamless sleep. It was the sleep of the dead. Nothing exhausted a man more than doubling his weight for hours on end.

When I awakened, I bathed and ate. Returning to the command deck refreshed, I found Yamada, Durris and Rumbold were gone. They'd been replaced by a skeleton crew of understudies.

Only Zye remained at her post. I approached her and touched her shoulder.

She looked up at me questioningly.

"Zye, you should take a break. Go take a shower or something. I need you functioning at your best when this battle begins."

"Captain," she said, "I've been studying the enemy vessel."

"Yes, we all have."

"Sir, I think there's something odd about it."

I let her show me what she was talking about. The data was confusing.

"The ship does seem to be... larger," I said, frowning. "But that's not possible—is it?"

"I don't think so."

Moving to Yamada's screen, I ran my hands over it and worked the controls. There was the monster ship, displacing an estimated tonnage that was mind-boggling. What was really disturbing, however, was the fact that the estimate was fully twenty percent higher than it had been when we'd first discovered the ship.

"Could they have some kind of light-bending technology?" I asked Zye.

She shrugged. "I'm not aware of such a thing—other than their ability to cloak their vessels."

"Get Yamada up here on the double."

A few minutes later, while we were still puzzling over the sensor data, she showed up with damp hair and slightly out of breath.

"Lieutenant," I said, "what do you make of these sensor discrepancies?"

She sat down, blinking, and went over the data we'd compiled. She was baffled at first, but soon began working numbers. In the meantime, I summoned my key crewmembers back to their stations. I had a feeling we might need them.

"Sir, the ship seems to be getting bigger the farther away it is from us. That's very strange."

"Obviously, it's some kind of trick," Zye complained. "The Stroj are always full of tricks."

"Yes," I said, "but it's up to us to figure out exactly how we're being fooled. Is it possible this ship we've been running from, this monster of the skies, is much smaller than it appears?"

Yamada shrugged. "I suppose. Maybe it's like their stealth tech. Think about it: a small ship wants to go unnoticed. A larger ship, however, might want to look bigger and more dangerous than she is."

Snorting and shaking my head, I was almost convinced. "Could we be running from a phantom?"

"It's possible," Yamada said, frowning. "But there's another possibility, sir. She could be looking bigger because she's closer to us than she appears to be."

I stared at her. "Explain."

"Well, what if she's projecting herself in a different location. The technology to do so would be somewhat simpler than total stealth. She could—"

Snapping my fingers, I walked over to Durris. "Plot her course."

"That's this yellow line here, sir," he said. "Running right by our ship."

"Yamada," I said, "swing your sensor array around and focus on that yellow line. Look for tritium trails."

She stared at me, then wordlessly got to work. For a tense ninety seconds, no one spoke. At last, she made a choking cry.

"She's alongside us, sir!" she shouted. "She's pacing us, and projecting herself as being far behind."

"The slowing of her engines..." I said thoughtfully. "It was a trick. We matched her, when really she's been roaring ahead to catch us."

Turning toward Zye, I gave her the only orders I could think of.

"Raise shields, Zye," I said.

"Captain," Durris protested. "They'll know we see them."

"Yes, but if we don't they could ambush us at any moment. Raise shields!"

Zye's hand reached up to her boards, and she touched them. The ship's defensive systems came alive in response.

-50-

The Stroj dreadnought was right on top of us. My first thought, other than initial shock, was that I should have foreseen the possibility. The enemy had demonstrated the ability to cloak their ships. If they were capable of that illusion, why not others?

"In short," Yamada said, "they're projecting their location, using a sensor-fooling system of some kind to appear to be far away when they're really quite close."

"That's why they appeared to be too large," Durris added. "Their projection is displaced, but since it's actually closer, the image is larger."

"The increased size is a flaw in their system," I said. "A give-away like the tritium trails. Let's hope they don't get any better at fooling us than they already are."

"Captain!" Yamada interjected. "The dreadnought is opening her gun ports and shifting course."

"New course and heading?"

"I—I'm not sure, sir. I don't know where they really are."

"First Officer," I said quickly. "Assume they're heading directly toward us. Use the tritium trail and the angle of flight to triangulate. We should be able to pinpoint their actual position."

"On it, Captain," he said, racing back to his nav tables.

Zye looked at me pointedly. "We should run… or fight. Your orders, sir?"

I studied the monstrous ship on the screens. She seemed even more threatening when I wasn't sure exactly where she was.

"They can't be in range," I said, "or they would have fired immediately. Wherever they are, we don't have much time. Angle away from the approaching vessel, Rumbold."

He looked startled and uncertain. "What heading sir? I don't know where they really are."

"Assume they're in the general direction of their illusion. Tack away at a sharp angle. Do so now."

He put his hands on the controls, glancing at Durris hopefully. As he was still working on the nav table, it was clear to Rumbold he wasn't getting any help from there.

Going by feel, he gave us a thirty-degree shift and we were pressed against our straps as thrust was applied.

"Enemy reflection is shifting course with us," Yamada said. "At least, it looks like they are. Their sensor image appears to be flying at nothing, but they have to be reacting to us."

"Durris?" I called. "I need a solution, Commander."

"On it, sir..." he said, but it was a full harrowing minute before he came back triumphant.

"I think I have it," he told me. "That last course change provided another point of reference. I've got them pinpointed."

"Range?"

He locked eyes with me. "About eight hundred thousand kilometers."

"So close? But they're not firing."

"The Stroj ships might not have extremely long-range weapons, sir. We've yet to see a ship of theirs that does."

"Alternately," Zye said suddenly, "like the smaller Stroj ships when cloaked, this dreadnought's displacement system might take too much power for them to fire while it's on. That would indicate they're getting close enough for a killing shot before they turn the effect off."

I nodded slowly. "That has to be it. They must realize we know they're displaced. But they're gambling that we don't have them pinpointed. Their best bet, in that case, is to get in close and blast us at point-blank range at a moment of their choosing."

Turning to Durris and Zye, I made a fateful decision. "I know we don't have a target-lock. But the target is fairly large, and we know where they are down to decimal places. We're going to lay down a pattern of fire hoping for luck."

Durris' mouth tightened into a line, but he said nothing. "Passing my algorithm to you, Zye. Target the projected coordinates."

"Particle beam cannons active," she said. "Charging up."

"Don't fire them all at once," I cautioned her. "Lay out a consistent barrage, looking for a hit."

Several tense minutes passed. At last, the cannon batteries were ready.

"Fire at will," I said.

Immediately, the ship shuddered. The big guns cycled and recharged while we anxiously awaited any kind of feedback.

"No evidence that we hit anything, sir," Zye said.

"I need better numbers out of your station, Durris."

"I know sir, I know!"

He worked, his face sweating, to give me a closer target. The math was complex, and while our battle computers were powerful number-crunchers, they weren't specifically programmed for such a situation. Guesswork was the specialty of humans.

By the time the cannons had cooled and recharged, he had a slight variation to offer. We fired again. After several seconds, the result was determined to be the same: nothing.

"They can't be too worried," Rumbold remarked. "They're still using their displacement system. If we were scorching their fins I bet they'd come out of hiding and start swinging back."

His logic was irrefutable. I moved to help Durris with the math. Both of us strained and slid formulas around on his table. The programming was intense, and I wasn't as well trained on the process as he was. Still, I managed to give him some options he hadn't considered.

"Let's try to flush them," I said. "Assume we're missing by a wide margin. Independently target every cannon in a bank, then fire them all at once like a rainstorm of fire."

"Won't do much damage if we hit."

"No, but it might scare them."

He looked at me seriously. "Sir, are you sure you want to engage this vessel in toe-to-toe combat? I believe Admiral Halsey—"

"Yes, I know. This isn't my choice. The enemy has crept up on us. We're firing defensively. If we don't even know where they are, how do we run from them?"

I could tell he was unconvinced, but he stopped objecting. At last, we had zeroed in on another region of space . We fired again, and this time the beams were all widely dispersed.

"Any response?" I asked.

Yamada didn't answer immediately. She looked worried, and she was staring into her scopes.

"Captain..." she said. "I don't understand it, but it looks like they just disappeared."

"Widen your scanning area. Look where Durris and I have been placing all these shots."

There was a tense moment or two while she swung her sensor array around and began studying a new region of space.

"I've picked her up again—she's close, sir!" Yamada called.

"How close?"

"Less than five hundred thousand kilometers."

"Battle stations!" I shouted. "Everyone strap in. Zye, unload our defensive measures and strengthen that aft shield. Rumbold—"

"I know sir—hang on!"

We began evading with a sickening lurch. Another sudden shift followed five seconds after the first.

"Zye, see if you can hit them now."

"Waiting on heat recycle."

"Fire in the yellow—we may not get a second chance."

"Enemy weapons charging up," Yamada said.

On the forward screens, I could see dreadnought now—the real ship, in her real location. The gun ports were open, and her wicked-looking cannons were tracking us. I calculated we were probably within her optimal range of fire. We were still firing at long range, meaning our guns could be effective, but they couldn't deliver their maximum punch.

"Missiles detected, but we have some time before they can catch us," Yamada said. "The enemy cannons are going off—they're missing us."

"Keep up the good work, Rumbold."

He tossed me a grin over his shoulder then went back to obsessively minding the helm.

That was as far as we got before one of those big, invisible beams caught up to us. The ship buckled with explosive impact.

"Port side shield down in one hit," Zye said. "Hull has minor damage."

"Invert!" I ordered. "Aim our starboard side toward them."

There was the sensation of doing a barrel-roll. *Defiant* spun itself on its keel axis to present an undamaged shield to the enemy. It was mildly sickening, but everyone held on determinedly.

"Keep evading, Rumbold. Don't spare the gas."

We were accelerating hard now, and it made my teeth ache.

"We hit their forward shield twice," Zye said. "No appreciable effect."

My heart sank. It was really true. We couldn't fight this monster.

We were entirely out-classed.

-51-

We ran. There was nothing else to do.

The next half-hour was a time of grueling pain. It was like being on the worst of roller-coasters but with none of the fun involved.

We lurched and slammed from side-to-side. Now and then, the enemy caught us with a sizzling beam in the guts. The hull was scored until it had blackened. I had no doubt that *Defiant's* exterior resembled the bark of an abused oak, scorched by flames and torn up by the claws of wild beasts.

Over and over we inverted, flipping a freshly recharged shield toward the enemy, only to have it blasted down again. The impacts were deafening, and I could hardly make myself heard over them.

Yamada said something after ten minutes of this abuse, but I missed her words.

"Repeat that, Yamada," I ordered.

"Sir, we've got a communication incoming."

I almost laughed. Was CENTCOM calling to complain about my not following orders? Were they considering a court martial for unauthorized enemy engagement?

"Tap it directly to my implant."

There was no point in taking a message on the screens now. It was impossible to converse normally. Vomit rolled on the decks and crawled up the walls. A few of the command crew had already passed out, and I knew more would follow.

Closing my eyes, I answered my implant and displayed the transmission in my head.

They appeared. They were not human—at least, not entirely. A trio of Stroj seemingly stood before me in my field of vision. They were disembodied, overwritten upon my retina.

My eyes snapped open, and they stood in a tight group before me. They all stared at me—as if they were just as uncertain of what they were looking at as I was.

"Well met," I said. "I take it you're from the ship I'm engaged with right now?"

"We command *Nostromo*," said the one on the left.

"*Nostromo*..." I said thoughtfully. "Which of you is the captain?"

"We share that duty. You are the captain of the Beta ship?"

"I am."

"You are a Basic?"

"That would seem self-evident."

They turned toward one another, exchanging glances.

"It's not permitted for Earth to have a ship such as this," the one on the right said.

I shifted my eyes toward him—or was it her? Yes... vestigial flaps for breasts gave it away. She'd evidently grafted the limbs of another, larger male onto her person—blending them with the features of her original form.

"Why can't we have such a ship?" I asked. I cared little for their restrictions, but I was curious about them.

"Beta ships are difficult to destroy. It's outside our thought-boundaries that you should be flying such a vessel."

"Well, I am. What are you going to do about it?"

"Destroy you, of course."

Chuckling, I shook my head. Talking to the Stroj was almost always a thankless chore.

"Is that why you're calling?" I asked. "To inform me of my scheduled demise? In that case, I have a ship to attend to, and I need to get back to the battle."

"This action is not a battle," the one on the left corrected me. "It is an execution. A correction of an error."

I began to get it then. These three didn't have organic brains. They were all linked—I could see the tubes interconnecting them now. They'd formed some kind of a joint command by plugging their artificial minds together. Under different circumstances, I might have found them fascinating.

"Is that all you wish to say?" I prompted.

"No. We desire information."

"What information?"

"Where is the creature known as Lorn? What did he tell you of our mission?"

Apparently, they'd detected the pinnace we'd left behind in hyperspace, but they weren't sure who was aboard. I hesitated before responding. Lorn, for all his faults, had kept up his end of every bargain we'd struck. He'd shown us how to exit the Stroj system. He'd brought us a code-key to do it as well. Unlike these machine-minded Stroj, he had a more or less human brain.

"I refuse to answer," I said.

"You're protecting a Stroj?" asked the one on the right—the female. "That's most unusual."

"It's as I expected," said the one in the middle, the only one who hadn't spoken up until now. He was taller and thinner than the other two. His connecting tubes ran to both of the other Stroj, which gave me the impression he was the leader of the trio.

"Lorn is a traitor," he said to his co-captains. "He's in league with these Basics, no matter what they say."

"Gentlemen—and Lady," I said. "I'm afraid I have to disconnect now. Unless you want to offer terms under which we both ceasefire…?"

They seemed grimly amused by the concept.

"Well then," I continued, "I need to get back to my duties."

"Wait," said the tall one in the middle. "You are that which is known as Sparhawk?"

"Yes, I am."

"We look forward to consuming your flesh. We've each pre-chosen a portion of your body to subsume. We would greatly prefer it if you eject from your ship now, so that your corpse won't be too badly damaged."

They all looked at me hungrily for a moment, and I disconnected without answering. Suppressing a shudder, I noticed that the impacts on our hull had subsided during my conversation with the enemy.

"Status?" I demanded.

"They've broken off," Durris said, "it's most peculiar."

"No it isn't," Rumbold objected. "My evasions made their task hopeless. They know they can't catch us, so they're retreating."

My hopes dared to soar. Could they be so anxious to capture me intact that they would break off the attack?

"You're wrong," Zye said to Rumbold.

We all looked at her.

"Stroj are creatures that abhor inefficiency," she said. "They've decided to take the easy route to our destruction."

"And what's that?" Durris asked.

"To head for Earth again, of course. Now that their projection tricks failed to get them in close enough to destroy us, they've gone back to their original plan."

"Which is?" Rumbold demanded.

"They'll fly directly to Earth and begin bombing," I answered before Zye could. Her logic was perfectly clear to me now. "They know we'll have to fight them to save Earth. We won't keep running if they begin to exterminate our population. Why chase us? All they have to do is head to Earth, knowing we'll intercept."

The rest of my crew looked glum as they pondered the undeniable truth of what Zye and I were saying.

There were many hours to fly as we turned back to our previous course. The Stroj ship was no longer displaced. We stayed out of range, shadowing her.

During the next thirty or so hours, we received many queries from CENTCOM. They were beginning to panic back on Earth.

"Sparhawk," Halsey told me grimly when we were beginning our final approach. "We've reviewed your logs, and the vids from your recent engagement with this enemy. I'll have to admit, I can't see where you could have done something different that would have been effective. Yes, you brought them to Earth—but they were clearly planning to attack anyway. Your discovery destroyed their invasion army and forced their hand. I can't see that as anything other than a job well done."

He looked extra tired in this latest recording. Almost beaten. His fingertips lingered at his right temple, rubbing the spot repeatedly.

"Despite your actions, this is going to be very difficult," he continued. "We've got ships, but they're untested. None of them can take the kind of beating that your ship has already received. They're more than destroyers, they're light cruisers. But compared to your battle cruiser, they're like tin cans."

I didn't reply. We were still too far out for interactive conversations. We'd just passed the orbit of Mars, and given its relative position to Earth, that delayed our transmissions by about nine minutes.

"The only thing that makes sense to us is to hit them with everything we've got, in close, and all at once. Your ship will have to be here, of course. Plan on rendezvousing with the rest of Star Guard at 0500 hours, GMT zero. We'll strike just as they get within range of Fort Luna."

Making a crisp response acknowledging the orders, I wished Halsey well and sent the message. After that I informed my crew about the battle plan, and most of them seemed pleased.

"About time we got a little credit," Durris said, smiling. "I was worried they'd shoot the messenger on this one. But they've got to know that the Stroj were always a threat, and the fact we discovered them early before they were ready has screwed up their plans. We couldn't have done any better in our service of Earth."

"No, probably not," I agreed.

Rumbold was the only one who didn't seem pleased.

"Their tone," he said, "I don't like it. They think we're doomed, don't they Captain?"

"I wouldn't go that far."

"No, of course not... Do you want me at the helm for this action, sir?"

I looked at him thoughtfully, then nodded. "You've done pretty well up until now, old man."

"Thank you sir," he said, and he manned his station proudly. He was the only oldster on the command deck—unless you counted the frequent visits by my aunt—and he was visibly proud of his service.

I chanced to look at the battle-clock then, and my smile faded.

We had less than two hours to go before we'd again come within range of those punishing guns.

-52-

On every screen, *Defiant's* course converged with the enemy warship. I tried to not squint as the Stroj dreadnought loomed, but it was difficult. We'd been abused by this ship. We knew what it could do, and that made it all the harder to pretend that this time would be different. That this time, we would defeat *Nostromo*.

"Star Guard's destroyers have formed up behind us, Captain," Zye said. "The cruisers are a little slower, they're leaving Earth orbit now."

"How long until the formation is complete?" I asked.

"Seventeen minutes. There will be a few more of the smaller vessels adding to the task force after that, but nothing of any significant size."

I eyed the tactical holo-maps. Many tiny ships, represented by a few pixels in some cases, struggled to come together in our wake. They looked like a school of small fish following their leader.

On the far side of the display loomed the monster that we must defeat. The dreadnought dwarfed everything Earth had.

"Give me the full battle roster we're expecting to have at the moment of contact, Durris," I ordered.

"Nine destroyers. Six of the new Orca-class cruisers. Twenty-six patrol boats and several hundred smaller craft, mostly fighters and pinnaces associated with the larger vessels."

"That sounds like one battle cruiser—meaning us—and fifteen small support ships. The rest of them are mere distractions."

"Well," Durris said, not bothering to argue the point, "maybe the small-fry will do their job and distract the enemy."

"You mean absorb some of their fire? I doubt the trio that commands *Nostromo* will be taken off-track that easily. They know that we're the real threat. They'll go right for us and do whatever it takes to knock us out."

Durris frowned thoughtfully. I could see he had something on his mind, but I didn't pry. I let him stew for another two minutes until he finally came up to my command chair and addressed me quietly.

"Maybe there's a plan in what you just said, Captain."

"How so?"

"What if we fell back? What if we forced them to either engage our smaller vessels, or plow through them to get to us?"

The idea was intriguing, but I shook my head. "I doubt it would work. *Nostromo* would simply slow down as well, taking their time about destroying everything we threw at them. Once they were finished, they'd lunge forward and finish us. They might be scarred at that point, but I wouldn't bet on it. The truth is that without our heavy armor taking the hits, most of these ships won't survive long."

"Yes, Captain," he said glumly.

"Besides," I continued, "CENTCOM would never go for the idea. They've laid out their battle plans, and they expect me to follow them."

He nodded and turned to go. "Just a thought," he said, and returned to his station.

His words haunted my mind as the battle grew closer to being a reality.

Halsey contacted me with less than three minutes until go-time.

"Captain Sparhawk," he said, standing at attention.

"Admiral Halsey."

"I don't need to tell you that this battle is one we can't afford to lose. You're to destroy the enemy ship anyway you can—even if that means the destruction of your own vessel."

"Understood, Admiral."

Halsey nodded. "I know you're a clever and resourceful leader. I wouldn't have put you in that ship if I thought differently. When the engagement starts, you're going to be in independent command as far as tactical decisions go. We can't second guess your every move from a half-dozen light-seconds away."

"I understand sir, I won't let Earth down."

"See that you don't. Good luck. Halsey out."

And that was it. They'd given us a battle plan, but it was somewhat vague on the details. We were to lead with *Defiant* up front to take the first punishing blows. The rest of the smaller ships were to sweep around, englobing *Nostromo*. When and where her shields buckled, everyone in range was to pile-on, driving the stake into her heart.

Flocks of missiles were already sailing toward the battle zone. They'd been launched hours earlier. They would strike shortly after our ships were locked in combat.

In the computer simulations, the battle plan seemed reasonable. In fact, there didn't seem to be much else we could do, given the circumstances.

What I didn't like was how predictable it all was. The trio of captains had to know what was coming. Despite this, they were rolling up toward us as if they didn't have a care in world.

The first salvo was launched even as this thought occurred to me—but it wasn't ours.

"*Nostromo* is firing, Captain," Yamada said.

"Did she miss us?"

"No sir—she just nailed one of the cruisers."

My eyes slid over the screens. There... a collection of bright green pixels were drifting apart, like scattering jewels. The Stroj warship had made her first kill.

"Halsey's right! They are built like tin cans!" Rumbold crowed unhelpfully.

"Increase speed by ten percent," I ordered. "Zye, get a lock on that ship as soon as you can."

"We have a lock, but we're still out of effective range."

"*Nostromo* is firing again, sir," Yamada said, "...another hit. A destroyer this time. The *Karachi* is gone."

"Damn it," I said under my breath. "Where are those missiles?"

"Two minutes out."

"They'll have destroyed all of our cruisers by then."

We watched as the battle continued to unfold. Our ships were racing forward now, throwing out all pretense of maintaining a tight formation. It looked like pandemonium, but at least no one was running. Our captains had never faced anything like this kind of firepower before.

"She's firing again—a partial miss."

Tapping as fast as I could, I brought up the Star Guard Cruiser *El Salvador* on my screen. She'd been grazed. Her forward shields were down, and the ship was venting badly—but she was still in the fight, still advancing.

"Contact *El Salvador's* captain," I told Yamada. "Suggest they should break off and fall to the rear."

"Yes sir," Yamada said, working her boards.

Before she could finish the message, however, *Nostromo* reached out again and finished the job she'd started. *El Salvador* was nothing but burning, spinning fragments.

"Are we in range yet?" I demanded. "Fire the moment we cross the boundary."

"Eleven seconds," Zye said. "Ten... nine..."

The countdown seemed unending, but at last our big guns discharged. We waited a few seconds, then our forward optics registered the results.

"A hit! Forward bow, target's shields knocked to eighteen percent."

I looked at Yamada incredulously. "Her shields are still up?"

"Yes. They must have transferred all their power to their forward shields. Their engines have cut out, and they're gliding forward on momentum."

"Shields and weapons. She's not giving any of her other systems any power. She means to destroy us all."

No one spoke. The evidence was clear.

"Recycle to green," I ordered, "and hit her again, same spot."

"Guns programmed, sir," Zye acknowledged.

"None of the other ships are in range yet, are they?" Rumbold asked. "They're like sitting ducks."

To illustrate his point, another of the cruisers was smashed. This time, the ship went into a flat spin. She dropped out of formation, crippled. Unlike the *El Salvador's* commander, when she got control of herself again, she limped toward the rear of the formation as quickly as she was able.

We fired again, and this time the crew whooped.

"Shield penetration confirmed," Yamada said. "At least fifty-percent of that one got through."

"Any serious damage?"

"The hull stopped it. But I think we might have taken out a bank of secondary guns."

"Mark that and transmit the intel to the fleet. We might be able to get through there, it's a weak point."

Again, the big ship lit up and her beams stabbed out. I kept expecting—hoping—that *Nostromo* would turn on us. We could take these shots where our comrades couldn't.

Hissing through my teeth, I watched as the volley caught the retreating, crippled cruiser and scattered her atoms. There was nothing left.

"As clean a kill as you like," Rumbold said sadly. "Core breach—at least it was quick."

"Why won't she fire on us?" I demanded.

"She knows we'll be hard to beat down," Durris answered. "She's knocking out all our support ships while they're bunched up. That's easier than chasing them all over the star system later."

I looked at him. "It was a rhetorical question, First Officer."

"Sorry sir."

The cruisers were in range at last. They began firing back. At about the same time, the missiles from Luna came onto our near-range scanners. They were moving in at an angle on *Nostromo's* port side.

For the first time, the big ship seemed to take notice of something besides its next hapless victim. She rolled to present her belly-shield to the incoming missiles.

"Hold fire!" I shouted the moment she did so.

Zye glanced at me in surprise, and she scrambled to cancel the auto-fire cycle she had the big guns following. The levels went green and stayed there.

"Wait until those missiles are almost on her. Then take out that shield she's presenting to them. Rumbold, swing us toward the missiles. We'll hit from the same side."

"Roger that."

We lurched, and there was an extended sensation of lateral motion. After several seconds, we were in position.

"The destroyers are coming into range now," Durris said excitedly. "I've relayed the plan to them. They'll all hit that shield when they can."

Secondary guns all over *Nostromo's* prickly hull began to light up. They were automated turrets, spraying fire at the incoming missiles to destroy them before they could make contact.

Missiles, hundreds of missiles, were destroyed. But hundreds more plunged inward.

I found myself leaning forward and holding my breath. The missiles made their final, suicidal thrust.

"That's close enough—fire Zye."

She did, and our cannons sang. The dreadnought's shield flickered. It wasn't down, but it was badly overloaded.

The destroyers fired a moment later. They poured beams into the weakened spot, and the enemy began to roll again.

"She's trying to take the strike with her armored superstructure," Durris said.

"It's too late!" Rumbold said triumphantly.

The missiles slammed home at last. Dozens took down the belly-shield, and a hundred more hammered the hull beneath in rapid succession.

"We've got venting," Yamada said, "we hurt her."

A cheer went up. It was the first time we'd ever seriously damaged this warship.

The dreadnought completed its slow roll, however, and now the rest of the missile-flock struck a fresh shield. The impacts were shrugged off.

Durris looked at me. "Which side should we go for?" he asked. "The topside shield? The rest of our fleet is peppering that area now."

"No," I said, shaking my head. "She'll just roll again. Go under her, bring us around, and hammer that belly region where the missiles got through. We have to beat down her defenses and hit her where it hurts."

Defiant moved in a new, sickening direction. We held on with our teeth clenched and bared.

It was then that the battle shifted.

"Sir... *Nostromo* is coming about. She's aiming her prow at us, now."

A cold feeling swept over me. The enemy was no longer confident they could destroy us all in turn, one ship at a time. *Nostromo* was wounded, and they were taking appropriate action.

I could tell even before Yamada confirmed it that every gun the dreadnought had left was now targeting *Defiant*.

-53-

The news that we were next on *Nostromo's* menu was met with a mixture of pride and fear. No one smiled, but we braced ourselves for the opening punches determinedly.

"Rumbold, set us into a gentle spin on our keel axis."

He worked the controls in silence, putting us into a continuous motion that would spread strikes over a wider area of our hull.

The next barrage of fire struck us without warning. Leaping out at the speed of light, *Nostromo* and *Defiant* were momentarily connected by a lance of energy.

"Our forward shield is down!" Yamada shouted over the din.

"Keep us rolling on the keel axis, Rumbold. Increase the spin-rate twenty percent."

"I am sir, I am!"

"And get us under that ship," I continued calmly. "Zye, hold your fire."

"Captain," Zye said, "I've got a shot now, and their shield capacitors are recharging. Are you sure you want to hold our fire?"

"Follow orders, Zye," was all I said in response.

On the forward screen—on every screen—the big ship loomed close. For two major warships, this was point-blank range. We couldn't miss. It was all a matter of timing, of delivering a blow that would punch through and truly damage the enemy.

The big problem we faced was that this enemy both took and dished out more punishment than we did. If we scattered hits here and there on *Nostromo*, she could brush them off. Her shields were layered and quick to recharge. Her hull was also unbelievably resilient.

But that belly region where we'd scored real damage—that was our hope in my mind. We had to dig deeper into that spot and strike deep in the vitals.

The next shot hit us hard. We lost the forward shield, and though we still spun, the bigger ship raked our hull with strikes that tore gouges into *Defiant*'s fortified exterior. It sounded to me as if giants were hammering on the ship, beating it with massive weapons.

"Deck six—no response. They've lost pressure, and I fear everyone's dead."

That was the medical deck. I saw Yamada look at me, but I grimly watched the screens. We hadn't been knocked out yet.

"All enemy shields are in the red," Zye announced. "Below fifty percent."

That was due to the relentless barrage of fire coming from our supporters. They weren't getting through, but they were constantly weakening every shield the enemy had.

Another blinding strike came in—I wasn't clear on how the Stroj were firing so fast. Either they had superior cooling technology, or they were only using one bank each time they fired, thereby increasing their rate of fire.

"We've lost main battery two, Captain," Zye said.

That got my attention. "Every gun on bank two has been knocked out?"

"Our fire control systems are dead. I'm not sure about the condition of the actual tubes, but I know we can't operate them from here."

Displays spun sickeningly, I turned away, feeling defeated. There was no way I could order a repair crew out onto the hull under these conditions. I wondered if I'd held onto my close-range barrage too long. Perhaps this had turned into a proverbial "use it or lose it" situation.

Trying to ignore these self-doubts, I waited until we were at the belly of the big ship. Finally, the moment came.

"There!" I shouted, leaning forward and straining against the straps that laced my body. "I can see where she's still venting."

"Aye Captain," Rumbold said, staring. "They haven't gotten the bleeding under control yet."

"Fire banks one and three on my mark... one... two... Mark!"

Everything we had gushed upward in a single precision shot. The dreadnought's flickering shields vanished, and the beams dug deeply into the hull.

"Hold that beam!" I ordered. "Continue firing until I order you to stop."

Zye glanced at me briefly, but she kept her hands on the firing controls and didn't let up. The heat graphs went red very quickly. After that, they continued to spike up until they flared white.

"Bank one in shutdown," Zye said.

"Override and keep firing."

"We'll melt the tubes, Captain," Rumbold said worriedly.

"We're dead anyway if this doesn't work. Maintain those beams, Zye."

Everyone fell silent. We stared together at the incoming video.

"Bank three in shutdown now... Bank one unresponsive."

"Override bank three."

The guns kept cracking off jolts of pure force. We were now directly below the enemy, passing beneath her like shadowy fish on the seafloor. The underbelly region we'd targeted was glowing orange-white. Molten globules were breaking away, vaporizing and expanding out into space. A vast cloud of particles began to grow between our two ships. I knew that this cloud would soon impede our fire if our cannons didn't melt away first.

In the end, it was our cannons that gave out.

"Secondaries, fire," I ordered. "Hit that same spot."

Zye looked at me and shook her head. She removed her hands from her boards. "The secondaries went down long ago, Captain," she said. "Recall that you ordered me to fire everything we had at once."

"So I did," I said, relaxing somewhat.

We watched tensely as the dreadnought slid away to our stern.

"She's still flying, sir," Yamada said. "We hurt her, and she's on fire inside. But I'm not seeing a core breach."

Hammering my fist on my chair, I came to a fateful decision. "Helm, come hard about. Accelerate at ten Gs."

Rumbold's eyes rolled around to look at me. His face was white, and he didn't say a word. Even so, I knew what he was asking.

"Yes, old friend," I told him. "We're going to ram her."

At those words, I sensed that every eye on the deck had fallen on me, but I didn't care. My orders were to stop this dreadnought. If that meant destroying both vessels in the process... well, so be it.

For the record, Rumbold never argued with me. Neither did any of the others. They knew the score. Too many souls below on Earth were depending on us. We simply must not fail.

Defiant slewed around with sickening agility. We had no weapons left that would be effective against the dreadnought—save for *Defiant's* prow, driven by our powerful engines. I planned to make a missile out of her and take the enemy down with us.

On screen, the dreadnought wheeled ponderously to face her tormentor. In comparison, her movements were slow and imprecise. I began to hope that if we struck her with enough of a glancing blow, we might barrel through the explosion and actually survive.

Nostromo was still shrinking in perspective on our screens. Although we'd spun around, inertia was still driving us backward. Slowly, we regained our footing and began a new charge.

Nostromo angled her guns directly upon us. I could see she was venting badly, worse than before. Bracing myself for a powerful blast, I was surprised when she struck us with only a spray of small, jabbing lances.

"She must be having significant heat problems now as well," Rumbold speculated. "That was the lightest touch she's delivered today."

We soon saw why. The breach in her belly was widening. It was burning—as if the metal of her hull was itself on fire. A burning mass of super-dense material was converting to energy. Plasma gleamed brilliantly against the black of space like an arc-welder's torch.

Still, her thin secondary beams clawed out and found us. They blasted down our tattered shields and scored our hull with deep furrows.

All around *Nostromo,* a swarm of smaller Earth-ships pressed the attack. Like jackals that sensed a giant beast was wounded, they darted and approached closer than they'd dared before. From their comparatively small guns a hundred needle-thin beams jabbed and sliced.

Then, the incredible happened. The enemy's shielding flickered out.

"Pull up!" I shouted at Rumbold. "All power to the aft shields the second we clear her. Cancel the ramming protocol, we'll do a fly-by, nothing more."

Rumbold dutifully tilted up our nose. We sailed past the crippled dreadnought instead of crashing into her. At our stern, a hundred tiny vessels closed and went to work. They were like ants chewing on an elephant that was floundering in dust.

After we'd passed her by, *Nostromo's* last operating cannons shot us in the rear ineffectually. We'd escaped death.

Our sister ships pressed in on all sides. Without shields, the dreadnought was naked. They surgically destroyed every jutting gun, sensor array and projector. The massive hull was soon as pockmarked as the Moon. They even fused shut every hatchway so the Stroj inside couldn't escape. It was a grim decision, but I hadn't made it.

The big ship turned again, one last time. But she didn't head for open space as I'd expected her to. She aimed herself instead toward the bright blue-white disk that was Earth.

Nostromo's big engines still operated, if sluggishly. She began a long burn, pushing the vessel toward our home planet.

"Come about again," I said grimly. "Match the enemy course and speed. If they're going to take out a city by turning *Nostromo* into a self-propelled meteor, we're going to have to nudge her off course the only way we can."

Again, no one objected, but I could see fear and disappointment in their eyes. For a few minutes there, we all dared hope we might live to see the morning.

For several long minutes, we stalked the great ship as it drove a glittering, burning arc across Earth's disk.

"They're trying to hit land," Durris said with certainty. His plotted course-arcs glowed up into his face. "They don't want to splash down in an ocean—even though that would make an amazing tidal wave. They're going to target the most significant density of civilization they can manage—possibly Central Command itself."

After reviewing the data, I was forced to agree with his conclusions.

"Sir..." Yamada said, touching her ear and frowning. "There's a call coming in."

"Transfer it to my implant," I said crisply.

I was sure it was going to be Halsey. This was the moment during which he'd tell me I had to sacrifice my ship and crew to stop *Nostromo* from achieving her final goal. I was already way ahead of CENTCOM on that point, of course, but I'd expected them to call and check up on me all the same.

When a trio of bizarre humanoids appeared inside my visual perception instead, I blinked in surprise.

It was the Stroj group-captain. The center figure of the three spoke up. "The creature known as Sparhawk has been promoted in significance," he said. "Your consumption has become the number one priority of the Stroj."

"Why would you call just to tell me that?"

"Because we desire revenge," he—or it—said. "We know that Basics fear the future. They imagine pain, and they thereby experience it time and time again in their imaginations before it ever becomes a reality. We wanted to make sure that you missed none of that well-deserved experience."

I gave them a savage grin. "Know then, Stroj Captains, that you've instead ignited joy in my heart. It is *I* who now tastes *your* fear. It is *I* who serves to witness *your* kind's greatest defeat. The fact that you're even sending such a petty message—"

The channel closed abruptly. I snarled and sat up.

"Reconnect me, Yamada," I said.

"But sir…" she said, pointing at the screen.

I followed her gesture, and I was rendered speechless. The screens were displaying a terrible sight, one that both stunned me and filled me with wonder at the same time.

Nostromo had gone into a slow, wobbling roll. Explosions wracked her hull, including a vast plume of gas that shot out of her aft exhaust ports.

Then, incredibly, she began to break up.

"Tell the destroyers and the last three cruiser captains to target that wreckage," I said quickly. "A big chunk could still take out a city."

"They know, Captain."

Star Guard ships were already racing ahead. They hadn't needed my prompting. Countless bolts of energy melted and sliced the biggest chunks of *Nostromo* into objects no more than ten meters across by the time these dense objects began to rain down upon Earth's atmosphere.

Like a thousand large meteors, the chunks disintegrated and vaporized into streaks of white light. From the ground, it must have been an amazing sight.

Only then did I know in my heart that it was over. The dreadnought *Nostromo* had been completely destroyed.

-54-

We limped home, with many subsystems having long since failed. Navigational niceties such as docking lights, steering thrusters and proximity sensors were all non-operational. Our hull had been so peppered with strikes, all such devices had been burned away.

Despite the fact we were in high orbit around Earth when the battle ended, it took us a full six hours to reach Araminta Station. Worse, we had a long line of ships ahead of us when we finally reached the docks. Many of them were in worse shape than we were. As much as we wanted to get off-ship and be debriefed, we had to wait in line like everyone else.

At last, Yamada called me from the command deck, and I lurched awake in my bunk. I'd drifted off after telling myself I'd only close my eyes for a second.

"I'll be right there," I said, straightening my kit.

When I reached the command deck, I was in for a surprise. Ambassador Grantholm was standing there, wearing a fine gauzy dress that was as black as space itself.

She looked as she must have during her first century of life. Her back seemed straighter and some of the worry-lines had been smoothed out of her face.

In front of her stood Admiral Halsey. His eyes were almost as bright as hers. He was grinning and rocking back on his heels. The two of them looked as though they were about to embrace.

Then, shockingly, they did so.

"Admiral," Lady Grantholm said as they separated, "it's so *good* to be back home."

"You did an amazing job, Ambassador," he said.

I wasn't the only one watching this display with a mixture of surprise and alarm. Rumbold sighed and turned away. No one else saw, but he slumped somewhat into the chair at his station, running fingers over his boards.

Could it be he'd harbored hope that a High Lady such as my aunt would recall their moments together? I thought of telling him she'd only been enjoying herself, but I wasn't sure if that would be an act of kindness or cruelty.

"Admiral Halsey," I said, stepping up and saluting him.

He took his eyes off Lady Grantholm and noticed me. "Ah, Sparhawk! The hero of the hour. Well done, sir! You fought your ship well."

"Thank you, Admiral. Many Star Guard captains can say the same today."

He let go of my aunt's hands and stepped toward me, nodding. He grabbed my right hand in both of his and shook it vigorously.

"Don't be modest now, Sparhawk. This is your day."

"Listen to him, William," my aunt advised.

I glanced at her, wondering what she was thinking. She was a cunning old bat. During our long voyage I'd come to suspect she was the most conniving member of my entire family—and that covered some serious ground.

My father could give a good speech, mind you, and his political instincts were legendary. But I'd learned during this mission that my aunt was a deeper planner than Dad had ever been.

Turning back to Halsey, I smiled and accepted his congratulations without reservation. After all, I knew I deserved them.

We spent an hour or so going over the damage to *Defiant*. It was extensive, but not irreparable. When we were done with this lengthy process, Halsey led me off the ship onto the station.

There, it seemed like everyone we met wanted to shake my hand and clap my back. I was beginning to feel pretty good about my ordeals—now that they were behind me.

When we reached his office, Halsey faced me and smiled.

"You did it," he said. "You really did it. When you were in action, did you realize how long the odds were on the continuation of your career?"

"A single battle cruiser is no match for a dreadnought in close combat, sir," I admitted. "But I thought I might win the struggle anyway."

He waved my words away and chuckled. "No, no, that's not what I meant. I'm talking about the Joint Chiefs. They wanted to crucify you every moment."

"Even after I destroyed *Nostromo*?"

"Of course. You brought her here, remember? In the minds of many officials, you nearly caused the extinction of our entire race."

This comment stumped me. My mouth opened, but no sound came forth.

"Yes," he said in a low tone, "it was that close for you. But do you know who saved the situation? Your aunt, that's who. I guess blood really is thicker than water. She's been online talking to the brass ever since the battle ended. Convincing them that they'd be better off playing you up as a hero than as a fool. She explained the people wouldn't stand for a court martial after a dramatic battle in space right over their heads. That they'd rather have a figurehead to attend their parades than a scape-goat to throw filth at."

My mind finally caught up with his words. "Who will play that role then, sir?" I inquired.

"What?"

"Who's your scape-goat? The man this world will blame for bringing us all so close to doom?"

We locked stares for a moment. His attitude undertook a sudden shift. He stood up and leaned forward with his fingers splayed on his desk. The computerized desk glowed around each of those fingers, uncertain what its master might want from it.

"Are you suggesting that *I* might be to blame, Sparhawk?"

"You sent me up there, sir. You authorized me to become *Defiant's* captain. In fact, as I recall, you insisted upon it. Who's the greater fool? The fool himself, or the man who promotes him?"

He glared at me for a moment longer before looking down and shaking his head. "Well-played. That was exactly what your aunt said—but you knew that already, didn't you?"

"I didn't discuss it with her. But it only stands to reason."

"A real chip off the old block, aren't you? No wonder your family has held political power for decades—well, it doesn't matter. The enemy has been defeated, and you're a planet-wide hero. Go to a few parties and enjoy yourself, Captain," he concluded—waving dismissively and looking mad enough to spit on me.

"I'll do just that, Admiral," I said calmly. "Would you mind joining me at a bar right now, in fact?"

He'd just begun toying with his desk again, but he halted. He looked at me with narrowed eyes.

"What's this then? An attempt to bury the hatchet so soon?"

I spread my hands. "We don't know how long it will be before the next colonist ship comes visiting. There's no time for petty squabbles. Besides, many good Guard officers were spaced today. I'd like to tip a glass to their souls."

He nodded slowly. "Me too... All right then, let's go."

We walked out and found the nearest bar. Naturally, a rowdy victory party was already in progress. Every spacer who recognized us bought us a drink, and we were soon blind drunk.

Eventually, I remembered to turn on my implants to process out the toxins. It was a wise choice, but one I made much too late. I ended up passing out and being carted back to my ship by a pack of singing yard-dogs from the station.

When I awoke the next morning, I was startled by the face of my Aunt. She was peering and frowning at me, tsking all the while.

"Captain Sparhawk," she said. "I'm too old for changing diapers."

I looked down in concern, but found my clothing was still on and unsoiled. She'd been speaking figuratively, to my great relief.

"You behaved abominably yesterday," she said, taking a seat behind my own desk.

Stretching and groaning, I clawed myself into a sitting position.

"Every man gets drunk now and then," I said, "especially after saving the world."

"I'm not talking about getting drunk. I'm talking about threatening Halsey. That was foolish."

I frowned at her thoughtfully. "Who let you in here, anyway?"

She rolled her eyes. "As if the commander of any mission in space wouldn't insist on a full set of door codes for every cabin aboard."

Thinking that over, I considered telling her that I didn't possess such a set of codes, but I passed on the idea.

"How did you know that I talked to Halsey? Or rather, what I said?"

She made that tsking sound again. "William, be serious. I know almost everything that happens on this ship. How else could I have gotten you placed in command of her?"

"Halsey didn't want to give me the command?"

"He wasn't the main obstacle. There were members of the High Command who tried to stop me. But they failed to derail us and place lackeys of their own aboard *Defiant*."

After a trip to the bathroom, during which I liberally threw handfuls of cold water into my face, I returned. She was still sitting there behind my desk like a patient spider.

My mind was finally operating. Why was she here? Just to scold me? Unlikely. She wanted to tell me something, or to get some kind of information from me. That's what her kind was always interested in. Manipulation of events, deal-making... little else interested her.

"Okay Aunt Helen," I said, "I'll bite. What do you want from me today?"

"This isn't over," she said, "this war between the worlds. I'd hoped we could reach out to these childish colonists diplomatically. That Earth's wealth and culture could control the barbarians that have been festering out there among the stars for so long. Unfortunately, that initial gambit has clearly failed."

"What's plan B?"

"War, of course," she said smoothly.

"Does it have to go that way?"

"Yes, I absolutely think it does. You've met plenty of these Stroj, William. Is it your educated opinion that they can be reasoned with? Do you think we can get them to sign a treaty of some kind, perhaps?"

"They might be convinced to do that."

She laughed. "They'd simply use it to slow us down before their next vicious attack."

"Probably so," I admitted.

"Sometimes, war is the only solution. Sometimes an enemy must be destroyed."

"Of course, but that isn't my call to make."

Her eyes followed me as I changed uniforms. Smart-straps wrapped themselves over my body with a slithering motion that caught on the hairs of my legs and arms.

"I'm going to call a private council among the elite of several political parties," she said quietly. "I want you to be there. I want you to help me convince them that they must act."

"You mean to build a fleet? We're doing that now."

"No. I think we have to go further. The plans we have now are purely defensive in nature. We need larger ships. Vessels capable of exploration and hunting, as needed."

"Starships? Like *Defiant*?"

She inclined her head. "Like *Nostromo*, possibly."

That was a thought. What would it be like to have the deck of a massive killer like that under my feet? Despite my better judgment, I was intrigued.

"I won't lie for you," I told her. "I'll report, and I'll give my honest opinion. That's it."

"Of course. I'd never expect anything less from you. In fact, your reputation for painful honesty is an asset I'm depending on in this situation. All you have to do is tell me what your real opinion is, first."

I was beginning to catch on. She wanted Earth to build an attack fleet. In order to get the blessing of the political "powers that be", they had to be convinced. Many would be adverse to shouldering such a massive expense.

Who could better convince them than the hero who'd saved them all from destruction in the skies right over their heads?

A series of things began to click in my mind following this thought. Had she come along on this trip to bear witness? Had she chosen me to captain this ship, not because she believed in my capacities, but because she could get me to support her conclusions in front of the right people? The people behind the scenes who made the big decisions?

And lastly, had she worked hard to give me the status of a hero only in order to further her goals?

The only logical answer to all these questions was: *yes*.

"All right," I said, looking her square in the eye. "I'll go with you. I'll make the case. But only because it's the right choice. We can't let Star Guard sit here and build fortifications forever. We can't let the Stroj choose the time and the place of our next meeting. We must seize the initiative."

She smiled and her artificially-regrown teeth gleamed. "I knew you'd come to the right decision. You've got a lot of your mother in you—much more than the thirty percent they give you credit for."

With that, she bid me farewell, and left.

-55-

I showered, dressed, and headed toward the docking tubes. I was tired of being trapped aboard *Defiant*, as much as I loved her. Even Araminta Station seemed like a welcome respite in comparison.

It was at the docking tubes that I met up with Zye. She'd clearly been waiting for me. Without anything more than a nod from each of us, she fell into step at my side.

"You think there might be more Stroj assassins on Earth?" I asked her.

"There probably are."

"Is that why you intend to follow me around planet-side?"

She glanced at me reproachfully. "I find your ingratitude distressing."

Heaving a sigh, I nodded. "My apologies. Please accompany me, Zye. I'm sure we'll both enjoy ourselves."

Mollified, she followed me down the sky-lift to the ground station. We moved toward the public transport—but we never made it that far.

Apparently, someone had alerted the media to our presence. The drones showed up first—a dozen floating cameras no larger than eyeballs. They swarmed, and they deftly dodged my fingers when I sought to slap them away.

By the time we reached the streets, I realized we weren't going to be allowed any peace whatsoever.

"Time for a change of plan," I said, "I'm calling for estate transport."

One of my father's chauffeurs swooped down less than five minutes later to pick us up. We scrambled inside, and a few of the camera drones became trapped in the car with us. I swatted them from the air and tossed them out the windows, which then slid themselves back into place.

"Driver," I said, "take me home, will you?"

"Can't do that, sir."

"Why not?"

"We've got a schedule. You're wanted at the Treasury Citadel. There's an event being held in your honor."

Closing my eyes, I opened them again slowly. "All right," I said, forcing a smile. "I'm sure I'll enjoy myself. Drive on."

Zye looked at me with a strange expression.

"What's the matter?" I asked.

"You're not behaving as you normally do."

I shrugged. "I've accepted my fate this time. It's for the good of the planet, after all."

"Master Sparhawk, sir?" asked the driver.

Glancing up with disapproval, I nodded to him reluctantly. A good driver didn't listen in and bother his passengers.

He grinned at me. "Could I have your thumbprint? It's for the wife—you understand."

"Of course," I said, smiling tiredly and pressing my thumb against the computer scroll he slid back to me. I really *was* beginning to understand my new existence.

* * *

Seven days and a dozen public events passed by in a blur. I'd reunited with my parents and been promptly paraded in front of every donor and VIP they could muster into my presence.

"That's right, he's my only son," Dad said, his arm wrapped around my shoulders and his face beaming.

He'd recovered well from his injuries of a year ago. He could stand unaided now, but not for extended periods. It was enough to allow for appropriately staged pictures, at least.

Like all offspring, I'd long sought my father's approval. The only thing that bothered me was that the change in his attitude was so clearly self-serving. Still, I knew I shouldn't pass up such a golden opportunity for rekindling our relationship.

In short, I went along with the charade, but I never felt completely at ease. I couldn't forget that his shift in attitude toward my naval career had come because it suited his purposes. My father had resisted my choices in life with every breath, manipulation and lengthy exhalation he made. Now, suddenly, he was all smiles, hugs and photo-ops.

I tried valiantly not to let this bother me. My parents were political animals, after all. They were like obsessed sports-fans, in a way, pursuing their passion viscerally. They had their habits and their personalities, and there was nothing I could do to change that.

Making peace with a difficult situation, I tried to love them for who they were and bask in the approval I'd sought for so long. If only they didn't make such a drama out of every moment, it would've been easier to believe in their sincerity.

"Yes, he *is* the best," my mother insisted, her hands pressing my chest and back simultaneously. "I raised him to be a warrior. That's just what Earth needs today, don't you think?"

I wanted to squirm, but I forced a tight smile instead. The journalist who was interviewing the two of us together seemed alight with personal interest. She was pretty, petite and her eyes moved quickly, like those of a bird.

"Captain Sparhawk," she said, "it's been said that you gained your command through political manipulation. Is that true?"

My mother's gushing smile vanished. "Come, William. We'll talk to a more serious person in the ballroom."

I locked eyes with the reporter. She stared at me, ignoring my mother, who was attempting to guide me away.

Resisting my mother's tug effortlessly, I took in a breath and nodded to the reporter. "Some have said that," I admitted. "Given my family history, I can understand why such a worry might concern any citizen. But it's simply not true. Check my record. I spent longer as a mere ensign than most Academy graduates typically do. The fact was that my officers hated me at first."

Sensing her opportunity, the reporter stepped closer. Her short hair hung in two curving arcs down around her chin. I found this intriguing.

"I did check it. They did hate you—no one could make another conclusion fairly. And your parents—they didn't want you to be a Star Guard officer either, did they?"

"No, quite the opposite. They resisted my service at every step."

My mother's hands turned into claws. She lifted herself up on her tiptoes and whispered hotly in my ear.

"Don't let her beguile you," she hissed. "You're ruining this."

Politely, I turned back to the reporter. "Perhaps at a later time," I said.

"I'd like that."

I was dragged away. I felt as if I was a child once more, and my mother had just caught me filling the bathtub with her e-docs all over again.

"I can't believe you're such a sucker for a pretty face, William," she scolded. "Why don't you go and make up with Lady Astra? You made such a cute couple."

At the mention of Lady Astra, I felt a pang. I'd seen her across the room since my return to Earth, but I'd yet to speak to her. Each time my eyes met hers by chance, she looked quickly away. Perhaps she'd heard about some of the affairs I'd had of late.

"Where are we going, mother?" I asked mildly. "Wherever it is, I'd like to stop off at the bar, first."

"Oh no, that's the last thing you need. You're already losing it."

"What do you mean?"

She took a breath and let it slowly out. "Listen, my son. You're not used to this. Adulation, fame, playing the role of the hero. I don't think it suits you. It seems to be grating on you."

I considered her thoughtfully. "Perhaps you're right," I said. "I like the praise—but I don't like the scrutiny. The whole thing feels unnatural to me. I've always been a Sparhawk, but I've never been the man on Earth that everyone wants to meet."

"Well, just try to keep your wits about you," mother said. "That's all I ask."

I nodded, and she finally let me go.

Turning toward the bar in relief, I didn't make it twenty steps before the petite reporter stepped in my way. One moment she'd been nowhere to be seen, and the next she was in my path. It would have been annoying, save for the fact that she had a martini in each hand.

"Here," she said, offering me one. "You look like you could use this."

"You're very perceptive."

I tasted the drink, and I almost gagged. Someone had put sugar and apple-flavoring into it. After the initial shock wore off, however, I found I was able to drink the sticky stuff anyway.

The reporter's name was Sara. We shared several drinks, some personal conversations, and eventually her bed in a neighboring hotel.

Sometime after midnight, we were rudely awakened by a pounding at the door.

Groaning and heaving myself into a sitting position, I looked around blearily in the dark.

Sara squirmed up against my back. She was nude, and seemed frightened.

"Could it be assassins?" she asked in a whisper.

In truth, the idea *had* occurred to me. One couldn't be too careful after destroying the pride of the Stroj fleet, after all.

"Wait here," I said, walking to the door.

I didn't open it, but instead reached for my saber.

That's when the doorjamb splintered, and the door itself was flung against the wall with a crash. A massive booted figure stepped in and caught the vibrating door on its rebound with a meaty arm.

I attempted to draw my sword, but a huge hand closed over my wrist.

Sara screamed and the lights turned themselves up in an automated response.

The intruder was none other than Zye. I looked up at her and frowned.

"You've simply got to stop doing this kind of thing, Zye."

"You left the party," she said in an accusatory tone.

"True.

"You left with this woman?"

"You are a sleuth, Zye."

She paused, glaring at me, then at Sara on the bed—who had pulled up the sheets to cover herself.

Sara's eyes were as big around as they could possibly be. I had the feeling she wouldn't be asking for a second date.

Zye let go of my wrist and relaxed somewhat.

"I'm sorry," she said. "Your mother—she said you were under the influence of a harlot."

Sara made an insulted sound of disapproval.

Looking at Zye, I pointedly gestured toward the hallway. "Well, why don't you go back downstairs and tell her it was all a misunderstanding?"

"I will. But first, may I examine the female?" Zye craned her head to stare past me at the rumpled bed.

"What?" squeaked Sara.

"No, Zye, that won't be necessary."

"But she might be a Stroj. They're becoming more sophisticated in their techniques."

"No, thank you," I said firmly.

Finally, with great reluctance, Zye retreated. I grabbed a tall-backed chair and wedged it under the doorknob to re-establish a little privacy. Still not satisfied, I pushed a heavy dresser against the chair.

When I returned to bed, I found Sara's attitude had changed. "She's crazy. That huge Beta—she wanted to kill me, didn't she?"

"She's overprotective," I said. "You have to understand, there have been many attempts on my life."

"She called me a whore!"

"Not exactly... she said my mother did."

Sara looked at me for a few seconds, then she burst out laughing. She sat down again on the edge of the bed.

"You aren't leaving?" I asked her.

"I think I'll stay awhile—after all, this is my room."

That made us both laugh. We touched again soon thereafter, and one thing swiftly led to another. Half an hour later, Sara and I were left exhausted and entwined on the bed. We stared at shadows that played on the ceiling.

"No wonder you drink," she said. "Does this sort of madness interfere with your duties at Star Guard?"

"Are you a reporter now, or a lover?"

She shrugged noncommittally.

"Well," I said, "I'll admit that I'm very glad I decided to have toxin-filtering implants installed years ago."

"That way, you can get drunk whenever you want without side-effects," she said thoughtfully. "Seems like a wise investment, since everyone around you is half-insane."

Pondering the truth of her words, I soon nodded off to sleep again.

-56-

It was nearly a month later that my aunt, the Lady Grantholm, showed up and asked me to escort her to an event. I questioned her on the nature of the affair, but she was determinedly vague.

"You promised that you'd back me up when the time came, William," she reminded me gently.

In sudden understanding, I offered her my arm. She had me do the driving—no chauffeur or guards of any kind. When we arrived at an ancient estate on the Hudson River, I still wasn't sure what was coming next.

We landed the air car politely at the main entrance, then drove up a winding gravel road to a formidable gate. The gate opened under power without any visible inspection from security.

"They know me here," my aunt said, giving me an encouraging smile.

I drove the car up to a looming mansion built with Romanesque columns and ivy-covered walls. The house was grand in an old-fashioned way that I hadn't seen for years. It gripped a mountaintop overlooking the river and was surrounded by tall trees. What famous personage had built the place centuries earlier? I could only imagine.

"This way Lady," said the doorman, who was an oldster with bristling white eyebrows. He gave me a brisk up-down appraisal. "Your driver will be comfortable in the garage, I'm sure."

I frowned, but my aunt put a firm hand on my arm. "He's my nephew. Surely, you've seen him in the news vids?"

The doorman's eyebrows bunched up, then rose in comic surprise as recognition set in.

"Captain Sparhawk? Can it be? You're so young..."

"Thank you," I said, taking his comment in the best possible light.

He flushed scarlet and ushered us into the great house without further delay.

Once inside, I was greeted by cold air, shadows and mildew. I expected to be escorted to the upstairs parlor, but instead we were led to a heavy door at the side of the great staircase. The attendant opened the door and urged us to continue through, unguided. Our path led beyond its worn sill and down winding steps into the dark sub-floors beneath the mansion.

"In less happy times," my aunt explained, "people of class sheltered in these places. The surface of our world was... unsavory."

I glanced at her in surprise. She must have been speaking of the days immediately following the Cataclysm. I'd heard people had lived in bunkers—but I'd never visited one before.

On the way down the steps, which wound farther and farther, ever deeper into the earth, I began to hear distant voices.

The voices were faint and indecipherable at first. Slowly, they broke up into conversations, then individual words. Those who spoke were almost whispering, and I began to wonder if I was overhearing the chit-chat of ghosts.

At last, we came to a landing surrounded by marble pillars. It struck me as very odd that anyone would bother to haul such heavy, gaudy things this far down into the ground.

"Don't worry," my aunt said quietly, "there's an elevator to take us back up to the top when this is over."

At her words, I glanced back up the way we'd come. The spiraling staircase corkscrewed around at least a dozen full revolutions above our heads.

We stopped at a tall door of dark oak. I wasn't surprised when it creaked as it opened.

There, in the dim-lit chamber beyond, was a gallery of sorts. Figures sat in a semi-circle, and when we entered the room we stood in their midst. Only then did I realize we'd stepped out upon a stage, and that we were in fact the center of their attention.

My aunt bowed deeply, and I did the same. The crowd quieted and regarded us soberly.

Without preamble, my Aunt Helen began to tell the tale of our long voyage to the stars. She talked about each planet: Our visit with the Connatic, the fateful run-in with the Stroj pirates, and the trio of planets, Ruby, Jade and Sapphire, which had all fallen into barbarism.

She kept talking, and they kept listening. At last, she came to the part concerning our battle in the skies over Earth. It was then that a single withered hand rose from the front row.

The owner of the hand was an exceedingly old person. He had a face like parchment, and a voice like sandpaper rasping over old wood.

The others simply called him 'the Chairman.' I recognized him at once—his face was on the credit pieces in my pocket.

"Helen of Grantholm," he said, "we know what you did among the stars. We know you brought death home to Earth. Why do you seek to council us now, after these great failures?"

She sucked in a breath and began to answer, but I took a step forward and interrupted. The thump of my boots on the old stage echoed, and all their glittering eyes turned to me.

"Hold on just a minute sir," I said, "the Stroj were already here among us. They were here before we took this journey, and I would hazard to guess that they're still here now, spying and waiting for the right moment to strike."

A murmur swept the group. My statements were unwelcome, but none of them offered a counterargument, so I pressed on.

"We aren't choosing this path," I said, "it has chosen us. More Stroj warships will come to Earth. They will not be denied."

"And why is this?" the Chairman demanded.

"Because they seek revenge. They see our existence, free and unsubmissive, as an affront to their dominance."

"What do you propose we do about it? Send more emissaries on bended knees? Fortify Earth?"

"Yes... and no," I said. "I've met these creatures in battle. They aren't like us. They're a blend of man, machine, and insanity. They must be destroyed. Diplomacy will only inflame their passions."

"My nephew speaks the truth," my aunt said at my side.

I glanced at her, but she waved for me to continue.

"I don't know what sins we've committed in the past," I said, "but whatever they were, the colonists seem to barely remember them now. The time has come to rejoin with our lost children. To provide the discipline they so desperately need."

"Discipline?" said a thin, corpse-like woman in the second row. "You're suggesting we do more than build up our defenses?"

"Yes. We have only a single world, a single star system. We barely know where these new bridges to the stars lead. There's much to learn and ignorance might mean extinction. We must build great ships and retake the stars."

They were silent for a time, but slowly, this silence gave way to a dozen separate conversations.

It was then that I began to recognize more of the people in that room. My eyes had finally adjusted to the gloom. My ears began to remember subtleties of voice that I'd heard before in documentaries and historical touch-texts...

These were famous people. People whose names were in the history books that our schools taught to children. Every one of them had long since been assumed dead—but the extremes of Earth's technology had kept them very much alive and filled with a disturbing vigor.

Grantholm was one of their kind. I understood that now. Frail and yet resilient, her lifespan had been artificially extended. All these people, these extreme oldsters, were anachronisms in the flesh. I could not begin to understand the nature of the special drugs, implants, cleansings and surgeries that kept them all among the living.

The truth was that Helen Grantholm was probably the youngest member of this esteemed group. She was important to them, I could tell, as she was still capable of moving among the young with effective grace. At the same time, she was ancient enough to understand them and be trusted by them.

"Colleagues," she said loudly, spinning slowly in place, "my nephew speaks the truth. Long ago, we cast our colonies adrift. We cut off our pathways to the stars. That decision has served us for a century and a half—but no longer. We aren't in control of this new situation. They've come back to us, our bastard children, those who we left out there to die in the dark."

"Cutting them off was the right decision back then," said the whisper-thin woman in the second row, "and it's the right decision now to leave them alone forever."

My eyes widened and fixated upon the oldster in that moment. Could it be true? Could it be that we hadn't been separated from the colonies by a natural disaster? That the Cataclysm had been an orchestrated event?

My mind reeled with the repercussions. What I knew of history was in flux.

I wasn't a babe born yesterday, mind you, no matter what the ghoulish people who sat in this dark dungeon might be thinking. I knew very well that throughout time there'd always been the accepted truth—and the *real* truth. When dramatic events had struck in the past, they'd rarely done so without someone lurking behind the curtains and pulling the levers of power.

But these oldsters that encircled me now—they knew the *real* truth. They knew what had actually occurred so long ago because they'd lived through it all in their youth. And by their own admissions, they were the very ones who'd pulled those levers.

What could have possessed them to set all our colonies adrift? Such a monstrous act it had been, destroying the economies of Earth and all her children at once…

Almost as soon as I asked myself the question, I knew the answer—they'd done it for power. To retain their grip on the world.

When people were insecure, when death, starvation and disaster stalked the world, rulers grew more powerful. Such had always been the way. Despots were forever born in moments of desperation, when the law-abiding feared their own shadows.

"There's another option," said the Chairman. "There's another way."

"What way is that, your Excellency?" my aunt asked tensely.

"We could do it again," he said. "We still have the power. The machines may be ancient, but they can be repaired. The signal will wipe away these bridges to the stars—just as it did the last time."

Eyes wide, I looked at my aunt. She seemed speechless. This was not at all how she'd thought things would go.

Again, I decided to interject myself into the conversation.

"Chairman," I said, "if I may be so bold?"

"Speak, Sparhawk. We owe you the breath in our dusty lungs. We'll hear your ideas—but know first that we on this council will determine our own path."

"I would not presume to know better than the wisest minds of Earth," I said, "but I would implore you to think of what such an act would do to Earth now. We've come so far! To erase all our technology—so many would suffer. So many would die. Even those here in this circle would be... well, out of respect... I'd best not say."

"Speak!" bellowed the Chairman, which caused him to explode into a fit of coughing.

When he'd regained control of himself, I forced a tight smile. "I'm young, as you've all noticed. But not so young that I don't know my share of oldsters. The last time the Cataclysm struck, you were all in your prime. Now... well... ask yourselves: could you survive hardship again?"

Quiet fell over the group. They seemed stubborn, but uncertain. My aunt stepped into this gap and seized the moment.

"No!" she said firmly. "Most of us would die! Perhaps *all* of us would die. I know I'm not capable of living through those times again. This recent voyage—it nearly killed me on a dozen occasions."

The group fell to muttering. A half-dozen separate conversations were spawned.

At last, the Chairman slapped his palm on the table before him. Hoarsely he announced, "Sparhawk makes a good point. Let's discuss how we might build this fleet. What it might entail."

We had them back on track. Aunt Helen began running vids on a holoprojector of great antiquity. In the center of the chamber, it depicted ships and designs for armament. She'd clearly gotten these files from Star Guard officials, who must have labored long and hard on them.

The group viewed the presentation stoically, but I could tell they were impressed by the scope of it, as was I.

The meeting continued after that, dragging on through a litany of complaints from possibly every member. But, in my opinion, they were now on a preordained path.

Eventually, they voted to build the fleet proposed in the imaginary graphics. A fleet such as had never been built before. These ships would be awesome weapons. Vessels designed to destroy entire worlds, if need be.

I couldn't help but imagine how this fleet would darken the skies when it was finished. It couldn't help but terrorize any opposition that dared threaten Old Earth.

Even though I was glad this dusty group hadn't decided to disconnect my world for a second time, I didn't feel at ease. The oldsters in this place were a strange lot. The more I listened to them and interacted with them the stranger they seemed to be.

As a group, they'd passed on into a new phase of their lives that I found unfathomable. They seemed to exist outside the normal cycle of life.

Throughout time, babies had forever become children. Those children had inevitably grown into adults, and the adults would inexorably slide into old age and decline—that was the familiar pattern of the past.

But these individuals had discovered a new, shadowy form of existence. It had warped them, in my opinion.

Decades earlier, they'd become reclusive. But that was only an early stage. Now, they lived lives that I almost couldn't imagine for myself. They reminded me of spiders, one and all. Creatures both strange and yet oddly familiar. *Things,* neither completely alive or completely dead, that had managed to live on inexplicably past their time, spinning their webs in the dark.

Even before that fateful council beneath the derelict stronghold broke up, I wondered how this would all turn out for humanity. These were powerful beings were unlike the rest of us. Together, they'd formed an ancient nucleus of selfish minds operating invisibly behind the figureheads of our government. Witnessing their discussions firsthand, I came at last to understand who really ruled Earth.

And as they drew up their plans, I had to wonder if I'd been fighting all my life on the side of light and hope—or in league with the very cause of darkness.

The End

More Books by B. V. Larson:

LOST COLONIES TRILOGY
Battle Cruiser
Dreadnought

UNDYING MERCENARIES
Steel World
Dust World
Tech World
Machine World
Death World

STAR FORCE SERIES
Swarm
Extinction
Rebellion
Conquest
Battle Station
Empire
Annihilation
Storm Assault
The Dead Sun
Outcast
Exile
Gauntlet
Demon Star

Visit BVLarson.com for more information.

Printed in Great Britain
by Amazon